# SIDNEY SHELDON'S
# THE
# PHOENIX

Sidney Sheldon was the author of eighteen previous best-selling novels (which have sold over 300 million copies worldwide), over 200 television scripts, twenty-five major films and six Broadway plays, ranking him as one of the world's most prolific writers. His first book, *The Naked Face*, was acclaimed by the *New York Times* as 'the best first mystery novel of the year' and subsequently each of his highly popular books hit No.1 on the *New York Times* bestseller list.

Tilly Bagshawe is the internationally bestselling author of seventeen previous novels. Tilly and her family divide their time between their home in Los Angeles and their beach house on Nantucket Island.

# SIDNEY SHELDON'S

# THE

# PHOENIX

## TILLY BAGSHAWE

HarperCollins*Publishers*

HarperCollins*Publishers* Ltd
1 London Bridge Street,
London SE1 9GF

www.harpercollins.co.uk

First published in Great Britain by HarperCollins*Publishers* 2019

1

Tilly Bagshawe asserts the moral right to
be identified as the author of this work

A catalogue record for this book is available from the British Library

ISBN: 978-0-00-822968-9

This novel is entirely a work of fiction.
The names, characters and incidents portrayed in it are
the work of the author's imagination. Any resemblance to
actual persons, living or dead, events or localities is
entirely coincidental.

Set in Sabon Lt Std 10.75/14 pt by Palimpsest Book Production Limited,
Falkirk, Stirlingshire
Printed and bound in the UK by CPI Group (UK) Ltd, Croydon CR0 4YY

*For Zac*

# PROLOGUE

**Outside Athens, Greece**

From the terrace of his elegant, whitewashed villa, former president Dimitri Mantzaris gazed out across Vouliagmeni beach to the clear blue waters of the Mediterranean Sea. He was an old man now and vastly fat, gorging himself daily on cheese and wine and baklava, the sweet, honeyed treats he'd always loved but had resisted as a younger man, back when his greed was at war with his vanity. At eighty years old, that war was over. The last vestiges of his good looks were long gone now, along with his political career. All the urges that had once driven and defined him – his naked lust for power, his insatiable sexual drive, his legendary avarice – had crumbled to dust, like the walls of the Parthenon. Eating was Dimitri Mantzaris's last remaining pleasure of the flesh, and he indulged it without restraint.

But not today.

Today, for the first time in decades, Dimitri Mantzaris had no appetite.

Stavros Alexandris, his former Minister of the Interior

1

and close friend, had brought him the picture this morning, on the third page of *I Avgi*, Greece's top-selling daily newspaper.

'I couldn't believe it when I saw it.' Stavros Alexandris's hands were shaking. A sprightly sixty, and as wirily thin as his former boss was obscenely fat, Alexandris had a reputation for both ruthlessness and calm. At this moment, however, the latter quality had deserted him. 'You don't think . . .?

'She's still alive . . .?' Mantzaris finished for him. *God I hope so.*

Athena Petridis. His nemesis. His conspirator. His muse. His angel. His betrayer. Except Athena had never been 'his'. Athena Petridis had never been anyone's, not even her husband's, the truly evil Spyros Petridis. Like her immortal namesake on Mount Olympus, Athena had condescended from time to time to meddle in the affairs of men. But only when it pleased her, and only ever for her own ends.

Dimitri Mantzaris had been president, the most powerful man in Greece, at the time of their affair. And yet not for one day, not for one moment, had he held the upper hand in their relationship. Athena Petridis had owned him the way other, lesser women might own a dog. She still owned him. Even though she and her husband had been dead for twelve years.

Mantzaris looked at the picture again. It showed a tragic but sadly all-too-familiar image of a drowned child, a little boy this time, washed up on the beach at Lesbos. With hopelessly overcrowded boats leaving Libya every day, Greeks were becoming indifferent to the relentless death toll of the migrants. In many places, in fact, attitudes had swung right through indifference, to anger and resentment. *Why did these people keep coming? Why did they put their own children at such appalling risk? Didn't they know that*

*Greece could barely afford to feed her own people, let alone open her doors to thousands of foreigners?*

Dimitri Mantzaris did not share these views. The pictures still moved him. He was not, despite what many believed, a man without a heart. Yet it was not the dead boy that stirred such profound emotion within him now. It was the insignia tattooed on his heel, like a slave brand. The ancient Greek letter 'L'. To scholars, this was the sign of the Spartan warrior, emblazoned on their shields in tribute to their home state of Laconia. But to Dimitri Mantzaris, along with many of the world leaders of his generation, the sign had a very different meaning. It was the secret, personal signature of Spyros Petridis, an illiterate peasant from Lagonissi who also happened to be both Athena's husband and the most successful organized crime boss since Carlo Gambino.

'It must be a hoax,' Stavros Alexandris babbled nervously.

Dimitri Mantzaris nodded.

'Or a coincidence.'

'Yes.'

'It can't be her.'

'No.'

'She's dead. They're both dead.'

'Exactly.'

'Even so, I think Daphne and I might get away for a while. Out of the country. Perhaps to Chile? Just until things die down. We have friends there . . .'

Alexandris left, and Dimitri Mantzaris lumbered out to the terrace and sank down into his favorite chair. He knew he would never see Stavros again. The mark on that child's heel was no coincidence and they both knew it. It was a message. A message only one person would have *dared* to send.

Closing his eyes, Dimitri Mantzaris let the memories wash over him. Athena's soft skin, her musky scent, her

3

deep laugh. With anguish he recalled the cloying desperation of her heavenly body, built for sex the way a Ferrari was built for speed.

'Athena . . .'

The word hung on his lips.

Mantzaris had friends too, people who owed him, who could help him disappear before it was too late. But he was too old to run.

He would stay here and wait for Athena to come for him.

It would be wonderful to see her face again. Even if just for a moment, before she put a bullet in his brain.


## Osaka, Japan


It wasn't until two days later that Professor Noriko Adachi saw the picture. The tattoo on the dead child's foot filled the screen on her office computer like cancer on an X-ray. Awful. Disgusting. Yet Japan's most famous living literary scholar couldn't stop herself from looking at it.

No sooner had charity workers on the beach noticed the unusual 'L' sign than theories began abounding on the web as to what it meant. Most were laughably wide of the mark. One or two came closer to the truth, more by luck than judgment in Professor Adachi's opinion, pointing the finger at 'people-traffickers'. But no one had yet said the word 'Petridis'.

*Most people still don't know*, Professor Adachi thought bitterly. *And those who do are too cowardly to speak out.*

Lovingly, she picked up the gilt-framed photograph in pride of place on her desk and traced a finger over the glass. Her only son, Kiko, was standing outside his dorm room in America, beaming with pride in his UCLA T-shirt. Above him, the dazzling California sky shone cartoon-blue. *Fifteen years ago next week.* What a perfect day it had been, so full of hope and promise.

A year after that picture was taken, Kiko Adachi was dead. The hardworking, diligent student and athlete, and love of his parents' life, had fatally overdosed on a new, lethally strong brand of cocaine, recognizable by the 'L' insignia on the baggies, specially shipped onto US college campuses by Spyros Petridis.

A year after that, Noriko and her husband Izumi, Kiko's father, had divorced. Izumi complained that his wife had become obsessed with Petridis and his glamorous wife Athena, by that time a UN special ambassador and world-renowned philanthropist whose charisma and beauty had so dazzled the world's most powerful men that her husband operated their empire with near impunity.

Izumi was right. Noriko was obsessed. She wrote countless articles about the Petridises' criminal activity, which no one had the balls to publish. She even penned a novel about her son's death, with the names and identities thinly disguised, but no one would print that either, despite the professor's fame. After two and a half years of fruitless effort, it was the happiest day of Professor Noriko Adachi's life when she woke up to the news that Spyros Petridis's helicopter had gone down in a remote part of Utah, killing him and his wife instantly in a white-hot ball of flames. All that was left of Spyros Petridis had been a few charred bones, just enough to confirm a DNA match. As for Athena – Lady Macbeth – the heat was such that she'd been completely incinerated. Burned to dust. *Erased.*

In the twelve years since, Noriko Adachi had returned to the University of Osaka and rebuilt her career and what was left of her life. Spyros and Athena had robbed her of her family, but she still found some solace in books, in the literature of tragedy and loss and rebirth that had been her academic world since her own student days.

Until now.

Her gaze returned to the screen.

One picture, one emblem, and it all came flooding back.

Another dead boy.

Somebody else's son.

*Nobody could have survived that crash*, Noriko told herself, forcing her rational brain to kick in, to override her emotions. *No human could have lived through that fire.*

But perhaps Athena Petridis wasn't human? Perhaps she was truly a monster, a devil, an evil spirit like the Japanese *Kamaitachi*, mythical sickle-wielding weasels who would slice off children's legs. Perhaps she was a witch.

Professor Noriko Adachi sat at her desk and let the hate take over, pumping like poison through her veins.

*If Athena Petridis is alive . . . I'll kill her.*

## Los Angeles, California

Larry Gaster pulled over on Mulholland Drive, his silver Bugatti Veyron gleaming in the sun. On the passenger seat, the image of the drowned child's branded heel filled the screen of Larry's iPad.

It was a struggle to breathe. Reaching forward, the legendary Hollywood producer opened the glove box, fumbled for the bottle of Xanax, and crammed three pills into his mouth, grinding them between his porcelain-veneered teeth with grim desperation.

A profoundly vain man, Larry Gaster looked much

6

younger than his sixty-five years, thanks to the efforts of LA's most talented surgeons and their patient's limitless funds. Larry's skin was smooth, his brown eyes bright, and his luxurious chestnut hair still only lightly flecked with gray. Unlike most of Hollywood's big hitters, Larry Gaster wasn't satisfied with having young actresses line up to go to bed with him simply because he was powerful and rich. He wanted them to *want* him too. To desire him, physically. These days, despite his best efforts, that was becoming harder and harder to achieve. Some people might put that down to his age. But Larry Gaster knew different.

It was Athena. Athena Petridis.

If only he'd never laid eyes on her!

Larry Gaster had been forty-seven and one of the most desired men in Hollywood when he had agreed to produce a biopic about the great Greek beauty's life. Athena met him at the Beverly Hills Hotel for lunch in a white flowing dress that made her look like an angel. It was the beginning of the end for Larry. He fell in love with her immediately and although they never slept together, never even kissed, Larry's obsession for Spyros Petridis's wife became the driving force in his life.

Athena was a victim. A good woman, a *perfect* woman, trapped in a violent marriage to a monster. That was the truth, and it was what Larry Gaster portrayed in his film. Larry wanted to rescue Athena from Spyros. He wanted to keep her in America, to build her a palace up in the Hollywood Hills where she could live, safe in his protection, eternally grateful for his gallantry like Queen Guinevere to Larry's Sir Lancelot.

But things hadn't happened like that. The day after production wrapped on the movie, Larry Gaster was kidnapped outside his office on Sunset Boulevard in broad daylight. No one knew what had happened during the week the producer was missing, and no one ever would. Larry had said nothing – to the police, to his family, to anyone. He'd simply shown up at the gates to his Beverly Hills estate one morning in a state of shock. The fourth finger of his left hand had been severed and the letter 'L' had been branded on the base of his right heel.

*L for Larry.* That was what he told people who noticed it in later life.

The film was never released.

And Larry Gaster never saw Athena Petridis again.

After the helicopter crash, little by little, Larry resumed his career, picking up where he'd left off. In the last decade he'd produced four blockbuster hits and remarried. Twice. Life was good. Until this.

Winding down the window, he picked up his iPad and hurled it out of the car, over the edge of the precipice that dropped down to the valley.

Then, like a small child, Larry Gaster began to cry.


**London, England**


Peter Hambrecht closed his eyes and lost himself in the music, his baton moving through the air with a grace and fluidity that set him apart from all the other great conductors. Hambrecht was *the* maestro, the undisputed best in the world. Every musician in London's Royal Albert Hall felt privileged to be there that night. Because to be swept up in Peter Hambrecht's genius, even for a moment, was to play to one's full potential. To shine like a star.

'Thank you, Maestro!'

'Wonderful performance, Maestro!'

After the concert, Peter shook hands and signed

autographs with his usual good grace. Then he put on his thick cashmere overcoat and walked the few short blocks back to his flat on Queensgate.

The next morning, he saw the picture, the same day it was published. An old friend emailed a copy.

'I thought you'd want to see this,' the friend wrote.

That struck Peter as odd. Who in their right mind would 'want' to see a picture of a drowned child? But of course, his friend was not referring to the child, only to the emblem burned into his flesh, as if he were an animal or a piece of meat. Peter winced, imagining the pain the poor little boy must have suffered.

Later, the friend telephoned. 'Do you think Athena . . .?'

'No.'

'But Peter . . .'

'Athena is dead.'

Peter Hambrecht had known Athena Demitris, as she was then, since they were children, and had loved her all his life. She was his best friend, his confidante, the sister he'd never had. In the tiny village of Organi where they grew up, blonde, blue-eyed Athena had been adored by everyone. Dark, shy, effeminate Peter, on the other hand, with his German father and his strange accent and the little piccolo he carried with him everywhere, was an outcast, a favorite target of the local bullies.

'Hey, Sauerkraut!' they would taunt him. 'Why don't you wear a tutu, so you can dance to that gay classical music you're always playing? You want us to make you a tutu?'

'He can borrow my sister's.'

'I don't think he wants a tutu. I think he wants us to jam that flute up his ass. You'd like that, wouldn't you, Sauerkraut?'

Peter never rose to their jibes. But Athena always did, roaring to his defense time after time like a lioness, taking on his tormentors, alive with righteous fury on his behalf.

'How can you let them talk to you like that? You have to fight back!'

'Why?' Peter would ask.

'They're calling you gay!'

'I am gay,' he shrugged.

'No,' Athena insisted, with tears in her eyes. 'You aren't gay, Peter. You love me.'

'I do love you,' he assured her.

'More than anything?'

'More than anything. Just not like that.'

Athena covered her ears with her hands. 'No, no, no. Stop saying that. You're confused. You'll change your mind, you'll see. When we're married.'

Peter laughed. 'It's not my mind that needs to change, Athena!'

But there was no stopping her. There was never any stopping Athena. They married the year they both turned twenty and moved to a minuscule apartment in London, where Peter had won a place at the Royal College of Music.

'You're happy, aren't you?' Athena would demand, every morning, as he pored over sheet music in their tiny kitchenette.

Peter had to admit that he was, blissfully happy. The bullies were gone, he was playing his beloved music twenty-four hours a day, and he got to come home to his best friend, the most magical, gregarious, and most *alive* person he knew. Giving up sex with men seemed like a small price to pay.

He was even happier when, a few months later, Athena fell pregnant with their first child, a boy.

'We'll call him Apollo,' she gushed, 'after the god of music and beauty.'

And beautiful he had been, so impossibly beautiful, for the twenty short minutes of his life.

CHD the doctors said. *Congenital Heart Disease.* 'He didn't suffer,' they told Athena. 'Not at all.'

But three hearts broke that day, and Athena suffered enough for all of them. Later, Peter came to realize that the girl he had known all his life had died along with their son. That the Athena who came after was not the same as the one who had been before. Weeks of mute shock gave way to months of deep depression. Desperate to help, Peter tried everything: dragging Athena out to dinner and the park, taking her to doctors and therapists and hypnotists. He still remembered how delighted he was when Athena looked up at him one night, after another silent, miserable supper, and suggested that she take a trip back home to Greece.

'There's a place on Mykonos, my mother told me about it. It's in a tiny village, between Kalafatis and Elia. They do "rest cures" and programs to help people through grief. It's not cheap . . .'

'It doesn't matter,' Peter assured her. 'Go. You must go. I'll find the money, don't worry about that.'

It was the first proactive thought Athena had had since Apollo's death, and Peter grabbed at it with both hands like a drowning man. He couldn't have known that that would be it. The end.

It was on that trip to Mykonos that Athena met Spyros Petridis. Or rather, it was there, at her lowest ebb, that she fell under his evil spell. She wrote to Peter twice, strange, formal letters that sounded nothing like her, explaining that she had met someone and fallen in love and that she wasn't coming back. Peter was gay and she needed more than a platonic relationship. The marriage would never have survived long term.

Only in the very last line she wrote did Peter hear what sounded like Athena's true, authentic voice. 'Every time

I see your face, I see his,' she wrote. 'It's more pain than I can bear.'

And so he'd let her go. That was thirty years ago now, and Peter Hambrecht had had other, great loves in his life, not to mention a wildly successful career. But he'd never forgotten Athena. Over the years, as her fame, and her husband's infamy, grew, Peter had watched Athena on television like a child watching a cartoon character. Or rather, characters, plural. The gracious socialite and hostess. The saintly goodwill ambassador. The untouchable beauty, *People* magazine's 'sexiest woman alive'. None of these was the real Athena.

Rumors swirled about Spyros Petridis's criminal dealings, his murder squads and his drug gangs and his people-smugglers. But nothing was ever proven. Athena's dazzling light, her aura of goodness, her magic, seemed to blind people to the dark underbelly of her husband's world.

Peter suspected the rumors were true. But he never blamed Athena, not then, not now. However she might have changed, he knew his Athena could never, ever be responsible for the death or suffering of a child. Even if she were alive, there was no way on earth that she would be connected to what happened to that poor little Libyan boy. No way.

But she wasn't alive.

She was dead, burned alive alongside her monstrous husband.

*May God rest her soul.*


**East Hampton, NY**


'Goddamn it!'

Mark Redmayne shielded his eyes from the sun as he watched his golf ball veer wildly to the left of the eleventh

12

hole before landing with an audible *plop* in the depths of the lake. He stiffened. *Damn.* A brilliant but ruthless businessman, Redmayne was in his early fifties, although he had the physique of a much younger man. Coupled with his stiff, soldier-like bearing, it helped preserve the aura of barely repressed violence that hung around him constantly, intimidating rivals and friends alike. Mark Redmayne was not a man one wanted to cross.

He was playing like an amateur today. Technically, of course, he was an amateur, but only because he didn't have time to play golf professionally, not because he wasn't good enough. Running a Fortune 500 company turned out to be a tiresomely full-time gig. And then of course there was Mark Redmayne's other job. His duty. His *calling*. That was even more demanding. Especially on days like today.

He'd come to the golf course this afternoon to try to detach. It wasn't working. His conversation of a few hours ago with Gabriel, one of The Group's very best operatives, continued to haunt him.

'It's her, sir,' Gabriel informed him bluntly over the telephone. 'She's alive and she wants us to know it.'

'She's not alive. She's dead,' Mark Redmayne said, as if by saying the words forcefully enough, he could make it so. 'We killed her.'

Pinching the bridge of his nose to try to shut off the headache hammering wildly inside his skull, he gazed out of his office window. Below him, Manhattan lay spread out like a dream, a glorious kingdom he had conquered. Mark Redmayne hadn't founded his company, but under his leadership he had grown it from the modest printing business his father had left him into a global multi-billion-dollar empire. It was incredible the effect a tragic childhood could have on one's ambition, one's determination to succeed at all costs. Business success, however, meant nothing to Mark

Redmayne compared to this. The Group, and the work they did under Mark's leadership – *that* was reality. That was what mattered.

'We killed them both,' he muttered, as much to himself as to his operative on the other end of the line.

'Maybe not,' said Gabriel.

'"*Maybe?*" . . . Don't you give me "*maybe not*"!' Redmayne exploded. 'I was there, OK? I watched that chopper go down.'

Most of The Group's agents were terrified of the boss's temper, and with good reason. Mark Redmayne wasn't known for his compassion; his retribution, once invoked, was ruthless. But Gabriel was one of the few people immune to his outbursts. Nothing could sway him from the facts.

'Athena Petridis's DNA was never found, sir.'

A muscle on the side of Mark Redmayne's jaw began to twitch.

'Because her remains were destroyed in the fire.'

'But her husband's weren't?' Gabriel challenged. 'They were in the cockpit together, side by side. If his bones didn't burn, why should hers?'

'I don't know,' Redmayne admitted grudgingly. 'I just know that they did. This discussion is over.'

He hung up, which was childish, but he didn't have the strength or the patience to listen to any more of the agent's doubts. Largely because they were his doubts too. As soon as he saw the picture, the dead child with his branded foot, he knew. Athena Petridis, *that bitch, that witch, that untouchable monster of a woman* . . . was alive.

Mark Redmayne had hated the Petridises for a very long time. There was a special place in his psyche for people who hurt children. The terrible secret of his own childhood – the single, awful event that had made him who he was and led him to The Group in the first place – had fanned the flames of his loathing into a raging, crazed, homicidal inferno which no force on earth could ever put out.

But what if somehow – impossibly – Athena Petridis had survived the crash that had killed her husband? And she was out there right now, laughing at them, laughing at *him*, for having the audacity to think he'd won. For twelve years, she'd played dead, lulling The Group, and the world, into a false sense of security. But now, with this sick, cruel message, this violation of an innocent child – L – she was back.

'I'll fetch you new balls, sir.' Mark Redmayne's caddy looked nervously at his employer. Mr Redmayne was not used to losing, and had a reputation for taking his frustrations out on the closest underling to hand. This time, however, to the caddy's relief, he seemed oddly calm.

'No need, Henry. There's nothing wrong with my old balls. I just need to remember I have them.'

'Sir?'

'And then I need to start playing a bit better.'

Back in his Bombardier Challenger Learjet after the round, Mark Redmayne made the call he'd been putting off since this morning.

'Let's say you're right.'

'Sir.' Gabriel waited.

'Let's say she's alive.'

'She is alive, sir.'

'So you say. But what leads do you have?'

'None yet, sir.'

'Well find some if you expect me to take you seriously,' Mark Redmayne commanded, and hung up.

Opening his briefcase, he looked again at the picture of the dead boy. No name. Just a tiny, maimed corpse, washed up on the beach like so much trash. That was how Spyros Petridis had treated the poor and the powerless. Like trash to be discarded. And his she-devil wife had helped him do it.

No governments had had the balls to take on the Petridises. It had been left up to them, to The Group, to do what needed to be done. To right what was wrong. To track down evil wherever it lurked, and destroy it whatever the cost. The Group operated outside of laws, outside of boundaries, outside of national interest or political or religious affiliation. They took risks no one else would take. And they covered their tracks. Always.

Killing Athena Petridis once had been Mark Redmayne's duty.

Killing her twice would be his pleasure.

## Sikinos, Greece

Sister Magdalena, Mother Superior of the tiny Convent of the Sacred Heart, bowed her gray head in prayer. Dusk had already fallen, and through the windows of the remote, Byzantine chapel set deep in the island's wilderness, one could glimpse the setting sun bleeding its dying rays into the sea.

*Forgive me my transgressions*, the elderly nun murmured, her arthritic fingers worrying at the rosary beads around her neck. *Help me to find the right path, Lord. Guide me through the darkness.*

Most of the nuns were at supper in the refectory, a simple repast of tomatoes, olives and vine leaves stuffed with wild rice. But Sister Magdalena always fasted on this day: the anniversary of Sister Elena's arrival.

Sister Elena and the visiting priest, Father Georgiou, were the only other souls in the chapel tonight. Across the stone-flagged nave, inside an exquisite, medieval carved wooden confessional, Sister Elena was receiving the sacrament.

*'Bless me, Father, for I have sinned.'*

The Mother Superior could hear only mumbling: first Elena's soft, singsong tones and then Father Georgiou's deep baritone. Although of course she knew the words by heart.

*'Name your sins, my child.'*

What sins could Elena possibly have? This kind, gentle, endlessly patient soul? This stoic, even cheerful, sufferer of torments that would have broken any ordinary human being? Poor Sister Elena. She had lost so much. Her youth, her beauty, her loved ones. Even now, all these years later, the doctors said she was in constant physical pain. And yet her faith remained as strong as ever, a shining beacon of hope through the dark night of despair.

*She should be leading us,* Sister Magdalena thought, for the thousandth time. *Not me. I'm like John the Baptist, unfit even to wash her feet.* And yet Sister Magdalena accepted that this was God's plan. Elena had come to them on the boat from Ios like baby Moses in his basket of reeds, a helpless refugee. Although she had never spoken of what or whom exactly she was fleeing, no one doubted the sincerity of her plight. Back then she'd been too weak to lead the community. Now she was too humble, too devoted to her own spiritual life of purity and sacrifice.

Sister Elena emerged from the confessional. Seeing the Reverend Mother kneeling there, she bowed her head once respectfully, then hurried back to her cell to begin her penance. Could words and prayers and fasting really right the wrongs of the past? Or the present, for that matter? It was a nice idea. Evil and goodness existing like numbers on some sort of balance sheet that could be moved around at will. *If only that were true.*

17

In the privacy of her bare room she began removing her garments one by one and laying them neatly on her bed. The heavy wool tunic, belt, scapular and veil, all black, followed by a black veil, extra-thick in Sister Elena's case, then a white one, and finally the white 'coif' or headdress worn by all the fully professed sisters at Sikinos. Finally she stood naked, relieved to be free of her torturous habit on this stiflingly hot night.

There was no mirror in the cell, nor any other accouterment of vanity, but at night the fifty-year-old nun could clearly see her reflection in the glass windowpane. Her figure was still beautiful, slender yet rounded, with full high breasts and a narrow waist tapering into softly curved hips and thighs almost as firm as they had been in her youth. From the neck down, she was still a beautiful woman. But her face was marked with sin.

*My face is my penance*, she reflected.

Then again, there was more to life than physical perfection. Power, for instance.

Reaching into the pocket of the tunic lying neatly on her bed, she pulled out the piece of paper Father Georgiou had given her, unfolding it carefully with slow, practiced hands. Newspapers were forbidden at the convent, along with all other contact with the outside world. Just seeing the words H Αυγή (Athens top-selling daily newspaper translated as 'The Dawn') at the top of the page after all these years gave Sister Elena a little thrill.

But not as much of a thrill as the photograph.

The dead child. The sign. Right there, for the whole world to see!

There were many of them out there, children and adults alike, branded like this young boy. Brothers and sisters in fire. In pain. Reaching down, Sister Elena ran her fingers over the grooves of the brand seared into her own flesh, at the top of her inner thigh. A simple letter 'L', the same mark as on the migrant boy. How ironic that it should be this child, this nameless refugee – this nobody – whose death had brought their signs out into the open. Put them on the front page of the newspaper, no less, and all over the television news.

*God bless you, child.*

Putting her hands up to her face, Sister Elena let the paper flutter to the ground, aware of an unfamiliar sensation she couldn't quite place.

Then, all at once, it dawned on her what that was.

Sister Elena had just done something that she hadn't done in well over ten years.

She'd smiled.

PART ONE

# CHAPTER ONE

Jim Newsome felt the sweat trickle down between his shoulder blades and the dust sting his eyes as the preacher droned on.

*'Mimi Praeger . . . good Christian . . . good neighbor . . . back home with the Lord . . .'*

The punishing sun made it hard to concentrate. A wiry outdoorsman in his late sixties, with thin lips and the erect, stiff bearing of a soldier, Jim Newsome stood beside his soft, round wife Mary, betraying no outward sign of his discomfort. But inside Jim was seething. Who in their right mind held a funeral service outdoors, at noon, in the height of summer? All around, the air shimmered with a dry, painful heat, all wind and dust and cracked earth. The kind of heat that made your throat hurt and your skin prickle with the whispered threat of fire. This was desert heat. Only they weren't in the desert. They were in Paradise Valley, California, at the Praeger ranch, an oasis of lush green pastureland. Or at least it had been, before the drought arrived, drying out the river beds and turning the meadows brown and brittle, like an old man's skin.

*'As we gather to scatter Mimi's ashes over the land she*

*loved . . .'* The pastor took a sip of water, mopping his brow with a handkerchief, his face tomato-red. *'Let us call to mind our own failings . . .'*

Jim Newsome tuned out. The rancher's failings were his own business, not some milksop of a preacher's, barely out of short pants. Jim would call them to mind when he was good and ready.

Instead, he scanned the faces of the mourners gathered outside old Mimi Praeger's cabin, a simple, pine post-and-beam structure that belonged to another era, another time. More than thirty people had shown up for the service, a good number, especially when you considered how much Mimi had always kept to herself. For years she'd lived totally alone up here, miles from the nearest gas station, and a full day's walk to the tiny convenience store on Prospect Road. Then the child had come along – Ella – and for a few years it had been the two of them, grandmother and granddaughter, like a pair of pioneer women against the world. But children grow. When Ella finally left the cabin for college in San Francisco, it had just about broken poor Mimi's heart.

A lot of people never forgave the girl for that.

'She's got a nerve showing her face here, if you ask me,' Jim's wife Mary had observed caustically, watching Ella Praeger talking to the preacher before today's service. In a fitted black shift dress and patent leather boots, and with her long blonde hair tied back severely in a single, too-tight braid, Mimi's granddaughter had certainly come a long way from the scruffy, oddball tomboy kid the locals remembered.

'She could hardly *not* come,' replied Jim. 'She's family, after all. Next of kin. And this is her land now.'

'Not for long,' Mary Newsome sniffed. 'You think she's going to want to hold on to this place, now she has her fancy-pants city life? She'll sell just as soon as she gets an offer, you mark my words.'

'Maybe,' said Jim.

Jim Newsome couldn't find it in his heart to judge Ella Praeger as severely as his wife – or the rest of the valley, for that matter. It must have been tough growing up out here, with only old Mimi for company. Both parents dead. No TV. No friends. No *fun*. Little wonder the girl had turned out strange. Withdrawn. *Brittle*. That kind of loneliness wasn't healthy for a young person. Or any person, for that matter.

Ella Praeger took the urn from the preacher's clammy hands and solemnly carried it to the foot of the oak tree. Her grandmother had loved this tree. Ella would watch her stroking it sometimes, running a gnarled hand up and down its ancient bark affectionately, as if it were a pet dog.

*It got more affection than she ever showed me*, Ella thought. But she wasn't bitter. Mimi Praeger was who she was: a survivalist and a loner who had chosen a life completely at one with the land. She had taught Ella the things she knew. How to chop down a tree, how to fix a roof and build a boat, how to start a fire and shoot a rabbit and gut a fish and clean a gun. She had tried to teach her how to pray. Ella knew that her grandmother had loved her, in her own reserved, uncommunicative way. She had done her best to raise her dead son's only child, a burden she never asked for.

When Ella was eleven, a woman had come to the cabin – she was from social services, Ella now realized, although back then nothing was explained – and after the woman's visit, Mimi had reluctantly allowed Ella to attend school in the nearest town. It was a two-hour journey, there and back, involving three buses and one long walk along a

25

frightening, unlit road, and it was Ella's first experience of life outside of the ranch. Of television and internet, of different clothes and cars, of pop music and fast-food restaurants and *people*. So many people. Ella observed all of it with a sort of detached wonder, like a visitor on a day trip to an exotic zoo. But while she excelled academically at Valley High, socially she never fit in. Never *tried* to fit in, her teachers believed. Ella brought home reports with words like '*aloof*' and '*arrogant*' mingled in with other, less damning adjectives. *Gifted. Exceptional.* Her language skills in particular were extraordinary, including a pronounced talent for computer languages, the newly voguish 'coding' that was becoming so highly prized by California colleges.

Unfortunately Ella's grandmother did not approve of computer science, for reasons that again were never explained to Ella, and those classes were dropped. But Ella's GPA remained stellar, even as her struggles with social skills intensified. Ostracized by her peers at school, for her old-fashioned clothes and standoffish manner – (with the exception of the boys who flocked to sleep with her, delighted by Ella's matter-of-fact promiscuity once she hit puberty and her complete disregard for the concept of 'reputation', so important to the other high school girls) – Ella's isolation intensified. She lived in two worlds – the world of school and the world of Mimi's ranch – but didn't fit in to either of them.

Mimi's horror when Ella accepted a place at Berkeley took Ella by surprise. She'd assumed her grandmother would be happy and proud of her achievement, but once again she seemed to have missed those all-important signals.

'But I thought you wanted me to go to college?' Ella said imploringly.

'What on earth made you think that?' her grandmother wailed. 'You can't go to the city, Ella. I need you here.'

26

'But . . . you always encouraged me to study.'

'Not so you would *leave!* After everything I've done for you, Ella.'

'What for, then?'

'For yourself!' Mimi banged a veiny fist on the simple kitchen table that the two women had eaten on every day for the last thirteen years. 'To fulfill your God-given potential. Not so that you could run off to one of those dreadful, godless colleges and expose yourself to . . . to . . .'

'To *what*, Granny?' Ella had shouted back, in a rare loss of temper. 'To *life*?'

'To danger,' the old woman replied, shaking a finger at Ella. '*Danger.*'

Feeling the clay urn in her hands, that conversation came back to Ella as though it were yesterday. What 'danger' had her grandmother been so afraid of on her behalf? What fate in the city could possibly be worse than the slow death by suffocation of life up here on the ranch, in the middle of nowhere? Especially these last few years, when it didn't even rain. Even God, it seemed, had abandoned them.

Turning around just once to look at the group of mourners assembled on the hillside, Ella wondered what these people were doing here. Most of them she recognized vaguely as the owners of neighboring ranches, or faces from church or the store. But not one of them really knew Mimi, or her. They weren't friends. Ella's grandmother didn't 'do' friends. Perhaps as a result, Ella had never acquired the skill of getting people to like her, of forging bonds of affection the way that other people seemed to do so effortlessly. Instead, like Mimi, she tended to say exactly what she thought, blurting out observations or responding to questions with a blunt honesty that frequently landed her in trouble.

27

There was one man among the mourners whom Ella didn't recognize, standing at the very back in a dark suit and mirrored sunglasses. Other than Ella herself, he was the only person present in 'city' clothes, and he looked as out of place among these simple, farming folk as a unicorn in a cowshed. He was tall and slim, and when he took the sunglasses off, Ella could see that he had a classically handsome face, like a model from a men's clothing catalog. Strong jaw. Tanned skin. She wondered briefly what he would be like in bed, before refocusing on his identity. *Maybe he's a real-estate agent, come to make an offer on the ranch?* Ella thought. It didn't occur to her that such an approach at a funeral service might be considered insensitive, even offensive. The man's presence made her curious, not angry.

Unscrewing the top of the urn, Ella peered inside at the dust – all that was left of her grandmother. Not even the hardy, rugged Mimi Praeger could outrun old age forever. These ashes were now the sole remnants of Ella's entire family, in fact. With more violence than she intended, she flung out her arm, scattering the ashes to the wind.

Mimi's neighbors gasped at the abruptness of the gesture, the shocking lack of ceremony. Ella sensed their disapproval but chose to ignore it, turning and walking purposefully back up the hill towards the cabin – her cabin, now – with her purse swinging jauntily over her shoulder and the empty urn in her hand.

'Like she's throwing out the trash,' Mary Newsome whispered to Jim, shaking her head disapprovingly. The small gaggle of ranchers closest to Mary murmured their agreement. *Poor Mimi. After all she did for that girl.*

'Come on, now. Let's not be too quick to judge. Grief takes people in different ways,' Jim Newsome reminded them. 'Remember, that young lady's lost just about everybody.'

Inside the cabin, Ella hurried into the bathroom and locked the door behind her. Sitting down on the toilet seat, she slumped forward with her head in her hands and massaged her throbbing temples. *Please no. Not now. Not with all these people here.*

The headache she'd woken up with this morning was coming back, although thankfully not as strongly as before. This morning, as so often lately, the white noise inside Ella's skull had been deafening, to the point where she couldn't get out of bed. And when she did, finally, stagger to her feet, an overwhelming nausea had seen her staggering to the bathroom in her tiny Mission District apartment, throwing up the entire contents of her stomach.

'It's a brain tumor,' Ella had informed her doctor two weeks ago, sitting in his plush corner office at San Francisco's Saint Francis Memorial Hospital. 'It's growing. I can feel it.'

'It isn't a brain tumor.'

'How do you know?' Ella demanded. 'How can you possibly know that?'

'Because I'm a neurologist.'

'Even so . . .'

'And because I've comprehensively scanned your brain with the very latest technology. There is no tumor.'

'You've made a mistake.'

The doctor laughed. 'No mistake, I assure you.'

'Yes. You must have made a mistake.'

He looked at his patient curiously.

'Do you *want* to have a brain tumor, Miss Praeger?'

Ella thought about this for a moment. On the one hand, a brain tumor was a bad thing. Brain tumors could kill you. *I don't want to die.* On the other hand, a brain tumor

29

might be an explanation for all the crazy shit going on inside her head. The headaches and vomiting were only part of it, the part Ella had told her doctors. It was the rest of it that really scared her – voices; music; high-frequency throbbing that sounded to Ella like some sort of coded transmission. That stuff had been going on for a long time. As long as Ella could remember, honestly, although in recent months it had gotten a lot worse. *If I don't have a brain tumor, I'm crazy. I must be.*

'Would you like to talk to someone?' the doctor asked, his amusement shifting to concern. 'A psychologist, perhaps? Oftentimes the sort of symptoms you describe can be brought on by stress. I could refer you to—'

But Ella had already gone, running out of his office, never to return.

The next day, her grandmother died. Peacefully, in her sleep.

'Were you close?'

Bob, a shy, balding, middle-aged man who worked at the coffee shop near Ella's work and was the closest thing she had to a friend, asked when Ella told him.

'She was my closest relative, yes,' Ella responded. 'My parents are dead.'

'Sure, but I meant emotionally. Were you close to her emotionally?'

Ella looked at him blankly. She liked Bob, but found him strange. Evidently he felt the same way about her, because when she'd suggested they sleep together months ago, he'd declined. Even though he wasn't homosexual.

'I'm married, Ella,' he explained.

'I know,' she smiled. 'So you like having sexual intercourse with women.'

For some reason Bob found this funny. 'Well, *yeah* . . .' he laughed. 'I do.'

30

'I'm a woman,' Ella pointed out, with an endearing *case closed* finality to her tone.

'You *are* a woman,' Bob agreed. 'A very beautiful woman. And I'm flattered . . . I mean, I appreciate the offer. But . . .'

'You don't want to have intercourse with me?'

'OK firstly, just a little FYI – people usually use the word "sex". "Intercourse" kind of sounds like a biology textbook.'

'Right,' said Ella. She'd been told this before, but her grandmother had always been a stickler for proper terminology, and old habits were hard to break.

'And secondly, it's not that I don't *want* to have sex with you, Ella. It's that I'm married. My wife would not be happy at all if I did that.'

Ella looked even more perplexed. 'But your wife won't know. She won't be there with us. Will she?'

'None of us will be there!' said Bob, who seemed to have accidentally stumbled into an episode of *The Twilight Zone*. 'Because you and me sleeping together is really not a great idea. Just out of interest, is this how you usually . . .? I mean, have you asked other guys you don't know that well if they want to, you know . . .?'

'Have sex with me?' Ella offered helpfully, pleased to have remembered the phrase *du jour*.

Bob nodded.

'Sure,' said Ella.

'And how have they responded?'

'They do want to. The married ones too. Unless they're homosexuals.'

'OK,' said Bob, rubbing his eyes. 'You know, you can also say "gay".'

*Mimi would have hated that*, thought Ella. Her grandmother hadn't exactly been 'evolved' on LGBT rights. 'I'm

31

tired of hearing about their rights,' the old woman used to say. 'We should be talking about their *wrongs*!'

'I've actually had intercourse – sex – with one hundred and fourteen people,' Ella informed Bob matter-of-factly, and not without a touch of pride.

His eyes widened. 'One hundred and fourteen? Wow, that's, er . . . that's a solid number. Again, just some friendly advice – you don't actually need to share that kind of personal information with everyone.'

'I'm not sharing it with everyone,' Ella smiled. 'Just you. Could I have another latte?' If she and Bob weren't going to have intercourse then she might as well enjoy another hot beverage. 'With almond syrup in it?'

After this conversation, for reasons Ella didn't fully understand, Bob began taking a more active interest in her welfare. It was Bob who'd explained to her that she would have to organize some sort of service for her grandmother. He'd even offered to drive her out to the cabin, if she needed company or a shoulder to cry on.

'You mean *I* have to go? Myself?' Ella sounded surprised.

'You don't "have" to go. But you're her next of kin, and she left you the ranch,' Bob explained. 'So, yeah. I'd say it's sort of expected.'

'Expected by whom?'

'By everyone.'

'Like who?'

Bob tried another tack. 'Your grandmother would have wanted it.'

'Would she?'

'I expect so.'

'OK but she's dead now.'

'Yes, I know she's dead, Ella. But she raised you. This is your chance to say goodbye.'

Ella frowned, like a mother being forced to explain

32

something painfully simple to a child. 'You can't *"say"* things to dead people, Bob. That's ridiculous.'

Still, in the end Ella had taken Bob's advice, because he was her friend and because he understood the world better than she did. She'd arranged today's service, and posted notices in the local paper, and had a caterer provide sandwiches and drinks, and worn the black dress Bob's wife Joanie suggested and carefully listened to Bob's instructions on how to behave. *'Just scatter the ashes, and if you can't think of anything else to say to people, just say "thank you for coming".'* So Ella had driven out here on her own, despite her terrible headache and having to pull over to the side of the road to vomit and despite her sadness that this was *not* her chance to say goodbye to her grandmother, whom she loved. She'd missed her chance to say goodbye, just like she'd missed it with her parents, and now she was all alone in this world and losing her mind and she didn't even have a brain tumor to explain it. And now here she was sitting in this tiny bathroom with the timber walls and the framed Bible verses hanging over the basin, in this cabin where she'd grown up so lonely she'd almost died.

*I almost died.*

*I would have died if I'd stayed here.*

*Anybody would.*

*Why couldn't Mimi understand that?*

A knock on the door broke her reverie.

'Ella?' It was the preacher. Reverend . . . Something. Ella couldn't remember any more. 'Are you all right in there, my dear? Your guests are starting to head inside. I know people want to offer their condolences.'

Ella splashed cold water on her face and popped two ibuprofen from the bottle in her purse. Opening the door she pushed past the preacher and hurried back out on to the porch, looking for the man in the suit. If he made Ella an offer for the ranch, she'd consider it. But he was nowhere to be seen, not outside or milling around the food tables with the rest of the locals.

Bob was wrong. It had been a mistake to come back here. Ella might be different but she wasn't stupid. She could feel people's eyes crawling over her, disliking her, disapproving, just as they had when she was growing up.

Ella had no memories of her life before she came to live with Mimi, other than sensorial ones: the smell of her mother's perfume; the cool touch of her hand, so different to the warm, bear-like grip of Ella's father. When Ella was four years old, her parents had sent her to stay with her grandmother while they traveled abroad together for a job. It was supposed to be for a few months. But they were killed in a car accident and never returned. Ella spent the rest of her childhood here, in the cabin. Yet it had never been 'home'. 'Home' was a place Ella could never reach. A place where her parents were still alive.

Just then she saw him. The man in the suit, closing the old wooden gate behind him as he hit the button to unlock his car, a sleek two-door Lexus that looked even more out of place here than he did. If that were possible.

'Hey!' Ella called out to him from the porch, but the man didn't register. Her voice must have been lost in the wind. 'Hey! Hold up!'

She set off at a run, back down the hill, past the oak tree where Mimi's ashes lay scattered, towards the gate. But before she was even halfway there, both man and car had gone.

'He a friend of yours?' Jim Newsome asked her when she got back to the house, nodding in the direction of the departed car.

'No,' Ella replied, still panting from the run.

Her headache, thankfully, was receding again, but the

idea of playing hostess to Mimi's uptight neighbors for the next two hours still filled her with dread. At least Mr Newsome wasn't as bad as some of them. The women were the worst, generally.

'D'you know his name?' the old man pressed.

Ella shook her head. 'No. I've never seen him before. Have you?'

'Nope,' said Jim. *Strange.* 'Drink?'

He'd already poured a generous glass of Jim Beam for himself, and now offered a second to Ella.

'Must be a tough day for you.'

Ella shrugged, declining the drink. 'I try not to consume alcohol at social functions,' she explained. 'It makes me uninhibited and that's . . . not always a good thing.'

'OK,' said Jim.

'When I'm drunk I'm more likely to have sex, you see,' she elaborated. 'Bob says I should try to do that less.'

Jim Newsome choked on his drink, coughing and spluttering until the liquor burned the lining of his nose. But his eyes were laughing. If this was sober, 'appropriate' Ella, he hardly dared imagine the drunk version. Poor, God-fearing Mimi Praeger must have been at her wits' end raising this crazy girl.

'Oh he does, does he?' Jim chuckled. 'Well "Bob" sounds like a decent sorta guy.'

Jim's wife Mary waddled over to the two of them, stiffly offering Ella her hand. 'Hello, Ella. I just wanted to say how sorry I am for your loss.'

Ella looked at her curiously. Mary Newsome hated her. That much was obvious. Yet here she was being kind. Sometimes – often – other people behaved in a way that made no sense to Ella at all.

'Here, have this. It's an alcoholic drink.' Not sure what else to do, Ella pressed the glass Jim Newsome had offered her into his wife's hand. Then, recalling Bob's advice, she smiled and added, 'Thank you for coming.'

Mary Newsome stared after Ella as she walked away.

Beside her, Jim's broad shoulders began to shake with laughter.

# CHAPTER TWO

Ella woke late the next morning with a different kind of headache. The kind you get from drinking half a bottle of bourbon on your own, once all the guests and caterers and preachers have gone home, then passing out, fully clothed, on your childhood bed.

The first thing she was aware of was the light, streaming in through every window like an assault. Ella's grandmother had not believed in drapes or blinds. 'A healthy person rises with the sun,' was one of her favorite sayings. A lot of Mimi Praeger's nuggets of wisdom began with the words 'A healthy person . . .' Most were variations on the theme of hard work, prayerfulness and self-sufficiency.

'*A healthy person never lets others do for them what they can do themselves.*'

'*A healthy person keeps a clean gun, clean shoes and a clean mind.*'

Ella learned early that she was not a 'healthy person'. At least, not by nature. She had to work at it, and she did work, to please her grandmother but also because, to put it bluntly, there was nothing else to do. Hunting and trapping and whittling and working with her hands became

Ella's 'games' – activities she learned to enjoy because, really, what was the alternative? After years of practice she excelled at them all, an achievement in which both she and Mimi took pride.

'Look at you!' Ella's grandmother used to say, flashing a rare smile as she watched the eight-year-old pop a rabbit from two hundred yards. 'There's not a junior shot in San Joaquin County better than you, my darling.' Once, when Ella was climbing rocks above one of their favorite fishing pools, Mimi told her she was as 'nimble as a mountain goat.' It was one of the happiest moments of Ella's life, a true compliment. Her grandmother's praise was sparing and hard won, but it meant everything to the little girl. Because of course, Mimi was all she had. And vice versa.

There had been such love between them in those days.

*What happened?*

Crawling out of bed, Ella staggered to the cabin's only bathroom (which hadn't been installed until she was twelve – running water had been another grudging concession to social services) and splashed ice-cold water on her face angrily, as if it could wash away the regret. So much had been left unsaid between Ella Praeger and her grandmother, but it was all too late now. Wasted thoughts and feelings and emotions were left to trickle down the drain, like water from a forgotten faucet.

*'A healthy person never wastes God's water . . .'*

Peeling off her crumpled funeral dress and black underwear, Ella freed her hair from its disheveled braid and stepped under the cold shower, gasping as the jets pounded into her bare skin like bullets. She had a good figure, toned and athletic with high, round breasts counterbalancing her narrow, boyish hips. Her hair was dirty blonde and unfashionably long, an old style she was oddly reluctant to part with. But it was Ella's face that really caught people's attention. Hers was a kooky, love-it-or-hate-it sort of beauty. Her green, wide-set eyes gave her face a look of aloofness when at rest, and her high cheekbones and pointed chin added to the overall feline effect. A childhood fall from an apple tree had left Ella with a permanent kink in the top of her nose, preventing her features from having the sort of perfect symmetry that might have left her looking cartoonishly 'pretty'. Instead Ella Praeger was what you might call 'striking'. 'Sexy' was another common epithet, among those who liked their women direct, to a degree that others found terrifying.

Pulling on her spare set of clothes – she'd only brought one change with her, a reminder to herself that she wasn't going to be staying long – Ella made a breakfast of beans and dry cured bacon from leftovers in the pantry, and drank two cups of coffee with powdered milk that she brewed on the stove. Then she found a shady spot on the porch, downed the last of her ibuprofen, which was like trying to put out a brush fire with a water pistol, and sat very still for an hour until her headache receded to something close to bearable.

Mentally, she began running through her to-do list. If she worked hard – '*a healthy person . . .*' she hoped to be able to tie things up and head back to the city tomorrow, or the following day at the latest. Before that, Bob had reminded her she still needed to settle up with the crematorium. And then her main job would be to empty out the cabin, packing up any personal or valuable items to take with her, boxing the rest and cleaning the place from top to bottom, so she could lock it up and leave it until she decided what to do.

The strange man in a suit yesterday had all but convinced her to sell. And he probably wasn't even a real-estate agent! In any case, Ella was confident that sorting through her grandmother's things wouldn't take too long. A survivalist to her bones, Mimi Praeger had only owned three dresses (two for church, one for every day) two pairs of pants (winter and summer), a couple of heavily darned sweaters and the overalls she'd been cremated in. The only book in the house was the Bible, and other than her guns, fishing tackle, a chess set and a few pieces of 'family' china, there were really no objects for Ella to salvage. The one, precious photograph of Ella's parents, William and Rachel, on their wedding day, which Mimi used to keep by her bed, Ella had taken long ago and installed in her own apartment in San Francisco.

That picture had been the cause of one of the worst fights she ever had with her grandmother. Ella showed up at the cabin the morning after her college graduation to try and sort things out with Mimi, but the old woman had been hurt and reacted angrily, unreasonably. She wouldn't talk to Ella, wouldn't listen. When Ella asked for the photograph, Mimi refused to give it to her.

'It doesn't belong to you!' she'd hissed unkindly, her wizened features twisting into an ugly mask of rage. 'You can't simply come here and take things, Ella.'

'But they were *my* parents!' Ella yelled back. 'It's the only image I have of them. The only link. You destroyed everything else.'

Mimi rolled her eyes. 'You're not still talking about those clothes, are you?'

Ella dug her fingernails into her palms so hard she bled. It was the one thing, as she got older, for which she found she could never forgive her grandmother. The suitcase her mother had packed for her, when she first came to stay at the cabin at four years old, and which had contained some of Ella's clothes and toys and a blanket that, in Ella's memory at least, still smelled of her mom, had disappeared from her room one day while she was at school. When Ella asked Mimi where it was, her grandmother replied nonchalantly that she'd 'got rid of it' – or rather burned the contents, as Ella later learned – because 'it's time to look forward, Ella, not back. What use do you have now for a little girl's clothes?' Those clothes, those few items packed with love by a mother who believed she would only be leaving her daughter for a few weeks, were Ella's last physical link to her parents. And Mimi had taken them and burned them, on a whim. Without permission, without thought, it seemed, for Ella's feelings. It was almost as if it had been done in anger, although what that anger could possibly have been prompted by, Ella had no idea, either at the time or later.

'I'm taking the picture.' Ella glared at her grandmother. 'I'm taking it and there's nothing you can do about it!' Marching into Mimi's bedroom like an amazon warrior, she snatched the framed photograph from the dresser. Her grandmother followed, frail arms flapping uselessly, shrieking at Ella like a trapped animal as she tried to grab the precious object back out of her hands. To her shame, Ella had physically pushed the old woman aside, years of her own pent-up rage exploding out of her as she stormed to her car and drove back to Berkeley without a backward glance.

The argument was never mentioned again. Nor did anyone apologize. As with Mimi's burning of the clothes, the entire incident was swept away. Buried. But in Ella's heart, all these things lived.

Healthy people perform jobs methodically, starting at the beginning and ending at the end. Ella packed and organized and scrubbed and disinfected the cabin from the bottom up, starting with the kitchen, then the living room, the tiny

41

bathroom and her own box bedroom, little more than a single built-in bed, a wooden chair, and a sawn-off plank that had served as a desk. To her surprise she found her mood improving as she worked, the exertion bringing a sort of peaceful satisfaction that drove away insistent memories of loneliness and pain. Lifting the striped rug to beat out the dust, Ella pressed down gently on the loose floorboard, her secret compartment where as a teenager she'd hidden such *verboten* items as a portable radio (Mimi strictly banned all 'technology', whether or not it had been invented in the 1920s), trashy, romantic novels borrowed from the school library (mostly Jackie Collins with all the sexiest parts double-folded at the corners of the page) and a small make-up bag and mirror. Later, Ella had added packets of Yasmin, her contraceptive pill, and miniature bottles of coconut Malibu liqueur that Jacob Lister, whose parents ran the Prospect Road convenience store, traded her in return for an opportunity to touch her bare breasts, an excellent deal in Ella's opinion: *win-win*. The board lifted easily, and although its contents were long since gone, Ella still felt a nostalgic thrill that this small act of defiance on her part had remained undetected.

By four o'clock, the entire ground floor was organized and sparkling. A growl from her stomach reminded Ella she hadn't eaten since breakfast. There was nothing but canned goods left in the pantry, so she opted for a plate of Spam followed by a tin of peaches with condensed milk, all of which tasted oddly delicious. Fortified and delighted by her swift progress – she would definitely be able to lock up and head home tomorrow – Ella climbed the ship's-ladder staircase to the loft space that had also served as her grandmother's bedroom.

For the first time all day, she paused. Here, where the smell of Mimi's skin still lingered on the pillowcase, and her shawl still hung from the back of the chair, the magnitude of what she was doing struck Ella. *I'm scrubbing out my childhood. Packing away Mimi's life, and a huge part of my own. Forever.* She waited for the sadness to hit her. The grief that she'd read about and been told about and been waiting for. But instead she felt something else, something terrible. She felt a sort of joy. Angry, defiant, exuberant joy. Survivor's joy. And it swept through Ella like a wave, lifting her up, filling her lungs with laughter and her limbs with an overwhelming urge to kick and punch and lash out with wild relief. Before she even knew what she was doing, she'd taken the bottle of cleaning fluid in her hand and hurled it with full force against the wall, splitting the plastic and splattering lavender-scented bleach over everything within a five-foot arc.

Laughing harder now, she picked up Mimi's solid oak cane and started lashing out with it like some sort of deranged ninja, slamming it into the floor and walls and then finally jumping up on her grandmother's bag and jabbing it hard into the ceiling. Most of the roof was made of split-log beams, impervious to Ella's blows. But there was one small plastered section directly above the headboard that seemed to Ella to be positively begging for destruction. With a banshee yell of delight and an almighty, full-arm swing, she connected the cane to the plaster like a bat to a baseball. White dust and debris rained down everywhere, on the counterpane and all over Ella's hair. Flinging herself back on the bed, she was still laughing when the rest of the plaster gave way and a cast-iron strong box, easily heavy enough to kill her, plunged out of the hole she'd just created, missing Ella's skull by millimeters.

'Jesus!'

For a full minute Ella stared at the box lying on the bed beside her. The near-death experienced had sobered her instantly. *If I'd died*, she wondered, *how long would it be before somebody found me? Weeks? Maybe a month?* Embarrassed by her earlier hysteria, her thoughts quickly shifted from herself to the box beside her. Clearly, Mimi must have hidden it. And not just hidden, but built an entire false ceiling to conceal the thing, to keep it safe. That must mean its contents were either valuable, or secret, or both. Ella couldn't imagine her grandmother hiding anything illegal. On the other hand, she couldn't really imagine her hiding anything at all. '*Healthy people are honest and open. There are no secrets from the Lord.*' It was strange that it took a person dying to find out things about them that you never knew.

Tentatively, Ella ran a finger over the box's clasp. Perhaps there were love letters inside, from Mimi's long-dead husband Bill? Or from someone else – a secret lover! The idea made Ella smile. It would be a relief to learn that her grandmother had not always been such a prude when it came to sex, but it was hard to imagine. Whatever was inside, Ella knew that once she opened the box, Mimi's 'secret' would be out. It would be too late to go back. She took a deep breath, savoring the sanctity of the moment, and lifted the lid.

*Letters.*

*I was right!*

Some were loose and folded, others slipped back inside opened envelopes, all lovingly tied together with a length of gingham ribbon. It looked as if there were cards at the bottom too, flashes of color and glitter glinting out from beneath the faded yellow parchment.

Carefully, Ella lifted the stack out of the box and placed it on top of the bed. With a gentle tug she untied the ribbon, picking up the first letter and unfolding it as delicately as she could with her long fingers.

'Dear Mother,' the letter began.

Ella's heart was already in her mouth. The letter was from her father!

'I don't want to argue with you any more. I know you disapprove of my work, and Rachel's. But not everybody sees the world as you do. What we're doing is important, not just for us but for the world. You think you're protecting Ella with this lie, but you aren't. It's cruel and it's wrong. Please, Mother, for her sake if not for mine, tell her the truth. Give Ella our letters. She doesn't understand now, but one day she will. Your loving son, William.'

Ella's hands trembled. She read her father's words a second and third time, trying to decipher every possible drop of meaning from the few short lines. What did he mean that Mimi 'disapproved of his work'? Both Ella's parents had been doctors. How could anybody disapprove of that? They were tending to the poor in India when the taxi they were traveling in was hit head-on by a truck, killing them both instantly.

And what 'lie' had her grandmother told her?

Most importantly of all, what were these letters her father mentioned? Had her parents really written to her? If so, surely Mimi would have kept those letters? She wouldn't have destroyed those too, would she, like she did with the suitcase of clothes?

Frantic, Ella shuffled through the rest of the stack, opening up letters and quickly scanning each for her own name.

'Dear Mother . . .' the next one began. And the one after that, and the one after that. 'Dear Mother', 'Dear Mother', 'Dear Mother' . . . And then at last there it was.

'My darling Ella . . .'

Ella ran a finger lovingly over the paper as if it were the Holy Grail, tracing each inked letter with infinite slowness.

45

'I hope you are well and helping Granny as much as you can around the ranch. I know you miss us, and we miss you too, very very much. I wish I could explain more to you, but it's not safe for you to be with Mommy and me right now. One day, I hope, it will be. But until then please know you are always, always in our hearts. Your ever-loving, Dad.'

Ella's eyes welled with tears. Why hadn't Mimi given this to her? Surely she would have known how much it would have meant?

There was no address at the top, but there was a date: 2 September 2000.

Ella stopped breathing. *That must be wrong. That's two years after they died.*

She looked at the date again, staring at it, almost in a trance. Then reaching down to the bottom of the pile of papers, she pulled out each of the cards – there were eight in total. Four for Christmas and four for her birthday. Trembling in disbelief, Ella read them all.

'Happy 6th Birthday!'

'Now you are SEVEN!'

A cartoon dog in a top hat held up a balloon. 'To the World's Coolest Eight-Year-Old.'

All of them were signed. 'All our love, Mommy and Dad.'

'No,' Ella said out loud. *No. She wouldn't have. She couldn't!*

*She told me they'd died.*

*She told me they'd died when I was five.*

Ella felt her breathing grow ragged. She felt dizzy all of a sudden, and sick. Sliding to the edge of her grandmother's bed, she leaned forward with her head between her knees.

Breathe in. Breathe out.

*She told me they were dead.*

Breathe in. Breathe out.

*She lied to me!*

Ella stood up, then sat down, then stood up again – a cartoon display of indecision. Her head began to hurt again, pressure building up inside her skull as if some evil sprite were in there, inflating a giant balloon. It wasn't voices this time, or static white noise – strangely she never seemed to get those symptoms at the cabin, only in the city – but it was debilitating nonetheless. She needed to read the rest of the letters but it was impossible. The whole room was spinning and images swam before her eyes.

*I need a doctor*, Ella thought, as the pain in her head brought her to her knees and she felt herself edging slowly towards unconsciousness. But there was no phone at the cabin and no cell reception for miles. If only she'd taken Bob up on his offer and let him come with her, he could have gone for help.

Her last thought was how ironic it would be if she died on the day she found out that her parents weren't dead after all. And how *dared* her grandmother die without explaining any of this to her?

# CHAPTER THREE

Gary Larson crossed his fat thighs and leaned back in his chair, a pained expression on his face.

'I'm sorry, Ella. But I'm going to have to let you go.'

Gary had landed the job of CEO at Biogen Medical Research two years ago by default when his friend Marti Gruber, the original CEO and founder, died in a freak snowboard accident in Tahoe. Everybody had loved Marti, the archetypal go-getting millennial entrepreneur with a passion for risk and pushing boundaries. Nobody loved Gary, his lecherous, talentless best friend and business partner, who had ridden Marti's coat-tails to success, Ringo-style, ever since High School. But fortune, it seemed, didn't always favor the bold. Sometimes it favored the fat, entitled and cowardly, leaving the bold to suffocate under six hundred tons of unexpectedly unstable snow.

'These unexplained absences of yours have become a habit, and one BMR can't afford,' Gary told Ella pomp-ously. It was over a week since Mimi's funeral, but this was the first day Ella had felt well enough to return to work at her boring, number-crunching job in the statistics division.

'OK,' she said calmly, standing up to go.

Gary Larson frowned. 'Wait!' he called after her. It was infuriating the way that Ella Praeger seemed immune to his authority. Even now, when he was firing her ass, the bitch wouldn't do him the courtesy of showing any emotion. He'd secretly hoped for tears, perhaps even some pleading. He'd imagined Ella on her knees, her strangely beautiful face turned up to his in desperation. '*Please, Mr Larson. I need this job. I'll do anything!*' But instead she was walking away and out of his life with no more concern than someone who'd just been told about a minor change to their bus timetable.

'Please, take a seat.' He gestured magnanimously to the chair Ella had just vacated. 'This isn't personal, you know. I've always liked you.'

'I know,' said Ella, still standing.

Gary softened. Perhaps he was being too hasty, letting Ella Praeger go? She was an oddball, certainly, and not popular with her colleagues. But she was a brilliant statistician and a hard worker when she deigned to show up. And then of course there was that body . . .

'You wanted to sleep with me from the day I joined.'

'I beg your pardon?' Gary flushed.

'My first day here, you put your hands on my buttocks in the elevator,' said Ella, mimicking the action with her hands.

'I have no memory of that!' Gary spluttered.

'I do,' Ella said calmly. 'Also, when I ate in the canteen you used to sit next to me and touch my legs with yours.'

'Ella, I assure you . . .'

'You also made repeated positive observations about my appearance,' Ella went on, 'which is another well-known indicator of sexual attraction.'

The CEO's face went from pink to red to puce.

'Now listen, Ella, there's no need for this to get ugly.'

Ella looked perplexed. *Why would it get ugly?*

'You're throwing around some pretty wild accusations there. I'm sorry if you misinterpreted some of my friendly overtures towards you, as your boss . . .'

'No need to apologize,' said Ella, her tone still maddeningly neutral. 'I didn't misinterpret them. I just ignored them because I didn't find you attractive. Goodbye.'

Gary opened his mouth to say something, then closed it again, like a dying fish on a line. Was she threatening him? Or insulting him? Or was this just Ella Praeger being her usual, baffling, socially awkward self?

She walked out of his office and this time Gary Larson let her go. As soon as she left he loosened his tie, which felt horribly tight all of a sudden, and picked up the phone to HR.

'Make sure Ella Praeger gets a generous severance package,' he barked. 'And when she takes it, have her sign a rider to waive any future claims against the company.'

'Of course, sir. And when you say "generous" . . .?'

'Give her whatever she wants,' Gary blurted. 'Just get rid of her.'

Noriko Adachi sipped her iced water as she listened intently to the man sitting across the table from her.

His call last night had been unexpected, but welcome. Professor Adachi still had no idea how this total stranger knew she was in New York, never mind the hotel where she was staying, her room number, and precise details of her itinerary. The seminar on early nineteenth-century feminist literature at NYU was hardly a well-publicized event, especially for those outside the academic world. And yet this polished, erudite American businessman, Mark Redmayne – a billionaire according to Google – seemed to know all there was to know about her.

In other circumstances Noriko would have shut him down immediately. She didn't appreciate being stalked. But as soon as she heard the word 'Petridis', he had her undivided attention.

'My condolences for your loss, Professor,' Redmayne began, the moment Noriko sat down at their corner table at The Finch in Brooklyn. 'From what we hear, your son Akiko was a fine young man.'

'Thank you. He was.'

It was odd the way he used 'we' instead of 'I'. He'd done the same thing last night on the phone. Noriko wondered who else he was speaking for.

'Fifteen years ago, wasn't it?'

'That's right.' Despite herself she felt the tears welling in her eyes. It was so long since anyone had talked to her about Kiko. Hearing his name brought it all back.

'But it feels like yesterday?'

'Yes,' Noriko cleared her throat. 'It's been hard to lay him to rest knowing his killers were never brought to justice. Worse than that, they were praised. Adored by the world.' A muscle began to twitch in her jaw. She twisted her napkin violently between her fingers, as if it were a chicken and she were trying to wring its neck.

'I understand, believe me,' said Redmayne. 'My Group – the organization I run – have been on to the Petridises for years. Decades. Oh, we tried to get the authorities to investigate. Governments, international agencies, local police forces. But no one took us seriously. In the end, we were forced to take matters into our own hands.'

Noriko listened, enthralled. 'What do you mean "take matters into your own hands"?' She paused for a moment, her clever mind racing to catch up as she answered her own question. 'The helicopter crash?' She lowered her voice to a whisper. 'That was you?'

Redmayne nodded. 'That was us.'

As their food arrived, he described his 'Group' to Noriko, albeit in very vague, shadowy terms. From what she could tell they appeared to be some sort of secret, vigilante society – a slick, well-funded one, if Mark Redmayne's credentials were anything to go by – targeting criminals that the police or politicians either couldn't or wouldn't bring to justice. Perhaps she should have listened in more detail, but her brain was still stuck on the Petridises. At long last she had met someone who not only believed her about Kiko and the destruction that Spyros and Athena had wrought, but who had actually *done something about it!* It was intoxicating.

'I read your article. The one *Newsweek* wouldn't run,' Redmayne told her. 'You were right about so much. I can feel your pain vibrating off the page.'

'Yes. Those were dark times,' admitted Noriko, too caught up in the moment to ask him *how* he'd found and read an article that had never been published. 'After the crash, things were better for a while. I started to let go. But then . . .'

'But then this. Right?' Mark Redmayne slid a high-resolution copy of the picture of the drowned migrant boy across the table. The 'L' on his foot was clearly visible.

Noriko bit her lip and pinched the bridge of her nose, determined not to cry again.

'Yes.'

'I can't imagine how painful it must have been for you to see that,' said Redmayne.

Noriko looked away, at the busy street outside the window. 'She's alive,' she whispered.

'It would seem that way,' Redmayne concurred.

'How? How could she have survived that crash?'

'We don't know,' he answered truthfully. 'There's a lot

we don't know at this point. But we intend to find out. And if Athena Petridis *is* alive, we will bring her to justice. You have my word on that.'

Noriko looked up sharply. 'Are you looking for justice? Or vengeance?'

'Is there a difference?' Redmayne cocked his head to one side. 'We can call it vengeance, I suppose. Righteous vengeance.'

For a while both of them fell silent. After a full minute, Redmayne began to wonder whether he'd done enough. But then Professor Noriko Adachi turned to him and uttered the words he'd been waiting to hear.

'I want to help, Mr Redmayne. Please – tell me more about your Group.'

Back in San Francisco, Ella's anxiety was building. In reality she felt a lot less sanguine about losing her job at Biogen than she'd let on to her now ex-boss. Walking home to her tiny apartment on Fillmore Street after their interview, she struggled to contain a rising sense of panic. *What now?*

After a week spent in and out of doctors' offices by day, getting second, third and fourth opinions after her collapse at the cabin (all depressingly the same – 'there's nothing physically wrong with you, Ms Praeger'; 'there may be a psychological trigger'), and in her apartment by night, reading and re-reading all her father's letters to her grandmother and herself, Ella was emotionally and physically exhausted.

True, her medical research job was boring, and Gary's clumsy come-ons a daily irritant. And true, the money wasn't great. But Ella's job had provided routine and stability, something tangible to hold on to. She needed that now more than ever. The events of the last three weeks had thrown her for a total loop – Mimi's death, going back to the ranch for the funeral, finding the letters, all on top of the intolerable situation with her headaches.

53

Bob from the coffee shop had helped her try to make sense of the letters at least.

'I wouldn't jump to conclusions,' he advised her. 'You don't know what your grandmother's motives might have been for keeping the truth from you. There are a lot of missing pieces here.'

Ella looked at him with anguish. 'It's not just Mimi. If my parents were alive, why didn't they come back for me?'

Bob hugged her. For someone so abrasive, and downright rude at times, Ella could be deeply sensitive, almost like a child.

'I don't know, sweetheart.'

'How could they leave me there, for ever? And why did they stop writing? The last letter was sent the year I turned eight. Do you think they stopped because I never replied? Do you think they thought I didn't love them?'

'No,' Bob said fiercely. 'I'm sure they didn't think that. Look at your dad's letters to your grandmother. He knew she was the one keeping their letters from you. He knew that she'd lied to you about the car crash.'

'And why was he the only one who wrote?' Ella asked angrily. 'What about my mother? Where was she all those years? Where is she *now*?'

'Look,' said Bob. 'These are all good questions. But the only way you're going to know anything is by finding out the truth for yourself. It seems to me the first thing you need to know is whether they're still alive.'

Bob had been so kind, as usual, and so practical. Ella wished she had his facility for breaking problems down into manageable parts. And he was right – she *did* have to take charge and discover the truth for herself, somehow. But something held her back. In her more honest moments, she realized that the 'something' was fear.

Tapping the code into the panel outside her building,

Ella slipped inside and climbed the creaky three flights of stairs to her attic apartment. Once inside she removed her shoes and placed them exactly symmetrically against the wall, as was her ritual. In front of her, the living-room-cum-kitchen was just as she had left it a few hours ago: neat, ordered and Spartan. The white Formica table gleamed like something out of a pathologist's lab, an impression only enhanced by the pervasive smell of bleach countertop cleaner. A single, bright red armchair faced the television, also dusted to within an inch of its life, with the only other furniture in the room a functional Ikea bookcase, on which a variety of novels and self-help books were stacked in strict, color-coded order.

*It's eleven o'clock on a Monday morning*, Ella thought, shifting her weight awkwardly from foot to foot as her panic returned with a vengeance. *What do I do now?* Growing up on the ranch there was always a job to be done, and a time for everything. In the city it was different. There were no guns to clean or rabbits to skin or fences to mend. To fill the days, one needed a job. A made-up purpose. Up until today Ella had had one. But now the terrifying prospect loomed of 'free time'; of long, structureless hours in which the voices in her head would be free to run rampant. They were already playing now, on low volume. A male voice had started reciting strings of numbers the moment Ella walked into the building. *Maybe the doctors are right? Maybe it is stress related?*

Moving aimlessly through to her bedroom, Ella sat at her desk and flipped open her computer, resisting the urge to open the drawer containing her father's letters. Last night she'd spent more than three hours obsessively studying the postmarks on all the envelopes Mimi had saved. The letters had come from all over the globe: Pakistan, Greece, South Africa, Fiji. *My parents explored the world together,*

55

*knowing I was stuck in that cabin, completely isolated, grieving a death that had never happened.* In the beginning, Ella had taken her father's side, blaming her grandmother entirely for the 'cruel lie' she'd been weaned on. But as the days passed she couldn't avoid the harsh truth that her parents had also been complicit. *They knew where I was. And they never came back.*

What Ella had to do now, and urgently, was to find another job. She couldn't allow the letters to consume her, not until her own life had stabilized. Scrolling through the positions listed on monster.com and the Berkeley alumni website, her heart sank. Even for the desk-bound, research or coding jobs, employers wanted 'outgoing', 'charismatic' staff with 'proven people skills'. Ella's academic credentials were stellar and she was always invited to interview. But that was where things inevitably went wrong.

'Tell us *why* you want to work for Humperfloop Industries?' the bright-eyed HR team would ask her.

'To earn money,' Ella would reply truthfully. This usually prompted laughter, but then that would be followed by other, trickier questions.

'What are your passions?' a middle-aged female interviewer at a tech start-up once asked Ella. 'Apart from coding.'

'*Apart* from coding?'

'Yes,' the woman smiled. 'We're looking for well-rounded individuals. People with more than one string to their bow.'

Ella's palms began sweating. All the responses she'd practiced were about coding. What sort of 'passions' did the woman mean? Bob had warned Ella vociferously never, ever to mention sex in these encounters. But what did that leave her with?

'I like . . . coffee cake,' she said at last.

The woman looked blank. 'Coffee cake?'

'I can shoot a deer from three hundred yards,' Ella blurted. The interviewer's horrified face told Ella at once that she'd made a misstep, yet some death-wish prompted her to follow up with: 'I can gut fish!'

'Very interesting. Well, thank you, Miss Praeger. Please, see yourself out.'

Landing the Biogen job a year ago had been nothing short of a miracle. Ella was pretty sure she'd only got that because Gary Larson fancied her. But now she'd lost it, thanks in part to her stupid headaches, which weren't getting any better and would probably ruin her chances at her next job, if she ever got one.

*Don't be negative*, she told herself. *Healthy people turn their lemons into lemonade.*

This time she would do better. She would follow Bob's example and break the problem down into small steps. Step One: get better at interviews.

Standing up, she positioned herself stiffly in front of the mirror. Many people had told her that 'tone of voice' was important, as well as body language and eye contact.

'A pleasure to meet you!' Ella grinned at her reflection, proffering her right hand. 'I'm Ella Praeger.'

*Hmm. No, Too gushing.*

'How do you do?' she tried again. 'I'm Ella.'

This time her smile looked like a rigor-mortis grimace.

'Thank you for seeing me,' she told the mirror, relaxing her jaw and tossing back her hair in what she hoped was a relaxed and natural manner. 'I'm Ella.'

'The pleasure's all mine, Ella.'

Ella spun around and screamed. Standing behind her, leaning nonchalantly against her bedroom door as if he had a perfect right to be there, and grinning like the Cheshire cat, was the man from her grandmother's funeral.

# CHAPTER FOUR

'Get out!'

Picking up a hairbrush from her perfectly arranged dressing table, Ella hurled it at the man's handsome head. He was even more attractive than she remembered him from the ranch, but this was no time to get distracted. The throw was accurate and lightning fast, hitting him painfully on the side of the skull.

'What did you do that for?' The man scowled at her.

'You broke into my apartment,' Ella retorted, reaching for a heavy-looking glass perfume bottle.

'Don't!' the man begged, covering his head protectively with his arms. 'I didn't break in to your apartment. The door was open.'

Ella's eyes narrowed. 'I always close the door behind me.'

'Not this time,' shrugged the man.

'Who are you?' Ella demanded, still clutching the scent bottle.

'That's not important,' said the man, his earlier confidence returning even as he rubbed the growing lump on his skull, already the size of a walnut.

'It's important to me. Why are you here?' said Ella. 'And why were you at my grandmother's service?'

'Put down that bottle and I'll tell you.'

The man smiled, and for the first time Ella allowed herself to take a really good look at his face. She'd already clocked him as attractive, but she saw now that his defining feature was his jaw. Strong and perhaps a little too wide, it gave him a rough, rugged look at odds with his otherwise sophisticated manner and dress. He had brown eyes, surrounded by fans of deep lines that marked him as older than Ella had thought at the funeral service. Forty, at a guess, but in good shape for his age and with no hints of gray at the edges of his thick, dark hair. He was wearing a suit again today, well cut and expensive, with gold cufflinks that glinted when he raised his arms to shield himself from Ella's impending blows.

While Ella looked at him, he returned the compliment, his gaze trailing languidly up and down Ella's body in a most disconcerting manner. The look in his eyes was part curious, part predatory. Ella felt an instinctive rush of blood to her groin. She gripped the perfume bottle tighter.

'Tell me, right now, who you are and why you're following me or I'll call the police and have you arrested for trespassing.'

'No you won't.' The man turned and walked into Ella's living room, sitting down at the table and stretching out his legs with a maddening lack of concern. If he'd had a cigarette, he would have lit it.

'I might,' Ella protested weakly, unsure how she'd somehow lost the upper hand in their interaction. 'Or for harassment.'

'No one's harassing you, Ella.' It was the first time he'd used her name. 'Sit down.' He gestured to the chair opposite him, as if this were his apartment, not hers. Ella contemplated refusing, but then decided it would look weak and churlish. Besides, now that the shock at being ambushed had passed, she felt more intrigued than threatened. Putting down the bottle she joined him at the table.

'Good.' He smiled again, flashing his white teeth like a wolf. 'Now, I believe you had some questions for me?'

'Why were you at Mimi's funeral?' Ella began.

'To see you.'

'But you didn't see me. You didn't introduce yourself. You left before I could speak to you.'

'I saw what I needed to see.'

Ella scowled. She'd never been a fan of riddles.

'What does that mean? What do you *want* from me?' Her exasperation was starting to show. 'You show up at my grandmother's funeral, uninvited. Then you walk into my home, unannounced, and actually at a really bad time. I lost my job this morning.'

The man shrugged, showing zero interest in this information, never mind sympathy.

*Christ, he's rude*, thought Ella. *Of all the obnoxious, self-centered . . .*

'You would have had to leave your job anyway,' he said matter-of-factly. 'You're going to be working for us from now on, Ella.'

Ella raised an eyebrow. 'Oh I am, am I? And who exactly is "Us"?'

The man leaned forward, suddenly animated. 'The organization I represent is a secret but powerful group. We work as a force for justice around the globe.'

Ella stifled the urge to laugh. What was this, a comic book? Next he'd be telling her that they all wore capes and lived in Bat-caves. But when he spoke again he sounded deadly serious.

'There are things I can explain to you today. Other

60

things will become clear over time. Once you start your training.'

*Training?* For the first time it occurred to Ella that perhaps this good-looking stranger was actually unhinged. Some sort of paranoid schizophrenic who'd seen her on the street or in the coffee shop and decided to stalk her. First to Mimi's funeral and now here, at her home. Perhaps she ought to be concerned for her safety?

'Listen, I'm sorry,' she said, getting up and walking, calmly, to the front door of the apartment. 'I'm sure you mean well, but I think you must have me confused with someone else. I'm not going to be doing any "training" or joining any group. I have an ordinary life. I work in an office.'

'I thought you said you were fired?'

*Wow*, thought Ella, frowning. *He has even worse social skills than I do.*

'Well, yes. I was fired. But that's not the point. The point is I need you to leave now.'

She held open the door. The man didn't move.

'Please go.' Nothing.

'I'm serious.' Ella's tone hardened. 'If you don't leave, I'll—'

'Your parents, William and Rachel Praeger, were both important members of The Group,' the man said, without looking up from the table. 'They devoted their lives to the cause.'

Ella froze. 'You knew my parents?'

'Not personally,' the man said. 'I knew *of* them, naturally. They were legendary in their time. Everyone in The Group knows about the Praegers.'

Ella closed the door. Her heart was beating so fast it was hard to breathe.

She looked at the man. 'You used the past tense. They "were" legendary.'

'Yes.'

'So . . . my parents are dead?'

'Yes.'

There was no soft-soaping. No 'I'm so sorry' or 'I thought you knew'. He answered her as bluntly as if she'd asked him the time, or some trivia question. *Tactless. Like me*, Ella thought again. Not that their similarities eased the blow.

Leaning back against the wall, she fought to steady her breathing. All her life, up until ten days ago, she'd believed her parents were dead, killed in a car crash when she was very young. But since finding the stack of letters hidden in Mimi's ceiling, she'd been living on hope. Angry hope. Confused hope. But hope nonetheless. That perhaps, miraculously, it *wasn't* too late. That one day she *would* see her mother and father again and they would explain everything. Make everything all right.

But now, with a single word, this stranger, this bizarre, arrogant, handsome man had extinguished that hope, like a priest at the end of Mass, casually snuffing out a candle.

'Are you sure they're dead?' Ella whispered.

'Quite sure,' said the man. 'They died on a mission for us in 2001.'

Two thousand and one. That was the year the letters had stopped.

'I believe you were eight years old at the time,' the man said.

'What sort of "mission"?' asked Ella. It didn't occur to her to wonder how he knew her age, or indeed anything about her. 'Are you trying to tell me that my parents were spies?'

He shrugged. 'We prefer the term "agents".'

'How did they die?' demanded Ella, who didn't give a damn what terms the man preferred.

He hesitated for the briefest of moments, then said, 'They were murdered.'

Ella swallowed hard.

*Murdered.*

For a few seconds she was left mute. 'How?'

The man held up a hand. 'I can't say any more, I'm afraid. Not yet. But you should know that your parents were both tremendously brave people, Ella. They did their best to protect you, to allow you to enjoy a safe and happy childhood.'

*Safe and happy?* thought Ella, bitterly. Those were hardly the words she would have chosen to describe life up at the cabin with Mimi.

'I want to know how they were killed, and why.'

'And you will,' said the man. 'When you're ready. It was always your parents' wish that one day you would join us. Carry on their legacy.'

The man continued talking, about 'The Group' and 'missions' and 'training', but Ella had tuned out. She didn't care about whatever cult it was that he was trying to persuade her to join. All she cared about was that this man knew things about her mother and father. Real things. Specific things. For the first time in Ella's life, someone was offering her answers – actual, factual answers, not the stream of lies and half-truths and platitudes she'd been fed by her grandmother, well intentioned or not.

'What else do you know about my parents?' she interrupted him, reclaiming her place opposite him at the table. 'You said you never met them.'

'No.'

'But other people in your group did?'

'There are people still in The Group who would have known them, yes,' the man answered cautiously.

'Who? Can I talk to them?'

'I can't give you names at this stage, I'm afraid.'

'What do you mean "*at this stage*"?' said Ella, growing more strident. 'And why can't you? They were *my* parents. I have a right to know.'

'As I explained, once you start training for your first mission, you'll be briefed more fully,' the man said calmly.

Ella rubbed her temples. This entire conversation had been surreal from the beginning, but all this talk of 'training' and 'missions' was going too far. She wasn't about to join this weirdo's cult, still less volunteer for any sort of 'special ops'. Whatever number these people had pulled on her parents' back in the day wasn't going to work on her. She wasn't Lara Croft. She was an unemployed statistician with questionable social skills and some sort of undiagnosed mental disorder that made her feel as if hundreds of little men with pickaxes were permanently mining the inside of her cranium, day in, day out. Most of the time it was a 'mission' for Ella just to get through the day.

Wearily, she pressed her splayed fingers to the side of her skull.

'Your training will help you with the headaches you've been experiencing,' the man said nonchalantly. 'As well as with the other side effects of your . . . gifts.' He chose the word carefully, turning it over in his mind, like a squirrel trying to select a particular nut. 'The nausea, hearing voices, all of that.'

Ella's stomach lurched. How on earth did this complete stranger know about the voices in her head? She'd never told anyone about them, not even her useless doctors.

'What do you mean my "gifts"?' Her voice came out scratchy and strained. 'How do you know these things about me?'

'Here.' The man reached into his inside jacket pocket and pulled out a silver USB memory stick that looked like an old-fashioned cigarette lighter. 'Look at this after I've gone. It will give you more clarity on the details. You're unique. But the important thing to understand is that there's nothing wrong with you, Ella. Your brain was simply designed differently to other people's.'

'Brains aren't "designed",' murmured Ella, gazing at the stick in her palm and talking as much to herself as to him.

'Yours was,' said the man. 'In vitro. Your parents were pioneers in gene editing. As individual scientists they were each brilliant, but as a team they pushed boundaries that none of their contemporaries dared even approach.'

'Wait.' Ella held up a hand. 'My parents were both doctors. Medical doctors.'

'That is not accurate,' said the man.

'Yes it *is* accurate,' insisted Ella, angrily. 'My grandmother told me—'

'Is this the same grandmother who told you that they'd died in a car crash?' The man gave her a pitying look. 'Surely you've realized by now, Ella, that your grandmother lied to you. Repeatedly. About many things.'

Ella bit her lip. She wanted him to be wrong, wanted to be able to leap to Mimi's defense. But she couldn't.

'What I'm telling you now is the truth,' said the man. 'Whether you choose to believe it or not. Your parents were not doctors, they were research scientists. Your mother was a neurologist and your father a geneticist, and they were two of the most brilliant minds of their generation. You were their greatest achievement.'

Ella waited for him to go on.

'The voices and messages you've been hearing aren't auditory hallucinations. They're all real,' he explained. 'They're electronic signals emails, texts, data and voice transmissions. You were genetically modified before birth to be able to receive and, theoretically at least, to unscramble them. We believe you have visual capabilities too, but we won't know the full extent of your gifts until we get you into the lab. It's really quite exciting,' he added cheerfully.

_Exciting?_ To be told that your own parents had conceived you as some sort of experiment? The words 'genetically modified' made Ella think of those perfectly round, red tomatoes that looked pretty on supermarket shelves but that tasted like tennis balls when you bit into them. _Fake. Ruined._

'You're saying my parents caused the problems with my brain?' she reiterated slowly. 'On purpose?'

'Not problems. Abilities,' said the man. 'You're looking at this all wrong, Ella. Just imagine the possibilities. You're gifted. You can access the unknown. You're like a . . . a human receiver.'

'Well if I am, I'm a broken one,' Ella snapped. 'I can't "unscramble" anything. All I hear is white noise until my head feels like it's going to explode. I'm sick, all the time. That's the only "gift" they gave me. The only "ability".'

There was no mistaking the bitterness in her voice. The anger.

'I understand it's a shock,' said the man, with an attempt at empathy that clearly did not come naturally to him. 'But those things will all improve. With training. Once you've learned how to master your abilities, we hope they will prove to be an invaluable asset to The Group, and to the greater good. Just as your parents intended.'

He stood up, pushing back his chair and straightening his silk tie with a perfectly manicured hand. 'I know it's a lot to take in. Download the information on the memory stick. Try to focus when you do, because once viewed it will automatically and permanently delete. I'll be in touch in the coming days about next steps.'

Ella stood up too. She couldn't just let him leave. She

no longer thought he was deranged, but at the same time none of this made the remotest bit of sense. How dare this man, this stranger, walk into her life and drop bomb after bomb after bomb, refuse to answer her questions, then saunter off, leaving Ella to pick up the pieces?

Reaching out, she put a restraining hand on his arm. 'Wait! Hold on. Please.'

'I'll be in touch,' he said, shrugging off her hand and heading for the door.

'You know what? Don't bother!' Ella yelled after him defiantly as he started down the stairs. 'Because I'm not joining any stupid Group. Not for you or my parents or anyone else. So don't come back here!'

The man kept walking.

'I have a life of my own, you know,' shouted Ella.

He stopped and turned to look up at her, his expression curious rather than angry.

'Do you? No job. No family. No friends. No real purpose.' He counted off Ella's deficiencies on his fingers, not spitefully but in a matter-of-fact way, like a scientist letting the data speak for itself. 'That's not what I would call a life,' he concluded. 'But perhaps we have different standards?'

Ella spluttered furiously, trying to think of a suitable comeback, but by the time it came to her the man had gone. She stood alone at the top of the stairs, the silver USB stick clutched in her hand, feeling as if a tornado had just swept into her life and upended every single thing in it. If the man had still been in range, she would have hurled the stick at his head and hoped she knocked him out cold. *Smug bastard.*

Well, if he thought he was going to determine her future, he had another think coming. Ella wasn't Frankenstein's monster, whatever her parents might have intended. The man could take his stupid Group and his training and his missions and stick them where the sun didn't shine.

*I'll show you, Mr 'perhaps we have different standards'? Mr . . .?*

It dawned on Ella in that moment that this man who claimed to know so much about her and her parents; this stranger who'd unlocked the mystery of her secret voices and solved the riddle of her past, hadn't told Ella a single thing about himself.

She didn't know how he'd come to join The Group, or what he did for them.

She didn't know how old he was, or where he lived.

She didn't even know his name.

# CHAPTER FIVE

Helen Martindale pushed her greying hair back from her doughy, round face and fixed it back in place with a bobby pin. She smiled patiently at the young woman opposite her, who hadn't looked up from the single-page contract Helen had handed her more than six minutes ago, reading and re-reading every line of text as if it held the answer to the meaning of life.

'It's just our standard vendor's agreement,' Helen explained. 'Shouldn't be any surprises in there.'

The young woman kept reading.

'We'll get you a fair price for the place,' Helen said reassuringly. She was delighted that Mimi Praeger's grand-daughter had chosen to list the valuable Paradise Valley ranch with Martindale and Jessop, rather than go with some fancy city realtor, offering all of those 'virtual tours' and 'social media presence' and promising pre-drought prices that locals like Helen Martindale knew couldn't be achieved any more.

'Is there something bothering you, hon?' Helen asked, once a full ten minutes had passed.

'Hmm?' Ella looked up, bewildered, as if suddenly seeing

the older woman for the first time. 'Oh, no. Thanks. Everything's fine. Do you need me to sign something?'

Helen Martindale pointed to the dotted line at the bottom of the page and handed Ella a pen. The poor child seemed to be in a world of her own. Of course, she'd always been a funny one, a few biscuits short of a breakfast, as Helen's daddy used to say. No wonder, given the isolated life she'd been forced to lead up at that ranch. Other than at school, she barely ever got to play with other children and learn how social interactions were supposed to work. But she seemed worse than usual this morning. Maybe parting with the ranch and saying goodbye to the cabin she'd grown up in was proving more of an emotional wrench than she'd anticipated.

'Are you staying on the property while you're here?' Helen asked, kindly.

'No,' said Ella. She didn't intend to be rude; she simply didn't have any facility for small talk.

'Well, that makes things easier from our point of view.' Helen smiled. 'Feels hard for you, I daresay, coming back to the valley now your grandmother's gone?'

Not sure how to respond to this observation, Ella stood up, shook Helen's hand stiffly, and left, closing the office door behind her.

Helen Martindale looked through the window as the girl stood on the sidewalk, swaying like a poplar tree in the wind, uncertain which way to go, before suddenly deciding to make a left on Main Street.

*Poor thing*, the real-estate agent thought again. She wondered whether the profits from selling the Praeger ranch would make her new client's life better or worse, and she couldn't quite shake the depressing feeling that it was probably the latter. Ella's problems, Helen Martindale rightly suspected, weren't the kind that you could fix with a check.

*

It did feel hard coming back to the valley, but not because Mimi had gone. Right now Ella was still too angry with her grandmother to allow in any other feelings. No, what was hard was the fact that she was still in limbo, with no idea what the next chapter of her life would look like. Stupidly, she'd put off her job search until she heard back from 'the man', who'd promised he'd be in touch again within a few days. It was now nine days since his un-announced visit to Ella's apartment, and she'd heard nothing from him since.

Not that she had the remotest intention of joining his 'group' or attending whatever nonsensical 'training' it was that he had in mind for her. But she'd been looking forward to delivering that defiant message in person. And, if she was honest, simply to seeing him again. Although she didn't like to admit it, the man's random appearances in Ella's life provided a thrill that was only partly connected to the tantalizing clues he offered about her parents.

But now he was entirely absent, leaving Ella to return to Paradise Valley feeling even more hopeless and deflated than she had at the funeral. Thankfully, so far, Ella hadn't run into any of her old high-school classmates/tormentors. That would really be the icing on the—

'Well I never! If it ain't Miss Ella! Ella Praeger, as I live and breathe!'

If it had happened to someone else, it would have been funny.

Danny Bleeker, blond, blue-eyed Danny, star pitcher on the Paradise High baseball team and bane of Ella's life from tenth grade right through to her senior year, was bounding across the street to greet her like an overexcited puppy.

'How the hell are you, Ella Praeger?' She wasn't the most adept at reading these social interactions, but the strange thing was, he seemed genuinely pleased to see her, smiling

71

broadly and placing both hands on Ella's shoulders, as if she were a long-lost cousin or cherished old friend. He looked the same, although possibly his dark blue mechanic's overalls gave him a slightly more mature look than he'd had back in High School. 'I thought it'd be a cold day in hell before you showed up back in town again. Things didn't work out in San Francisco?'

'My grandmother died,' said Ella, with her usual directness.

'Sorry to hear that,' said Danny.

'I'm selling her land.'

Danny Bleeker whistled. 'That must be worth a pretty penny. So you're rich now, huh? Or you will be. Well that's great. Good for you.'

Just at that moment a deafeningly loud babble of voices, like a hundred crossed wires, exploded in Ella's head like a burst speaker. She clapped both hands over her ears and doubled over, wincing in pain.

'What is it?' Danny asked, instinctively wrapping an arm around her. 'What just happened?'

Ella froze, waiting for the shrieking voices to recede – they usually did within a few seconds – before wriggling out from beneath his arm. 'Nothing. Only a headache.'

'You still get those?' he sounded concerned. 'You know you should really see a doctor. That shit's been going on for years. D'you remember in Miss Haelstrom's class, you—'

'Danny?' Ella asked.

'Yeah?'

'Why are you acting nice?'

He laughed loudly. 'I'm not acting! I am nice.'

'No,' said Ella, sincerely. 'You aren't. You are a cruel and spiteful person.'

He frowned, seeming genuinely taken aback.

'Hey, look, I know I was a bit of an ass in school.'

72

'You were horrific.'

'I'll admit I was kind of full of myself back then. But, you know, I was a kid. I was seventeen!'

'Everyone in twelfth grade is seventeen,' Ella pointed out, unsure why he'd brought up what seemed to her an irrelevant statement of fact.

'What I mean is—'

'You told people we'd had intercourse.'

Danny blushed. 'Did I? I don't remember that.'

'You said I'd begged you to have relations with me. "Begged". That was the word you used.'

Danny held up his hands in a 'mea culpa' gesture. 'Jeesh, OK. Wow. Well I don't know what to say. I was a jerk and I'm sorry. But it's ancient history, isn't it? I'm married now,' he brightened. 'You remember Beth Harvey?'

Ella didn't, but Danny pulled a photograph out of the breast pocket of his overalls and pressed it into her hand. It showed an ordinary-looking dark-haired girl, whom Ella may or may not have seen before, with two fat, bald babies, one perched on each hip.

'Those're our twins,' Danny said proudly. 'Nate and Charlie. You got kids?'

'No!' Flustered, Ella looked around for a means of escape that wouldn't involve either pushing past Danny or turning on her heel and running.

'Married?'

She shook her head vehemently. But no matter what Ella did, or said, Danny just kept smiling, like some sort of madman. Why was he asking her these questions? Why was he even talking to her? She liked him better when he was a bully. At least then she knew where she stood. What did one say to a 'nice' Danny Bleeker?

'I get it,' he nodded, his eyes blazing with the well-intentioned but utterly vacant expression of someone who

73

categorically did *not* get it. 'You're all about your career. Right? Well, I guess you always were real smart. Underneath the crazy,' he added, but it was said affectionately. 'You went to Cal, didn't you? So what'd you end up as? Doctor? Lawyer? No? Don't tell me: Rocket scientist!' he laughed. 'You work for Elon Musk or somethin'?'

'No,' said Ella. 'I used to be a statistician but I got fired. Officially it was because I took too much time off, but actually it was because I declined sexual relations with my boss. He was extremely unattractive,' she added by way of explanation. 'I have to go back to my hotel now. Goodbye.'

Danny Bleeker turned and scratched his head as he watched his old classmate speed-walk away from him towards the rundown Double Tree, the only hotel in town. Watching Ella Praeger leave was always a pleasure. She still had a great ass. But if anything, the years since school seemed to have made her even weirder. Danny had wanted to sleep with her so bad back then. All his taunting and cruelty had been a clumsy attempt at flirtation, an effort to get Ella's attention. But with hindsight he reckoned he'd had a lucky escape.

Back in her bland hotel room, Ella lay back on the ugly brown bed and closed her eyes. She was mentally bracing for more voices to ambush her. So far this trip she'd had two debilitating 'episodes' while out on Main Street, and a string of more minor ones here in the hotel, as if a radio were hidden somewhere in her bedroom, crackling out static as its signal veered between two stations.

Since the man had left her apartment, apparently for good, Ella had had ample time to ponder the outlandish theory he'd given her to explain away her symptoms.

*'The voices are real. They're electronic transmissions, of varying types. You were genetically modified before birth*

74

*to be able to both detect and unscramble them. It's a unique ability.'*

Her longing for an answer to the debilitating condition made her want to believe him. But even the most cursory of reality checks made that hard to do. *Genetically modified before birth?* Come on. Was that even possible? Ella's brief Google search suggested it was not, any more than exposure to gamma radiation could turn you into a giant green brute, or a spider bite could imbue you with web-spinning hands. Clearly the man, whoever he was, was deliberately playing on her weaknesses, telling her something she wanted to hear in order to win her trust, to draw her into the clutches of 'The Group'. He'd successfully latched onto Ella's twin Achilles heels – her thirst for knowledge about her parents, and her desperate search for a cure to her crippling headaches; a way to stop the voices that babbled at her day and night – cruelly using both to try to manipulate her. Was his disappearing act now yet more manipulation, Ella wondered? If so, it was working.

But why? That was the question. What did he want from her? What did he hope to gain?

Those were the questions that haunted Ella, night after night, along with all the 'hows'. How did he know so much about her symptoms? She'd told no one about the voices that plagued her, not a living soul. If her parents had been brainwashed by whatever cult it was that the man belonged to, and if they really were genetic scientists, then his explanation for the white noise in her head seemed at least possible, even if it was outlandish. *Genetically modified.* It wasn't exactly comforting, but it was an answer of sorts. A place to start, even if it posed as many problems as it solved.

Reaching into her pocket as she lay on the bed, Ella coiled her fingers around the USB stick that the man had given her. She still hadn't looked at the contents. Some combination of fear and defiance held her back, narrowly outweighing curiosity.

*He wants me to look at it*, thought Ella, *which is exactly why I mustn't. Doing what he wants, letting him set the agenda. That would be handing him the upper hand on a plate.*

The man clearly saw her as naïve. As malleable, a sheep to be led. Ella intended to show him just how wrong he was. But how *could* she show him if he disappeared on her? What if he never came back, and this stick was the only clue to the truth about her condition?

Her fingers traced the grooves in the metal, warm now from the heat of her hand and slightly clammy with sweat. Pulling the USB stick from her pocket she stood up and placed it on the desk, next to her computer. The voices hadn't come back, yet. All was quiet, in the room and in Ella's head. She locked the door.

*If I plug it in now, no one will know that I looked at it. No one but me.*

*He can't manipulate me unless I let him.*

She plugged the device into her laptop and waited for something to appear.

Nothing happened.

Ella clicked on 'file' and searched in 'contents'. It was blank. The stick was completely empty.

'Bastard!' she said aloud. Was this his idea of a joke? Anger welled up inside her. She wanted to hit something, break something, *hurt* something – ideally him.

But then something strange started happening to her screen. First, it went black. Then it flashed brightly back to life, Ella's desktop popping back up with its neatly arranged files and programs seeming to oscillate and shimmer, like signs in a heat haze. Finally, to Ella's astonishment, then horror, her applications began disappearing, popping like balloons in front of her eyes, one by one.

*What the . . .?*

At the bottom of her screen, a counter had popped up, showing the 'used' memory levels dropping slowly at first: 225GB . . . 200GB . . . 160GB . . . then very, very rapidly indeed, 8GB . . . 1GB . . . 470MB.

The stick was wiping her drive! The man wasn't giving her information – he was stealing information! Ella yanked the device out of her USB drive, but it was too late. With a dying flicker, like an old man's last wheezy breath, her screen faded to black.

Shaking, furious at herself for her own stupidity, Ella sat mute, staring at the nothingness in front of her. After a few seconds her computer gave a crackle, the same white noise she often heard in her head, only this was external, real. Then a face appeared. It was a man's face, half in shadow, and it was immobile at first, a freeze-frame on an old-fashioned video. Another crackle and it – he – began to move, leaning forwards out of the shadows, gazing into the camera.

Ella gripped the side of the desk. *No. It can't be.*

'My darling Ella.' Clearing his throat, William Praeger started to speak. 'If you are watching this, then you already know I have left this world. I can't be with you any more, and for that, my darling, I am so very sorry.'

'Dad!' Ella gasped, fighting for breath. That voice! Ella hadn't heard it for twenty-two years. Had completely forgotten it, in fact – or so she'd thought until now, as it assailed her like an old friend, enchanting and intoxicating, conjuring up lost love like a cruel yet beautiful magic spell. Instinctively she reached out and touched the screen, as if her fingers could somehow connect with him, transport her back into the past. But of course they didn't.

'You will have been contacted by someone from The Group. And I am sure that will have left you confused, and maybe even frightened. Please, don't be.'

He looked so young, early thirties at most, and was wearing a white T-shirt and a string of beads around his neck. His hair was long, like a hippie's or a surfer's, and he was also deeply tanned, none of which tallied with Ella's few, snatched memories of him. But his mannerisms, his movements, his smile; all of those were the same. She watched, transfixed, hanging off his every word.

'Your destiny, like your mother's and mine, has always been intertwined with The Group and its work. Our work. I know it may not feel like it right now. But that destiny is also a privilege, perhaps the greatest privilege a person can have. You were born to do good, Ella. To do good in ways that other people might not understand.

'It's not an easy path. There is evil in this world, Ella; evil of a pitch and intensity that most people can't imagine. Sadly, those few who can see it usually choose not to act. They put their heads in the sand. They wish it away. Unfortunately, this often includes our own government.'

Ella's stomach lurched. She loved her father, and over his long years of absence had come to idolize him, and her mother too. Yet on this recording, William Praeger sounded like every other brainwashed cult member she'd ever seen on TV, ranting on about conspiracy theories and corrupt governments and how only 'The Group' understands the truth.

'Ella, you are blessed with unique gifts. You are the product of love, but also of science. Your brain can function in ways that nobody else's can. The Group will explain everything to you when the time is right. Right now, we don't know exactly how far those gifts will take you, or what their potential will be. But your mother and I know that you will use them for good. We believe in you, Ella. We love you.'

Silent tears streamed down Ella's face. She wanted to climb into the screen and hug him, and kiss him . . . and then yell at him and shake him till his head hurt as much as hers did. How could he do this to her? Her own father! His so-called 'gifts' had condemned her to an existence of daily misery! To headaches, and paranoia, and a loneliness the depths of which he couldn't possibly understand. How dare he and her mother play God with her life, trying out their experimental genetic bullshit on their own child? Or any other innocent human being, for that matter.

'Stay true to yourself, my darling,' William went on. 'Trust in The Group and try to be patient. What you don't understand now, you will eventually, believe me.' Her father's eyes welled up with tears then, and Ella could see the effort he was making to contain his emotion. 'Above all, please Ella, never forget how much your mother and I have loved you. Give your grandmother a kiss for me. Goodbye, my precious Ella Mae.'

There was another final hiss of sound, and Ella's screen went blank a final time.

'No.' Ella whispered under her breath. 'No, no, no, no, no!' That couldn't be it? He hadn't told her anything about her mother. Where was she? Why wasn't she in the video?

Desperately she plugged the stick back in, trying everything to bring the footage back up again, to rewind. But it was nowhere. Gone, wiped, just like the man said it would be.

*Nooo.* Ella stood up, pulling at her hair in frustration that bordered on panic. There had to be more! It was bad enough that her mom was missing from Mimi's box of letters and cards. But why wasn't she on this footage? Why wasn't she here on Ella's screen, sitting next to her father, offering her own explanations, saying her own goodbyes?

Hadn't Rachel Praeger cared about her daughter at all? Had Ella been nothing more than an experiment to her, a sacrificial offering to the all-powerful 'Group'?

Ella was starting to hate this Group. Who *were* these people, to mess with people's lives, to separate parents from their children, then return years later and 'claim' those children as their own?

Slamming her laptop shut, Ella tossed it angrily onto the bed. It was useless now, ruined, its hard drive hopelessly corrupted. *Like my life*, Ella reflected bitterly. She paced the room like a trapped animal, feeling at once exhausted and yet full of restless energy. She had an overwhelming urge to know, to understand. And yet it seemed the more she did know, the more tantalizing nuggets of information were drip-fed into her life, the more maddened with uncertainty and curiosity she became. Was she really even a person at all, a human being with a soul and an identity of her own? Was she her parents' daughter, or their science project? With each new blow she could feel her self-esteem crumbling. But like an addiction, Ella's need to understand drove her, even though she knew that it could destroy her too.

Seeing and hearing her father had been exquisite joy and yet, at the same time, agonizing torture. Because of all the things he hadn't said. Because he was here, but then he was gone. And because he hadn't said sorry.

He owed Ella an apology for so many things. But mostly for never coming back.

Ella ran a bath and climbed into it, making the water as hot as she could stand. She watched as her skin reddened like lobster flesh, willing the unpleasant, burning sensation to drown out her emotional anguish. It didn't.

*You have two choices*, she told herself, steam rising up and enveloping her in a thick, heady cloud. *You can sink. Or you can swim.*

*You can control your own life. Or be controlled.*

The footage she'd just watched had confirmed the man's story about her scientific origins. Her mother and father really *had* tried to program her, like a computer. So she could be useful to 'The Group'. *Seriously. George Orwell couldn't have made this stuff up.* Ella's parents had believed they had the right to control not just her mind and her body, but all her future decisions as well. Her 'destiny', as Ella's father had put it. Clearly the Praegers had been brainwashed by 'The Group'. And now, from beyond the grave, they wanted to send Ella off to be brainwashed too.

*No. No way.*

Ella had already resisted her grandmother's idea of 'destiny' – a life of isolation and Christian piety up at the ranch, cut off from the rest of the world. It had been painful to break away, but Ella had done it. And she could do it again.

OK, so her brain had been messed with. That was a problem. But it was a problem she could fix on her own, without the help of the cult that had screwed her up in the first place. She could still lead a normal life if she chose to. The kind of life that Bob had, in the city, with a job and a family and friends. She could do it. Bob could teach her how to do it.

*Except* . . . the voices. The headaches, the nausea, the endless roar that wouldn't ever switch off. They would drive her mad in the end. How could she hope to hold down a job, or a relationship, when at any moment deafening tangles of noise and pain could ambush her, bringing her, sometimes literally, to her knees?

She had to learn how to control the voices. How to master the unwanted 'gift' that her parents had given her. Because unless she could do that, no life she chose would be worth living.

81

Climbing out of the bath, dripping wet, Ella lay back on the bed and let the cool air of the room suck the heat out of her body.

However she felt about the man – however profoundly she hated him right now – he was the key to her future. Not because she owed a damn thing to him, or her parents, or their stupid Group. But because he might, just might, be able to teach her how to master the voices in her head. Or at least to introduce her to people who could. Maybe, just maybe, if *those* voices stopped, she might stand a better chance at interpreting the real voices of those around her. Of reading social cues. Of fitting in.

'Where are you?' Ella shouted out loud. 'Where the hell are you, you son of a bitch?'

'Close your eyes.'

Ella spun around, grabbing the throw rug from the foot of the bed, scrambling to cover her naked body. His voice was so clear, at first Ella thought he must be standing in the room. She looked around, her eyes darting to every corner of the hotel suite, but there was no one there.

'You'll hear me better if your eyes are closed,' the man repeated.

Only then did Ella realize, with a sinking heart, that his voice was actually coming from inside her head. Unlike all the others, though, it was crystal clear, like a telephone call on a perfect, crackle-free line.

*He's transmitting to me?*

Despite herself, she was fascinated. How the hell was he able to . . .?

'Don't try to answer me,' he instructed her. 'It won't work. You can receive but you can't transmit. Just listen.'

*Perfect*, thought Ella bitterly. *So you're in control. Again.*

'I'm glad you saw the footage,' the man continued. 'I expect you have questions.'

82

*Just a few.*

'You'll have a chance to ask them at training. It starts tomorrow at our upstate facility. They're expecting you.'

*Of course they are.*

'Find something to write with. The information I'm about to give you is important. Do not share it with anyone.'

Perhaps it was a blessing Ella couldn't respond, as his dictatorial tone was really starting to tick her off. After about twenty seconds of silence, he gave her some map coordinates, which he repeated twice. Ella scribbled them down. There were just the numbers, nothing more. Then came a curt 'goodbye' and the man's voice shut off, as suddenly as it had begun.

Feeling marginally less agitated than she had before, Ella climbed under the covers.

Tomorrow, she would see this 'Group' first hand. She had no intention of joining them. Of being brainwashed and corrupted the way her parents had been. And she certainly wasn't going on any 'mission' for this bunch of lunatics. Instead, Ella would turn the tables. She would take what *she* needed from them, on *her* terms. She would make them teach her how to control and perhaps even switch off the 'transmissions' that were making her life so unbearable. To disable her 'gift'. And, she'd extract more information about her parents, especially her mother. The least this cult could do after all the havoc they'd wreaked was to fill in the gaps. When she was done, she would leave, free of her headaches, free of her grandmother, free of her parents' expectations, free of everything. She would begin building the normal, happy life she wanted. The life she deserved.

For the first time since Mimi's funeral, Ella fell almost at once into a deep, contented sleep.

# CHAPTER SIX

Daphne Alexandris turned to her husband Stavros. 'Did you hear that noise?'

'What noise?' Stavros looked up from his iPad.

'That . . . clattering. There it is again!'

The Alexandrises were sitting at opposite ends of the grand drawing room in their colonial mansion in Putre, Chile. A friend of Stavros's had sold it to him for a song back in the days when Stavros had been riding high as Greece's interior minister and Dimitri Mantzaris's right-hand man. In exchange, Stavros had green-lighted some apartment developments in a slummy part of Athens, that might or might not have fully complied with Greek fire regulations. In any event, the house in Putre was an oasis of calm and peace, a place where Stavros and his wife could escape the pressures of Greek politics – or anything else they might need to escape. Set back from the ancient *pueblo* of the pretty mountain town, with the peaks of the Taapaca Volcano rising up behind it like benevolent deities, the mansion was at once luxurious and supremely comfortable, furnished with an array of priceless South American antiques. One could live like a king in Chile on reasonably modest means, and the Alexandrises' means were far from modest. Good security, of course, was a must. But luckily they could afford that too.

'It's probably just foxes or possums,' said Stavros, yawning. It was late, and he was no more than one more good brandy away from his bed. 'Scrabbling at the trash. I'll send Juanita out to take care of them.'

Reaching to his left, he rang a small silver bell on the table beside him, like a Victorian lord of the manor. Sure enough, the housekeeper arrived like a summoned genie.

'Go and see what's making that racket would you, Juanita? The noise is bothering Señora Alexandris.'

'I don't know how you can be so calm, Stavros,' Daphne Alexandris hissed, her thin neck straining with stress so that the sinews bulged beneath the crepey, sixty-year-old skin. 'What if it isn't foxes? What if it's *her*? No one close to Mantzaris is safe. You said so yourself. That's why we're here, isn't it?'

Walking over to his wife, Stavros laid a skinny hand on her shoulder. 'We are here because it *is* safe here, my darling,' he reminded her. 'Athena's business – if she truly *is* alive – is in Greece. Trust me, Chile will not even be on her radar. She wouldn't waste resources sending somebody trekking all the way up here, to the top of the world, just to find the likes of us.'

Turning away from her, he walked across to the bar and poured himself a large measure of Frapin Extra Grande Champagne Cognac.

'Will you have one more, Daphne? Calm your nerves before bed?' he asked, reaching up for a second brandy glass. 'Daphne? Did you open a window? It's terribly—'

Turning around he froze, letting both glasses drop to the floor and shatter into a thousand pieces across the Persian carpet. His wife sat just as she had been before, perfectly still, her eyes wide open. Except that now there was a bullet hole right through the middle of her forehead. The sash window behind her stood open, its lace curtains fluttering in the evening breeze.

A slow, cold terror crawled over him, rooting him to the spot.

Stavros had heard nothing. *Nothing!* Not a shot. Not a breath. Not a sound.

Black spots swam before his eyes.

*Why? Why Daphne? Why not him? Surely it was him she wanted. That bitch! Dimitri's she-devil . . .*

He looked around him at the empty room, and the darkness beyond the window, wild panic in his eyes.

Then, like a hunted animal, he turned and ran.

'Shall we?'

Ella looked up again at the two-foot-thick wooden gates in front of her. Set into a barbed-wire fence, they were twice her height, and would have looked vast anywhere else. But here, deep in the California forest, dwarfed by redwoods that towered over everything like a battalion of ancient giants, they seemed almost comically small, like the gateway to a children's fort.

The journey here had been long and bizarre. It had been a six-hour drive from Ella's hotel to the coordinates the man had given her last night. If, indeed, what she'd heard as she lay on the bed really *was* the man trying to contact her, and not a sign that she had finally lost the plot and needed to check herself into a mental facility as soon as possible, whether she liked it or not.

Her satnav had sent her on a narrow road that wound higher and higher into the hills. The scenery was breathtaking. Wilder and more rugged than the rolling pastures of her grandmother's ranch, but every bit as beautiful, this part of the state was like a Tolkienian fantasy, all pines and rocks and deer and bears and dazzling blue skies that seemed to stretch to eternity. Watching eagles soar above her, and waterfalls cascade down the rocks beside the road, so close in places that if Ella opened her driver's window and stretched out her arm she could almost touch them, she found herself forgetting everything else as she lost herself in the wonder and majesty of nature. Her grandmother's rigid version of religion had never appealed to her, never seemed real. But places like this – the peace, the beauty – made Ella want to believe in God, or at least in something outside of herself, something bigger and more important. Something she could trust in.

The tranquility was interrupted by the next leg of the journey. Ella was met at the designated coordinates by a young woman called Agnes, who led her on a two-mile hike up a steep escarpment, littered with loose rocks, and then insisted on blindfolding her in the back of an expensive-looking Range Rover Velar for a bumpy, tortuous forty-minute drive through the forest. Disorientated and exhausted, Ella had been on the brink of demanding to go home. But after eight, grueling hours, she had to see this through.

The property Ella glimpsed looked more like a well-maintained hotel than the prison camp suggested by the gated front. Small white bungalows were dotted amongst neatly mown lawns, and soft outdoor uplighters revealed lovingly planted flower beds and charming brick walking paths snaking throughout the grounds. Here and there, parked golf carts, some piled high with bags of what looked like dirty laundry, only heightened Ella's feeling that she was checking in to the San Ysidro Ranch, and not potentially risking her life at the mercy of some obscure and secretive cult.

'Pretty, isn't it?' said Agnes, registering her passenger's surprise. 'The training program can be pretty intense, so Mr Redmayne believes it is important that members should have a pleasant environment to return to at the end of the day. Not luxurious, but relaxing.'

Ella listened. She wondered whether the man who had visited her was in fact 'Mr Redmayne' and, if so, when he would appear in person.

'Accommodations are divided up by gender,' Agnes went on. 'You'll be staying in the female quarters, obviously. Whoah, hold up!'

She slammed on the brakes. A group of disheveled and exhausted-looking women had staggered into the road in front of them. They were wearing army fatigues and most were filthy, their hair matted and their faces splattered with mud. They were also all strikingly thin. As Agnes screeched to a halt, one of them turned and looked right at Ella before sinking to her knees, and vomiting violently. That fairly comprehensively ruined the San Ysidro vibe.

'Oh my God!' Ella reached for the handle of her door.

Agnes's arm shot out to stop her. 'What are you doing?'

'I'm going to help her, of course,' said Ella. 'Didn't you just see that?'

'She's training,' Agnes said, as if that explained everything. 'And she's with her unit.'

'Training for what? Armageddon?' Ella asked, watching the other women stagger on while their teammate fell back against the tarmac, apparently unconscious. 'And her "unit" just left her there.'

With a growing sense of foreboding, she waited for them to arrive at check-in, or registration, or wherever it was they were going. But instead, after only a few hundred more yards, Agnes pulled over outside one of the bungalows, gesturing for Ella to get out.

'These are your quarters,' she told her, jumping out herself and retrieving Ella's backpack from the back of the truck.

'OK . . .' Ella said hesitantly.

'Is something wrong?'

'No, it's just . . . don't I need to sign in? Let somebody know I'm here?'

Agnes laughed loudly 'Oh, Ella! Everybody knows you're here, my dear. Where else would you be? We've all been waiting for you.'

Ella tried not to think about Bob's 'Jonestown' warnings. Whatever she had let herself in for, it was too late now.

*You're here by choice*, she coached herself. *Not for them. For you. To get what YOU need. To take back YOUR life.*

*Then you get out.*

'Community dinner's in an hour,' Agnes chirped. Ella reflected that the poor women she'd just seen didn't look as if they'd eaten dinner in weeks, community or otherwise, but she kept the thought to herself.

'If you need anything before then, your roommate should be able to help.' Handing Ella her backpack, Agnes hopped back into the driver's seat. 'Welcome to Camp Hope!' she said cheerfully, driving away.

Tentatively, Ella opened the bungalow door. 'Hello?'

She was met by a squeal, a strong waft of perfume, and the slightly disconcerting sight of a buxom blonde in a skin-tight pink T-shirt bounding up to her like a puppy. This girl certainly hadn't been starved. If anything she looked as if she might have eaten the other women's food, every ounce of which had made its way to her enormous boobs.

'Oh my *God*. You're here! You're finally here. I do not believe it, oh my God oh my God oh my *God!*'

89

The blonde looked to be about Ella's own age, although there was something distinctly teenagerish in her manner, from the gushing welcome to the look-at-me clothes. The room was split into two halves, each with a single bed and a washbasin. While Ella's side was bare, the girl had kitted hers out in a sea of pink, complete with fluffy rainbow pillows and 'Hello Kitty' bedding. Décor-wise at least, it was less 'spy' and more 'pre-pubescent Japanese schoolgirl'.

'You must be Ella.'

'That's right.'

'I'm Christine. Christine Marshall. Sooooooo happy to meet you.' Drawing her into a hug, Christine squeezed tightly and let out another, only slightly more muted, squeal.

Extricating herself from Christine's enthusiastic embrace, Ella put her stuff warily down on the bed.

'You're probably exhausted,' Christine said kindly, taking a step back. Everywhere she went, an aura of perfume followed her like a miasma. 'I know I was when I first arrived. But if you have any questions, any questions at all, just fire away.'

Ella had a lot of questions, but they were for the man to answer, not this human Barbie doll.

'I'm looking for someone,' she told Christine, describing the man as best she could. Stocky. Dark hair. Strong jaw. Well dressed. As she spoke it occurred to her how vague and generic she made him sound.

'He's the person who recruited me, and I really, really need to speak to him. Tonight, if possible. Do you know him?'

Christine's face fell. 'I don't think so. Sorry. Although I wish I did from your description. But if he's at camp then he'll be at community dinner. Everyone comes to community dinner.'

'Everyone?' Ella mentioned the group of women she'd

passed driving through the camp just now. How they looked half starved.

'Ah, yes, well they were probably on operations,' replied Christine, echoing Agnes's confidence that somehow that made it all OK. 'Discipline and self-denial are all part of the program.'

At that moment a very fat man with a straggly beard and long hair growing down on either side of a premature bald patch burst into the cabin, a look of almost maniacal excitement on his face. 'You're here at last then?' he said, staring fixedly at Ella.

'Do I know you?' Ella frowned.

'Not yet,' his smile broadened. 'But I know you. Everybody does. You're quite the celebrity around here, Miss Praeger. Jackson.' He thrust a bear-like paw towards her. 'I'm a friend of Chrissie's.'

'He's a pain in my ass,' corrected Christine, although it was said with obvious affection. 'Jackson thinks he's more important than the rest of us because he works in systems and is a genius.'

'She's just being bitchy because she wants my body and knows she can't have it,' Jackson told Ella, deadpan. Ella hesitated, then laughed.

'Look,' she said, 'I don't know what you've heard. But I'm not part of your Group. I'm only at Camp Hope because of a man who turned up to my grandmother's funeral. He told me he had information about my parents and . . . other things. Maybe you've heard of them? William and Rachel Praeger? They joined The Group decades ago, before I was born.'

Jackson and Christine exchanged glances.

'Sorry, I don't know about them,' said Jackson. 'But we've heard about *you*. That you have special capabilities that could be vital to our work.'

'And that it's super-important we make you feel welcome,' Christine added, sincerely.

'So, you know: Welcome,' said Jackson.

'Thanks,' said Ella. 'But you haven't heard of my mother and father?'

Both Jackson and Christine shook their heads.

'Perhaps *you* know the man who recruited me?' she asked Jackson, describing him again. 'Christine said she doesn't.'

'Sorry. It's not ringing a bell for me either,' Jackson said, apologetically.

No one seemed to know anything, other than the fact that Ella herself was 'important' and 'expected' and 'different', like some sort of magical unicorn they'd been told to wait for, and who had now miraculously appeared among them.

*I'm like the messiah of a religion I've never heard of and don't understand*, she thought. A mix of fatigue and extreme anger washed over Ella.

'I'm sorry.' She stood up abruptly. 'I seem to have made a mistake. I should never have come here. I need to leave.'

'Leave?' Christine looked aghast. 'But, you can't *leave*. You've literally only just arrived.'

'Sorry,' said Ella again, to Christine and Jackson. 'Good luck with everything. It was nice to meet you both.'

She grabbed her suitcase and turned on her heel out of the cabin without a second glance. It had been a long and grueling day, coming here, and her hopes had been so high after last night. But it had all been for nothing. The man had lured her here under false pretenses. She didn't believe that anyone at Camp Hope knew her parents. The man had delivered Ella to his group of misfits and weirdoes, like a good little brainwashed boy, and then disappeared. Again.

Jackson seemed pleasant, and perhaps Christine was nice enough too in her own pneumatic, giggly way. But it was a carefully controlled 'nice'. A cult nice, a 'be patient, all will be revealed' nice, designed to suck Ella into whatever cause it was that 'The Group' believed in, without actually answering any of her questions.

She marched up the winding maze of paths towards the front gates. She passed only a few people along the way, some of whom gave her curious glances, although no one intervened. Everybody else was obviously on the way to community dinner. Reaching the gates at last, her heart pounded as she approached the two men on duty.

'I need to leave,' she blurted. 'Now.'

'Leave?' the first man looked puzzled.

'Yes,' Ella said firmly, although inside her panic was mounting. What if they wouldn't let her out? What if they tried to keep her a prisoner here?

'Are you sure?' the second man asked, compounding Ella's anxiety. 'It's very late. Where will you go?'

'Just open the gates,' Ella demanded.

He hesitated.

'Open them!'

To her surprise and relief, the man shrugged and did as she asked, pressing a button that caused the camp gates to swing open. Outside, beyond the softly floodlit glow of Camp Hope, the pitch-dark forest stretched endlessly out in front of her. Ella hesitated. *Where* am *I going to go?* she wondered. It suddenly struck her that she had no idea in which direction her car was parked, and Agnes must have driven her at least a few miles away from that spot. There'd be bears out there, and mountain lions, and heaven knew what else. Her phone was dead and she was unarmed. Should she turn back and wait till morning?

'Leaving us so soon, Ella?' Ella spun around. The man's voice rang out in her head as clearly as if she were watching television or listening to the radio in her room. As ever he sounded supremely calm and unconcerned. Amused, almost. It was infuriating.

'Where *are* you?!' Ella's exasperated voice rang out through the trees. There must be a camera up there somewhere, hidden in the canopy, but in this light she couldn't see it. 'Answer me!'

'No need to shout. You're free to go at any time, of course,' he continued, his voice patronizingly slow and patient, as if Ella were the crazy one, not him. 'This isn't a prison.'

'It might as well be,' Ella yelled into the darkness, aware that anyone listening to her must think her completely insane, having a confrontational conversation with an imaginary friend. 'Everyone inside is completely brainwashed.'

'Don't be so dramatic.'

So there were listening devices out there too? There must be, or how could he be hearing her?

'How are you doing this? How are you speaking to me? Transmitting . . .?'

'Be patient,' said the man. 'The answers you seek are all here, Ella, I promise you that. About your parents. Your past. Your future.'

'No,' she shot back. 'They aren't. No one knows anything.'

A long sigh. 'They do. Trust me.'

'Why should I?' said Ella furiously. 'Why should I trust you when you won't tell me who you are, or where you are, or anything at all? And if you really have the answers, why won't you just tell me them now? What are you waiting for? For me to be brainwashed too? Because I'm telling you now, it's not going to happen.'

There was a moment's silence. Total silence. Ella wondered whether the man had gone, 'hung up' on whatever line it was he seemed to have into her head, her psyche. But then he spoke again, more kindly than before.

'Stay here tonight.' It was less of a command, more of a suggestion. 'The woods aren't safe and you need to sleep.'

That much at least was true, much as she wished it weren't.

'Someone will brief you by the end of the day tomorrow. If you still want to leave after that meeting, then I'll help you get safely back home.'

Mute and exhausted, Ella nodded. Wordlessly, she trudged back down the hill towards her bungalow, watched by the two bewildered guards.

She didn't trust the man. Not as far as she could throw him. *But she didn't trust the bears either.*

Tomorrow.

She would leave tomorrow.

One day at Camp Hope wouldn't kill her.

# CHAPTER SEVEN

*They're trying to kill me. They are actually trying to kill me.*

Ella sank to her knees, unable to move another step. Her lungs were in agony. After an eight-mile run in punishing midday heat, she felt as if she'd inhaled a bag of razor blades. Her skin burned, the blisters on her feet screamed and a dreadful feeling of nausea rose all the way from the pit of her (empty) stomach to her parched throat. Forget the Marine Corps. The first day's 'introductory' physical training at Camp Hope had clearly been devised by an experienced torturer, possibly headhunted by The Group from a Malaysian prison.

'All right, ladies. One-minute water break and then you're in active recovery. That means a light jog back to base. No walking.' The tracksuit-wearing giant from yesterday smiled at Ella and the two other young women slumped on the ground beside her, as if he'd just done them a favor. He'd apparently abandoned yesterday's tag-team of skeletons to initiate Ella and the other new recruits into the joys of ops training, an experience Ella would categorically *not* be repeating after today. Astonishingly, both the other girls smiled weakly back at him, earning themselves a withering glare from Ella. These brainwashed, cult groupies were too much for her. She could tell they were intimidated by her anger, but she couldn't have cared less if her life depended on it.

Jogging back through the forest, she felt her frustration building, even as the agony in her lungs began to recede. She'd heard nothing from the man today, about this 'briefing' she was supposed to receive, or anything else. The voices in her head had gone completely silent. She didn't have a watch on, but she reckoned it must be three o'clock at least, judging by the position of the sun, and the long, grueling hours she'd been out training. She'd longed to tell the Adidas giant where he could stick his barked orders, but having come this far she didn't want to do anything to jeopardize the promised meeting and explanation. Now, however, she was beginning to think that the man was simply stringing her along again, dangling carrots he never had any intention of actually delivering.

Back at the camp, Ella stopped for a moment to catch her breath before heading straight up the path that Christine had told her led to the administrative offices.

'Praeger!' the giant boomed. 'Where do you think you're going? The showers are this way.'

Ella's only answer was a succinct middle finger raised above her head as she kept walking, to audible shocked gasps from her training mates. A few minutes later, pulling open the door to the main office so violently it might have come off its hinges, she stood like an angry bull in front of the reception desk, sweating and panting. 'I demand to see whoever's in charge of this dump,' she snapped at the young man behind the desk. 'Right now.'

The young man didn't bat an eyelid. 'Of course, Ms Praeger,' he smiled. 'Ms MacAvoy's been expecting you.

Can I get you a glass of water or would you prefer to go straight through?'

Thrown by his reaction, Ella hesitated. Before she could answer, the glass door behind the reception desk swung open and an attractive, professional-looking woman in her early fifties stepped forwards.

'Ah, Ella. I thought it was you. I'm Katherine MacAvoy, the supervisor here at Camp Hope.' Extending her arm she shook Ella's hand warmly. 'Do come in.'

Inside the office was bright and clean, with a lot of white, modern furniture and chrome accents. An enormous picture window provided panoramic views of the redwoods and distant pastures beyond, and there were photographs of waterfalls and autumnal scenes on the walls. Katherine MacAvoy's desk was bare except for an open MacBook Air, a charging iPhone and a single beige manila file with Ella's name typed on the front.

'Please.' Sitting down at the desk, Katherine gestured for Ella to take the chair opposite. 'You must be exhausted. I remember my own first day of training. It's no picnic, is it?'

She smiled but Ella didn't reciprocate. No way was she falling for these people's charm offensives.

'I'm not interested in your training. I'm not a member of your stupid Group, OK? I came here to learn more about my parents, William and Rachel Praeger, and what they may or may not have done to my brain. That is literally the only reason I am sitting here right now. Because I was promised answers. Not because I'm buying into this, or you, in any way.'

Katherine MacAvoy nodded calmly. 'I understand.'

'No you don't!' Ella snapped. 'How could you possibly?'

'You're agitated,' the older woman said gently. 'Why don't you—'

'The man who contacted me, who came to my

98

grandmother's funeral and told me about this place . . . he claimed that my mother and father used to be part of your organization. He showed me a video file of my father that seemed to confirm it. He also said that my parents were scientists and that they'd . . .' She searched around for the right word. '. . . *edited* certain parts of my brain.'

'That's right,' the older woman assented.

'I was brought up to believe that my mother and father died in a car crash in 1998. Is that correct?'

Katherine MacAvoy met Ella's hostile gaze with her own steady one.

'It is not correct, no. But I imagine the man you met explained that to you already?'

'He said my parents were murdered.'

Katherine cleared her throat. 'I'm afraid that's true, Ella.'

'Yes, well, you'll excuse me if I don't take your word for it,' Ella hissed, as impotently furious as a trapped snake. 'I want to see proof.'

'I see. Well . . .'

'I also want proof that it really was my parents and not you people who messed around with my brain so that I hear these goddamn . . . *things*. *All the time!*' Ella banged the side of her temples with her fists. She felt as if years of repressed anger and fear and frustration were in imminent danger of bursting out of her. As if her skull might literally explode, like a grenade. 'Because he said that too, this man. And he said coming here would help me, but it hasn't helped me, and he promised me again last night, sending goddamn audio messages into my brain like he has some right of access, *which he doesn't,* and I actually think all you people are full of *shit!*' She banged her fist on the table, sending the manila folder skidding across the polished wood of the desk. Seeing her name on the front, Ella picked it up.

'So this is for me, is it?' she demanded, still furious.

'It is.' Katherine MacAvoy's calm demeanor never wavered.

'And is it proof?'

'No,' said Katherine. 'The "proof" you're looking for doesn't exist, Ella. But what Gabriel told you is true.'

*Gabriel?* Somehow Ella couldn't imagine that being the man's name.

'This file,' Katherine patted the manila folder, 'contains a briefing document on us and our work, and some preliminary information about your first mission. I hope it answers some of your initial questions. But perhaps you should read it first and then we can talk further?'

'No.' Ella stood up, shaking her head. 'No more. This ends here. This man – *Gabriel* – told me last night that if I wasn't satisfied after my meeting today, I could leave and he would help me get back to San Francisco. So I'm leaving. Right now.'

Katherine MacAvoy studied Ella's face. There was no regret there, no hesitation. Only a very dangerous combination of disgust and determination. *If she leaves now, we've lost her. She won't come back.*

'How did Gabriel contact you last night?'

Ella had already turned to leave. The question felt like an arrow in her back.

'He transmitted directly to your brain, didn't he?' Katherine MacAvoy pressed her advantage. 'You heard his voice internally. In your head.'

Ella nodded grudgingly. 'I told you. He does that sometimes. He cuts through all the other noise.'

'How?' asked Katherine. 'Surely the only way he could do that would be if he understood the changes your parents made to your brain chemistry? Think about it, Ella. We *know* who you are. We *understand* why you're different. Nobody else does.'

'Then tell me!' Ella roared, turning around to face her. 'Tell me right now, today, or I will leave here and I will not come back. I want to see this Gabriel. I want him here, in person.' She jabbed a finger down on Katherine's desk. 'I want *him* to tell me everything he knows about me and about what happened to my parents. And if he doesn't then I'll leave and I'll . . . I'll go to the police and tell them about this place.'

Katherine's expression darkened. 'Don't do that, Ella.' The calm tone still hadn't wavered, but underlying it now there was an unmistakable note of threat.

'Why shouldn't I?' Ella's entire body seemed to quiver with defiance.

'Just don't.'

For a moment a heavy silence fell. Then Katherine continued.

'I will request that Gabriel attend Camp Hope in person during your stay,' Katherine went on. 'I will also commit to providing you with more detailed, written evidence about your parents' time with us, and specifically their last mission and the circumstances of their deaths.'

'When?' asked Ella.

'I'll need a few days. Perhaps a week.'

'A *week*? No. I won't stay here for a week. I can't.'

'Of course you can,' Katherine said briskly, smiling again. 'Young women your age pay thousands of dollars to go away on fitness retreats.'

'I don't,' said Ella. 'And this isn't a fitness retreat.'

'You're right. It's much more,' Katherine agreed. 'The physical side of things is only a part of your training.'

Ella let out an exasperated sigh. 'What is the point of training me for a "mission" I've already told you I'm not going to be going on?'

Katherine looked at her intently. 'Because I believe you

are a good person, Ella. A moral person. I believe you are your parents' daughter. And, as such, once you understand the work we do, and how vital it is,' she handed the manila envelope back to Ella, 'I'm convinced you'll choose to join us. Eventually.'

Ella took the envelope in silence.

'But,' Katherine added, leaning back, 'if I'm wrong and you don't decide to join us, then try to look upon this time as an opportunity; a chance to get fit, to learn more about your abilities, to push yourself to new limits. A chance to discover your true strength, Ella.

'I'd like to start by sending you to see Professor Michael Dixon. He should be able to help you right away with your headaches.'

'Help me how?' asked Ella warily, aware that once again she'd been talked around, bamboozled into staying with precious little to show for it. 'Is he a doctor?'

Katherine's smile broadened till she looked positively beatific. 'In a way.'

'You can't be a doctor *in a way*,' said Ella. 'Either you are or you aren't.'

'You'll like him, I'm sure,' Katherine said brightly. 'Gordon at the front desk will show you where to go. You can see yourself out.'

'You want me to meet this person right now?' said Ella.

Katherine looked amused. 'Do make up your mind, my dear. I thought you were the one in a hurry?'

Professor Michael 'Dix' Dixon turned out to be a tiny gnome of a man, barely over five foot tall, with a mop of wiry gray hair, a pronounced stoop and a face so wrinkled it reminded Ella of the pickled walnuts that Grandmother Mimi used to preserve in jars back at the cabin. His tiny, jet-black eyes were set deep into the sockets, like two raisins

102

pushed too far into the dough on a gingerbread man. He wore a thick, brushed cotton shirt and knitted waistcoat that made Ella sweat just to look at them, teamed with baggy corduroy slacks and a pair of immaculately polished brogues. And when he spoke it was with an upper-class British accent straight out of *Downton Abbey*.

'Ella Praeger! As I live and breathe.' He looked Ella up and down appraisingly as soon as she walked into his lab, from the outside a rather nondescript, breeze-block building with a row of square, high-set windows, but inside a gleaming example of technological innovation at its best. 'We all thought you were a myth, my dear. An urban legend. But no! Here you are, in the flesh, and come to talk to me of all people. Well I'm honored, my dear. Honored.' Turning to a group of technicians huddled over a computer screen in the corner, Professor Dixon scowled disapprovingly. 'For heaven's sake. Would one of you young hooligans get Miss Praeger a chair?'

Two young men leaped to attention, one of them scurrying over with a plastic seat for Ella, depositing it on the ground without making eye contact before darting back to the safety of the group.

'A cup of tea, perhaps?' Professor Dixon asked solicitously.

'Thank you,' Ella smiled. 'That would be nice.'

It was impossible not to warm to this sweet, avuncular old man, especially as he appeared so enamored with her. 'Sorry,' Ella blushed, as her stomach growled audibly. 'I haven't eaten since breakfast.'

Clapping his hands imperiously in the direction of his junior lab partners, Professor Dixon demanded, 'Tea and biscuits and cake, pronto! Honestly, I don't know what's wrong with these fools in operations,' he said to Ella convivially. 'I mean physical training's all very well. But if

103

I've told them once, I've told them a thousand times. An army can't march on an empty stomach. Now then, Miss Ella Praeger. Where to begin? What, my dear, *dear* girl, can I do for you?'

For the first time, Ella felt her cynicism about Camp Hope starting to thaw at the edges. If this man had chosen to devote his life and talents to The Group, they simply couldn't be all bad.

'You obviously know who I am, Professor Dixon,' she began tentatively. 'I mean, my name was familiar to you?'

'Well of course it was. It is.' The old man nodded seriously. 'The Praeger name means something to all of us here, Ella. May I call you Ella?'

'Of course.'

'Thank you,' he beamed. 'And you must call me Dix, everybody does.'

Ella nodded. 'OK.'

'All of us in The Group have been waiting for you for a long time, Ella. Scientifically speaking you're . . . well, you're unique.'

Ella took a deep breath. 'Professor—'

'Dix,' he corrected her.

'Dix. Sorry. How much do you know about the procedures performed on my brain before I was born?'

'Well now, let's see.' He smiled encouragingly, rubbing his hands together as if Ella were a DIY project he couldn't wait to get his hands on. 'I suppose I know as much as anybody knows who wasn't actually there at the time. I've seen all your medical notes, and the notes relating to your mother's pregnancy. I was also lucky enough to inherit the genetic neurology papers that your parents were working on during their time here. So I'd say I have a fairly decent insight into what they were *trying* to achieve. As for how successful they were – the scope and limits of your powers today – well, that *none* of us will know fully until we start working together. That's why it's so incredibly exciting that you're—'

'Can you help me get rid of the headaches?' Ella interrupted him.

Dix looked at her thoughtfully. It was telling, and sobering, that this was her first question. The poor girl must have suffered more than he'd realized.

'I hope so,' he answered seriously.

'And what about . . . other things?' Ella bit her lip anxiously. Dix waited for her to explain. 'I'm not always very good with other people,' she blushed. 'Reading their emotions, or knowing what to say. I make mistakes.'

'We all make mistakes,' Dix said kindly. 'I'm confident that together we can reduce some of your . . . uncertainty . . . in social situations.' He was choosing his words carefully. 'It can't be easy, trying to interpret others, when you have a riot going on inside your own mind.'

'It isn't,' said Ella, deeply grateful for the professor's simple understanding.

'Of course, changing the habits of a lifetime won't happen overnight, any more than mastering your gifts will. You must be prepared to put in the work.'

'Oh, I am,' Ella insisted. 'Believe me. I'll do anything.'

'Good.' Dix smiled. 'And I apologize for rabbiting on at you earlier. Letting my excitement run away with me, I'm afraid. We'll be discovering an awful lot together in the coming days and weeks, Ella. But are there other questions that I can answer for you now?'

Ella thought about it. There were so many questions, it was hard to know exactly where to begin.

'Gabriel, the man who recruited me,' she said at last. 'He said that the voices I've been hearing in my head are electronic signals. Is that true?'

105

'Well, it's a bit of a broad-brush description,' Dix muttered disapprovingly. 'But yes. In layman's terms, you could say that.'

'And that I'm a sort of "receiver"? He said the headaches come because I haven't learned how to unscramble all the data coming in?'

Dix wrinkled his nose disdainfully. 'I do wish these operations Johnnies would leave the scientific explanations to the scientists. It sounds as if "Gabriel" has given you half a picture at best.'

'But about the headaches?'

'About the headaches, yes, he's correct. It's true that once you gain mastery of the auditory side of your capabilities – once you learn how to tune into certain signals and out of others – your headaches should stop. Or at least vastly reduce.'

Ella exhaled. If nothing else good came from this bizarre chapter of her life, putting a stop to the debilitating migraines would make everything worth it.

'You said the "auditory side",' she noticed. 'Is there another side to my . . . to the changes my parents made?'

'Oh yes!' Dix's eyes widened. The uncontained enthusiasm was back. 'Absolutely. We believe . . . we hope . . . that you have the capability to develop all sorts of visual data interpretation skills.'

'I'm sorry?' Ella looked baffled.

'You already hear things,' Dix explained. 'But you ought to be able to see things too, things that other people can't. And to *store* and *interpret* that information in unique ways. For example, I'm hoping to teach you how to use your eyes like cameras, to take and record a "mental picture" of what you observe.'

'Like photographic memory, you mean?' Ella asked, remembering the ease with which she'd been able to study for tests at school, retaining information at a glance.

'A much, much more detailed version of it, yes. Only in your case, theoretically at least, we might be able to download stored images *directly from your brain!*' The little man was practically hopping from foot to foot with excitement. 'Imagine that? We're not there yet, of course, but once we start working together, who knows? The sky's the limit! And speaking of the sky . . .'

Ella found herself willing him to take a breath.

'Satellite technology has of course advanced very considerably since your parents edited your genes. I'm hopeful that you should eventually be able to receive and interpret all sorts of GPS data. And obviously the strategic applications of something like that are pretty much limitless. You could use satellite coordinates to navigate, for instance. To visualize vast areas of land or sea, or even space. Theaters of war.'

*I'm not going to war*, thought Ella. *I'm going to fix my headaches, learn more about my family, and go home.* But at least coming from this kind, excitable old man, she didn't resent the assumption. If anything she felt worried about how to let 'Dix' down gently.

'Did you know my parents?' she asked him, changing the subject.

He took Ella's smooth hand in his gnarled ones. 'Only by reputation, I'm sorry to say. But I have the greatest respect for both of them. As scientists and as people. They were fearless.'

'That's probably why they're dead,' muttered Ella.

Most people might have winced at the bitterness of such a blunt comment, but Dix seemed to find Ella's perspective amusing. 'Ha!' he laughed loudly. 'I daresay it might be! Well said, my dear! How refreshing you are.'

Ella was pleased. Whatever else happened at Camp Hope, Dix was clearly going to be a kindred spirit. 'Refreshing'

107

was not a word often used to describe her. Most people opted for 'tactless' at best and 'outrageously rude' at worst. Ella liked 'refreshing'. She would have to tell Bob that one.

The professor's colleagues returned bearing a tray of tea and food, and Ella suddenly realized how ravenous she was. Dix watched, delighted, as she inhaled three slices of specially imported Fortnum's fruitcake, washing them down with a large mug of Twinings Earl Grey tea.

'Now. No one's told me how long you're staying here,' Dix told Ella, as she drained the dregs of her cup. 'But for as long as you're at Camp Hope, I'd like us to work together at least four days a week, if that's all right with you. My mission is to have identified the full scope of your gifts and to have you mastering as many of them as possible before you leave. How does that sound?'

'Fine,' said Ella. 'Good,' she added, trying to echo at least a fraction of his own enthusiasm.

'You don't sound very convinced.'

'I'm sorry,' Ella sighed. 'It's just, to you, my brain is a "gift". But to me, it's always been more of a curse.'

Dix looked at her intently. When he spoke it was with a kindness and empathy that almost made her cry.

'I understand, Ella. You've suffered. But your brain – your unique, enhanced, incomparable brain – *is* a gift. It is. A potent, fascinating, wonderful gift, not just to you but to the entire world. To science!' He grasped her hands again. 'I hope, once you discover how to use it, you will begin to see it that way.'

'I hope so too,' said Ella sincerely.

'And now, speaking of gifts,' he said, clapping his hands together and grinning in an attempt to lighten the mood. 'I have something for you. Follow me.'

Ella trailed behind him as he walked slowly up some metal stairs to a raised platform that seemed to be his personal lab-space. Opening a drawer in his desk, Dix removed a small box. Grinning like a schoolboy, he pressed it into Ella's hand.

Ella turned the box over curiously. 'What is it?'

'Something I've been working on for the past two years,' Dix said excitedly, 'ever since Redmayne decided it was time to make contact with you. They're a bit of a gimmick,' he admitted, 'but I hope they'll be a useful tool to get you started, on the auditory side at least. That's where you seem to be getting the strongest signals so far.'

*Redmayne.* It was the second time in the last forty-eight hours that Ella had heard that name, but her questions receded in the face of the professor's endearingly childlike joy. 'Open it! Open it!' Dix squawked, squirming with anticipation like a small child with a full bladder.

The box slid open, like a packet of matches. Inside, nestled in a bed of Styrofoam were what looked like a pair of hearing aids.

'Put them on,' instructed Dix.

Ella tried.

'No, no, not like that. Inside the lobe. Here, let me.' Gently he inserted the tiny devices into each of Ella's ears. 'Comfortable?'

She nodded.

'Good. Now, hang on a tick.' Turning his back to Ella, Dix began tapping something into an iPad. Ella started and clutched her head as a wave of sound, voices and static and loud, tuneless beeps exploded inside her skull. Leaning over gingerly, Dix turned a small dial on each of her earpieces. As if by magic, the wave receded, and only two voices were audible, both as clear as day.

'That's incredible!' said Ella.

It was just how Gabriel's voice had sounded last night when she'd tried to leave, and that evening at her hotel in

Paradise Valley. It was as if all the other transmissions had been switched off, somehow, and only a single, crystal-clear channel remained.

'How did you do that?' she asked Dix.

He put a finger to his lips, watching her eagerly. 'Just listen.'

Ella did. Both the voices she heard now were male. At first she wasn't sure what they were talking about, but eventually a pattern emerged. Coordinates and wind speeds and . . . was it tides?

She looked up at Dix. 'The coast guard?'

'Bingo!' he clapped his hands excitedly. 'Marvelous, marvelous. Very good, Ella. That's exactly what we'd hoped for. Right, take them out.'

Ella did as she was asked, handing over the hearing aids. 'So, what are these? How do they work?'

The old man grinned. 'They're very simple filters. Eventually, you'll learn how to do this yourself, organically. There's a technique I'll teach you, similar to mindfulness if you've ever heard of that? It's not complicated but it does require practice. Once you've got the knack, you'll be able to turn down certain signals and turn up others, by yourself. But until you've mastered it, these will help. I must say, I'm delighted they seem to work so well!' He beamed, clearly gratified with his handiwork.

Ella sat silently for a moment, processing this information.

'What would happen if *you* put these in your ears?' she asked him.

'Nothing,' Dix confirmed. 'I have nothing to filter. No data inputs. You, on the other hand, have rather more than you can handle. Hence your headaches.'

'Can these switch the noise – data – off completely? Like a mute button?'

'No. They're not sophisticated enough for that. To mute

110

the signals you're receiving completely, at the moment we have to use an external firewall. We block all data at Camp Hope as a matter of course, for security reasons. When you heard the medley of sounds earlier, it was because I'd temporarily disabled the firewall to allow them to reach you. So we could run the test.'

'So, I'll *always* hear some voices? No matter what?' Ella looked crestfallen.

'I didn't say that,' Dix smiled. 'These earpieces aren't capable of shutting down your brain's receiving capability. But *you* can do it. You can do it with visual stimuli as well. I'll teach you how.'

'Really?'

'Really,' he said firmly. 'Your brain is probably the most sophisticated machine I'll ever have the privilege to work with, Ella. We don't know everything about it yet. But we do know it can do incredible things.'

Again, Ella took a moment to digest this before resuming her questions.

'If someone else were to know how this thing in my brain works – like you do – would they be able to transmit to me directly? So they would come through louder, not just as background noise?'

'Yes!' Dix seemed delighted by the question. 'That is exactly right. You have a primary neurological frequency that naturally overrides the secondary ones.'

'And is that how Gabriel was able to speak to me last night?'

Dix cocked his head to one side, confused. 'I'm sorry. Did you say that *Gabriel* transmitted to you? Last night?'

Ella nodded.

'Here? At the camp?'

'Yes. I mean, *I* was here,' Ella confirmed. 'I don't know if he was. I was trying to leave, as it happened, but he sort of talked me round.'

111

Dix looked utterly furious, his wrinkled face practically quivering with rage.

'Talked you round, did he?' he muttered. 'Hmmm. That sounds about right. He's good at that.'

'Does that mean he *was* here? Physically?' asked Ella. 'Or close by, at least, to be able to transmit to me?'

'Not necessarily,' said Dix. 'In general it's true that the closer a transmission is, geographically, the louder you will "hear" it.'

'Like being within Wi-Fi range?'

'Sort of.' He frowned. 'I'll explain more later, but the point is that in Gabriel's case, that doesn't necessarily hold true, because he has remote access to our systems here. It sounds to me like he disabled the firewall from wherever he was, so he could transmit to you directly behind my back. The little . . . so-and-so.' The old man seemed to be talking to himself as much as to Ella, his whole being alive with indignation. 'When I get my hands on that boy—'

'He's transmitted to me before,' said Ella, stoking the flames of Dix's fury. 'The night before I came to camp. That's how I knew how to get here. Where to find you.'

'And where were you when *this* transmission happened?' asked the incredulous Dix.

'In Paradise Valley,' said Ella. 'Where I grew up. It's kind of out in the sticks. I never normally hear voices there, but I heard his. So, would he have been close by *that* time?' She was still very confused by the mechanics of all this.

'Probably,' said Dix. 'Although I suppose in theory he might have . . . if he'd somehow managed to hack into the . . .' The professor's grumblings were no longer audible, but from his expression Ella surmised that Gabriel was sinking ever further into his bad books.

'I couldn't talk back to him though,' she told Dix.

'No. You wouldn't have been able to,' he replied.

'Because I can't transmit, right? That's what Gabriel said. I'm just a receiver.'

The professor snorted. 'I would strongly advise you to take everything Gabriel says to you with a large pinch of salt.'

'I'll bear that in mind,' said Ella, amused. 'So, *can* I transmit?'

'Theoretically? Yes. You probably could. But there wouldn't be much point.'

'Why not?'

'Because the other person wouldn't be able to hear *you*. As far as we know, you are the only person in the world whose brain is capable of receiving data in this way. Your parents' experiment has never been repeated. You are unique, Ella,' he added, looking at her in genuine awe. 'That's why we need you. It's why the world needs you.'

*Yes, but I don't want to save the world!* Ella thought. *I want a normal life. I want to be normal. I never asked for any of this.*

'Together we will learn to make the most of your abilities,' Dix went on, his kindly manner diffusing Ella's frustration. 'Starting with the auditory signals. The experiment we just did here was a start, but it was artificial. Because of the firewall, all frequencies inside the camp were blocked except for the coast guard, who use a simple radio transmission. Your friend Gabriel doubtless used something similar last night. So his voice, directed to your primary neuro-channel, was all you heard. But in the real world, there will of course be multiple, conflicting signals. Part of your training here will involve learning how to differentiate between them. To become your own tuning device, if you will.'

Ella looked doubtful.

'We'll get there, my dear.'

Dix was so reassuring, so kind, that Ella started to well up. 'Oh, now, now, heavens, there's no need for all that,' the

113

old man spluttered, embarrassed. Like most Englishmen, excessive emotion clearly wasn't Professor Dixon's thing. 'I have a question for you, if I may,' he said, deftly bringing the conversation back to practical matters. 'Are you in possession of a mobile telephone?'

'A mobile telephone?' Ella laughed. That was the kind of expression Mimi would have used. 'Sure, but it doesn't work here. I lost reception about a hundred miles east of the camp. Plus I think the battery's dead.'

Dix made a dismissive *tsk-tsk* sound and flapped his arms about again. 'Never mind that. Bring it to the lab, would you? I'm going to download a wonderful little application for you. It's called Babbel.'

'The language thing?' asked Ella. She'd heard it advertised on the radio. 'Isn't that like Rosetta Stone?'

'Exactly.'

'What do I need that for?'

'For your mission training, my dear,' said Dix absently. 'Helping you to understand your special abilities is one piece of my job – the most interesting piece – but it's not much good intercepting and interpreting vitally important signals if they're all in another language, is it?'

*Another language?* Ella rubbed her eyes. She couldn't keep up.

'I thought Mrs MacAvoy would have explained already,' said Dix. 'But, no matter. We have plenty of time.'

'Plenty of time for what?' Ella asked wearily.

Dix patted her on the shoulder benignly. 'For learning to speak Greek, of course.'

# CHAPTER EIGHT

Gabriel leaned back against the soft leather seat of his Maserati and pressed his foot down hard on the accelerator. He smiled to himself as the car leaped forward, surging up the empty but familiar road like a panther. God, it was good to be back in California. And even better to be here to see the intoxicating, and yet distinctly obstinate, Ella Praeger. Gabriel had thought about Ella a lot since their last encounter. Most of those thoughts had been distinctly X-rated, something he'd wisely chosen not to share with the boss.

'This is probably the most important mission The Group has undertaken in a decade,' Mark Redmayne had reminded him, unnecessarily, on last night's conference call. 'We need that girl on board. But she's still stalling.'

'Yes, sir. So I understand.'

'She wants more information,' Katherine MacAvoy chimed in. 'Not just about her capabilities, about her parents too. She wants to know the truth about what happened to them.'

'I don't care what she *wants*, Katherine,' Redmayne snarled. 'Just get her ready. That's your job.'

The Camp Hope supervisor swallowed hard. Mark Redmayne had led The Group to some of its most brilliant successes. But he was also a bully. Like most of his senior team, Katherine MacAvoy was afraid of him.

'I know that, sir, and I'm trying to do it. I just don't believe she'll commit to us unless she perceives we're committing to her.'

'Then make her perceive it.'

'How?'

'I don't know! Not by telling her about her parents, that's for sure. Do it by force if you have to, but we need Ella Praeger on that plane.'

'Forcing her is a stupid idea,' said Gabriel, who seemed to be missing the self-preservation/fear gene that drove Katherine and everybody else when it came to Redmayne. 'If she's not committed to the mission, it will fail.'

'Hmmm,' Redmayne grunted. As usual, though he hated to admit it, Gabriel was right. 'So what do you suggest?'

'Let me talk to her. Ella knows me. We have some degree of . . . rapport.'

Mark Redmayne hesitated. He could imagine the form Gabriel's 'rapport' with Ella might take. The man had bedded more women than anyone could count. Bizarrely, from Mark Redmayne's perspective, as he was clearly somewhere on the autism spectrum and about as tactful as a bag of spanners in the face, the last thing they could afford around the woman who might yet become The Group's most valuable asset.

'Ella *has* asked to see Gabriel in person, sir,' Katherine MacAvoy added nervously. 'Several times.'

She decided not to mention that, according to Professor Dixon, Gabriel had already been in contact with Ella at Camp Hope, transmitting directly to her neuro-receivers, something he could only have done by hacking into the lab's computer systems. The fact he'd spotted her trying to leave meant he must also have wangled access to the camp's CCTV feed, none of which said much about the state of their security. Redmayne was in a foul enough mood already. The last thing any of them needed right now was for him to go off the deep end. Katherine would tackle Gabriel about the breaches of protocol herself when he got here.

And so it was that Gabriel found himself speeding through the California redwoods, charged with changing Ella Praeger's mind. He was actually relishing the prospect – he'd always enjoyed a challenge.

Reveling in the engine's roar, he pushed the Maserati even faster. The boss didn't like the fact that Gabriel drove an expensive car. Mark Redmayne himself might be filthy rich, but he preferred his operatives to lead more modest lives. To 'blend in', as he put it. 'Be the "gray men in the crowd".' That had never suited Gabriel.

Back before he *was* Gabriel – when he was still a child, with his old name, his old life – his father, a carpet salesmen from Rockford, Illinois, had been a 'gray man'. Gabriel's dad lived a gray life in a gray house full of gray dreams, and he'd died of that grayest of diseases, lung cancer, at the pathetically young age of forty-seven. Those were not footsteps in which Gabriel intended to follow, on any level.

His dad's morals had been gray too. A serial, yet oddly joyless philanderer, he had broken his wife's heart and spirit until she too became gray, a shadowy ghost of her former self. People told Gabriel that his mother's depression had been a lifelong illness, that it began long before she'd even met his father. But the little boy didn't buy that. Not at his mother's funeral, when he was eight years old. And not now. His father had broken his mother. That was the truth.

Gabriel had vowed never to break a woman. Having inherited his father's high libido, abstinence was never a

117

realistic option. Instead, a far neater and simpler solution presented itself: never marry. Never commit. A loner by nature, the solitude had suited him well. For the last decade he'd been 'married' to The Group, as passionately devoted to the cause as the most ardent lover to his bride, and as addicted to the adrenaline as any junkie. He'd changed his name, partly in dedication to his new life, but also to leave behind a childhood he wanted desperately to forget, to sever like a rotten limb.

His new life wasn't perfect. It was true he didn't like Mark Redmayne, but then who did? He hadn't joined The Group to make friends, or to gain anyone's approval. As for romance, while it was true that scores of beautiful women had come and gone from his life, none of them had had their hearts broken. Gabriel wasn't in the 'hearts' business, and he never made promises he couldn't keep. All in all, it was a highly satisfactory way of living.

Leaving his car in the usual place, he pulled out his day-pack and began the final, two-mile trek up to Camp Hope on foot. He remembered it well from his own training, and always felt a frisson of excitement, returning to the place where it all began. But today was different. Today the 'frisson' had become a raging fire in his chest. His eagerness to see the girl was bordering on the worrisome.

*You're here to do a job*, he reminded himself. *A vital job.* He forced himself to think about the drowned child on the beach, about the evil insignia burned onto his tiny foot.

*Focus.*


'Looks like you've got a visitor.' Christine nudged Ella in the ribs and pointed breathlessly to the handsome man walking up the path towards their cabin.

'He's waving at you!' Christine squealed excitedly. 'Oh

my God, is that the guy who recruited you? You never told me he looked like Ryan Gosling!'

'He doesn't,' said Ella tetchily, pulling out her earphones and scowling in the man's general direction. More casually dressed than the last two times she'd met him, in Nike running pants, sneakers and a black sleeveless T-shirt, and with a light film of sweat glistening on his muscular shoulders, she had to admit he was looking disarmingly handsome this afternoon. She, on the other hand, looked 'clean', having come straight from the shower after training, but with her scratched, make-up-free face, wet hair and skinny legs covered in bruises, she was hardly at her most alluring.

'You took your time,' she hissed at him, once he came within earshot.

'You're lucky I came at all,' he drawled. 'Believe it or not, Ella, I have other things to do besides hand-holding you. But when the camp supervisor said you'd begged to see me—'

'*Hand-holding?*' Ella spluttered, so angry it was hard to speak. '*Begged?*'

Ignoring her, Gabriel turned to Christine, his eyes roaming admiringly and unashamedly over her ample assets, displayed to considerable advantage in the tiny denim hot pants and pink bikini top she was wearing. 'I don't believe we've met.'

'I don't believe we have,' Christine panted, staring with an equal lack of shame at his ripped torso. 'I *definitely* would've remembered you.'

'Likewise.'

'I'll give you two some privacy, shall I?' Ella said archly, gathering her things furiously and stuffing them into the bag at her feet. '*Begged*' to see him indeed! If she'd begged for anything, it was the information he'd promised her and then deliberately withheld. If it weren't for Dix and the progress she was making controlling the voices in her head, she would have walked out of here a week ago, with or without Gabriel's help.

'Don't be silly,' he said patronizingly, his eyes still locked with Christine's. 'I've come here to talk to you. We're going for a drive.'

'Oh no we're not,' said Ella, folding her arms across her chest defiantly. 'Anything you have to say to me you can say right here.'

Ella gazed sullenly out of the Maserati's passenger-side window as the last of the trees sped past, giving way to open fields and even the occasional ranch.

'Are you always this moody?' Gabriel asked, a smile playing at the corners of his lips. 'Or is it me?'

'It's you,' said Ella.

Silence resumed.

'They told me your name was *Gabriel*,' Ella said eventually, pronouncing the word as if it offended her. 'You don't look like a Gabriel to me.'

'Don't I?' No one had ever commented on his adopted name before. It was a bit disconcerting.

'No,' said Ella. 'The angel Gabriel? That's definitely not you.'

He grinned. 'Not all of us Gabriels are angels. How are you enjoying your training?' he asked, changing the subject before she decided to quiz him any more on his name. That was a conversation that could lead them back to his past, and he definitely didn't want to go there. Especially not with Ella.

'It's appalling,' Ella said bitterly. 'It's utterly inhumane.'

'You realize that the mission you're being trained for launches very soon?'

'*You* realize I'm not going on any mission?'

He gave her a 'whatever you say' smile that made him look even more infuriatingly handsome. 'How's the Greek going, by the way?'

'*Ante gamisou,*' snapped Ella.

'Impressive,' he beamed. What Ella had just said translated into something distinctly unsuitable for children. 'Let's eat.'

With a sudden, violent swerve, he turned the car up an unsigned single-lane road that swiftly led them to what looked like an old adobe farmhouse.

Warily, Ella stepped out of the car. 'This is a restaurant?'

'When it needs to be. It belongs to The Group. The couple who live here are retired but they make it available when needed. We're expected.'

The latter was clearly true. Ella followed Gabriel into a pretty, whitewashed dining room. Inside, a farmhouse table had been laid for two with a feast of hot and cold dishes, fresh flowers, a pitcher of iced water and a chilled bottle of vintage Chablis.

'Help yourself,' said Gabriel, taking his own advice and spooning mountains of lamb stew, saffron rice and various green salads onto his plate before taking a seat. 'We can talk freely here.'

Ella gave a cynical laugh. 'Talk freely? Does that mean you'll actually answer my questions?'

'Some of them,' he replied, admiring the way Ella's still-damp hair coiled down around her shoulders as far as her breasts. She'd changed into a simple yellow sundress for their excursion, of the sort that would have looked demure on any other woman, even frumpy, but that somehow clung tantalizingly to Ella's body like a second skin. 'If you'll answer mine. Wine?'

'No thank you.'

Reluctantly, Ella took some food and a glass of water

and sat down opposite him. Pouring himself a large glass of Chablis, Gabriel took a long sip and got the ball rolling.

'Shall we take turns?'

'All right,' said Ella. 'Who goes first?'

'I do,' Gabriel announced imperiously. 'If you aren't going to go on the mission, why are you still at Camp Hope?'

For a moment Ella was silent. It was a good opener.

'I told you I'd help you get back to the city if you chose to go. But you didn't. Why not?'

'I had no way of contacting you,' mumbled Ella awkwardly.

'Bullshit.' Gabriel took another sip of his wine. 'Katherine could have reached me easily. You never tried.'

'OK,' said Ella, her blood already up. 'I also stayed because of Dix. He's been helping me control the noises in my head. To understand what they are, and where they come from and to tune certain signals in and out. He's helped me with other things too, like how to interpret people better and handle social situations, things I never got the chance to learn as a kid. And I'm getting better. I am! Dix seems actually to know what's wrong with me, which is more than any other doctor has ever been able to do.'

'There's nothing wrong with you,' said Gabriel. 'You have a—'

'Don't say gift.' Ella held up a finger in warning. 'Don't you dare say gift. You have no idea, any of you, what it's like. Anyway, my turn. How did you know that I was trying to leave camp that day? You must have been spying on me.'

'Don't be so paranoid,' he said breezily.

'I want to know how,' insisted Ella. 'Are there hidden cameras? Or do you have people inside following me and reporting back to you?'

'Maybe,' he leaned towards her slowly, 'I can read your thoughts. See into that tangled, beautiful brain of yours. Did you ever think of that?'

Ella felt a sick feeling build in the pit of her stomach and her breath start to shorten. That couldn't be true. Could it?

'No,' she said with a confidence she didn't feel. 'I never thought of that because it's baloney. Dix already told me I can only receive information, not transmit it.'

'What if dear old Dix is mistaken?' Gabriel teased her. 'He's not God, you know. He makes mistakes.'

He moved even closer, sliding a warm, dry hand over Ella's. The sick feeling intensified but it was mingled with something else, something which Ella recognized but refused to acknowledge. Not now. Not for *him*.

'What if I told you I knew *exactly* what you were thinking, right now? Would that scare you?'

Ella swallowed. 'No.'

'I don't think I believe you,' he smiled, making no effort to hide his enjoyment at making her squirm. 'What is it you're trying to hide from me, Ella?'

'Stop it.' She snatched her hand back. 'You cannot access my thoughts.'

He sat back and laughed loudly. 'OK, you're right. I can't. There are cameras, OK? At the gatehouse and at various places around the camp. And yes, I might have snooped a little bit. Just to check you were OK. Which, on that particular night, you weren't. So I stepped in to help. You're welcome,' he added, in response to Ella's stony glare. Taking a bite of lamb, he gestured to Ella to eat as well. 'You're too thin.'

'Oh really? And whose fault is that? Working me to the bone every damned day,' Ella grumbled. But she took a spoonful of rice anyway.

'My question,' he continued, while she ate. 'How's it going with Dix?'

'It's going fine.'

'What does "fine" mean? How long till you can fully use your . . . whatever you want to call it? Till you can tune into the things you want to and shut out the rest?'

'I have no idea,' said Ella truthfully. 'I've never done this before. Neither has Dix. A few months, maybe? He's given me some exercises. It's a sort of mindfulness, almost like self-hypnosis. I have to—'

'Could you crack it in ten days?'

'What? No!' said Ella. 'Of course not. It's not like flicking a switch, you know.'

'If you had to?'

'I don't have to,' said Ella. 'And before you say one more word about this "mission", I'll tell you what I told Katherine MacAvoy. I'm not going anywhere or doing anything for you people until someone tells me something about my goddamned parents.'

Gabriel hesitated. Mark Redmayne had specifically told him not to stray into this territory under any circumstances.

*Screw it.* He could handle it.

'Your mother and father joined The Group together in 1990,' Gabriel told her. 'By the time you were born they had become committed members, although the peak of their active service occurred later, around the time that they entrusted you to your grandmother's care.'

Ella leaned in, hanging off his every word.

'Their work involved their scientific expertise. As I told you before, your mother was a neurologist and your father was a pioneer in gene replacement theory. Typically they worked together, although your mother eventually achieved a more senior rank within operations than your father and sometimes worked with other operatives.'

'Really?' said Ella, intrigued by this small, humanizing detail. Both of her parents had become shadowy figures, but now her mother felt even more opaque than her father. He at least had written letters and cards, leaving something tangible for Ella now that she had got her hands on them. The place where her mother's memory should be was just an empty space, with nothing more than snatched fragments of remembered words, touches and smells, and even those were fading as each year passed.

'Their missions were classified,' Gabriel went on, 'so I can't talk about them.'

'Only the government can classify things,' said Ella, annoyed. 'Do you even realize how self-important you sound?'

'They died in 2001,' Gabriel said, ignoring Ella's outburst.

'You mean they were murdered,' said Ella. 'That's what you told me before.'

'Yes,' said Gabriel.

'You also said you'd tell me how they were killed. Once I started training,' Ella reminded him.

'I believe I said, I would tell you when the time was right. When you were ready.'

'And when will that be?' Ella raised her voice furiously. 'In your high-and-mighty opinion?'

'When you leave for your mission,' said Gabriel, finishing the last of his wine and refolding his napkin, placing it neatly on the table.

'Enough,' said Ella, too tired to have the same argument with him again. 'I'd like you to take me home now, please. Like you promised. To San Francisco.'

'OK,' said Gabriel calmly. 'If that's what you want.'

'It is.'

He nodded. 'We'll go now.'

They walked in silence back to the car. Opening the door

for Ella in an uncharacteristically chivalrous display, he waited for her to buckle up before getting behind the wheel and starting the engine.

'Dix will be sad you didn't say goodbye,' he observed as they headed back along the narrow lane towards the main road.

'I'll miss him,' said Ella. 'He's a good man. Please tell him I'll keep practicing the techniques he taught me, and that I'm very grateful for everything he did.' Wistfully, she pulled the earpieces the professor had given her the day they met out of her pocketbook and laid them on her lap. 'At least I'll still have these to remember him by.'

'I'm afraid not,' said Gabriel, holding out his hand. 'We're going to need those back.'

'What? No,' said Ella, snatching the earpieces away. 'These are mine. Dix gave them to me.'

'While you were working with us,' said Gabriel. 'Anything conceived and/or manufactured in our labs is proprietary technology. You must return them.'

'And what if I don't?' said Ella. She was growing heartily sick of Gabriel's *musts*. 'What are you going to do about it? Call the police? Report me for theft?'

'No.'

'No,' she mocked him. 'Of course you aren't! Because you know as well as I do that the authorities will be a sight more interested in what *you* and your friends are doing up in those forests. Brainwashing people and half starving them and having them sign their lives away to a cult that sends them off to commit crimes and get murdered and calls that "justice".'

With a scream of brakes and a terrifying spray of gravel, Gabriel brought the car to a halt. Turning off the engine he turned on Ella in white-lipped fury.

'Is that really what you think? That we're a cult? After

all this time, after all that's been done for you and shown to you and shared with you?'

Ella wanted to shout back that she hadn't asked for anything to be 'done for' her. That all she wanted was to be left alone, to grieve for her family and get on with her life as best she could, in peace. But something about his face, his hurt, angry, ridiculously attractive face, held her back.

'Do you think Professor Dixon is the kind of man you can brainwash?' he demanded.

Ella had to admit that she didn't. 'But Dix is an exception.'

'No!' Gabriel roared. 'Not an exception. Except*ional*, yes. Brilliant. Committed. Honorable. Brave. But then so are all of our operatives, in their different ways. Michael Dixon had a life and a career back in England, Ella. He had endless opportunities to make money and an academic name for himself. But instead he chose to sacrifice those things for a greater good. He devoted his gifts to the good of others, to the betterment of mankind, to something bigger than himself.'

'So you keep saying,' Ella shot back, taking comfort in her own cloak of righteous indignation. 'But what "greater good" are you talking about? You never explain it. You never explain anything, not really. Instead you ask me to put my life on the line for a "cause" without a name. Why should I, Gabriel? Why *should* I?'

Gabriel looked away for a moment. He was under direct orders not to divulge anything to Ella until the mission was underway. Until she was in the air, en route to the target, committed. Until it was too late for her to turn back. Gabriel had gone along with it up till now, but it had felt wrong from the beginning. Her question was a good one. Why should she go, based on nothing but trust and platitudes?

She deserved an explanation. Not the whole truth perhaps. But she deserved something.

'Everybody joins The Group, and takes these risks, for their own reasons,' he began. 'In my case it was a woman.'

'Why am I not surprised?' said Ella, but the look on his face told her instantly this was not a time for quips.

'When I was in college, I took an internship with a technology firm in India. I spent six months in Bangalore,' said Gabriel. 'I became close friends with a young woman there. Her name was Mira. Mira Saluja.'

Ella listened intently.

'Mira was five years older than me. Brilliant, very beautiful, from an educated Punjabi family. We dated for a few months but her parents didn't approve. They had already decided on a husband for Mira. I think maybe she would have gone against them and stuck with me if I'd made a commitment to her,' he mused. 'If I'd proposed marriage. But I didn't. She thought I wasn't serious about her.'

'Was she right?' asked Ella.

Gabriel looked pained. 'No! I loved her. She was perfect. But I'm not the marrying kind.'

Ella nodded understandingly. 'Me neither.'

'In any case it didn't matter in the end because, six weeks before my internship was up, Mira was brutally raped and murdered.'

He said it so matter-of-factly, Ella was shocked. 'By whom? The Indian husband? Or his family?'

Gabriel shook his head grimly. 'No. Although a lot of influential people devoted a lot of time and effort to trying to frame it as an honor killing. But no. Sanjit, Mira's fiancé, was a good guy. No, Mira was killed by a senior American diplomat by the name of Scooter Ryan. You might have heard of him.'

Ella blanched. She wasn't into politics and rarely read

the papers or turned on the TV news. But even she had heard of Scooter Ryan – devoted patriot, family man and father of three, killed by a car bomb outside Boston in one of the only unsolved, unclaimed terrorist attacks to take place on US soil in the last decade.

'*The* Scooter Ryan? The republican, family-values guy?'

Gabriel nodded. 'Yup. Also a rapist and a killer and a liar.'

'Wasn't he an ex-marine?' Ella asked, as the Boston car-bomb story came back to her.

'That's right,' said Gabriel. 'Scooter came on to Mira one night at a hotel bar, close to the US consulate. She wasn't interested. After Mira turned him down, he followed her, beat her, raped her, and finally strangled her with her own scarf. Then he dumped her body on a trash heap fifteen miles north of the city and kept going to his country retreat, where he spent the weekend playing polo with a bunch of visiting State Department families.'

'He wasn't arrested?'

Gabriel stared down at his lap. 'No, he was not.' He said the words slowly, as if he'd been taught them by a therapist whose job it was to keep him calm. 'Because that's not how it works, apparently, not in the "real world". Rumors were denied, evidence suppressed, money changed hands, and diplomatic immunity was invoked. Mira was buried, the press fell silent, and Scooter went home to the States, with no more fuss than if he'd accidentally killed a stray pheasant on the road.' Looking up, his eyes bore into Ella's. 'So I was angry about that.'

The understatement hung in the air between them like a charge of lightning.

'A few weeks later I found The Group. Or maybe they found me, I'm not sure exactly how it went down. I was drinking a lot. But that's what The Group do, you see.

When the powers of the "real world" let you down; when they take the side of the powerful, no matter whether those people are good or bad, right or wrong, The Group steps in to make sure that justice prevails.'

After a silence that felt like forever, Ella asked him flat out. 'Are you telling me that you – that The Group – murdered Scooter Ryan?'

For the first time since he began the story, Gabriel smiled. 'I don't believe I told you that. I'm simply explaining what happened to my friend Mira, and how it led *me* to this life. I'm telling you that Mira was *my* emotional hook. Because you want to know what *yours* is. Why *you* should join a group you know next to nothing about.'

'Did you kill Ryan?' Ella asked again. She wasn't about to be deflected that easily.

Gabriel's returned her gaze. 'Sometimes, usually, doing the right thing means saving lives. Sometimes it means exposing what's been hidden, or hiding what others would like to expose. Sometimes it means breaking the law in pursuit of a greater good. And occasionally – yes – it means killing people. Bad people. The world is full of Scooter Ryans. Of people who believe they are above the law. From drug lords, heads of state and CEOs, right down to lowly people-smugglers, pedophile priests and corrupt prison officers. The Group isn't Greenpeace, Ella. But we aren't a cult either. We are a secret, elite, moral force. To be invited to join us is both a privilege and a responsibility. How you choose to respond to that call will be your free choice.'

'So you did kill Ryan.'

He suppressed a smile. 'If you say so, Ella. All *I'm* saying is that whatever I did, I did for Mira. And I believe that whatever *you* do, should you choose to join us, you'll do for your parents. They're your hook. So if you're looking for a reason to go on this mission, how about avenging their murders?'

Ella stiffened. He had her attention now.

'The mission has something to do with my parents?'

'It does.' Gabriel nodded. 'I can't tell you more than that. I shouldn't even have told you that. But yes. It does.'

Restarting the engine, he set off again. A few minutes later they reached the T-junction with the main road.

'San Francisco's that way.' Gabriel nodded to the right. 'And Camp Hope's to our left. Your choice.'

*My choice*, thought Ella. In one direction lay danger, uncertainty, and being forced to place her trust in a group that told her next to nothing, while expecting her to blindly obey its orders. In the other lay safety, calm, and at least the possibility of a normal life.

*But I wouldn't have avenged my parents' murders.*

*I wouldn't have righted the wrongs of the past.*

*I would have to live the rest of my life never knowing what might have been.* Wordlessly, Ella pointed left. The decision was already made and they both knew it.

She couldn't back out now.

They drove the rest of the journey in silence. At the usual parking place in the woods, where the hiking trail began, a young man Ella vaguely recognized from around camp was waiting to meet them. Gabriel waved a greeting from the car but showed no sign of getting out.

'You're not coming?' Ella asked.

He shook his head. 'No. I have to get back to my own assignment. But I'll be in touch. Good luck.' Lowering his voice, he added, 'And don't tell anyone what I told you.'

'When will they tell me more? About this mission?' she asked, suddenly panicked about the idea of Gabriel leaving. She couldn't say why exactly, but for all his arrogance and abrasiveness, he was a link to reality, to the outside world and her old life. A way back. Like him or loathe him, Gabriel was Ella's lifeboat. She didn't want to have to watch him sail away.

'You knew about Scooter, about what he'd done,' Ella reminded him. 'You told me that *you* found The Group. That you sought out your revenge. It's not like that for me. I still don't know anything about this mission. I don't know who killed my parents, or why, or where they're sending me. I mean, obviously there's a Greek connection or Dix wouldn't have made me take the Babbel classes, but other than that . . .'

'Ella.' Gabriel rested a hand briefly on her arm. 'Let it go. Commit to The Group. They'll tell you more when it's safe to do so. But they won't be rushed. My guess is that you won't be fully briefed till you're on the plane.'

Ella rolled her eyes. 'If this turns out to be some wild-goose chase, I'm holding you responsible.' Opening the passenger door, she jabbed a defeated finger in Gabriel's direction. Without thinking he reached out and caught it, their hands suddenly entwined.

'Don't rely on me, Ella,' he said gruffly, his voice catching in his throat. 'Don't rely on anyone. Only on yourself.'

'Fine,' said Ella, her own throat dry and hoarse all of a sudden. She climbed out of the car, straightening the creased skirt of her sundress. 'I won't.'

'Goodbye,' said Gabriel, starting the engine.

*That's it? 'Goodbye?'*

Ella studied his face, but his expression had switched back to neutral, as unreadable as a Sanskrit tablet.

With a sinking heart, she watched him drive away.

For better or worse, her new life was about to begin.

# PART TWO

# CHAPTER NINE

'Mood! Mahmoud!'

The fat policeman, Thalakis, clapped his hairy, sausage-like hands in front of the prisoner's face. It was stiflingly hot in the cell. Not the dry, desert heat of Libya, where Mahmoud 'Mood' Salim grew up in a sleepy village sixty miles from Murzuk. This was the stinking, fetid, heavy heat of Greece, a country Mood had already come to hate with every fiber of his being. The air here smelled of sweat and fish and cheese and lies, of the stinking breath of men like Inspector Thalakis. *Not men. Beasts. Animals, devoid of compassion.*

'Speak, man!' Flecks of spittle flew off the policeman's swollen lips and landed on the prisoner's skin. 'Answer the question,' Thalakis commanded. 'Answer, or it will be worse for you!'

*Worse for me.* In other circumstances, in his old life, Mood would have laughed. How did this ignorant pig of a man imagine that anything could possibly be worse for him than it was now?

'Who did you pay for your passage? Tell me!' The sausage fist slammed down on the cheap Formica table. 'Who brought you here, Mahmoud? Your family . . .'

135

It happened before anyone knew what was happening. The prisoner rose up out of his chair with a primal roar, like a monster from the depths of the Aegean, and lunged at Inspector Thalakis, wrapping his powerful, giant's hands around the fat man's neck.

'Don't you speak of my family!'

The giant hands tightened. Thalakis's face turned red, then purple, his eyes bulging out of their sockets like grapes about to burst their skin. The two guards present threw themselves at the prisoner, Mood, pulling him back with all their combined strength, but to no avail. It was like trying to pry a barnacle off the keel of a boat with a plastic spoon.

*He's going to kill him!*

Thalakis was losing consciousness. In panic, one of the guards pulled out his pistol. Turning it over, he brought it down hard, handle-side, on the back of the prisoner's skull. There was a loud crack, then blood, then silence. Like a felled tree, Mahmoud Salim slid to the ground. Inspector Thalakis fell forward onto the table, gasping for air like a dying fish.

The last thing Mood remembered, before the blackness engulfed him, was the cold swell of the final wave. That, and the sound of his six-year-old daughter's screams as she was swept away . . .


Mood Salim had been born into a large family of goat herders in Libya's southwestern Fezzan region. The youngest of six sons, his childhood had been Spartan but happy. There were no toys or televisions or other modern-day luxuries. The Salims lived as countless generations had before them, and about as far removed from the politics of Tripoli and the world beyond as it was possible to be. Mood's playmates were his brothers and cousins, and the endless Saharan *ergs* or sand dunes had been his playground. His mother was his teacher, his father his god, and his goats his purpose. He never knew hunger, and would not have considered himself poor, not having experienced any other way of living.

That Libya was gone now, the stuff of storybooks for Mood's own children. He and his wife Hoda had been blessed with two daughters. Parzheen, the older girl, was black haired and dark eyed and as quick-witted and cunning as a little sprite. Her younger sister Ava was softer, rounder, sweeter, with a laugh that sounded to Mood like water bubbling up from a desert spring.

'Her laugh is like life, like a gift from heaven,' he used to say to Hoda, watching the tiny toddler crawl around in their cramped apartment in Tarhuna. Hoda would smile and kiss him. She adored her husband's romantic streak, the poetry in Mood's soul that she felt sure must have come from his upbringing out in the desert. Her own childhood had been the polar opposite: educated, middle class, urban, and not particularly happy. Her parents divorced when she was eleven, leaving Hoda and her brother Khalil to fend mostly for themselves.

Everybody commented on how the Salims were a marriage of opposites, a classic case of the old and new Libya colliding, although nobody could question the success of the union. Mood, as broad and strong as an ox, six foot five in his bare feet and tiny, elfin Hoda were utterly devoted to each other and their children. Their modest flat in Tarhuna had positively buzzed with happiness.

Now there was nothing left of it but rubble.

The politics and war and misery that had spread through the Middle East had hit the Salims late. But when it came it was like a tsunami, destroying everything in its path, annihilating what had gone before and casting a deep, dark cloud over what might be to come.

When the first boats began to sail from Sabratha, heading across the Mediterranean either to Italy or to Greece, it no more crossed Mood's mind that he and his girls would one day seek passage on them than that they would fly to the moon. But the medieval horrors of IS – the waves of evil fanatics swarming through Libya from Syria and Iraq like a black plague – swiftly changed his mind. Before long Mood, like so many of his neighbors, had sold everything he owned in order to buy himself and his girls a guaranteed spot on a boat bound for Lesbos.

The man who sold it to him was a fellow Libyan, but pale skinned and a few years younger than Mood. He wore an imported suit and an expensive watch and aftershave, all three insulting luxuries in a city where people had nothing, where scores of old people and children were dying of starvation. 'You're making the right choice, brother,' he told Mood, grinning as he took his money.

'It's not a choice,' Mood replied. 'And you are not my brother.'

But the deal was done.

Everybody told him the same thing: conditions on the worst boats were subhuman – tiny, decrepit fishing vessels, overloaded with more than three hundred people. No life jackets. Collapsing decks. Some of the most pitiless people-smugglers had taken to offering 'bad weather' discounts to families so poor they had no choice but to set sail during winter storms, sometimes in open rubber dinghies, or offering 'free rides' to children under three, as if this were a holiday cruise. Mood had taken pains to get a place on a better boat than that, a mid-sized fishing boat, wooden but in good repair, that would carry no more than forty migrants. Even so, the journey would be both arduous and dangerous. But at least this suffering, this danger, involved some action on Mood's part. It was something he was *doing*, to rescue his girls. As opposed to waiting passively in Libya to be bombed or shelled or starved or tortured to death by the latest band of unhinged madmen. Europe – Greece – offered at least the chance of life. Of a future. Of hope.

The week before they left, they befriended another family staying in the same safe house outside Sabratha. The father had been killed, but the mother Zafeera and her three children, twin boys Parzheen's age and an infant girl, were paid passengers on the same boat as the Salims. Mood remembered Zafeera as an oasis of calm in the desert of fear and uncertainty that was all of their lives back then, as they waited for word that they could board. 'Sleep prepared,' the smugglers had told them. 'We may knock for you at three a.m. You must come at once or we sail without you.'

'Trust in Allah,' Zafeera would tell Mood and Hoda, her round face radiant with goodness and faith, as another night passed and no knock came. If the boat didn't leave soon they might all be burned in their beds.

'He blesses the innocent,' Zafeera assured them. 'He will protect us and our children.'

He didn't.

It was pitch black the night they climbed aboard, the darkness so thick you could barely see your hand in front of your face. Even so, Mood counted at least eighty souls on their 'no-more-than-forty' berth, and the rotten wood beneath his feet sagged ominously with each heavy step he took.

'This isn't what we paid for!' another man complained loudly to one of the smugglers, who instantly pulled out a machete and held it to the man's throat, pressing down dangerously close to the jugular as he pinned him to the wall.

'Be quiet!' he hissed. 'No more noise. Any more noise and we cut you. All of you!' He spun around to snarl at the terrified masses crouched in the dark. Hoda and the girls clung to one another. With sadness but no shame, Mood manhandled an old man out of his way in order to seize four life jackets from the stack of no more than thirty in the boat's hollow center. Then he returned to his family and fitted everybody's vests before spreading his outstretched arms over the three of them, like an oak tree. It was as much protection as he could offer in that moment. Seconds later, the rotting vessel surged out to sea.

The voyage reminded Mood of an old joke his father-in-law used to tell about seasickness. How on the first night it's so bad that you're scared you might die. 'And on the second night it's so bad, you're scared you might not!' Poor little Ava vomited for hours on end, until her exhausted body could take no more and she collapsed into sleep in her mother's sodden arms. Parzheen fared only slightly better, and had to be forced to swallow some of the bread and dates Hoda had brought to keep them going till they reached land. Mood was also sick, more from the dreadful smell of other people's vomit than the rocking boat itself, although a storm six hours into the crossing had left every-body clinging to the sides and praying, convinced they were going to capsize or simply be smashed to smithereens by the next colossal wave.

But they weren't. And after twelve more relatively calm hours, everyone's frayed nerves began to ease. If they didn't veer wildly off course, they could expect to make landfall by midnight at the latest, either on Lesbos as planned or on one of the other islands, if the coast-guard patrol boats were out in too overwhelming a force.

Mood remembered looking at Hoda as the girls both slept; he smiled at her – neither of them had the energy left for conversation. But his beautiful wife had smiled back and squeezed his hand, and hope and gratitude had flowed between them. After that, more exhausted than he'd ever been in his life, Mood finally fell asleep.

When he woke, he was in the water. Later, on the rescue boat, a British girl with red hair and glasses told him that they'd been struck by another migrant vessel from the side and that both boats had sunk within minutes. But in the moment he knew nothing except darkness and icy cold, his body plunging deep under the waves and then, as if he were tied to a bungee rope, shooting back to the surface, his life jacket propelling him upwards and into the air like a flying fish.

He remembered so little now. Snatches. Screaming the children's names, and Hoda's. Straining his ears to try and distinguish their voices from the blood-curdling cries of anguish and terror all around him, like a ewe searching for her lost lambs in a vast field of bleating despair. He remembered blackness. Disorientation. Panic. His own heartbeat, loudly and mockingly proclaiming his survival when all he cared about was theirs.

And then suddenly he saw her. A momentary flash of light and there she was: Parzheen, floating, flailing, her skinny arms reaching out for purchase, for anything that might save her.

'Parzheen!' *Could she hear him?* 'Parzheen, it's Papa. I'm coming!'

The light was gone but he swam blindly towards her. There was nothing now but his daughter and the water between them. With each stroke he stretched out his arms, his fingertips reaching, clawing, seeking her tiny body somewhere in the vast ocean. And then suddenly, like a

miracle, she was there. In his arms. Clinging. Breathing.
'*Papa!*'

'It's OK, Parzheen. It's OK, baby. I've got you.'

The world came back then, what little he could see and hear of it, in a wild rush to his senses. Another flash of light – where was it coming from? – and a dinghy. Rubber, afloat, half empty. With his daughter on his shoulders he swam towards it like a man possessed. A wild hope stirred in his breast that perhaps Hoda and Ava might be there? His life jacket and Parzheen's had saved their lives. There was no reason to believe that his wife and baby hadn't made it too.

He reached the dinghy. With one giant, slippery hand he grabbed onto the side and hauled himself up. He recognized one of the men on board as one of the smugglers.

'My daughter,' Mood wheezed. 'Take her. Take the child.'

The man seemed to hesitate. But then he crawled forwards, stretching out his arms to lift Parzheen off her father's shoulders.

She screamed.

It was the scream of a small child more frightened of letting go of her father in that dark water than of the two of them drowning together. It was a scream of love, the most beautiful scream in the world, and it was the last sound Mood heard before the wave slammed into both of them and his world ended forever.

Sarah Wade leaned over the giant Libyan man, stroking his hand as he slowly regained consciousness. Sarah had been working on the *Constance*, a rescue boat working 24/7 off the Greek coast, for almost five months now, but you never got used to it. The daily drownings, so many of the victims children, washed up like dolls with their eyes rolled back in their heads. The survivors' howls of grief. The traffickers' utter lack of remorse. And the Greek locals' indifference to the epic human tragedy unfolding all around them.

Sarah's boss, Pascale Dutroit, told her that that was unfair. 'It's human nature, when death becomes commonplace, to learn to live with it. No one can spend years of their lives sobbing and tearing out their hair – and even if they could, what good would it do?'

But Sarah felt differently. Perhaps because she was only twenty-three and an 'idealist', according to her parents. But if she could cry for these people every day, why couldn't the citizens of Lesbos? In Sarah's view it was because the Greeks didn't see the African migrants as 'people'. The harsh reality was that indifference was probably the kindest, most compassionate emotion shown to the boat people. Many locals felt an active rage, bordering on hatred, for the swarms of desperate families overwhelming their islands. They used words like *eisvoli* (invasion), *panoukla* (plague) and *zoyfia* (vermin). Pascale Dutroit argued that, in their own poverty, the Greek islanders could not be expected to bear such a huge influx. 'If you want to blame someone, blame the EU. Blame the UN, the rich countries of the world, for doing nothing.' But Sarah Wade didn't want to blame someone. She just wanted people to show a little humanity. Perhaps, if they worked on the boats as she did . . .

The big man groaned and coughed, spewing out a mixture of seawater and phlegm. He was coming round.

'You're OK,' Sarah spoke calmly, pulling her red hair back from her face as she leaned more closely into his. 'You're safe. We're taking you to Lesbos where you'll see a doctor.'

He sat up, with the look of wild desperation on his face that Sarah had seen so many times before. 'My daughters!' he gasped in Arabic. 'My wife?'

Sarah steeled herself not to cry. 'I'm sorry,' she replied in English. 'There were very few survivors. A handful.'

'Yes, but maybe . . . they was . . .' His English was faltering and he was still straining for breath. 'Hoda Salim. My wife. She's small with dark hair. And my girls. They were wearing . . .' He reached down to touch his orange life vest but it was gone.

Sarah Wade laid a hand over his against his sodden chest and forced herself to look him in the eye.

'I'm so sorry. All the survivors are adult males. The coast guard are still searching . . .'

Her voice trailed off. But her face had already told Mahmoud Salim all he needed to know. He lay back and closed his eyes, too numb with shock to do anything more than breathe. The girl continued stroking his hand and talking. Another vessel had hit them. Both boats had capsized. They'd done all they could but almost everyone on Mood's boat had been trapped underneath as she sank. Only the experienced smugglers and a handful of other strong men had made it out.

*And Parzheen*, thought Mood. *She fought. She fought for her life. Maybe . . .?*

But the hope was too painful to sustain. He couldn't. He had to block it out, to try to protect himself.

'When you leave this boat you'll be taken to see a doctor at one of the camps. You're entitled to food and shelter and technically to a legal representative, although you likely won't get one. The local police will want to interview you when you're well enough to talk. What happens then will be up to the Greek authorities, but most likely you'll be sent back home.'

*Home.* For Mood Salim, that place no longer existed.

The redheaded English girl was the last kind face he'd seen, and the last person to treat him like a human being.

From the moment he set foot on Greek soil, he was no longer Mood Salim, husband, father, son and brother. He was an animal, a thing to be herded and prodded, glared at and insulted and despised. But that was OK.

Mood didn't want compassion.

He wanted revenge.

Inspector Georgiou Thalakis clutched his throat, grateful to be alive. Staggering to his feet, he looked in the mirror at the line of deep purple bruises already forming on his neck, one for each of the monstrous Arab's fingers. How much longer would he be expected to deal with these pieces of scum? These violent, deranged foreigners, these animals, worse even than the Turks. They all claimed to be fleeing violence, and perhaps they were. But somewhere along the way, that same violence had infected them too. And now it was spreading here, to Greece, like some foul disease for which no one, apparently, had the cure.

'Is he dead?' Thalakis glared down at the prisoner sprawled out on the stone floor of the cell, a pool of blood around his head like a devil's halo.

One of the guards crouched over and put a finger to the giant's neck. 'Not yet. Should I call a doctor?'

Thalakis considered. One more dead Libyan was a problem solved, in his opinion. On the other hand, he wanted the name of the bastard in charge of this particular trafficking gang. Thanks to the meddling, do-gooder charity rescue boats, he had the boat's so-called 'captain' and his ragtag crew of smugglers. But Georgiou Thalakis wasn't interested in six monkeys. He wanted the organ grinder.

The smugglers were a lot more afraid of their bosses than they were of the Greek police and would never give up a name. Which meant he needed one of the survivors, either this brute Mahmoud or his sobbing buddy in the cell next door.

Just then the door opened and Thalakis's colleague, Inspector Vallas burst in. 'I think we've got him!' he grinned. 'My boy didn't have a name but we got a positive ID from a photo. Andreas Kouvlaki. What happened here by the way?' He glanced without much concern at the collapsed prisoner and the pool of blood.

'He slipped,' said Thalakis, equally uninterested. *Kouvlaki*. How did he know that name?

All of a sudden it came to him. 'Andreas Kouvlaki. Any relation of Perry Kouvlaki?'

'Bingo,' Inspector Vallas smiled. 'Andreas is Perry's little brother.'

'So Alexiadis is behind this?' Inspector Thalakis rubbed his sore neck again. 'I knew it!'

Makis Alexiadis, or 'Big Mak' to his friends and cronies, was the de-facto leader of the Petridis crime operation, a vast network of illegal businesses that were still going strong twelve years after its eponymous founders were killed in a 'tragic' helicopter accident in the United States. Perry Kouvlaki was well known as Alexiadis's right-hand man and chief lackey. If Perry's little brother was in Libya, recruiting cargo for the death boats, then Petridis Inc. was branching out into the migrant business. Which made sense. Even in this modern world of Bitcoin and cyber fraud, there were still fortunes to be made in good old-fashioned slavery and all of its many nefarious offshoots – prostitution, illegal farm labor, organized crime, even armed robbery. Once on European soil the migrants had no rights and no money and were ripe for exploitation by the likes of the Petridis gang.

Of course, no court would accept the word of a penniless Libyan as evidence that Makis Alexiadis was involved in people-trafficking, or that he was anything more than the legitimate businessman he claimed to be. Like Spyros Petridis before him, Alexiadis was a slippery customer, with more expensive lawyers at his disposal to protect his 'good name' than your average Congolese dictator. But a positive ID on Perry Kouvlaki's brother was a start. Now all they had to do was find the bastard.

'Shall I call a doctor?' Inspector Vallas asked his colleague.

Inspector Thalakis looked down again at the man who'd just tried to kill him.

'Sure. Go ahead.'

The lead on Andreas Kouvlaki had put him in an unusually forgiving mood.

Lying stock-still on the floor, Mood Salim – conversely – felt anything but forgiving.

If the Greek bastards thought he was unconscious, so much the better. He no longer cared about his interrogators, any more than they cared about him. He had a name now. Three names, in fact:

Andreas Kouvlaki. Perry Kouvlaki. And Makis Alexiadis.

Mood wouldn't rest until all three men were dead and buried.

Until their rotten, murderous souls burned in hell.

Just like his.

# CHAPTER TEN

Makis Alexiadis stood on the balcony of his sumptuous modernist villa, watching his guests arrive. They were an impressive group, models and movie stars, tech billionaires and real-estate moguls, rock stars and politicians, and even a smattering of European royalty, the women all draped in couture and the finest Israeli diamonds, the men flashing their Louis Moinet Meteoris watches, fresh off their Heesen superyachts and BD-700 private jets.

*Ah, Mykonos in the summer!* Surely life didn't get any better than this?

Named after the grandson of the great god Apollo, Mykonos had always been the jewel of the Aegean and, in Makis Alexiadis's opinion, Greece's most beautiful island. It might not be lush and green like the others – the constant, fierce winds made it hard for vegetation to thrive, leaving a landscape renowned for its steep, barren and rocky hills, plunging dramatically down to azure waters – but Mykonos boasted a unique, windswept, desert-like beauty all its own. Simple whitewashed fishing villages clung to the beaches, while up in the hills around Ano Mera, larger, grander villas perched like eagles, braving the winds in exchange for spectacular views of Delos, and beyond.

Lying between its more modest neighbors, Tinos, Syros, Paros and Naxos, at eighty-five square kilometers, Mykonos was by far the largest and 'flashiest' of the Cyclades, and had attracted the world's elite, playboy class to its idyllic shores long before Makis Alexiadis became one of their number.

Classically handsome in the Greek fashion, with thick, tar-black hair, olive skin and gray eyes like sea mist in the morning, Makis was of average height and stockily built, like a bull. Even when he was poor, growing up in a rundown apartment building in the Athenian suburb of Sepolia, women had been drawn to him like flies to honey. But Makis Alexiadis wasn't poor any more. A career that had begun, aged only fifteen, as Spyros Petridis's gopher-cum-driver-cum-golf-caddy-cum-all-round-lackey, had flourished twenty years later into wealth and power beyond even Makis's wildest dreams. Since his boss's death, 'Big Mak' Alexiadis had run the Petridis crime empire day-to-day, simultaneously growing his own 'front-of-house' business as a property developer, tycoon, philanthropist and all-round Greek media superstar. By exploiting the 'synergies' between his two lives, Makis Alexiadis had amassed a fortune that now rivaled his mentor Petridis's net worth back in his heyday.

These were good times.

In a paradise awash with billionaires, there were naturally numerous contenders for the title of Mykonos's most luxurious private residence. But Makis's beloved Villa Mirage must surely have made most people's top three. Fifteen thousand square feet of glass and marble, perched on the top of a cliff in Agios Lazaros, nestled amid five acres of manicured, formal gardens that glowed emerald green amid the surrounding red rock, Villa Mirage commanded ocean views so beautiful they had been known to make Makis Alexiadis weep. Which was quite an achievement. It would be an understatement to say that 'Big Mak' Alexiadis was not a sensitive man. Those who had been unlucky enough to cross him in business, or in life, knew him to be as stone-hearted as the huge boulders scattered around his beloved island, said by legend to be the petrified testicles of the Titans, mythical giants supposedly slain by Hercules on this very spot.

Makis Alexiadis's platinum Samsung Galaxy S III buzzed in his jacket pocket. He frowned. He only used this particular cell for his most private and important business, and it never left his side, not even while he slept. Theoretically a text at this time of night might be good news, but in this case he doubted it. He was right.

Pulling out the phone he read the message. 'Cargos lost at Lesbos and Chios. Two vessels sunk, one seized. More to follow.'

'Damn it!' Big Mak cursed aloud. That was the fourth lost shipment this month alone. *Four hundred and twenty migrants at an average total profit of three thousand euros each . . .* He totted up the value of the lost human life as if they were so many corn husks or sacks of sugar. Not that it was the money itself that mattered most. In the grand scheme of the Petridis empire that Big Mak presided over, 1.2 million euros was small potatoes. But the growing business of people-trafficking and, in particular, control of the profitable Aegean route, could be worth hundreds of millions to whichever gang gained ultimate supremacy. Losing not one more boat, but two on the same day, was a major setback. *We'll look like a laughing stock*, Makis thought bitterly.

Worse, he would have to explain this to the one person

to whom, nominally at least, he still answered. That was not a prospect he relished, quite apart from the fact that any communication with this particular person exposed both Makis personally and the organization to serious risk, not to mention the logistical challenges involved.

It wasn't easy, communing with the dead.

'There you are, Angel.' Tatiana, Makis's live-in Ukrainian companion, stepped out onto the balcony and coiled her lithe limbs longingly around him, like a hungry snake. 'I've been looking for you everywhere. People are asking for you, baby. Is everything OK?'

Two inches taller than Makis, with a mane of brunette hair, swollen, bee-stung lips and a cartoonishly sexualized body that she'd barely covered tonight in some sort of woven gold, chainmail attire, Tatiana was every red-blooded male's fantasy. At that moment, Makis felt simultaneously aroused and so irritated he could have happily wrapped his bare hands around her slender, gazelle's neck and snapped it like an irksome twig.

'No,' he snapped, grabbing her hand and placing it over his rock-hard cock anyway, more from habit than desire. 'Everything's not OK. Tell them all to leave.'

Tatiana laughed nervously. 'I can hardly do that. The French president is here, my love, and the—'

She gasped as Makis spun around and grabbed her by the hair, pulling her face so violently towards his own she thought for a moment he was going break her nose with the top of his skull, the way she'd seen him do to other underlings who'd annoyed him.

'Would you defy me?' He snarled at her like a dog.

Terrified, she shook her head vehemently. 'No, Mak. Never! I'll do whatever you want. I'm sorry.'

Mollified by her groveling and the unmistakable look of fear in her eyes, he let her go.

'Get me a pencil and paper,' he growled. 'And get Frankie up here. Now.'

He watched the girl scurry away and realized that, despite her physical perfection, he was bored. Time for a new model soon.

Seconds later, a maid appeared with the pencil and paper he'd asked for, swiftly followed by Frankie Goulakis, a toothless peasant boy whom Makis Alexiadis had picked up at the side of the road one day out of curiosity and amusement, rather as one might a stray dog, and then kept around for the same reasons. Frankie was simple but reliable with straightforward tasks, and fanatically loyal to his master.

'Take this to the caves.' Scrawling a short note, Makis folded it and handed it to the boy. 'Leave it in the usual place.'

Frankie nodded and left.

Glancing down again at the obscene display of wealth and modernity milling around in the gardens below him, Big Mak Alexiadis reflected once more on the ironies of doing business in modern Greece. Especially illicit business. While he received crucial information via encrypted text to his phone, the only way for him to safely pass on that information was via a piece of paper given to an illiterate boy, who would take it by donkey to the mouth of a cave where he would wedge it into a predetermined crevice. From there, another peasant would retrieve it and begin the long and arduous journey to *his* master, and from then onwards up an elaborate chain to Makis's superior. The whole process might take up to two weeks, a frustrating but necessary set of precautions.

Technology was evolving as rapidly here as everywhere else in the world. But it brought with it a new set of risks. Detection. Interception. Trackability. As a result, the old

152

ways were still very much alive and well in Greece. Makis Alexiadis's superior insisted on them.

Sweat ran down the man's face and back, his skin itching and burning beneath his simple woolen trousers and linen shirt. The sun, always fierce, seemed to burn today with a particularly fevered intensity. Almost as if he were being punished for toiling up the winding, rocky path to the convent. But of course, that couldn't be. Father Georgiou had told him he was doing the Lord's work by retrieving these messages from the cave and bringing them to Sister Elena.

'Mother church needs you, Bazyli.' That's what Father Georgiou said. 'Yours is not to reason why. You do your part and let the good sister do hers.' Deeply pious and devoted, Bazyli would have loved to become a priest himself, but he knew in his heart he was not worthy. Instead he had devoted his life to humbly serving those greater and holier than he. That included Father Georgiou and, of course, Sister Elena herself, although the revered nun was surrounded by an aura of mystique that confused Bazyli, and sometimes frightened him. There was something else about her too: something womanly and of-the-flesh, something that belied the spiritual life she'd chosen and that made the simple man feel simultaneously happy and guilty in her presence. He dismissed these things as symptoms of his own sinful nature, and did his best to put them aside.

The journey to Sikinos had been long and arduous, on foot and on horseback along thorny back-roads and, the worst part for Bazyli, the sea crossing that always made him vomit, no matter how calm the waters. Usually, by this point, just a few hundred meters below the appointed meeting spot in an orchard adjoining the convent walls, he would be feeling relief. Soon the journey would be over, the message safely delivered to the first link in the chain, and Bazyli could return to his smallholding on Paros, to his chickens and his sweet peas and his Bible. But today the heat made relief impossible. All he wanted was to stop and rest in the shade, right now; to sink his face into a cool pool of water and to drink and slake his raging thirst, like an animal.

Shielding his eyes against the blinding light, he looked once more up the hillside. And then, like a miracle, there she was, a black-and-white robed figure gliding down to greet him. Her face was veiled, hidden as always from the lustful eyes of men, and her female form completely covered by her habit. And yet the way she moved; her walk; the small, graceful movement of her hands, all mesmerized the messenger like some rare exotic drug.

'Sister.' Bazyli bowed his head as she came closer, dropping to his arthritic knees in both deference and exhaustion. 'For you.'

With trembling hands, he passed her the folded paper, panting like a dog.

'Thank you.' The soft cadence of her voice flowed over him like oil. Sister Elena rarely spoke. In the three years he'd acted as messenger for Father Georgiou, Bazyli couldn't have heard her utter more than ten words in total. Yet he knew that, in paradise, that voice would return to him; that he would bask in her words for ever.

'Please.' From beneath her robes she extracted a large, plastic bottle of water and handed it to him in exchange for the note, which she slipped into a pocket, unread. After he'd drunk about half of it, she produced a slab of cheese wrapped in paper, two large tomatoes and some bread.

'It's not necessary, Sister,' he protested, but she insisted, pressing the food into his hands. Then she laid a single palm on the top of his head in blessing, before turning and gliding back up the hill to the convent gate, as smoothly and silently as she'd arrived, like a ghost.

*She is goodness and kindness personified*, Bazyli thought. *The perfection of womanhood, like Our Lady, her life devoted to Christ.*

He had never been tempted to read any of the messages he delivered, even though, unlike Frankie Goulakis, he knew how to read. He'd already sullied Elena's spiritual purity with his own base, wanton thoughts – his desires long suppressed but never conquered. This was why he wasn't a priest. But he wasn't about to compound his sin by looking at that which was intended for another. For someone so far above Bazyli, he didn't even know their name. Although he assumed Sister Elena must know it . . .

Finishing the water, he tucked the food into his knapsack and hurried back down the hill.

It took Sister Elena fifteen minutes to reach the glade, a secret, completely secluded spot surrounded by thick pines and with a tiny, spring-fed stream trickling through it with water that was always ice cold, no matter how boiling the sun. Because it belonged to the Order of the Sacred Heart, no locals ever came here – they were a respectful lot, the islanders, as steeped in religious obedience and social propriety as any medieval serf. Being outside the convent walls, the glade was considered 'off limits' by Elena's fellow nuns too. It was her private kingdom, a place where – uniquely – she could be 'herself'.

Whatever that meant.

*So many reinventions. So many different identities. Different lives. Each of them 'real' in their own way.*

It wasn't like that for other people, she'd observed. In her fifty years on this earth, Elena had watched others grow and change and mature and evolve in a way that bore no relation to her own experience. Their lives weren't static, exactly. But they were *continuous*, moving along in a straight line past recognizable milestones: birth, childhood, adolescence, youth, middle age, old age, death. Through it all you were still *you*.

But not for her. Elena had existed as several distinct people, with no continuity at all. There was her childhood self: happy and calm. Her adolescent self: passionate, idealistic, sensual. Then came her longest, most significant role – her adult self, alive with a dark energy that annihilated all that had gone before. It was in this incarnation that she had met someone who was to change not just her own life, but the life of the world. Someone she still served, in a way, to this day, as the brand on her thigh reminded her.

And yet, that self had died too, the day she arrived at the convent. And from her ashes had risen 'Sister' Elena. Quiet, patient, devoted, calm, a blessing to all her sisters and to everybody else whose path she crossed. Separated from the world by choice, no longer an influencer or even an observer, but a recluse, a willing outcast.

In the beginning, life at the convent had felt like a curse. A punishment. But over the years Elena had come to cherish the deep peace of the nuns' routine as a blessing. It was a privilege to be free of it all: the striving, the passion, the conflict, and to devote oneself exclusively to God. To work and pray and sleep and leave no space in your heart for anything else.

She sighed. Such a pity it had to end.

*Nothing lasts for ever.*

Being 'Sister' Elena had been wonderful. But the letter in her hand meant that she was needed now for another role. She could no more stop this latest transformation than a caterpillar could refuse to spin its cocoon. It was time to shed her habit.

Someone who was greater than Sister Elena could ever be was soon to rise, Lazarus-like, from the dead.

The letter in her hands was from Makis Alexiadis. An important man, certainly, and yet not fit to kiss the feet of the one who was coming.

*Athena Petridis.*

*Athena!*

Just the name sent chills like an electrical current through Sister Elena's veins.

Pulling out the note that Makis Alexiadis had taken such pains to get to her, Sister Elena unfolded it and read it slowly. Her stomach soured, and she felt a tension in her body, her arms and hands and neck, that was at once alien and yet distantly familiar. This was bad news. Very bad. Two more lost shipments, the boats gone down with scores of lives lost. It was almost as if someone were trying to sabotage Athena's glorious return, her reclaiming of her birthright from Makis Alexiadis.

*Makis.*

*Big Mak.* That was what people called him now, the eager, scrawny little lad whom Spyros Petridis used to take everywhere with him, like a dog. He was, he claimed, still loyal to the couple who had plucked him from obscurity and thrust him into a world of inconceivable power, influence and wealth. But was he really? What if Makis was the one setting Athena up to fail? Allowing the lucrative Aegean migrant route to slip through her fingers? Laying the groundwork for a plot to usurp her?

What if Makis Alexiadis couldn't be trusted?

Of course there were many others to be feared. Old enemies. In particular 'The Group'. They were the ones who had sabotaged the Petridises' helicopter that day. The day they died.

Only of course, Athena hadn't died. Somehow she'd

survived the terrible flames of the wreckage, defied the searing heat like a witch. 'Someone' must have helped her.

Sister Elena chuckled to herself.

The drowned, branded boy would have let The Group know they'd failed. If Elena's memory served, they didn't take kindly to failure. Like all fanatics, they would fight on to the death. Till the job was done. They wouldn't stop until they'd driven a stake through Athena's heart.

Through the tall pines, Sister Elena glimpsed the walls of the convent that had been her home, her sanctuary, for so many long years. She would have preferred to delay her departure, just for a few more months. To prepare, emotionally. To ready herself for her duty, for what was to come. But the branded child washed up on the shore meant that time had run out. Today's note from Makis Alexiadis merely confirmed it.

The second coming was nigh.

# CHAPTER ELEVEN

The assassin crouched in the darkness, curled under the overhanging bay bushes that surrounded the bastide. His legs ached and his fingers had grown numb with cold. He felt as if he'd been waiting here forever. But these things mustn't be rushed. The guardians of Andreas Kouvlaki's estate, Monsieur and Madame Jamet, had only retired to bed half an hour ago. He must wait until both were deeply asleep before he made his move.

Andreas Kouvlaki's holiday villa in the south of France was a surprisingly tasteful property. Not for him the flashy, modern, glass and steel mansions overlooking Pampelonne beach or one of the grand gated estates in town. Instead the wealthy people-trafficker had chosen a converted seventeenth-century farmhouse in the hills above Ramatuelle, its secluded grounds ringed by woodland and completely hidden from the prying eyes of the locals. Perhaps he felt that the bastide's isolation was security enough? Was that why he'd hired only the elderly Jamets, a single, bored night watchman and two Doberman pinschers as protection? Or perhaps he was simply too arrogant to believe that his enemies would dare risk a strike against him?

His brother, Perry Kouvlaki, had been much more careful, installing elaborate alarm systems and trip wires and surrounding himself with a small army of bodyguards. Not that it had mattered in the end. The assassin had successfully dispatched Perry last month in Paris, beating him to death with a claw hammer in the back room of a deserted former nightclub, before branding his mangled body with a letter: 'A'. Once he'd discovered the older Kouvlaki's penchant for Arab boys, the younger the better, it had been easy to lure the revolting pedophile away from his various layers of protection to his death. He'd considered branding Perry while he was still alive. God knew the bastard deserved it. But once the hammer was in his hand, it was as if a red curtain descended and righteous, murderous rage took over. Perry was dead in seconds. In the end, he'd struggled to find enough unbroken skin on the corpse to leave his mark successfully, eventually opting for what had once been Perry Kouvlaki's shoulder blade.

Next time he must try to slow down.

Andreas knew of his brother's fate, although he assumed Perry's grizzly murder had been at the hands of a pimp, or the 'friends' of one of his playthings. Not sharing his brother's perversions, Andreas did not perceive himself to be at risk. Charming and handsome, with a slender frame and an immaculate taste in bespoke tailoring, the younger Kouvlaki was popular and well liked, playing the part of the respectable businessman to a tee. Women flocked to him and men competed to become his friend, oblivious to the raw human misery on which his business empire was based.

But Andreas had become complacent, and sloppy. No one was infallible, as the assassin well knew. And he was here to carry the job through. The day of reckoning had arrived.

Slowly emerging from his hiding place, wincing as the blood flowed back into his straightened legs, he moved towards the guardian's cottage. If his calculations were correct, the dogs should pick up his scent in approximately fifteen seconds, beginning a cacophony of barking that he must extinguish as soon as possible.

*Fifteen, fourteen . . . ten . . .*

Reaching into the bag slung across his chest, he pulled out the two dripping steaks, each generously laced with an odorless horse tranquilizer, holding them in front of him like a talisman.

*Two . . . one . . .*

Right on cue the Dobermans leaped out of the darkness like twin hell hounds, barking loudly, but the steaks stopped them instantly in their tracks. He hung back as they sniffed, then ate, unaware of the sedative racing into their bloodstream. Both animals were on the ground unconscious within a minute.

Screwing the silencer onto his gun, he knelt down and stroked each of their sleek coats. He wished he didn't have to do it, but it couldn't be helped. With a heavy heart, he shot a bullet deep into each animal's brain.

*They're Kouvlaki's victims, not mine*, he told himself as he reached the door of the cottage, easily unpicking the lock. Moving swiftly up the stairs, he paused for a moment at the Jamets' bedroom, looking at the old couple sleeping side by side, their sun-weathered faces still visible in the shadows, peeking out above the duvet like two pickled walnuts. He climbed up onto the bed and held a chloroformed rag over monsieur and madame simultaneously before either had a chance to stir. Less than a minute later, with both the guardians knocked out cold and handcuffed to a bedpost, he was back outside, headed towards the main house.

The last remaining obstacle was Laurent, Andreas Kouvlaki's lazy and useless night watchman. Most large homes on the Cote d'Azur employed such a person these days, supposedly to deter car thieves or would-be burglars, although most of the young men who accepted these deathly boring jobs were unemployed local youths, totally untrained and of considerably less use than the guard dogs. Nonetheless, it made people feel better to know there was somebody patrolling their homes with a flashlight while they slept. And Kouvlaki had at least gone to the trouble of providing Laurent with a gun, putting him one step above the rest.

At five foot eight and slightly built, however, Laurent was no match for the assassin. Approaching the boy from behind and clamping a third rag over his nose and mouth, just as he had with the guardians, he soon had Kouvlaki's last line of defense bound, gagged and locked in an outdoor toolshed.

A chill wind blew as he jimmied open a ground-floor window and climbed easily into the dark bastide. But he didn't feel the cold any more. Instead a slow, satisfying warmth crept through him as he considered what he was about to do and why.

*I am an angel of vengeance.*

*A servant of the righteous.*

*A destroyer of evil.*

Smiling, the assassin began climbing the stairs.

Inspector Anjou rubbed a jaded hand across his eyes.

'*La vache!*' He whistled through his teeth. The scene in front of him was like nothing he had ever come across in over twenty years of police work. What had begun in the evening as a couple's bedroom now looked like an abattoir. Like one of those appalling videos that animal rights activists or militant vegans post online. Except that the mutilated

162

corpse in the center of the carnage did not belong to a calf or a sow, but to a young man in the prime of his life.

'Is the girlfriend talking?' Inspector Anjou asked one of his officers, his eyes still fixed on the slashed, bloodied mulch that had once been Andreas Kouvlaki.

'Not really, sir,' the officer replied. 'Screaming, mostly. She's still in shock.'

'Did she see it happen?'

'No,' said the officer. 'She was drugged and tied to the bed. The intruder dragged Kouvlaki outside. That was the last she saw of him alive, apparently. When she woke up he was . . .' The young man nodded towards the body but averted his eyes. He already looked green and fit to puke. Inspector Anjou didn't blame him.

'She called us though, didn't she?'

The young officer nodded. 'The killer deliberately placed the phone next to her on the bed. He must have wanted her to get help.'

Inspector Anjou grunted. 'Oh yeah. He was a gem of a guy, all right.'

'Of course not, sir. But it is striking that he didn't harm anybody else on the property,' the young man pointed out. 'Apart from the guard dogs. I mean, it was clearly Mr Kouvlaki he was after.'

*And boy did he get him.*

Anjou knelt next to the body. He was careful not to touch anything, but roamed over Andreas Kouvlaki's injuries in as much detail as he could, examining the killer's handiwork with disgust. The face had been battered into an indistinguishable pulp, probably with a fist or the blunt handle of a gun. Most of the other wounds had been administered with a knife, although the killer clearly had a gun as well. There were bullets in the feet and lower legs – perhaps used to stop the victim when he tried to run?

163

The throat had been cut, repeatedly. But the most striking features on the corpse were the two mutilations that, Inspector Anjou hoped, had been inflicted after death.

One was a letter 'P' scorched into the chest like a cattle brand.

And the other was the right hand. It still bore the victim's gold and diamond rings. Whoever did this clearly wasn't interested in money. But the index finger had been cleanly severed.

*He kills dogs*, Inspector Anjou thought. *He's wildly violent. He leaves 'signs' on his victims and he keeps body parts as trophies.*

*But . . . he leaves a phone for the girlfriend to call for help. And he lets all the staff live.*

What kind of psycho *was* this?

Back in the safety of his rented room, the assassin showered, changed into sweatpants and a clean T-shirt, and lay back on the bed. He was exhausted, physically, but he knew he wouldn't sleep. Nothing could calm his frantic, buzzing mind.

It wasn't killing that was the rush. That gave him no pleasure. He wasn't a monster, after all. But it was the sense of completion. Of justice served. Of a mission, not yet completed, but in motion. He was doing his duty, not for himself, but for others.

Andreas Kouvlaki had been a clever man. Like his brother, he'd pleaded for his corrupt, worthless life. But unlike his brother, he'd had a strategy – offering to lead the killer to the most important target of them all.

'I can get you access to the Athens townhouse,' he'd babbled to his killer. 'That's where he is right now. Believe me, I hate him as much as you do. Everything I did, I did because he forced me to.'

The assassin hadn't believed him. Not for a second. But his promise of access was interesting. Interesting enough to delay his death.

'How? How can you get me in?'

'The codes to the outer perimeter gates and the front door are saved on a memory stick in my safe,' said Kouvlaki. 'I'll give that to you now. The safe's in one of the guest bedrooms. But the codes will only get you so far. At night he sleeps with the master bedroom laser-alarmed. You need biometric access to get in, and I'm one of only four people who have it. You'll need my help.'

The assassin looked thoughtfully at the groveling man at his feet. He remembered the first time he'd seen Andreas Kouvlaki, far, far away from here. On that day the sun was shining, and Andreas too had shone, radiating authority and confidence, his power and wealth in stark contrast to the poverty and misery and desperation all around him. Like a silver dolphin, swimming through a sea of filth.

How the tables had turned.

'Please!' Andreas begged. 'We can do this together. You need me. Let me help you.'

'Thank you,' the assassin said quietly. 'I will.'

And he had. Reaching into the bag by the side of his bed, he pulled out the night's two treasures, holding each lovingly.

The first was a memory stick, containing the access codes to his next victim's estate.

And the second was Andreas Kouvlaki's right index finger, the biometric 'key' to the master bedroom suite, tightly wrapped in a bag of ice.

# CHAPTER TWELVE

Ella pressed her forehead against the plastic plane window as they dropped down through the last layer of clouds towards Eleftherios Venizelos, otherwise known as Athens International Airport. Having never left the United States before, she was fascinated by everything she saw. Even from fifteen thousand feet, it was clear that she was entering not just a different country, but a different world.

A sky so bright blue it looked like something from a child's coloring book shimmered over a patchwork of brown and green fields, crisscrossed with tiny roads, along which were scattered white buildings of various shapes and sizes. Beyond the fields, an aqua sea lapped at a white-sand coast. The plane continued its descent and soon Ella could make out rivers and churches and what might have been an amphitheater, or some sort of ruin? A lone red sailboat headed out into open water. *It all seems so peaceful*, Ella thought.

Thanks to the briefing that she'd finally been handed at San Francisco Airport, and had read over and over again for the last ten hours straight, she now knew that this strange, colorful place was Attica, the region surrounding Greece's capital.

She also knew that, somewhere down there, her parents had lost their lives.

*Not 'lost'*, Ella corrected herself. William and Rachel Praeger had been robbed of their lives, brutally murdered. Now, at long last, Ella knew who to blame.

Her father William had died first, shot in the head at point-blank range by members of an organized crime gang run by a man named Spyros Petridis. He'd been on assignment in Europe, part of a team attempting to expose a vast money-laundering operation headed by Petridis and involving numerous senior European government officials. According to Ella's briefing, William was killed somewhere on the Greek mainland. Although his body was never found, The Group had since intercepted multiple communications from within the Petridis empire confirming his murder.

Ella's mother Rachel had suffered an even more appalling end. Lured to Greece by the Petridises, in search of her husband (in reality already dead), Rachel was kidnapped, taken to a remote beach and drowned in the Aegean by Spyros Petridis himself, while his wife Athena looked on. Personally enraged by the damage that William Praeger had done to his 'business interests', he had vowed to wreak a vengeance on The Group that went beyond just William's murder. Killing William's wife, and in such a sadistic manner, had been an act of rage and of terror, designed to strike fear into the uppermost echelons of The Group's anonymous leadership.

Instead, it had the opposite effect. Revolted by the murder of the Praegers, two of its most brave and brilliant young operatives, The Group struck back, successfully assassinating Spyros Petridis and his wife Athena the following year by sabotaging a helicopter in which they were both passengers, causing a fatal crash. Until a few months ago, the world believed that both the Petridises had perished in this 'accident'. But recent events suggested to The Group, and those in the know, that Athena Petridis might in fact have survived the crash and had been in hiding all this time.

Ella's mission was to establish whether this was true and – if it was – to find Athena Petridis. Find the woman who had stood by and watched while Ella's mother was drowned, like a rat. The Group hoped that Ella's unique abilities to receive and interpret data transmissions, as well as her personal investment in the mission, would help her succeed where traditional operatives had failed. 'Once located,' Ella's briefing asserted bluntly, 'the target will be destroyed.'

At first Ella was disappointed by the lack of detail about her parents' deaths. In a seventy-page briefing, less than two pages were devoted to the murders of William and Rachel Praeger. The other sixty-eight pages focused on the Petridis criminal empire, past and present, and what little concrete information The Group had so far on the possible where-abouts of Ella's target, Athena Petridis.

But as Ella read on, she found herself putting her parents' murders to one side as she began to comprehend the scale of the Petridis gang's crimes; if you could even call such a vast and sophisticated organization a 'gang'. The depths of misery that Spyros Petridis and his henchmen had inflicted over the years was breathtaking, especially for a group that, until today, Ella had never even heard of. Even if only a fraction of the report was accurate, these people had to be right up there with the Mafia and the Triads on the torture-and-killing stakes, and perhaps were even more successful when it came to white-collar crime, amassing eye-watering levels of wealth. As well as vast fortunes made from illegal activities such as prostitution and narcotics, the Petridises had defrauded, embezzled and intimidated their way into countless 'legitimate' businesses, from real estate to shipping to mining and investment banking. At the end of their reign of terror, in the years immediately prior to the crash, they'd even expanded into education, investing heavily in private, inner-city schools in the United States. Ironically, this had proved to be one of their most profitable sectors to date, a simple business model that involved luring poor but aspirational white and immigrant families into a lifetime of debt and, effectively, servitude to the Petridis machine.

*Even if they hadn't killed my parents*, Ella thought, *these people were evil to the bone.*

Closing her eyes, she decided to practice Dix's technique. Allowing the receiver part of her brain to open, she tried to tune in exclusively to the dialogue between air-traffic control and the cockpit. To her delight, she found she could do it easily. Not that the jargon-filled exchange meant much to her. But it was incredible to think that just a few short weeks ago, all she would have heard was an incomprehensible crackle, accompanied by a nausea-inducing headache.

Grudgingly, she admitted that she did have The Group to thank for some things.

With a single, hard bump they were on the ground.

'Welcome to Athens. We hope you had a pleasant flight.'

'It's like, a billion degrees here! And two billion per cent humidity. I'm melting like the Wicked Witch of the West.'

Ella was talking to her friend Bob a few blocks from her hotel, struggling to hold on to her cell phone with clammy, sweat-soaked hands.

'I mean, I only came out to get a soda, but I seriously need to take all my clothes off and jump in a fountain or something.'

'Don't do that,' said Bob, who both loved and hated the

fact that Ella had called him at four in the morning his time, after three weeks of radio silence – from *Greece* – but was now acting as if they'd just spoken yesterday. Like everything was normal.

'You didn't die in the woods, then. That's good.' He rubbed his eyes sleepily.

'What woods?' asked Ella.

'California woods. Weird Suit Guy. Coordinates. The cult?' Bob reminded her of their last conversation, on her drive up to Camp Hope.

'Oh, no,' said Ella, in an 'old news' tone of voice. 'I didn't die. And it's not a cult. Well, not exactly. I mean I guess you could say it sort of is . . .'

'Jesus, Ella.'

'Why are you whispering?'

'I'm whispering because it's the middle of the night and Joanie's sleeping next to me,' Bob explained. 'What are you doing in Greece?'

'I can't really tell you.'

'Or you'd have to kill me?' Bob joked.

'Don't worry. I would never kill you,' Ella replied, deadly seriously. 'Even if they asked me to.'

Bob sat up in bed. 'Ella, what's going on? You do realize this is not normal? Like, none of this is remotely normal. Can you tell me where you are exactly? Or how long you plan to be?'

'Sorry,' said Ella.

'Well, can I at least go check on your apartment while you're gone? If you're planning to be gone a while, which I really hope you're *not*. I want to do something, Ella. I'm worried about you.'

'Thanks, but you don't need to be. I just wanted to call to let you know I'm OK. Also to say sorry for asking you to have . . . to sleep with me. Before.'

170

Bob could feel her blushes down the phone. 'That's OK, Ella.'

'No, it wasn't OK. I see that now. I've been working on controlling my impulses.'

'Well . . . good,' said Bob. Perhaps there was some silver lining to Ella falling in with this bunch of weirdoes. 'That's good. So you're *not* going to take your clothes off and get in that fountain. Right?'

'But it's so *hot!*' Ella groaned. 'Oh my God, you have no idea.'

'And don't ask random Greek men to have sex with you,' Bob added, hoping her last comment was a joke.

'I won't,' said Ella. 'Take care, Bob.'

'No, no, no, don't hang up yet!' pleaded Bob. But it was too late.

Ella looked up for the waiter.

'*Chimos portokali, epharisto,*' she instructed him confidently. He nodded and disappeared.

Ella's spoken Greek was improving by the day, and her accent already natural enough that locals didn't immediately take her for a tourist. But Gabriel wasn't impressed.

'It's still not good enough,' he'd informed her bluntly, on their last phone call before she left Camp Hope for the airport. 'Work harder.'

'Thanks for that, Obey One,' Ella took umbrage. 'That's super encouraging.'

'In the field, the way you speak is as much part of your cover as anything else,' he explained, unapologetically. 'It can be the difference between life and death.'

'Oh yeah? Well if you wanted my Greek to be fluent, maybe you should have trained me for six months, not six minutes,' snapped Ella. 'It's not as if the language is all I have to learn. I'm with Dix four hours a day, plus there's physical training. You try it!'

Ella's orange juice arrived, inexplicably without ice – either the Greeks didn't feel the humidity or they were suckers for punishment – and Ella sipped it slowly, drinking in the scene around her. Just a few blocks away was a busy road, narrow but choked with honking traffic and roaring with all the usual sounds of city life: babies screaming, merchants yelling, music playing on corners and in open-fronted bars. Yet here, on this tiny square, it was almost eerily quiet. Apart from Ella and a handful of other patrons, the café was empty. The few brave souls who'd ventured out in the heat at all were wisely sticking to the shadows, smoking under trees or porches, or sitting silently on the steps of the tiny church. One woman dressed all in black, who looked so ancient she surely ought to be dead already, muttered over her rosary beads in a corner like a wicked peddler-woman from a fairy tale. Ella tried to imagine being that old, or belonging to this old world with its church bells and rituals and strange mingled scents of incense, coffee, onions, jasmine and sweat. Sitting here, the modern world she'd just left back in America already felt like a dream.

Then again, most of the last month felt like a dream to Ella, and one from which she was no longer sure she wanted to wake up. She was, she admitted to herself, excited.

The clock on the church belfry told her it was now three in the afternoon. In three hours, one of The Group's Greek agents was coming to pick her up from her hotel lobby to take her for a 'briefing dinner'. Enough time for her to return to her room, shower (again), change, and perhaps read the information Gabriel had given her for the hundredth time. Her limbs ached and she longed for sleep after her journey, but she knew that the moment she closed her eyes, no force on earth could wake her.

*

'Ella. *Ella!*'

The boat was rocking. Waves, huge waves, were crashing over the open deck and threatening to throw her overboard, pulling her exhausted body from side to side.

'Ella, wake up!'

She sat up in bed, panicked and utterly disorientated. A fat, middle-aged man with the hairiest forearms Ella had ever seen had both his hands clamped on her shoulders. Her face was dripping in water, so cold it had her gasping for breath.

'What . . . who are you?' she wheezed at the gorilla, who smiled back at her broadly, revealing two rows of heavily yellowed, cigar smoker's teeth.

'I am Nikkos. And you are late!' he beamed. 'But that's OK. You are a woman and this is Athens. *Hari ka pousas gnorissa.*'

'Don't tell me you're pleased to meet me! You just threw water in my face!'

'I couldn't wake you,' he shrugged apologetically. 'You were snoring. Like this.'

Throwing his round head back so it lolled on his neck, Nikkos did an impression of Ella, opening his mouth wide and emitting the most appalling, pig-like grunting noises.

'I'm sure I didn't sound like that,' said Ella, drying her face and trying to suppress a smile. There was something warm about him, an instantly endearing quality that made it hard to maintain one's anger. 'How did you get into my room?'

He raised an admonishing finger and made a 'tsk' sound with his tongue. 'Very very easy. You didn't double-lock. You must take more precautions, OK?'

Before Ella could say anything he was up and pacing, clapping his pudgy hands like a jovial drill sergeant. 'Come, come, hurry up, we must be at the restaurant. Very quickly and right now. We have much to discuss.'

'OK,' said Ella, dropping the towel she still had wrapped around her from the shower and walking stark naked, and apparently quite unconcerned, into the small dressing room. 'Just let me change. I'll be one minute.'

Nikkos blushed to the roots of what was left of his hair as she bent down to pull some clean underwear out of her suitcase. Who *was* this crazy woman? The boss had warned him Ella Praeger could be 'eccentric' but he hadn't expected *this*.

'I will wait in the car. Outside,' he called out, belatedly averting his eyes.

Dinner turned out to be at a bustling taverna right in the center of Athens' tourist district at the foot of the Acropolis, in the shadow of the famous Parthenon. Although not more than two miles from the hotel, Nikkos drove them on such a circuitous route it took almost forty minutes to get there.

'Are you worried about being followed?' asked Ella, taking a seat at a corner table and perusing the delicious-looking Greek menu.

'Not worried!' Nikkos assured her. 'Worrying is a waste of time. But prepared? Yes, always.' Lighting up a fat cigar, in clear defiance of the 'No Smoking' signs posted on every wall, he flagged down the waiter and immediately started ordering for both of them. *Gavros tiganitos*, plates of tiny deep-fried fish, slabs of feta cheese smothered in olive oil, tomato and kalamata salad, pan-fried octopus in garlic, and *dolmathes*, vine leaves stuffed with savory rice and onions. Waving away Ella's objections, he followed this up with a request for a large bottle of retsina and some bread and olives 'to begin'.

'Do you usually choose the food for your dinner companions?' Ella asked, not angry but a little bemused. 'Because I don't think I can eat a fraction of that.'

'Not with another man, no, no of course not,' Nikkos explained hastily. 'But with a woman, yes. Naturally, the man will choose the food that he pays for. This is the way in Greece.'

'But what if the woman doesn't like what the man chooses?'

'You don't like the food?' He looked hurt.

'I'm sure it will be delicious,' said Ella. 'It's just, well, don't you think your attitude is rather sexist? I mean, what if the woman pays?'

Nikkos threw back his head and laughed heartily at this idea. As he did so, an attractive middle-aged woman a few tables away suddenly turned and stared at him.

'Oh dear.' Nikkos blanched, hastily stubbing out his cigar as the woman made a beeline for their table, and began loudly and dramatically berating him, first in her native Italian and then in Greek. Even without her trusty Babbel tapes, Ella would probably have gotten the gist of the conversation from the woman's furious expression and wildly gesticulating hands. As it was she distinctly heard the words *pseftis* (liar), *apateonas* (cheat) and *choiros* (pig), were all repeated several times. Nikkos defended himself as best he could from her verbal, and occasionally physical blows, cowering like a berated dog while the waiters arrived bearing plate after plate of the feast he'd just ordered, apparently oblivious to the drama. At last the woman burned herself out and, like a tornado, whirled back to her own table, where she continued to look daggers at her hapless former flame.

'I apologize for that person's very rude behavior,' he mumbled to Ella, heaping both their plates with a mountain of food and pouring two brim-full glasses of the ice-cold wine, one of which he drained almost completely in a single fortifying gulp.

'She did seem rather upset,' Ella observed, spearing a *polpi* tentatively with her fork.

'She's Italian,' Nikkos asserted, as if this explained everything. 'I speak very good Italian,' he added boastfully, his natural ebullience already returning, like the tide. 'I am polyglot.'

Try as she might, Ella found it impossible to dislike this man. He seemed to her like an unreliable, greedy, generally badly behaved Santa Claus.

'She's upset because you cheated on her,' she told him, taking a sip of her own wine.

'No, no,' Nikkos waved away the accusation with another big slurp of wine. 'It was a misunderstanding, I assure you.'

'She said you had sex with two other women behind her back,' said Ella.

Registering his shocked face, she grinned. 'I am polyglot, too. Well, almost. I also have sexual relations with a lot of different people,' she added matter-of-factly.

Nikkos spluttered, choking and coughing until retsina came out of his nose.

'You are very different to Greek women,' he told Ella, as soon as he'd regained his breath.

'I'm very different to everyone,' she shrugged.

'Yes,' said Nikkos suddenly serious. 'I know. About your history and your . . . abilities. Are you using them now?'

Ella nodded. 'I'm learning to turn them on and off. I had training at the camp.'

'OK. So right now, can you "hear" anything?'

'Yes.' She lowered her voice. 'The man by the door in a red shirt is exchanging texts with his drug dealer. They're arguing over the price of a gram of cocaine.'

Nikkos's eyes widened. 'Really? You hear that? Or see it?'

'Neither exactly,' said Ella. 'It's hard to explain. But I'm

176

aware of it. Thousands of electronic signals are flowing through my brain day and night. I'm learning to tune in and out as I please. Also to detect different frequencies and radio waves. Like the Greek police outside.'

'There are police outside?' Nikkos spun around.

'Yes,' said Ella unconcerned. 'The ones who followed us. They're surveilling you, but they don't seem to know who I am. It's a good thing you never worry,' she teased him, tongue in cheek.

Nikkos put down his knife and fork and gazed at Ella in awe.

'That is very impressive. I understand now why they sent you and I pray you can help us. Succeed where others have failed.'

Ella leaned forward eagerly. 'They said you would brief me on stage one of the mission. Tonight? Now?'

'Mmm hmm,' said Nikkos, tearing off a hunk of warm bread and dipping it pensively into a bowl of hummus. 'Sit back,' he told Ella quietly, without looking up from his plate. 'Relax. Keep eating and drinking. We are having a normal, boring conversation over dinner, hm? Nothing for anyone to be interested in.'

Ella did as he asked, adjusting her body language and returning her attention to the delicious pile of fried anchovies that Nikkos had scooped onto her plate.

'I understand you already know the name and background of your target?' Nikkos began.

'Mm hm,' said Ella.

'Good. So this will be a two-part operation,' Nikkos went on. 'Phase one will be intelligence gathering. As you know, we have received recent reports suggesting that she, Athena Petridis, may be alive.'

'The brand on the drowned boy.' Ella shuddered.

'Yes, there's that,' said Nikkos. 'And other, older

rumors from the US about a badly injured woman being carried from the wreckage. But remember,' he pronounced it *Chhhreememberr*, rolling every 'r' to within an inch of its life. 'The crash site was incredibly remote. The likelihood of anyone being close enough to see what happened, never mind to help and rescue one of the passengers, must be very small and tiny.'

'You're saying you don't believe those reports?' Ella sounded surprised enough to earn a warning look from Nikkos. *Stay calm. Don't attract people's attention. This is a boring dinner conversation, remember?*

Ella got the message and lowered her voice.

'You don't think Athena survived?'

'Probably not,' he said after a pause.

Ella was shocked. Nikkos's skepticism about Athena Petridis's survival was in sharp contrast to the confidence of the rest of The Group. The way it had been put to Ella, establishing the *fact* that Athena was still alive was almost a formality at this point. The brand on the dead boy's heel proved it. The real purpose of Ella's mission was to locate her, so that a hit squad could move in and do the rest.

'That she survived the helicopter crash at all would be a miracle,' Nikkos explained, refilling both their glasses and ordering a second bottle. 'But the idea that not only did she survive the impact, but that someone saw her, pulled her from those flames, carried her maybe fifty kilometers to the nearest town, and then somehow kept it a secret, for long enough to smuggle her across the world? To me, this sounds like a fable. Like a Greek myth, hm?' he chuckled, pleased with his own analogy.

Ella sipped her wine in silent contemplation.

'You know my parents were working to bring the Petridises to justice. When I was still a small child. It was their last mission.'

'Yes. I know.' Nikkos looked down at the tablecloth, uncomfortable suddenly.

'Did you know them?' Ella asked. 'They would have been older than you, but not by that much. And if they both came to Greece, perhaps you met?'

'I never met your father. But I knew your mother,' Nikkos admitted, clearing his throat. 'Not well, but . . . our paths crossed.'

'What was she like?'

Nikkos looked away. 'She was a remarkable lady.'

'Remarkable in what way?'

Ella leaned towards him again, wide-eyed and eager for more, for any details he could spare her, like a starved dog hoping for dropped crumbs from its master's table. But Nikkos seemed uncharacteristically reticent.

'Many different ways. She was passionate. She was kind. Highly intelligent, of course.'

'Well, am I like her? Do you see similarities?'

It was a child's question, innocently asked, and it sent a pang, that felt an awful lot like guilt, through Nikkos's heart.

'I don't know yet if you are like her,' he said quietly. 'I hope you are. You're going to need your mother's courage in the weeks ahead, Ella. That much I know.'

The second bottle of wine arrived and Nikkos ignored Ella's protests, refilling her glass to the brim.

'Your purpose here, as you know, is as an intelligence-gathering tool. Hopefully your abilities are going to give us the edge on that score. Through you, we hope to find out whether Athena Petridis really is alive, or whether the mark on the boy was some sort of cruel hoax. A stunt, designed to make us and others believe that she is still out there.'

'But why . . .?'

179

Nikkos reached out his hand and placed it over hers. 'Too many questions,' he told her, not unkindly. 'To stay safe and be successful you must concentrate on the job at hand. For now that means forgetting about Athena and focusing only on *this* man.'

Reaching into his jacket pocket, he pulled out a crumpled piece of newspaper and passed it to Ella. It was taken from the society pages of *Eleftherotypia*, and it showed a glamorous group in white tie standing in front of the presidential mansion in central Athens. In the center of the group was a handsome, barrel-chested, dark-haired man, who clearly projected his dominance over the others with unspoken yet undeniable signals in his body language, expression and stance.

'Makis Alexiadis,' Nikkos said casually. 'They call him Big Mak. Very famous in Greece.'

'Who is he?' asked Ella.

'That depends who you ask. Some say he's a successful businessman. Others call him a playboy. This Greek word here,' he pointed to the photo's caption, 'I think you would say in English "*influencer*". It means politicians court him. Ordinary people watch him, on social media and on the television, and they copy his ways. His style.'

'And what do you say about him?'

Nikkos scooped the last of the feta greedily onto his plate.

'I say,' he took a leisurely bite, 'he is a killer. He is a sadist. He is . . .' He muttered something in Greek, searching for the right English word. '. . . a *blight* on this earth. Like a cancer.' Dropping his voice to a whisper, he leaned forward and continued, stroking Ella's hair as if he were murmuring sweet nothings into her ear. 'For many years, OK, Makis was Spyros Petridis's number two. Since the crash, he has been number one, the gang's de-facto leader. Later tonight

180

you will receive an anonymous package at your hotel with more details about him and his operations. But for now I can tell you that one of his "businesses" is kidnapping young children, mostly from the Middle East, and selling them to wealthy Western clients.'

'Selling them?'

Nikkos nodded.

'For sex?'

'Sometimes.'

Pressing her napkin to her mouth, Ella fought back her feelings of nausea.

'In the last three years we – The Group – have successfully targeted several of his "clients",' said Nikkos, taking his knife and slicing it purposefully through a tomato to indicate exactly what form this 'targeting' had taken.

'But not him?'

'No.' Nikkos made a face, as if this fact were a particularly bitter source of personal regret. 'Not him. Unfortunate to say, but if Athena *is* alive, then Makis Alexiadis is our closest remaining link to her. He may even have been in contact with her. We don't know. But we believe that whoever put that mark on the drowned child's heel was sending a signal to Makis as much as to us, or anybody else. A warning.'

'What sort of warning?' asked Ella. 'What does the mark mean? The "L"?'

'It was the sign Spyros Petridis used to signify his dominance over others. His power. Some believed that the "L" was for Lagonissi, Spyros's birthplace. Perhaps it was.'

'But?' Ella prompted. 'It sounds as if there's a "but".'

Nikkos looked uncomfortable. He should never have opened up this particular can of worms.

'But "L" wasn't the only ancient Greek letter used by the Petridises on their enemies or their subordinates during their heyday. From time to time there would be an alpha or an omega or a pi. We would find the signs on corpses, or sometimes even branded into living people who'd crossed them in some way. Restaurant owners, businesses who refused to pay them protection money. Even a famous Hollywood producer, a guy named Larry Gaster, reportedly had an "L" burned into his foot, as punishment for "flirting" with Athena. Before Spyros's marriage to Athena, the "L" was definitely his mark. So maybe it did mean Lagonissi back then. But in later years, that changed. If "L" was for Lagonissi, what was the significance of "O" and "A" and "P"?'

'Maybe they were places from Athena's past?' Ella suggested.

Nikkos shrugged. 'Maybe. We don't know. What we do know is that only Spyros or Athena ever used the letter brands, and Spyros is dead. We also know that Makis will have seen these photographs, of the boy on the beach. So the first phase of your mission will be to get close to him and gauge his reaction to those images. What has he said about them, and to whom? Was he surprised? Or did he know in advance they'd be published? Was he angry? Pleased?'

Ella nodded. 'OK. I can do that.'

Nikkos pressed a pudgy finger onto the newspaper clipping, obscuring Makis Alexiadis's handsome face. 'Do not attempt to confront him. Under any circumstances. Do not compromise your cover. Find out anything you can about the pictures and about Athena's connection to them, if there is one. Use your . . . you know, your brain thing . . . if you can.' He pointed vaguely to his skull, just in case Ella had misunderstood. 'Then return to Athens.'

'*Return* to Athens?' Ella raised an eyebrow. 'Doesn't Makis live here?'

'Not in August he doesn't,' Nikkos replied. 'Only fools and tourists stay in Athens in high summer. It's far too hot,' he explained, as if Ella hadn't noticed. 'Don't worry. He stays at his villa on Mykonos. It's very beautiful there and not so far. You will leave at the weekend.'

'The weekend? Why not tomorrow?' asked Ella.

Nikkos chuckled. 'You will understand when you read tonight's package. It will take a short time to put together your cover. Your new identity. And then, yes, you must practice a little bit. It is not so easy, my dear. Becoming somebody else overnight.'

*That's what I used to think*, thought Ella. *Before I met Gabriel.*

They agreed to leave the restaurant separately, with Nikkos going first to draw the car following him safely away from Ella.

'You're sure the police are still outside?' he asked, paying the bill and leaving a fat wodge of cash as a tip.

'Quite sure,' said Ella. 'I'll be fine. I'll stay here for twenty minutes and then go back and sleep. I'll look at whatever documents you send over in the morning, I'm too tired tonight.'

Kissing her on the cheek, Nikkos took his leave, being careful to give his disgruntled ex-lover's table a wide berth.

She was right about the cops. They followed him all the way home, but he made no attempt to shake them. After all, it was no secret where he lived, and he hadn't done anything illegal – yet.

Back in his modest Exarcheia apartment, Nikkos kicked off his shoes, poured himself a large ouzo and put a call in to the boss, as expected.

'How did it go? How was she?' Redmayne asked in his usual brusque, charmless manner.

'She was fine.' Nikkos rubbed his brow wearily. 'She understands the objective. She agreed to go to Mykonos.'

'She didn't question it?' Redmayne sounded surprised, but pleased.

'No,' said Nikkos. At that precise moment he couldn't bring himself to say 'sir'.

'Did she have any questions?'

'Not many,' Nikkos lied. 'She did ask about her parents, though. Whether I'd met them. What they were like.'

'You deflected her, I trust?' said Redmayne, a familiar note of threat returning to his voice.

'Of course I did. What else could I do?' retorted Nikkos, with more emotion than he'd intended, or than was probably wise. 'Tell her the truth about how we threw Rachel Praeger to the wolves? Just like we're doing now, to her daughter? I doubt Ella would have stayed to finish dinner if I'd said that.'

'No one "threw" anyone anywhere,' Mark Redmayne pronounced coldly. The edge to his voice was unmistakable now, sharp enough to cut through Nikkos's alcohol-fueled haze. 'Remember, I knew Rachel well. Very well.'

*Oh, I remember*, Nikkos thought bitterly.

'She was a committed agent who welcomed risk and fully understood what she was doing when she came to Greece,' Redmayne went on.

'Well her daughter isn't,' Nikkos replied stubbornly. 'Ella is young, she's naïve. I walked right into her hotel suite today. The door was unlocked and she was lying there asleep, out cold! Makis's men could have slit her throat in seconds.'

'Ella is a unique resource. She's a weapon, a powerful weapon, and the time to use her is now,' said Redmayne, as calmly collected as Nikkos was emotional. 'We're talking about *Athena Petridis* here. Are you forgetting who Athena is? What she does? She and her gang of monsters?'

'No,' Nikkos sank down wearily on his couch, rubbing his eyes. 'Of course not.'

'No, *sir*,' Redmayne shot back.

'No, sir,' Nikkos replied dutifully. 'I am not forgetting.'

'So don't you dare tell me it isn't *right* to use Ella, to use every resource we've got. If Athena is still alive, still out there, then it *is* right. It's essential.'

'Sir.'

'And if word ever reaches me that you've undermined this mission in any way – if you warn the girl, or give her information she doesn't need that might jeopardize our success – there will be grave consequences. Do you understand?'

'Yes, sir. I do.'

'No one agent is bigger than The Group. No life is worth more than the mission,' Redmayne barked. 'Rachel Praeger understood that better than anyone.'

*Yeah, and look what happened to her!* thought Nikkos. Aloud he confined himself to a respectful, 'Sir', and hung up.

On one level, the boss was right. Ella Praeger had literally been *created* to serve The Group. You could argue that all she was doing now was fulfilling her destiny. And it wasn't as if Ella herself was unwilling. Yet Nikkos still felt sick to his stomach. Because the fact remained that in a few days they would be sending an inexperienced child to Mykonos to spy on Big Mak Alexiadis. To 'get close' to a psychopath That was like throwing a kitten into a lion enclosure, and no amount of Redmayne's self-justifying spin could make it otherwise.

Nikkos tried to tell himself he was being too emotional. But he ended up needing a lot more to drink before he was able to fall asleep that night. And when he did, dreams of Rachel Praeger haunted him, her reproving face mingling with the sweet sound of her daughter's voice. Ella. So determined. So trusting:

'Am I like her?'

*God, you are like her!*

*So very, very like her.*

With all his heart, Nikkos wished it weren't so.

# CHAPTER THIRTEEN

Makis Alexiadis walked into Mythos, Mykonos's elite beach club, pausing for a moment as he weaved past the bar to enjoy the sensation of having all eyes swivel in his direction, the men's with envy and the women's with desire. It was a familiar sensation, yet he never grew tired of it. It felt good to be a king.

Heading to his usual spot, a velvet-lined, Moroccan-themed booth occupying the premier position in the restaurant's roped-off VIP section, just above the beach, he and his entourage settled in as the staff scurried around them, bringing silver trays of mojitos and caipirinhas, and peach bellinis for the girls. Makis had brought three with him tonight: Arabella, a willowy English It-girl and the daughter of a duke, added a touch of class to his harem. Lisette, the French movie star, brought the fame factor. And Miriam, the Persian princess, had the sort of curves that made other, lesser men crash their Bugattis into the sea. Mak had bedded all of them over the last few days, but none of them had truly inspired him sexually. Tatiana was a tough act to follow in that regard, although it was still a relief to be rid of her cloying, attention-seeking presence around the villa. Thankfully she would no longer be bothering him, or anyone with her whining demands. *What was it about genuinely stunning women that made them so deeply insecure?*

Makis didn't know, and tonight he didn't care. A free man again, he allowed his eyes to rove lustfully around the room, picking out the most beautiful specimens from a female clientele that could have been ripped straight from the pages of *Sports Illustrated*. Every now and then an ugly 'friend' or diamond-encrusted matriarch wedged their fat asses into one of the seats at the bar or usurped a spot on the dance floor. But these were rare blemishes on an otherwise perfect-skinned fruit. With its spectacular sunsets and thumping Arabic music, Mythos was the place to go for the hottest, youngest, most sought-after models on the island, the favored haunt of Mykonos's 'beautiful people'. Nammos and Cavo might be better known amongst the nouveau riche American crowd, but the Kardashians were welcome to that tacky scene. Mythos was where the real power players hung out on a summer night. Big Mak Alexiadis never went anywhere else.

Almost immediately, a girl sitting at the end of the bar caught his eye. In black cigarette pants and a man's smoking jacket, she already stood out from the rest of the barely dressed girls strutting their stuff, hoping to catch some billionaire's eye. Her tousled, pixie-cut hair was streaked with white-gold flashes, and she wore no jewelry, not even a watch. But it was her face that really held Mak's attention. He couldn't decide if it was beautiful or ugly. Neither word seemed to fit. *Compelling* was the only adjective that came to mind to describe the huge eyes set wide on either side of a not-quite-straight nose, the cheekbones so high you could have launched a missile from each one, and the small, rosebud lips tapering into an almost elfin chin.

Clearly he wasn't the only one who thought so. The girl was sipping a martini in between bites of her salmon nigiri, and making what looked to Mak like bored, polite conversation with the handsome man next to her, who seemed to be trying and failing to make an impression.

An imperious click of Mak's fingers brought Jamie French, Mythos's British manager, running to his side. Jamie was an encyclopedic fount of information about all his clients, and the go-to man for the latest island gossip.

'Who is that?' Mak asked, his eyes still glued to the girl.

'That's Persephone Hamlin. Heiress to an American real-estate fortune.'

'She's American?' Makis was surprised. She looked too chic to be a rich Yank tourist. 'And she's not at Nammos with her posse?'

Jamie chuckled. 'No. Persephone was raised in Los Angeles but her mother was Greek, hence the name.'

*And the class*, thought Makis.

'She was docked on a yacht a couple of days ago, but her friends sailed on to Santorini without her,' Jamie went on. 'I believe she's now slumming it in the presidential suite at The Grand.'

This was another surprise. The truly rich rarely stayed in hotels, at least not on Mykonos. It was strictly yachts or villas only.

'Is she staying there alone?' Mak asked.

'So I'm told.'

'Married?'

'Yeeees,' Jamie nodded, 'But not for long, I think. The husband has big addiction problems. Word is he fell off the wagon in St Tropez in July in spectacular style – binges, hookers, the lot. She came here to get away.'

Mak dismissed him, feeling emboldened. This was the sort of backstory he could work with.

He stood up and crossed the floor to where she was sitting.

'I'd like to introduce myself. Makis Alexiadis.' Stepping directly in front of the man she was talking to, he held out his hand. 'Persephone, isn't it?'

'That's right.' She shook his hand, but with more curiosity than enthusiasm. 'How do you know my name?'

'This is Mykonos.' He flashed her his most charming smile. 'If you're here for more than two days, everybody knows everything.'

'Erm, excuse me.' The man behind him tapped Mak on the shoulders. 'The lady and I were just in the middle of a conversation.'

Turning around, Mak looked at him with the cool, raw hatred of a killer.

'Do you know who I am?'

Belatedly, the man recognized him. A knot of fear slowly started to form in his stomach. He nodded.

'Good. Now go away.'

He was gone by the time Mak turned back around.

'Sorry about that,' he smiled at Persephone, settling himself onto the man's vacated bar stool. 'Where were we?'

'I don't think we were anywhere,' she replied, draining the rest of her cocktail and signaling to the sushi chef for the check.

'You're not leaving?'

'I *am* leaving,' she corrected him. 'That was very rude, what you just did.'

'Nonsense!' said Mak, placing a hand on her arm. 'It was chivalrous.'

Removing his hand, she gave him a withering look. 'Chivalrous?'

'Absolutely. He was boring you. I could see it from across the room. I just rode to your rescue.'

190

She ran a hand through her boyish hair (the sort of cut Makis usually detested) and fixed him with a look that could only possibly be interpreted as expressing profound dislike.

'Well thank you, Mr Alexiadis. But I'm not the sort of girl who needs to be rescued. I suggest you go and terrorize the companions of one of your other . . . friends.' She glanced in the direction of Makis's booth, where Arabella, Miriam and Lisette were all looking daggers in her direction. 'I'm sure they would all appreciate your chivalry.'

'Let me buy you a drink, at least,' said Mak, who was enjoying the thrill of the chase. It was a long time, a very long time, since a woman had shown no interest in him. 'I'm sorry if we got off on the wrong foot.'

Signing her check, she stood up and looked at him, that same appraising, curious expression in her eye.

'This being Mykonos, you must already know I'm married.'

'I might have heard something,' he confessed, not taking his eyes off hers. They were even bigger close up and the same green as vermouth. All of a sudden his desire to sleep with this woman, but more than that, to conquer her, to make her want *him*, felt almost overpowering. 'Do you never cheat on your husband, Persephone?' he asked, his voice hoarse with lust.

'Sometimes,' she answered nonchalantly, not a hint of desire in her own voice. 'But only when I feel a strong attraction. I'm afraid that's not the case with you. Goodbye.'

The entire club watched, astonished, as this strangely dressed American girl crossed the dance floor and walked out, leaving Makis Alexiadis sitting there like a jilted schoolboy. You could have cut the tension in the air with a knife. Big Mak was not a man you would choose to humiliate, or offend in any way. Not if you valued your life.

But when Mak walked back over to his group, he was

191

grinning from ear to ear. Ordering another drink, he pulled an ecstatic Miriam onto his lap and distracted himself with her ample bosom.

'*Goodbye!*' She hadn't even said 'goodnight'. It was 'goodbye' – so cutting, so deliberately final, as in 'goodbye for ever.' 'Get lost.'

The hardness he felt between his legs owed more to Persephone Hamlin's curt dismissal of him than it did to Miriam's spectacular breasts.

What a triumph it would be to hear that feisty little bitch moaning out his name in pleasure, begging him to take her, again and again and again. With all the recent stress over the lost shipments and the millions of dollars sunk in the Aegean, he could use a distraction.

Tomorrow he would find out all there was to know about Miss Persephone Hamlin.

Back in her suite at the Grand Hotel, Persephone slipped off her clothes and walked naked into the bathroom, observing herself in the gold rococo mirror.

It felt good to be Ella Praeger again, despite the lingering sexual frustration clinging to her body after her first encounter with Makis Alexiadis. Dear God, the way he'd looked at her! Like a hungry lion locking eyes with a gazelle. It was all Ella could do not to rip off her clothes on the spot and wrap herself around him, so overwhelmingly sexual and masculine was his aura. She could feel her groin throbbing and her throat was dry just thinking about it, and about all the things the animal in her would like the animal in Makis to do to her. Persephone Hamlin might be a model of decorum and restraint, but Ella Praeger wasn't at all used to having to rein in her sexuality. Between resisting Makis *and* Gabriel, this had the potential to be a grueling and frustrating mission.

Observing her naked reflection appreciatively, Ella ran a hand through the short, boyish hair that she still couldn't get used to. Back in Athens, after receiving a ten-page 'background document' on the mythical Ms Hamlin (Gabriel had concocted an impressively detailed persona, complete with schooling, siblings, complex parental relationships and a skiing accident when she was nine years old that accounted for the kink in her nose), Nikkos had dispatched her to the hairdresser's for a complete new look.

'Any color is fine,' Ella told the stylist in increasingly fluent Greek. 'And any style, within reason. Just please, don't go super-short.'

With the very first cut, a foot of her precious blonde hair hit the salon floor.

'What are you *doing?*' Ella screeched. But the man just shrugged.

'Mr Nikkos already gave me directions. He paid me, very good money,' he added, rubbing his fingers together with satisfaction.

*It's not enough that the men here choose what women eat?* Ella thought furiously. *They get to pick their hairstyles too?*

'Why that nasty face?' Nikkos asked when he came to pick her up. 'You look very beautiful. Very sexy.'

'I hate it,' Ella growled. 'I look like a boy.'

'It's not for you. It's for Makis. He will like it,' Nikkos insisted. 'It's . . .' he searched for the right word. 'Striking.'

'Strikingly gross,' Ella mumbled, like a sullen teenager, although secretly she had to admit that the bright blonde pixie suited her more than she'd thought it would. Afterwards the hairdresser, a woman named Grace, took Ella to some sort of spa where her eyebrows were shaped, her lashes tinted, and hair was removed from every conceivable part of her body. It was agony.

'I feel like a plucked chicken!' she berated Nikkos over the phone. 'And just so you know, I won't be having inter . . . I won't be sleeping with this guy, so what the hell was the point? He's never going to know what I've got going on down there.'

'It's Mykonos,' Nikkos said, grateful Ella wasn't there to see his blushes. 'You will be wearing a bikini sometimes. In Greece, men don't like—'

'Screw Greece!' Ella cut him off waspishly. 'I'm Persephone Hamlin and I didn't come here to find a Greek boyfriend. I came here to get over my asshole, coke-head husband and his latest prostitute girlfriend.'

'Called?' Nikkos quizzed her.

'Katya,' Ella answered, not missing a beat. 'They met at Les Caves nightclub in St Tropez, the day after Nick celebrated six months sober and I kicked him off the yacht the next morning. I've got this Nikkos. I'm ready.'

In reality, Ella was by no means sure she was ready. It was true that, ever since Camp Hope and starting her brain training, she was growing in confidence. With the white noise in her head under her own control for the first time in her life, she was starting to feel different. It was as if a thick layer of cloud had cleared, and she was seeing the world as it really was – the way everyone else saw it. Socially she felt less awkward. And in a strange way, taking on a cover story, an alter ego, made it even easier to practice her newfound skills. Even so, she knew she had a history of saying the wrong thing. If she made a misstep as Persephone Hamlin, the consequences could be grave. It wasn't just her own life she'd be risking.

On the other hand, if she didn't project confidence to Nikkos now, she might never get another chance to avenge her parents. Destiny was calling, and ready or not, Ella wasn't about to miss her shot.

In the distance, the church bells tolled once for one a.m. Tonight had gone well, better than she'd expected. Makis Alexiadis wanted her. She'd sensed it in the club, and confirmed it waiting for her cab outside, when to her delight she'd managed to tune successfully into his cell-phone communications. Since leaving Camp Hope, Ella's attempts to use her powers on her own had proved worryingly hit and miss, despite her daily mindfulness practice, as prescribed by Professor Dix. But on this occasion, Makis's calls came through loud and clear.

'He requested two different escorts, both to have short blonde hair, within ten minutes of me leaving,' Ella told Gabriel after her shower, in what would be the first of their regular nightly debrief calls. 'That means he is very interested.' She wisely chose not to add the part about her own, powerful attraction to Makis, the ruthless killer with the raw sexual magnetism of a young Marlon Brando on steroids.

'Good,' said Gabriel, although nothing in his tone suggested that he thought Makis's intentions towards Ella were 'good' at all. 'Stay close and let me know of your next contact. And be careful, Ella.'

'It's Persephone now,' she corrected him, teasingly. 'And don't worry. I will.'

She found it hard to sleep that night. Not because of the white noise traffic from her fellow hotel guests – she was now mostly able to lower that fairly easily to an almost comforting hum – but because of the adrenaline coursing through her veins, mingled with a raging river of untamed and unquenchable lust. It seemed impossible to think that only six weeks ago she'd been Ella Praeger, lonely data analyst at Biogen Medical, working for the loathsome Gary. And now here she was, an international spy, on a mission to seduce a crime boss and help bring down his evil, global network. And hopefully, in the process, exact vengeance on the woman who'd stood by and watched her mother drown.

Thinking about her mother's death brought Ella back down to earth. Would vengeance bring closure? Ella didn't know. But for the first time in her life she felt she had a purpose; that her actions and decisions mattered. Being Persephone Hamlin was going to be an adventure, but an adventure that meant something.

It felt good.

Ella was still finishing breakfast, a delicious buffet of creamy Greek yogurt, honey, fresh fruit and various different breads and cheeses, when she got the first call.

'Good morning, Miss Hamlin. This is Makis Alexiadis. We met last night.'

His voice sent shivers down her spine, and then directly between her legs, but Ella quickly pushed them aside and jumped into character. *You can do this.*

'It's *Mrs* Hamlin,' she said primly. 'And how did you get my number?'

'I'm a resourceful man,' Mak replied smoothly. 'I wanted to apologize.'

'I see,' said Ella. Her tone wasn't rude, but neither was it exactly inviting. 'For what, exactly?'

'You found me to be impolite last night. I would hate to leave you with that impression.'

'Thank you. I accept your apology,' Ella said regally, and hung up.

Sprawled out in his four-poster bed in Villa Mirage's sumptuous master suite, Makis laughed out loud.

*Bitch!*

Who the hell did Persephone Hamlin think she was?

*

The next call came that afternoon. Ella was reading by the pool, a new biography of Lincoln. (For reasons best known to himself, Gabriel had declared Persephone Hamlin to be a history buff.)

'Persephone. May I call you Persephone?'

'Mr Alexiadis.' Ella sighed. 'Is there something else I can help you with?'

'As a matter of fact, there is. I'd like you to have dinner with me tonight. And I insist that you call me Mak.'

'Mak.' She softened just fractionally. 'Look, I do appreciate the invitation. Truly. And I admire your persistence. But as I told you last night, I'm married.'

'To a man who isn't worthy of you,' Mak shot back.

'Oh, and you are, I suppose?' she retorted archly.

Sitting at the desk in his glass-walled study, Mak felt a surge of triumph. The cold Lady Persephone was beginning to defrost. Only slightly. But there was definitely a playfulness in that last response that hadn't been there before.

'Have dinner with me and find out,' he purred.

She hesitated, just long enough to give him hope.

'I can't tonight, I'm afraid. But thank you again.'

For the second time in a day, she put the phone down on him.

*It's a gauntlet*, thought Mak, feeling happier than he had in years. *She wants me to chase her.*

*Be careful what you wish for, Mrs Hamlin.*

It was almost two weeks before 'Persephone' finally relented and agreed to a 'date' of sorts. Two weeks that were every bit as hard on Ella as they were on Makis.

'You did *what*?' Gabriel erupted when he heard the news. 'Are you out of your mind? No. Cancel.'

Ella was perplexed. 'Why should I cancel? You were the

one telling me I was in danger of stringing this out too long. You literally instructed me to accept him.'

'Yes, for *dinner*.' His voice quivered with frustration and anxiety. 'Surrounded by other people, and where you stand a chance of intercepting any email or cell-phone communications he might receive. Not on a *boat!* Alone! With no cell reception, no means of rescue. He's a killer, Ella. You seem to have forgotten that fact.'

'Of course I haven't,' said Ella, slightly sheepishly because the truth was she often *did* forget it, especially when Mak gave Persephone his hungry lion look. 'But a boat is more intimate than dinner,' she countered. 'Just the two of us, on the open waves.'

'That's exactly what I'm afraid of.'

'But I'm here to get close to him. To invite confidences. Isn't that the whole point?'

'No!' Gabriel said angrily. 'The whole point was for you to use your special abilities to gather intelligence about Athena. Which you can't do, alone on a boat or some godforsaken private beach with a psychopath.'

'Mak wants to seduce Persephone, not kill her,' said Ella stubbornly. 'I'll be fine.'

*You hope*, thought Gabriel despairingly. He hated these calls with Ella, hated not being close enough to help her if she needed it. Nikkos Anastas was the 'man on the ground' for this mission, but Nikkos was so fat and slow these days he could barely break into a jog without risking a heart attack, never mind execute a daring, last-minute rescue mission, should Ella need one. They had to provide Ella with some sort of backup.

'I'm surprised Big Mak suggested a fishing boat, and not a superyacht,' he said, trying to drag the conversation back into calmer, more civil waters. 'That's hardly his usual style. He's normally so flashy he makes Kanye look low key.'

'True, but Persephone isn't, remember?' said Ella. 'She's the opposite. And flashiness was one of the things she came to hate about her husband. The fishing trip was her suggestion.'

Gabriel groaned. He wasn't going to win this one, but he didn't like it.

He didn't like it at all.


Miriam Dabiri didn't like it either.

Watching through the blacked-out windows of her town car as Makis Alexiadis helped the odd-looking Hamlin woman down from the jetty into a simple, rustic wooden fishing boat, she felt a lump of bile lodge painfully in her chest. Mak looked as dashing as ever in a sea-green polo shirt and Ralph Lauren shorts, his dark hair slicked back and his eyes hidden behind tortoiseshell Prada shades. The girl, Persephone, by contrast, appeared to have made no effort at all, and in fact looked more like a boy than ever in loose-fitting harem pants and a black tank top, teamed with a simple headscarf and flip flops.

*Who are you?* Miriam thought bitterly as she watched the two of them push laughingly off into open water. *Where the hell did you come from?*

Two weeks ago she, Miriam, had had the great Makis Alexiadis eating out of her hand, begging for her attention. True, there had been other girls around. But no one Miriam was confident she couldn't outclass, in bed and out of it.

'You have a body built for sex,' Makis had told her, the first night they made love. 'You're incredible.'

It was true. She did. And she was. Until all of a sudden this androgynous, small-breasted, American Uma-Thurman-lookalike appeared out of nowhere and somehow managed to blow Miriam out of the water. She wasn't even pretty, for God's sake! Not to mention her rude, sullen manner. It was beyond Miriam what it was about Persephone Hamlin that had her almost-beau so utterly obsessed.

*I'm watching you, bitch.*

Miriam Dabiri might look like a sex-doll, but she was far from stupid. Nor was she about to let a hot ticket like Big Mak Alexiadis slip through her fingers without a fight.

There was more to Mrs Persephone Hamlin than met the eye.

Miriam intended to find out what it was.

Mak watched as Persephone sat perched on a cushion at the bow of the boat, trailing her delicate fingers in the water while he rowed. How he wished those fingers were caressing his naked body instead, clawing at him, begging him to make love to her harder, faster, deeper . . .

The fantasy faded away as the physical demands of fighting against the waves asserted themselves, making his arms burn and his chest heave. He tried to remember the last time he had been in a rowboat, never mind actually sat at the oars. Long enough ago that he'd forgotten how good it felt to have the wind on his face and the salt spray on his arms; infinitely nicer than working out on his state-of-the-art ergo machine back at the villa.

*I must do this more often*, he thought, then laughed at himself for the ridiculousness of that idea, and for how much he'd already let this bolshie young woman affect him.

'How much further to the beach?' she asked, her voice half lost on the wind as she turned to face him.

'Not too far,' he panted. 'Around the next headland.'

'The beach' turned out to be a private cove on one of a string of tiny islands that Makis had bought up over the years, bribing his way around the notoriously complex Greek property laws. As they approached the thin strip of white sand, it was hard to imagine a more peaceful, idyllic spot. Or a more romantic one. The ruins of Delos were just visible on the horizon, but apart from those and a single, shabby fishing trawler in the distance, there was nothing to see but sea and sky. The island itself was utterly deserted, with only the occasional hardy olive tree, rooted stubbornly on the shoreline, braving the warm but relentless wind. For the first time Ella felt a pang of nervousness, remembering Gabriel's warnings. '*You're alone with no cell reception, no means of rescue. He's a killer.*'

'What would you like to do first, my lady? Fish, eat or swim?' Mak asked, looking absolutely nothing like a killer as he spread their picnic blanket on the ground, securing it with rocks he found scattered beneath the trees. In fact, he was so handsome and charming, so flatteringly solicitous of her happiness, that Ella had to consciously remind herself that: a) it wasn't her he was interested in but Persephone Hamlin, a figment of Gabriel's imagination; and b) he *was* in fact, as Gabriel never failed to remind her, a psychopath. More than that, he was a man who sold children to predators, who traded in human life as if people were mere goods to be profited from, and who might be the key to finding the woman who murdered Ella's parents. She was ashamed of her powerful sexual attraction to him, and worried that the shame didn't seem to make it go away.

As if on cue, Gabriel's voice suddenly rang out in Ella's head like a bell in an empty church. '*BE CAREFUL.*'

*Are you kidding me?* thought Ella. Somehow the bloody man was managing to transmit to her, even here. Worse, she seemed unable to tune him out. *Where is he? And how is he blocking out all my frequencies?* The last thing she needed right now was a back-seat driver.

Looking around, her eyes were drawn to the fishing trawler out towards Delos. *Could it be?* She tried to remember what Professor Dix had said about hacking into

201

local transmitters remotely. Could Gabriel or Nikkos have used the boat as a sort of mobile radio station?

'I *am* being careful!' she replied, waspishly – and foolishly, as she knew Gabriel couldn't hear her.

'What?' Makis looked at her, his dark eyes narrowing.

*Shit*. Ella's heart plunged into her stomach as she realized to her horror that she'd spoken out loud.

'I'm being careful . . . with what I eat.' Persephone scrambled, smiling reassuringly at her date. 'I saw all the baklava you packed for us. Let's swim first. Make sure we've earned it.'

'Sure.' Mak brightened, thrilled by the prospect of seeing more of Mrs Hamlin's body at last. He passed her the simple cotton bag she'd brought with her on the boat, assuming it contained a bikini. Hopefully a skimpy one. 'After you.'

'*NO!*' thundered Gabriel. '*Tell him no. Keep your clothes on!*'

Ella rubbed her temples, trying desperately to turn Gabriel off. Didn't he know he was distracting her? She desperately tried to recall some of the other tricks that Dix had taught her. Why was nothing working?

'*Tell him you forgot your swimsuit.*'

'I can't!'

'Can't what?' Makis asked. 'Is something the matter, Persephone?'

*Jesus. I did it again.*

'No, no. Everything's fine. I was just thinking that I can't decide between swimming and fishing. I mean, I haven't fished in years, but there's something rather romantic about catching one's own food, don't you think?'

She touched Mak's arm lightly with her hand and turned her head to one side coquettishly, successfully diffusing his irritation. *Thank God.*

'I suppose there is,' he answered gruffly, laying his own, warm hand over hers. A jolt of desire surged through her, so violently that she worried whether Gabriel might pick up on it.

'You know . . . you remind me of someone,' said Mak, his expression subtly changing.

'*Very careful!*' boomed Gabriel. '*He's trying to . . .*'

'Do I?' Ella smiled at Mak, trying simultaneously to interrupt Gabriel's signal with one of Dix's mind-control techniques. If he didn't stop distracting her, she was going to make another mistake, and one more might prove fatal. But to her immense relief, this time she succeeded in blocking him out. Gabriel's voice was gone.

'Mmmm,' said Makis. 'You do. And the strangest thing about it is that I can't think who. But when you smiled just then, I saw it.'

'What did you see?' She moved closer to him. Dangerously close.

'Something I recognized.' Reaching out, he ran a slow, languid finger down Ella's face and along her jaw, stopping just before he reached her lips. For a moment she thought she might be about to spontaneously combust with arousal. It took every ounce of her self-control not to show it.

'I don't know.' Smiling, Mak withdrew his hand. 'Maybe we met in a past life. Isn't that the sort of thing you Californians believe in?'

'Not all of us,' said Ella, clearing her throat, and deciding that Persephone Hamlin would be much too down to earth and practical for any of that 'past lives' nonsense.

She walked over to the two fly rods that Makis had propped against a sandbank a few yards from the water's edge. Makis followed. Handing her the smaller rod, he stood behind her, his strong, hard body pressed against hers as he instructed her on the correct grip.

'Casting a fly is an art form.' His breath felt warm in Ella's ear and she could smell his cologne, some heady mixture of patchouli and pine. She could have wept with longing. 'But it's also a knack, like juggling or riding a bicycle. Once you know how you'll never forget.'

His warm, smooth palm closed over her hand as he guided her rod up and backwards, before jolting it to a stop with a little flick. *He's evil. He's a psychopath.* Ella's brain kept re-sending the message, but her body kept returning it to sender. Another shiver of desire shot through her as a second twitch of the wrist sent her line flying forwards and her fly landing on the water, with a rather inelegant splash. She tried not to think about the frantic warning messages Gabriel was no doubt trying to send her right now.

'You see, Persephone?' Makis whispered.

'I think so,' Ella rasped, forcing herself to step forward so that their bodies were no longer touching. 'Let me try.'

'It's not easy at first, so don't get frustrated,' he told her, moving a few yards along the shore with his own rod.

*If only he knew how frustrated I am!* thought Ella. Out loud, she said, 'I won't,' nodding brusquely and flipping up her rod, performing a cast so exquisitely graceful and perfect it was like watching ballet. Mak watched in awe as her line sailed through the air, twice as far as it had when he'd helped her, and her fly descended onto the water as softly as a piece of thistledown.

'You've done this before,' he said admiringly.

'Once or twice,' Ella grinned. 'Up at the ranch where I grew up, I used to go fishing all the time.'

He frowned. 'The ranch?'

Ella's stomach lurched as, too late, she realized her mistake – and this time it was unforced. Persephone Hamlin grew up in the city. They'd made small talk about their differing childhoods only a few hours ago at the jetty. Mak had told her about the poverty he knew in his Athens tenement block, and 'Persephone' had described her family home in Los Angeles's luxurious Brentwood Park neighborhood.

*Oh God, how could I have been so stupid?*

'Well, I mean, didn't literally "grow up" there,' Ella scrambled, hoping her face was not as red and her heartbeat not as loud as she feared they were. 'I grew up in LA. The ranch was more of a vacation place. My grandmother lived there.'

'Really?' said Mak, his gaze shifting out to the water as he cast his own line. Or was he looking further out? Towards the trawler? Surely he couldn't suspect . . .

'That sounds nice. What was her name?'

Ella panicked. *Shit, shit shit.*

'My grandmother?'

'Mmm hm.' He watched intently as his fly began to move.

'Lucy,' said Ella, the name popping into her brain out of nowhere. 'Hey, I think you've got something!'

Mercifully, the fish on the end of his line enabled her to change the subject. And Mak seemed happy enough to drop it as he struggled to land a decent-sized sea bream, eager to impress Persephone once again. Ella hoped she'd got away with it this time, but it was a stupid, stupid mistake.

With a sinking heart, she realized she would have to tell Gabriel about it tonight.

'What were you *thinking*?'

The anger in his voice seemed to crackle like a hot, white flame.

'I'm sorry. It just slipped out,' said Ella.

'You even gave her a *name*?'

'He asked!' Ella protested. She was lying on the bed in her hotel room in a pair of striped silk pajamas, holding the phone away from her ear to shield herself from Gabriel's yells. 'What was I supposed to do?'

'Stick to the story! You were supposed to stick to the story. That's what "undercover" means.'

'Oh really? Well what about you, deciding to tag along for the ride without warning me? Using that damn boat as a transmitter? Monopolizing all my frequencies? Putting me off my stride with all your "*do this, do that . . . Be careful.*" As if I hadn't thought of that!'

'If today was you being careful, I dread to think what a reckless mission might look like,' Gabriel answered waspishly. He wasn't about to admit that she had a point about him ambushing her. And he definitely wasn't about to admit that he couldn't resist interrupting Makis's dangerous attempts at seducing her.

'You didn't trust me to handle Makis on my own.'

'And now you know why!'

Ella sighed. 'I came up with the most generic name I could, OK?' she said defensively. 'I mean, I know it was a mistake, but is it really such a big deal? Couldn't Persephone have had a grandma named Lucy?'

'Of course she *could*,' Gabriel explained, lowering his voice and drawing on reserves of patience he never knew he had. 'But that's not how these things work, Ella. Grandma Lucy wasn't in the story, and now she'll have to be. That means I need to create another, entire online presence to validate this new person's existence. And that's complicated. There needs to be a ranch, with deeds in her name, and a sales history. She needs a birth certificate and a death certificate and a reference in the electoral roll, so she seems real if anybody goes looking for her. Because if Makis Alexiadis suspects anything – *anything* – believe me, he will go looking. He's already run searches for Persephone Hamlin and Nick Hamlin, but we covered all that before we sent you in. Mocked up wedding shots, mentions in the society pages, all of that. That's your armor, Ella, do you understand? And today you just . . . took it off.'

'How do you know he's run searches?' Ella asked.

'Because we can track any hits to the links we planted online, and we've had some. Who else would be researching a woman who doesn't exist?'

'I'm sorry,' Ella said again, feeling foolish. All the adrenaline and bravado of earlier had left her now. She wasn't an invincible spy after all, it turned out, but an amateur, making rookie mistakes. It had taken her almost five full minutes to get around Gabriel's blocking techniques and shut off his distracting voice. Back at Camp Hope she'd had that down to seconds, but in the pressure of the moment, things were very different. Worse, deep down she knew that part of the reason she'd been resenting his intrusion was that she'd been trying to impress Mak at the time. She wanted to deny it, but the uncomfortable truth was she was attracted to Makis Alexiadis.

'It's OK,' Gabriel reassured her. 'I'll work through the night tonight and make sure we get this covered. But you must be more careful in future.'

'I will be. As long as *you* back off and let me do my job. Anyway, I do have some good news,' said Ella, eager to please him and earn her place back in his good books.

'Oh yeah, what's that?'

'Mak asked me to move into his villa. I'm checking out of here in the morning.'

The pause on the other end of the line was so long that at first Ella thought Gabriel had hung up. When at last he spoke, his voice sounded different, high pitched and strangled.

'So you, er . . . you hooked up today then, did you? After we lost contact.'

'Hooked up? No.' Ella sounded surprised. 'Was I supposed to?'

'No! No, no no. Absolutely not! No one expects you to make that sort of sacrifice,' said Gabriel, audibly relieved.

*It wouldn't be* that *much of a sacrifice*, Ella thought, but she wisely kept that to herself.

'I just assumed, when you said he'd asked you to move in to Mirage.'

'No. He was quite the gentleman about it,' said Ella. 'I'll be staying there as his guest. I'll have my own suite, my own living room and bathroom and all that.'

'That's great,' said Gabriel, genuinely pleased. 'Great that you'll be inside the villa. You need to get as much information out of there as you can.'

*You think?* thought Ella, but again she held her tongue.

'Try to get us something concrete on Athena,' Gabriel went on. 'And then get out, as soon as you can. But for God's sake, Ella, you really must be careful this time. You're in the lion's den now.'

'Understood,' said Ella, adding wistfully, 'I mean, obviously he *wants* to sleep with me. But I'm holding him off.'

'You see that's what I mean. You *must* stay in character. No more slips. He doesn't want to sleep with *you*, he wants to sleep with Persephone Hamlin,' Gabriel reminded her stiffly. 'Persephone's holding him off.'

'Right,' said Ella. 'For now.'

Gabriel hung up.

He did not feel comforted.

He did not feel comforted at all.

208

# CHAPTER FOURTEEN

Makis Alexiadis felt the burning sensation in his shoulders intensify as he plowed his way through the water, his strong arms propelling him forwards on the last of his one hundred lengths. He'd always found swimming a great stress reliever, ever since his early days working for Spyros Petridis, when he'd had to learn to execute innocent people for his master and then go to sleep at night with the sounds of their screams and pleading playing on an endless loop in his head.

Of course, 'innocent' was a subjective term. Usually the marked men were bad debtors, businessmen who'd taken loans from Spyros and then failed to make their interest payments.

'That's theft,' Spyros would instruct the teenage Makis. 'They are thieves and liars. And it's not as if they haven't had warnings.'

That part at least was true. Torched homes, kidnapped loved-ones, even severed fingers were all a part of Spyros's repertoire of 'warnings' back in those days. As he got older, Makis was expected to participate in all of them. The stress was appalling, but swimming saved the young boy's sanity.

There was a community pool in Athens he used to go, to swim and swim and swim until his skinny arms could no longer move, and his lungs were screaming for air. And when he emerged from that water, he told himself his guilt was washed away, and he taught himself to believe it.

*I'm a survivor. My only duty is to survive.*

These days his stresses were different. Persephone, damn her to heaven, still refused to sleep with him, and was even talking about returning to America to 'have things out' with her husband, whatever that meant. If she were less well connected, and less rich, he would have forced himself on her by now, and/or had the useless coke-head husband conveniently disposed of. But wealthy American heiresses tended to have people looking out for them, not least an army of lawyers, and Makis couldn't afford that sort of mess, not with everything else going on right now. More disturbingly, however, he had a sneaking suspicion that he might actually be developing feelings for this woman. Real, deep, affectionate feelings, of the kind he hadn't had since . . . well, not for a long time. There was just something about her, some magical quality, not unlike the one that the world had associated with Athena Petridis, back in the day.

*Athena.* Even the word filled his chest with tension and rage. She, of course, was the other source of his stress, rising like a kraken from the depths after all this time to try to take back her empire, to curtail his hard-won power. Oh, she was all reassurances, of course, whenever they corresponded. Makis had done a wonderful job. She was too old and too tired and physically depleted to try to take back the reins full time. He, Makis, would remain in charge day to day and she would merely offer strategic advice. 'Like a chairman to her CEO', as Athena put it. (Not an analogy Mak favored. CEOs reported to their chairmen.) But her analogies didn't matter because Makis didn't believe a word of it. Actions spoke louder than words, after all, and what was the brand on the migrant boy's heel if not a surefire sign that Athena's years as a silent partner were over?

'L' didn't stand for Lagonissi, as some fools had been suggesting. Not any more. That had been Spyros's sign, before he ever met Athena. The simple mark of a peasant risen to power. But Spyros was long gone, and Athena was no peasant. *Her* 'L' represented something very different, and Mak knew it. It was one piece of a much larger puzzle, a far more complex mosaic. Just weeks ago, not one but *both* the Kouvlaki brothers, Perry and Andreas, two of Makis's most trusted subordinates, had been brutally murdered and had their corpses branded with different letters – 'A' and 'P'. Athena herself may not have been behind the killings. But whoever ordered the Kouvlakis' murders knew her intimately and understood her secret code and what it meant. How it spoke of her past loss and present rage. Of her need to reclaim control, no matter what the cost. Her need to dominate. To win.

These signs were not to be taken lightly.

Heaving himself up out of Villa Mirage's indoor, Olympic-sized lap-pool, he rubbed himself dry and walked over to the poolside table where Cameron McKinley was waiting for him. The Scottish lawyer-cum-fixer had risen to become a central player in Big Mak's inner circle over the last few years, advising him on almost every aspect of his business empire. Tall and thin, almost to the point of emaciation, Cameron was albino pale, with translucent skin and pale, wispy, reddish-blond hair and ice-blue eyes, the physical opposite of his employer. Frankly, he'd always given Mak the creeps with his long, bony fingers and his mealy-mouthed way of talking, so softly spoken that he seemed to be almost whispering. Thankfully it was rare that they had to meet in person. Cameron was based in London, and the two men typically communicated only by phone. (Mak had trust issues when it came to lawyers and emails.) But on this occasion the matter in hand was so sensitive that only a face-to-face meeting would do.

'What do you have for me?' Mak demanded, taking a seat opposite the suited Scotsman in his damp Vilebrequin swim trunks.

'Sister Elena's still at the convent,' Cameron whispered. 'But my guess is she'll make a move soon.'

'Based on . . .?'

'Her daily routine's been changing. Subtly, but it has. She's spending more time outside the walled cloister, more time by herself. And some of Athena's old allies have been making moves too.'

'Who?'

'Konstantinos Papadakis, for one. He just turfed his long-standing tenants out of his fortified guesthouse on Corsica. He also brought his plane to Athens last week with a full-time pilot on standby.'

Konsta Papadakis was an old friend of Spyros Petridis's and had been best man at his wedding to Athena.

'You think he may be trying to move her?' Mak asked.

Cameron nodded. 'I do. And he's not the only one gearing up.' Cameron went on to list a string of Athena's past admirers and wealthy Petridis loyalists who'd transferred funds to the same anonymous Cayman Islands bank account in the last month. 'She's been reaching out to old friends for sure.'

The tightening sensation in Mak's chest intensified. He ran a hand through his wet hair.

'I must be seen to support her.'

'Indeed,' said Cameron.

'People need to know I welcome her return. That I've

only ever seen myself as a caretaker. In accordance with Spyros's wishes.'

'Quite.'

Makis leaned back in his chair. 'If anything were to happen to her it must appear to be an accident. Or some sort of natural event. Like a heart attack.'

Cameron's watery blue eyes didn't blink. 'Not impossible. She's in late middle age now, and her body's been through considerable trauma.'

'Or a fall?' Mak was thinking out loud.

'That happens.'

'Into water, perhaps?'

Cameron nodded. 'There are some dangerous currents throughout the islands.'

Mak bit his lip and relapsed into thoughtful silence. If Cameron was right, and Athena was already lining up supporters and an escape plan from her present hideout, then the time to act was now. Fortune favored the bold and, although Mak wasn't bold enough to take Athena on directly (he knew enough of his former master's wife to be deeply afraid of her and her capacity for vengeance), he also wasn't about to roll over like a puppy while she waltzed in and took what was his. What he'd *earned*.

'How about this?'

Leaning forward, Mak outlined a plan while his fixer listened intently. It was risky, certainly. But it wasn't impossible. Saying it out loud lifted his spirits. For the first time in days, Makis Alexiadis began to wonder if there might just be a chink of light at the end of the tunnel.

While Makis and Cameron plotted strategy, at the foot of the cliffs a man stood still as a statue watching every movement up at Villa Mirage, just as he had for the last two days. He knew every delivery truck that went in or out, and the times of every household servant's arrival in the morning and departure at night. He knew the timers on the pool lights and the morning and evening routine of the master of the house. When he took his shower; had his morning coffee; exercised; ate dinner; made love; slept. He learned the rhythms of the house like a loyal dog, memorizing the movements of its master, anticipating his every need.

And he waited.

Mark Redmayne smiled magnanimously as Gabriel approached his breakfast table.

'Please. Sit.'

The two men had never warmed to one another. Redmayne found The Group's star agent rude and challenging to the point of insubordination, while Gabriel considered his boss to be an arrogant, card-carrying narcissist, and about as trustworthy as a snake-oil salesman at a con artist's convention. This morning, however, Redmayne at least was in a forgiving mood.

For one thing he was in Paris, and staying at his favorite hotel in the world, the Georges V. A serendipitous business conference had offered him a cast-iron excuse to come to Europe and check up on The Group's various ongoing missions there. For another thing, his wife, Veronica, had decided to stay in the Hamptons this time around, leaving Mark free to enjoy all that Paris, and specifically the girls at the Crazy Horse, had to offer. But best of all, after a shaky start, Ella Praeger had finally broken her duck last night and intercepted some priceless information. If the stars were aligned, the girl might lead them directly to Athena Petridis.

Taking the seat opposite his boss, Gabriel was immediately provided with a fresh cup of the finest Peruvian coffee.

'Are you hungry?' Redmayne asked. 'The avocado toast is incredible.'

'No,' Gabriel replied, employing all of his customary charm and tact.

Redmayne stiffened. 'Suit yourself. To business, then?'

'I assume you've seen the intel?'

'I have.' Redmayne smiled broadly. 'I knew we were right to send her in there. The stuff she's been intercepting from inside that villa? Gold dust.' He took another satisfying bite of his own breakfast. 'Could this "Elena" be her? Could she be Athena?'

'It's not impossible,' admitted Gabriel.

Redmayne frowned. 'Well what are the alternatives? In your view,' he added pointedly.

'She could be a close associate. A go-between,' said Gabriel, not entirely convincingly.

'I don't think so,' said Redmayne. 'The location would have been perfect for Athena all these years: remote and secure. Plus Ella's been intercepting communications between Alexiadis and multiple close associates that suggest "Elena" is much more than just a "go-between." She's clearly a vitally important figure within the Petridis organization. Ella's intercepts also suggest a borderline obsessional interest in this "Elena" on Makis's part. All of that points to Athena herself.'

'Like I said, it's possible,' Gabriel admitted grudgingly. 'Ella's also picked up web activity indicating that Mak's been researching various access routes to the convent on Sikinos, including tidal patterns.'

'A surprising level of effort and direct involvement for a man of his importance if it *isn't* Athena,' Redmayne pointed out.

'True,' Gabriel nodded. 'But, we won't know until we know.'

'Exactly,' said Redmayne. 'Which is why we need an agent in that convent. How soon can Ella be extricated from Mykonos?'

'Ella?' Gabriel scowled into his coffee. 'Ella's not the best operative for the job, sir. She's far too inexperienced.'

'Oh, I don't know. I'd say she's done pretty well so far, wouldn't you?' Redmayne brushed the crumbs from his lips with a linen napkin.

'Yes, sir. But her work on Mykonos was different.'

'I don't see how.'

'It was intelligence gathering,' said Gabriel, through gritted teeth.

'So is this,' said Redmayne. 'We send her in, she takes one of those "mental photographs" of hers that Professor Dixon keeps waxing lyrical about, confirms Sister Elena's identity and leaves.'

'With respect, sir, that's ops. If Elena *is* Athena, Ella will be in significant danger and you know it.'

'In case you haven't noticed,' said Redmayne, choosing to let the insolence go, 'she's been under the same roof as Makis Alexiadis for weeks now. Arguably one of the most dangerous men on the planet.'

'Which I advised against,' Gabriel reminded him.

'Hmm,' Redmayne grunted. 'Well, I don't know what to tell you, Gabe. You were wrong then and you're wrong now. The young lady is far more capable and more resourceful than you give her credit for.' He waved a hand airily, as if he could swat away the risks of the Sikinos expedition like a pesky fly. 'She's brave. Like her mother,' he added, a dreamy, nostalgic look flitting briefly across his face.

Gabriel could have punched him. How could he bring up Rachel Praeger at a time like this? Had he no shame at all?

'Ella's already proved she can handle Big Mak, which is no mean feat as we both know,' Redmayne went on. 'All she has to do is identify "Elena", not engage her. She'll be fine.'

'Sir.'

Gabriel gritted his teeth, but inside he simmered with anger like a slowly boiling kettle. The boss was trying to frame his negligence for Ella's safety as some sort of compliment, a sign of his 'faith' in her, when in fact all he wanted was to hurl her recklessly into the lion's den. It was almost as if he wanted something terrible to happen to her. Wanted her to be killed. Although, of course, that made no sense.

'You said yourself last week that Ella needed an exit strategy from Villa Mirage,' said Redmayne, sensing Gabriel's disquiet and cleverly using his own words against him. 'That she couldn't be expected to hold Makis Alexiadis off forever. That she'd already gleaned whatever useful information was to be had from inside that house and we ought to pull her out.'

'I meant pull her out and bring her *home*,' snapped Gabriel, exasperated. 'Or at least back to relative safety in Athens. Not pull her out and send her to confront one of the most dangerous women in the world.'

'*Potentially* most dangerous,' Redmayne replied archly, reminding Gabriel of his own doubts about Sister Elena's identity. 'As you said yourself, she *may* just be a go-between. Besides, Ella's eager to go.'

'You already discussed it with her?'

'Via Nikkos Anastas,' Redmayne said nonchalantly, ignoring his agent's dismay. 'She was keen.'

'Well of course she was keen,' Gabriel said bitterly. 'After what you told her about her parents' deaths? She wants vengeance.'

'What *we* told her,' Redmayne corrected him sternly. 'You're a part of this too, Gabriel. In case you'd forgotten.'

Gabriel hadn't forgotten. He shifted uncomfortably in his seat.

'Sometimes we have to tell people what they need to hear,' Redmayne rationalized, the way that people without a conscience seemed to do with such blithe ease. 'Never lose sight of the big picture, Gabriel. The greater good.'

He drained the last of his coffee, setting the cup back down with finality.

'So. You're to let Ella know we'll be extracting her from Mykonos very soon and bringing her back to Athens, to prep her for the Sikinos mission. I've given Nikkos four days to organize her new cover.'

Gabriel shook his head but said nothing. Four days wasn't long enough. It was nowhere near long enough. But Redmayne wasn't about to change his mind. Besides which, even Gabriel could see the importance of getting someone inside the Convent of the Sacred Heart as soon as possible, before 'Sister Elena' pulled another disappearing act. If indeed she *was* Athena Petridis, the last time she vanished, nobody heard so much as a whisper from her for twelve long years.

'Remember, all Ella has to do is take the shot and ID her,' Redmayne said, trying to sound reassuring. 'If it *is* Athena, we'll have an experienced team ready to go in afterwards and do what needs to be done. I won't put Ella at any more risk than I have to, you have my word on that.'

*Your word!* Gabriel thought bitterly. *As if that's worth the paper it's written on.*

'I heard about what happened to the Kouvlaki brothers,' he observed, deadpan, changing the subject in a way he knew would disconcert Redmayne, and hopefully wipe the smug smile off his face. 'The murders. The brandings.'

'Hmmm.' To Gabriel's irritation, Redmayne gave nothing away. 'Nasty business.'

'An "A" and a "P" apparently,' said Gabriel. 'Some sort of message from Athena?'

'One assumes so,' drawled Redmayne.

'Unless she was set up,' muttered Gabriel. 'Someone using her calling card to make it look like she ordered the hit?'

Redmayne didn't flinch. 'I don't think so. Not that it matters vastly. I mean, obviously we won't be shedding any tears over Perry and Andreas.'

'Obviously,' nodded Gabriel. 'So you don't know anything more about the killings then?'

Redmayne raised an eyebrow languidly. 'More?'

Gabriel looked at him directly. 'Are we sure Athena was behind them?'

Redmayne returned his glare without blinking. 'You tell me, Gabriel. *Are* we sure? I am. But perhaps the question is, are you?'

Walking down the rue du Boccador a few minutes later, Gabriel tried to block out the sinking feeling pulling his heart down into the pit of his belly. He had Mark Redmayne's 'word' on protecting Ella. But too many of the boss's words had turned out to be lies over the years, or at least half-truths – like whatever it was he was hiding about the Kouvlakis' killings. Redmayne's lies were always in the service of The Group, of course, and the 'greater good'. But the ease with which falsehoods slipped off the man's tongue was unsettling. It reminded Gabriel of his father, someone he did his best on a daily basis to forget.

As for not putting Ella at risk, was that the truth? Gabriel couldn't get a handle on the boss's motives when it came to Ella, and it bothered him. On the one hand, he obviously prized her highly as The Group's new secret weapon. As the human receiver, the biological super-camera, an intelligence tool beyond the dreams of even the CIA, he wouldn't want anything to happen to her. On the other hand, as a human being he appeared at best indifferent towards her and at worst to harbor an active dislike, despite his nostalgic 'affection' for her mother. It was almost as if Mark Redmayne feared Ella Praeger in some way. Although again, Gabriel couldn't for the life of him imagine why that might be.

Redmayne's word meant nothing. Gabriel could only pray that, in the end, Ella's precious abilities would protect her, not just from Redmayne but from all the other myriad dangers that a life in The Group would expose her to.

Because the bitter truth was that Gabriel couldn't protect Ella. Just as he'd been unable to protect Mira, all those years ago.

That was the part that hurt the most.

# CHAPTER FIFTEEN

Miriam waited for Persephone Hamlin to finish her espresso, watching from the Gucci boutique across the street as her rival pulled some notes out of her purse and left them on the table.

Miriam had thought about leaving Mykonos numerous times since Makis Alexiadis threw her over. Lisette and Arabella had long since cut their losses and run, knowing as Miriam did that they were lucky to be alive. Rumor had it that not all of Mak's exes had survived to tell the tale. And it wasn't as if Miriam didn't have options. Another wealthy admirer had invited her to join him on his yacht in Ibiza, and an ex-boyfriend whom Miriam had stayed close to over the years had extended an open invitation for her to come and stay at his 'party bastide' in St Tropez.

'Forget the Greek,' he'd texted her just last week. 'Come hang at the Voile Rouge for a few days and let your hair down. You know you want to!'

It was tempting. But not as tempting as knocking the strange, boy-woman Persephone off the pedestal that Mak had decided to put her on. Miriam could give up Makis Alexiadis if she had to, but she wasn't about to cede her position as his sex object of choice to this alien-faced, kookily dressed freak who, if the rumors were true, was *still* rejecting his advances.

Frustratingly, a week of research had so far yielded nothing that Miriam could use against her. The few fragments of Persephone's 'story' that Miriam knew all appeared to check out when she searched online: the addict husband, the rich American parents, the house in Los Angeles. But still, Miriam's instincts screamed that something about this chick was off. That if she just waited – and watched – a little longer, she would catch her out.

In the beginning, Persephone spent almost all her time in the luxurious confines of Villa Mirage. On the rare occasions when she ventured out, she and Mak were always together. For two people who claimed not to be a couple, they looked suspiciously close. Mak was always opening doors and pulling out chairs for her. There was a lot of laughter too between them. Intimate asides, private jokes, his hands placed lovingly on one of her shoulders or the small of her back. It rankled, watching him lavish affection on this unworthy American in a way he had never done with her. But the worst part for Miriam was knowing that she wouldn't see anything significant or incriminating while Mak was present. She needed to catch Persephone alone.

Today might finally be the day!

Hiding the entire top half of her face behind a pair of oversized, Oliver Peoples sunglasses, Miriam slipped out of the store and followed at a safe distance as Persephone left the café and walked down the steep hill towards the harbor. This was the third morning in a row she'd ventured out into town without Makis. On each occasion she'd drunk a single coffee by herself and then simply wandered the streets, not shopping or going to the spa or *doing* anything, other than occasionally checking her phone.

Today she seemed to be following the same pattern, weaving her way through the morning crowd of tourists, pretending to look at boats. Except this time, she was more anxious than usual, stopping frequently to look around and behind her. More than once Miriam had to duck into a store or double back on herself so as not to appear to be following her, but Persephone didn't seem to notice her at all. Instead, apparently satisfied that she was safe and alone, she departed from her usual route and took a sharp left turn into an alleyway behind the Friday fish market.

This was not a part of town where any wealthy foreigner had any business being. Rotting fish heads and empty crates, still reeking of the previous day's catch, littered cobblestones still slick with blood and scales and spilled drinks, the detritus of a busy morning's trade. Two large, ugly plastic trash cans were wedged against a crumbling wall on one side, while on the other a pair of mangy cats eyed one another jealously as they searched for scraps.

While Miriam hung back behind a plane tree on the corner, out of sight, Persephone made a last check before pulling a cell phone that Miriam hadn't seen before out of her rattan purse. She made a call of around five minutes' duration. Miriam was too far away to hear anything that was said, but the urgent way in which Persephone's lips moved and her agitated hand gestures implied it was a fraught conversation. When it ended, Miriam watched, wide-eyed, as Persephone disassembled the phone, discarding the separate pieces – battery and handset – in different trash cans before slipping what must have been the SIM card into her pocket. Moments later, having once again checked she was alone, Persephone exited the alley by the other end and hailed a taxi, hopping inside and speeding off before Miriam had a chance to follow.

Not that she needed one. What she'd just seen was enough.

Her heart pounding, she dialed Mak's private number. Predictably it went straight to message – the days when he automatically picked up Miriam's calls were gone. But this time, Miriam knew he would call her back. His reluctance at engaging with former lovers was nothing compared to his paranoia. She made sure the message she left sounded suitably alarming.

'I have something important to tell you,' she whispered. 'As a friend. You may be in danger.'

When he called back, she would insist they meet in person. And she would downplay the incident. *'Perhaps it was nothing, but . . .' 'There may be a simple explanation . . .' 'I just thought you'd want to know . . .'*

If Persephone Hamlin really was trying to double-cross Mak, she'd just dug her own grave.

Ella looked critically at her reflection in the mirror, fiddling with the diamond drop earrings Makis had given her last week and wishing her hair weren't so short. In a full-length, clinging, backless gown in midnight blue silk, and five-inch silver Louboutin heels, she felt like a little girl playing dress up. Gabriel had insisted she 'make an effort' for tonight's dinner; to be sure that, for once, she looked the part of the wealthy heiress and that, when she departed Alexiadis's presence, she left him wanting more.

'He wants more anyway,' Ella responded bluntly. 'He's attracted to the fact that Persephone *doesn't* make an effort.'

'Tonight is different,' Gabriel insisted. 'He won't want you to leave. You must give him some sign that *you* don't want to either. That you are trying to keep his interest. That you will return to him. If he believes that, he's more likely to let you go.'

Ella wasn't convinced of the strategy, if that's what it was. All these conflicting signals and double bluffs were making her head spin. But she'd gone along with it anyway, partly because she didn't want another battle with Gabriel, who was already upset about her being sent undercover to the convent on Sikinos, and partly because she was nervous. What if Mak didn't 'let her go'? It wasn't her personal safety that bothered Ella so much as the idea that she might miss her window to find Athena Petridis. To confront the one person still alive who was responsible for her parents' deaths, and for all the misery of her childhood, not to mention that of countless other childhoods. Gabriel and Redmayne might still be harboring doubts, but Ella had convinced herself that the mysterious 'Sister Elena' and Athena Petridis would turn out to be one and the same. It was true because Ella needed it to be true. She told herself that this entire past month on Mykonos with Mak had been nothing to do with her growing attraction to him sexually, or the exhilaration, the illicit thrill of playing both huntress and hunted. It had all been purely in order to track down Athena and exact righteous vengeance for her parents' deaths. If Ella didn't leave now, or very soon, it might all have been for nothing. If Sister Elena left the convent before she got there . . . No. It didn't bear thinking about.

All Ella's recent interceptions had confirmed what she already suspected – that Mak was growing tired of waiting for Persephone to go to bed with him and that his excitement at their cat-and-mouse game was waning. In a short space of time, Ella had come a long way from the geeky teenager from Paradise Ranch who couldn't hold on to a boyfriend. But a virile, sexually rapacious man like Mak could only be pushed so far or dangled on a string for so long. She had no wish to find out what happened when he was dragged beyond his limits.

Downstairs, Mak was already seated in the villa's smaller, 'private' dining room, a circular space with two enormous picture windows and a glass roof that opened to the stars. In a beautifully tailored Zegna suit and a silk shirt in sky blue, open at the neck, he too had clearly made an effort tonight. The room was full of flowers (peonies, Persephone's favorite). But, most tellingly of all, the table had been set for two. Ella had been expecting two other couples, business associates of Mak's and their wives.

'Your friends aren't joining us?'

'No.'

Looking up, Mak took a moment to marvel once again at her beauty. More than beauty. Her *radiance*. That charisma, that presence Persephone had that he could no more describe than he could capture. She looked particularly ravishing tonight, in that dress that seemed painted onto her body, and that showed such tantalizing expanses of skin. Her smooth back. Her long, slender arms. And she was wearing the Graff earrings he'd bought her, for the first time.

'I thought it would be nicer just the two of us. Do you mind?'

'Of course not.' She smiled at him warmly, taking a seat as the waiting staff glided in bearing a variety of salads and fish dishes. 'I feel like I've hardly seen you these last few days.'

He didn't respond, but seemed to be watching her even more intently than usual. Ella felt her stomach begin to churn with nerves. Something felt different.

'Please don't think I'm complaining,' she said, projecting

226

a poise she was far from feeling while her wine and water glasses were filled. 'You've been so generous, having me here. I hope you know how grateful I am.'

His eyes wandered from her face, to her body, gift-wrapped in silk for his viewing pleasure, then slowly back up to her eyes. The expression on his face made it crystal clear what form he wanted her gratitude to take.

'It's been my pleasure to have you here, Persephone,' he said eventually. 'And you're right, business matters have kept me preoccupied for the last few days. But I'd like to make that time up to you. I've decided to spend the rest of the month on my yacht. I'd be honored if you would join me.'

Ella's throat went dry. This was a major curve ball. Was it a test? He hadn't mentioned any plans to leave Mykonos this summer before now. Whatever his motives, she knew she must play this very, very carefully.

'Where will you be sailing?' She played for time.

'I'm not sure. Perhaps to Italy eventually. Sardinia. But maybe to some of the smaller Greek islands first. Paxos. Alonissos. I've heard Sikinos is beautiful this time of year. Do you know it?'

Ella could hardly breathe. Sikinos was where Sister Elena's convent was. *Why would he mention that to me? Does he suspect I know something? But why would he? How could he?*

'No, I'm afraid I don't.' She buttered a slice of bread with Oscar-worthy nonchalance. 'Unfortunately, I won't be able to join you, at least not for the first part of the month.' She toyed with her earring thoughtfully. 'Although perhaps I could come aboard later, once you reach Italy?'

A small muscle began to twitch at the edge of Makis's jaw.

'Why can't you come now? You have plans?'

She sighed deeply and continued eating. 'I'm afraid I do. I've decided to divorce Nick.'

Mak sat back in his chair, surprised. 'Really?'

'Mmm hm,' she nodded, avoiding his gaze in a coy manner that *might* have implied he was a part of the reason for her decision. 'Being here has given me a lot of time to think. I needed that.'

'I see,' his voice softened.

Mak's conversation yesterday with Miriam Dabiri had troubled him deeply. It was no secret that Miriam was jealous, that she resented his interest in Persephone and the fact that he'd tired so suddenly of her. And yet, he believed the story she'd told him, about the animated call and the disassembling of the 'burner' phone. It simply sounded too elaborate and specific to have been made up.

'Be careful,' Miriam had warned him. 'As a friend. I don't think you can trust her.'

His first instinct had been to agree. Persephone must be spying on him, although for whom and to what end he couldn't fathom. But if she was divorcing her husband, perhaps there was another, less troubling motive for her secretive calls? She might be trying to hide money from her soon-to-be ex, or conceal an affair, or she might be hiring some shady investigator to look into *his* affairs and not want those calls traced. Divorce and secrecy often went hand in hand.

'I have to go to Athens to see some lawyers,' she told him now. Reaching across the table, she stroked his hand with what felt like more than just friendly affection. 'For various reasons it makes sense for me to file here, in Europe. Depending on how Nick responds, I may also have to fly back to the States.'

'For how long?'

She squeezed his hand. 'I don't know yet. But I leave for

228

Athens in the morning. I'll know more after my meetings there.'

'You leave tomorrow?' he frowned. The thought was painful.

'Not for ever.' She tried to sound reassuring. 'If he doesn't contest it – and there's a good chance he won't – I would love to join you on the yacht in a week or two. But I have to do this, Mak. You understand, don't you?'

He nodded.

'Once I'm divorced . . . things will be different,' she promised him.

Gazing into her eyes, Mak wanted to believe her.

After dinner, they sat out on the terrace talking for a long time. Afterwards, as usual, he walked her back to her own suite of rooms. But this time, when she placed her hand on the door, he moved in behind her, pressing his body close against hers.

'I don't want you to go.'

Ella closed her eyes. She could feel his warm breath in her ear and the heat of his body against her bare back. She was afraid of him, but excited at the same time, his desire triggering her own. Turning around she kissed him, only once but with a passion that, to her shame, she didn't have to fake.

'I don't want to go either,' she whispered afterwards. 'But I must. Goodnight, Makis.'

Turning the handle she slipped inside her rooms, closing the door behind her, her heart pounding as she waited to see whether he would force the issue and follow. To her combined relief and disappointment, he didn't.

Back in his own bed, feeling elated and frustrated in equal measure, Mak stared up at the ceiling. The kiss was real. That much he knew for sure. As for everything else

Persephone had told him tonight, on balance he believed her. But Miriam's warnings still hovered in the back of his mind like an unwanted black cloud.

*Better safe than sorry.*

He would speak with Cameron McKinley first thing tomorrow morning about having her followed. Persephone Hamlin would be free to go to Athens. But until the hour she joined him aboard his yacht, *Argo*, Makis Alexiadis would be watching her every move.

# CHAPTER SIXTEEN

Detective Inspector Jim Boyd pulled back the plastic sheeting and winced at the remains on the medical examiner's slab.

'Female, obviously,' Lisa Janner, the medical examiner explained. Helpfully, as it was far from obvious to Jim Boyd that the slimy mess he was looking at was even human. 'And as I said on the phone, Asian. Even with the facial features largely destroyed, you can tell from the hair. See?' Lisa lifted up a thick strand of glossy black hair between two gloved fingers, for DI Boyd's perusal. 'Probably early fifties. Well off, judging from the manicured hands, expensive dentistry. Dead long before she was submerged.'

The body, what remained of it, had washed up on the banks of the Thames not far from Westminster Bridge in the early hours of this morning, wrapped ineffectually in three layers of black plastic bin bag that had done very little to protect it from the foul ravages of the river. Some poor student out for a dawn jog had found it and spent twenty minutes heaving his guts out before he had the strength to call 999. *That'll teach the smug bastard, turning his body into a temple while the rest of us are still in bed sleeping off our hangovers*, thought Jim Boyd. Although he was damn glad he hadn't found 'her' in her original state. If what he was looking at now was the cleaned-up version, he dreaded to think . . .

'Cause of death almost certainly blunt force trauma to the back of the skull,' Lisa went on, gently turning the slimy orb to one side to reveal the wound. 'Although there are other relevant injuries that might have resulted in—'

'Where's the mark? The letter?' It was the first time Boyd had spoken. The first time he'd felt confident he could open his mouth without vomiting.

'Ah. That's down here.' Mercifully covering up the melted remnants of the woman's features, Lisa Janner lifted the base of the plastic tarp. One foot had been completely, and very cleanly severed, as if with a guillotine. But the other had been marked along the entire sole with a large letter: 'P'.

'What is that?' Jim Boyd looked closer. He felt more comfortable down at this end. 'Not a tattoo?'

'No. It's a brand,' the medical examiner informed him. 'Like a cattle brand. It was made with hot metal. Burned into the flesh.'

'After death?' Boyd asked hopefully, wincing again.

'Impossible to say.'

It took Jim Boyd a few moments to remember where he'd seen something similar recently. In the newspaper. The little toddler, washed up on the beach in Greece. Branded like an animal, and on the foot too. But that kid had been a migrant, stuffed onto one of those Libyan death boats, the poorest of the poor. What could a child like that have in common with a rich, middle-aged Asian bird stuffed into bin bags in London.

'Sir?'

Harrison, Boyd's sergeant, stuck his eager, ruddy-cheeked face around the door.

'We've got a name, sir. Probable anyway. Professor

Noriko Adachi. She's an academic, apparently. Lives in Japan.'

'Japan?' Boyd raised an eyebrow.

'Yes, sir. The techs were able to trace a bar code on a library card found with the body. It's from Osaka University. One of Professor Adachi's students there officially reported her missing three weeks ago.'

Boyd frowned. 'What was she doing in London?'

'Don't know, sir.' Harrison shrugged. 'Holiday? She entered the UK from New York on a tourist visa five weeks ago. She was in regular Skype contact with her students, but that stopped abruptly about a month ago. That's all we have at the minute.'

'Do you want to see any more?' Lisa Janner asked Boyd. 'As I say, there were other wounds . . .'

'It's all in your report, I assume?' asked Boyd

'Of course.'

'Then no. Thank you.'

He turned and walked grimly from the room. Professor Adachi had not been in London on holiday. Of that much he was certain. Brandings and severed feet and bodies in bin bags tossed into the Thames? These were not random, thoughtless acts of violence directed towards a tourist. This was not a rape or mugging gone wrong. It was the calculated work of a professional killer who had reason to wish Miss Adachi dead. Someone who either feared her, or hated her, or both.

'*What did you know, Noriko?*' he muttered aloud to himself under his breath. '*What did you know?*'


Constantin Pilavos loaded a second reel of film into his Nikkon FE 35 mm and waited patiently in his parked van until Persephone Hamlin emerged from the building.

Her divorce lawyer, Anna Cosmidis, was one of the

biggest legal hitters in Greece. Hence her offices, which occupied the entire top floor of a landmark building on Poseidonos Avenue, one of the most exclusive streets in Athens. Mrs Hamlin had been inside for almost two hours – God knew how much that would have cost her! – but Constantin's orders were to take pictures of her arriving *and* leaving, and then to follow her to wherever she went next.

At long last she reappeared, looking businesslike in a cream skirt and fitted jacket and with her eyes hidden behind oversized sunglasses. Rolling down his window and adjusting the zoom lens, Constantin began taking more shots. Mr McKinley, his boss, had insisted on the old-fashioned camera and hand-developed prints. Makis Alexiadis, *his* boss, was a stickler for avoiding electronic communication wherever possible and paranoid about emails or phone calls being intercepted. It was a lesson he'd learned from his mentor, Spyros Petridis, and never forgotten.

The whole thing was overkill in Constantin Pilavos's opinion. But as he was paid by the hour, he wasn't complaining. So far, the Hamlin woman had done nothing more interesting than visiting her lawyer, strolling in the park, and twice attending a local gym. Constantin had captured all of it, although he failed to see of what interest his pictures would be, to Makis Alexiadis or to anyone. If Big Mak suspected Persephone of having an affair, he was wrong. As far as Constantin could tell, the woman didn't even have any friends.

He continued snapping until she was out of sight, then started his engine.

Nikkos Anastas sat his ample backside down on an empty bench in the grounds of the Parthenon and opened his newspaper.

234

It was another sweltering day, hot enough that there were few people milling around at this midday hour. By the time Ella arrived and sat down on the adjoining bench directly behind him, two damp circles of sweat had already begun to spread under Nikkos's arms and the skin on his hairy legs was starting to burn below the line of his shorts.

'You took your time,' he said in Greek, without looking around or acknowledging her presence in any way.

'Divorce is a complicated business. Anna had a lot of questions.'

'You were able to answer them? No slip-ups.'

'No.' Ella spoke to the ground. 'It was fine.'

'He's still following you?'

'Mmm hmmm,' she confirmed. 'But I can't pick up anything from him. If he has a phone he doesn't use it.'

'So nothing from Mak?'

'Not that I can detect. Sorry,' said Ella.

Nikkos grunted. It was frustrating. Knowing Ella was being watched by Alexiadis, she had to go through the motions as Persephone Hamlin while in Athens, which made it harder than usual for the two of them to meet and plan the next stage of her mission. Nikkos had hoped that at least the goon tailing her might have provided Ella with a continued window onto Makis's movements and plans, particularly in so far as they concerned Athena. The radio silence was an added blow.

'When can we talk properly?' Ella asked, her own frustration beginning to show. 'Gabriel said you would give me instructions this week.'

'Yes, yes, yes,' said Nikkos impatiently. 'It has not been easy. Is that him? The Fiat van, next to the tobacco store?'

Ella glanced down the hill. 'It is,' she murmured, taking out a book from her purse and pretending to read.

'OK,' said Nikkos. 'Tomorrow night there's a big party

being held at the house of Stavros Helios. It's a political fundraiser. Persephone Hamlin's on the guest list.'

'Who's Stavros Helios?'

'A very rich man. One of the first Greeks to invest in Bitcoin,' said Nikkos. 'He's also one of us.'

'Does he know about me? About the Sikinos mission?'

'No, no, no. Don't worry about any of that. Just show up tomorrow night. We can talk properly there.'

'What about van man? He's bound to follow me. And for all we know, Makis may have other people watching.'

'Leave all that to me,' said Nikkos. 'And don't leave here for at least ten minutes. Your Greek's improving by the way.'

'Thank you,' said Ella.

But Nikkos had already folded up his paper and lumbered off down the hill.

Stavros Helios's estate was the second grandest mansion in Athens, right after the presidential palace. Designed by the same architect in the mid-nineteenth century, both were vast, white wedding cakes of buildings, complete with the usual 'classical' Greek touches of Doric columns, supported on enormous stucco plinths and crepidoma, and topped by an entablature depicting a variety of the ancient myths.

Of the two, however, Helios's house had by far the larger and more beautiful grounds. Surrounded by towering poplar trees and at the end of a quarter-mile-long drive, the mansion fronted onto a series of tiered lawns, fountains and formal gardens, each with a different theme. The rose garden, occasionally opened to the public, was said to contain more rare varieties of rose than any other in Europe, including the world-famous specimens at the palace of Versailles. But it was only one of a series of different outdoor 'spaces', each exquisite in their own way, including a Japanese garden, a water garden, a desert garden, a sculpture garden, and a bonsai 'forest'.

Climbing out of the chauffeur-driven limousine that Nikkos had arranged for her, Ella immediately felt underdressed in her simple white evening gown. Gazing at the other women emerging from their Bentleys and Lamborghinis in astonishing couture gowns, their bodices hand-stitched with dazzling beading, many of them sporting trains and even tiaras, she tried to remind herself that Persephone Hamlin took pride in being a rich woman of relatively simple sartorial tastes. Even so, arriving on her own and in a plain Calvin Klein sheath, Ella felt uncomfortably naked.

Removing the stiff invitation card from her silver clutch-bag, she handed it to the 'greeter' at the gate, an elegant woman in her fifties wearing a beautifully understated, pale pink Prada gown and with her dark hair pinned up in a bun like a ballerina.

'Welcome, Mrs Hamlin,' she smiled at Ella. 'I hope you enjoy the evening.'

'Hey. You!'

Constantin Pilavos froze as a heavy male hand clamped down on his shoulders.

'I'm from *Kathimerini*,' he explained, turning around to face his assailant, a giant brute of a man in an ill-fitting black suit, and pulling an elegantly forged press pass for the well-known Greek newspaper from his inside jacket pocket. Ahead of him, he could see Persephone Hamlin take a flute of champagne from one of the waiting staff before disappearing into the growing throng.

'I don't think so,' growled the giant menacingly. 'You need to leave.'

'I can assure you, my paper is on the approved media

list.' Constantin stammered nervously. He didn't wish to anger this monster, who could crush him like a baby bird if he put his mind to it. On the other hand, if he didn't come back with photographic evidence of Mrs Hamlin's one and only social night out in Athens, he'd have Mr McKinley to answer to, an equally unappealing prospect.

'Please,' he urged the giant. 'If you'd just check the list? Mr Helios specifically invited us to cover tonight's event.'

'Yeah? Well he's changed his mind,' grunted the giant, in a tone that made it crystal clear the conversation was over. 'I'll see you out.'

Lifting Constantin off the ground with no more effort than a child picking up a doll, he physically carried him back down the driveway and out of the gates. Worse, when he set him down, he proceeded to grab his camera, pull out the film, and thrust it into his pocket.

'Don't come back,' he snarled. 'We'll be watching.'

'Is he gone?' Ella asked Nikkos.

'He's gone. But I need you to listen carefully. Cameron McKinley won't let Persephone out of his sight for long. We don't have much time.'

They were sitting alone on a terrace at the rear of the property. Below them, in the sculpture garden, Athens's ruling political class were milling around, sipping Stavros Helios's vintage champagne and generally behaving as if they'd never heard of the word 'austerity'. Ella didn't think she'd ever seen such a vast gulf between the lives of the rich and the poor as she had since she came to Greece. Which was saying something for a girl who lived in San Francisco. But now wasn't the time for philosophizing.

Pulling an iPad out from the pocket of his capacious evening jacket – his entire suit was more tent than apparel – Nikkos pulled up a map of Sikinos.

'So, this is the island. Very small, as you can see. Not much there except the convent, two farms and a fishing village. Boats can access here and here.' He jabbed at the screen with a pudgy finger. 'But you don't need to worry about that; you will be going in as one of the staff at Maria's bakery, They're based on Folegandros, a neighboring island. Sikinos isn't big enough to support a bakery of its own. The nuns generally bake their own bread, but they occasionally order in cakes or pastries for special occasions. Next Wednesday is the feast of St Spyridon, patron saint of the Cyclades islands. They've already put in an order for madeleines and *portokalopita*, the traditional orange cakes of the region, as well as fifty special loaves. Delivery will be Wednesday morning, early.'

'Do I have a name? A cover story?' Ella asked, surprised by the strength of her excitement. For the first time since she left Mykonos, this felt real. And once again, she couldn't help but feel the tug of destiny – being a part of this mission felt strangely like coming home.

'Your name is Marta and you're from Patras.'

'That's it?' Ella looked worried. After all Gabriel's admonitions about the importance of a detailed cover story and sticking to it – all the endless complications of being Persephone Hamlin – this felt like something of a turnaround.

'No one will question you,' said Nikkos. 'You're delivering cakes. When you arrive, the sisters should still be at Matins. You need to make an excuse and slip out of the kitchens. Find Sister Elena. If you can, you are to take a "mental picture". Apparently you know what that means?'

Ella nodded.

'Good. It's unlikely there'll be much electronic traffic in the convent itself for you to pick up on, but you never know. If Elena does turn out to be Athena, then she must have had some means of communicating with her network. So. Be prepared. Be aware. But above all, we need eyes on Sister Elena.'

Ella nodded gravely. 'How long will I have?'

'Usually, the delivery girls are offered a meal and invited to pray with the community before they take the boat back,' said Nikkos. 'We hope that will give you an hour inside, perhaps a little more. Whatever happens, whether you've found Elena or not, make sure you rejoin the rest of Maria's staff before they leave and that you take the boat back to Folegandros with them. Someone will debrief you afterwards.'

Ella scowled. 'I can't leave without finding Athena.'

'Certainly you can,' Nikkos replied robustly. 'Don't forget, Sister Elena may not *be* Athena.'

'She is,' muttered Ella. 'I feel it in my bones.'

Nikkos rolled his eyes. 'Bones, schmones, my dear. Your job is to make sure.'

'If it *is* her, and I get her alone,' Ella mused, 'I'd have a chance to strike.'

'Strike?'

'I'd have a chance to kill her.' Ella's eyes met his. 'Shouldn't I take it?'

Nikkos gripped her firmly by the shoulders. 'Absolutely not. No. That's not your job.'

'But, The Group have been looking for her for twelve years,' Ella protested. 'What if this is our chance. Our only chance?'

'It won't be,' said Nikkos.

'You don't know that!' Ella snapped, frustrated. Why had she gone through all that physical training at Camp Hope if she was never going to be allowed to use it?

'Think it through,' said Nikkos calmly. 'If Sister Elena is Athena Petridis, and *you* kill her, or harm her in any way;

and if you're discovered, which you would be; then you'll be arrested and charged. Remember, as far as the Greek state is concerned, Athena Petridis was a philanthropist and campaigner for children's rights. She was never convicted of any crime.'

'Which is ridiculous,' Ella muttered, outraged. 'Everybody knew what she did.'

'Not everybody,' said Nikkos, shaking his head. 'Had *you* ever heard of her or her husband before you joined The Group?'

Ella had to admit that she hadn't.

'Exactly,' said Nikkos. 'And besides, suspecting – even knowing – and proving are not the same thing. If you act rashly, your cover will be blown, The Group's anonymity will be at risk, and years of hard work undone. You will likely go to jail. We won't be able to save you. And your gifts, the precious abilities that your parents gave you? Those will be wasted. Lost, to us and to the world. For ever.'

Ella considered this for a moment. When she spoke again it was quietly, but with an unmistakable edge of steel. 'Athena Petridis stood by and watched while her husband held my mother's head under the water. While he choked the life out of her. She deserves to die.'

Nikkos took her hand and squeezed it. 'Yes she does. No one's disputing that. And she will. But we are all cogs in the wheel that will crush her, Ella. That's how The Group works. No single one of us *is* the wheel. Not even you. Your part is to locate, to identify, to trap. Remember, if it hadn't been for you, we wouldn't even have known about Sister Elena. We'd never have looked at the convent.'

Feeling only slightly mollified, Ella listened as Nikkos outlined the rest of the plan. Tonight marked the end of Persephone Hamlin's existence. Cameron McKinley's men would be waiting, but they would never see their quarry

241

again. Instead, like a caterpillar spinning its chrysalis, Ella would sleep here tonight, at Helios's mansion. In her guest suite she would dye her hair dark brown, add some fake tattoos to her upper arms, and slip into the simple, worn clothes of Marta, the baker's assistant from Patras. At five a.m. she would be awoken and smuggled out of the estate by van, at the bottom of a hamper of laundry. By six fifteen a.m., Marta would be on a fishing boat on her way to the Cyclades.

The way Nikkos spoke about it, it sounded so simple. As if it had already happened, and Ella's transformation were already complete.

'Follow these directions *exactly*,' he told her, standing up and taking his leave, 'and you will be fine. Once I've gone, wait ten minutes and then go inside the house through those doors.' He pointed to a set of French doors opening onto a lawn about fifty yards to their left. 'Someone will be there to meet you and escort you to your rooms. Everything you need is there. Good luck.'

Ella watched as he walked away, his burly, bear-like frame looking even bigger than usual in his oversized suit. Signals and voices buzzed in her head – this house was a veritable hive of activity – but she shut them all off, unable to isolate a single, useful channel, or to focus on anything. Exhausted suddenly, she longed to be able to retreat to her room and sleep.

But first, of course, she must change. Shed her old skin, like the snake she was becoming, and assume her new role, her new identity. Just as her parents had before her.

It was frightening how much she was looking forward to it.

Anna Cosmidis looked again at her Pearlmaster 39 Rolex watch, her irritation building. The fabled divorce attorney had already been paid for her time, but she still objected on principle to being kept waiting.

'Renate.' She buzzed her secretary again. 'Still no word from Mrs Hamlin?'

'I'm sorry, ma'am. I've tried to reach her but the number I have no longer seems to be working. Should I cancel the appointment?'

Anna Cosmidis sighed. She'd liked Persephone Hamlin. But she hadn't gone into this business to make friends, and life was too short and trade too good to put up with unreliable clients.

'Yes. Cancel it,' she replied brusquely, her razor-sharp mind already moving on to the next challenge. 'You can show in Mrs Froebbel.'

Outside in his van, Constantin Pilavos waited.

And waited.

And waited.

He rubbed his bloodshot eyes, a hideous churning sensation in his stomach creeping down towards his bowels.

Somehow he must have missed Persephone Hamlin leaving the party at Stavros Helios's estate last night. He'd waited back at her hotel, but she'd never showed there either. Not last night. Not this morning.

Her nine a.m. meeting with her divorce lawyer had been Constantin's last hope. As the minutes ticked by, then the hours, fear turned to panic.

He could go back to Cameron McKinley and admit he'd lost the target.

Or he could run for his life, drive far away from Athens and never return.

With tears in his eyes, he started the engine.

*

Makis watched from the upper deck of the *Argo* as the tender drew closer. Aboard was Cameron McKinley, his thin, sandy hair blowing unattractively in the wind, like Donald Trump's on a golf course. He had a briefcase in his hand and an unreadable expression on his pale, watery face.

*He's come in person.* That meant the news was either very good, or very bad. Mak would say this for Cameron McKinley: the man had balls. He didn't cringe and cower around Mak, the way that everybody else did when they feared his wrath.

One of these days, Mak would punish him for it. But not today. Not with the threat of Athena's return still hanging over his head like a toxic cloud.

'What's happened?' he asked bluntly, as his fixer climbed aboard the yacht. 'You have pictures?' he gestured toward the briefcase.

'Yes.'

'Is she sleeping with somebody else?' Makis braced himself for the answer. If it was 'yes', he would kill the man, whoever he was, and then, when the time was right, punish Persephone.

'No,' said Cameron, handing the case to his boss.

The rush of relief was instant, but it was also brief. 'Who's this?' Mak asked, pointing to the fat, bearded man standing close to Persephone in numerous different pictures.

'His name is Nikkos Anastas,' said Cameron. 'Or so he claims. Ostensibly he runs a clothing business on the outskirts of Athens, but if he does then he's a *very* silent partner. We never saw them speaking together directly, but he kept popping up. Either he's surveilling her and doing a shitty job of it, or they know each other in some capacity. He's a concern.'

Mak could see at once in his fixer's pale blue eyes that something else was wrong.

'What?' he demanded, angrily, tossing the photographs aside. 'What is it?'

Cameron McKinley cleared his throat.

'We've lost her.'

Blood drained from Makis's face. 'You've *what?*'

'We haven't seen her since the night of the fundraiser at Stavros Helios's estate. I think she's left Athens—'

'You *think?!*' Mak's voice was a roar. Without thinking, he shot out both hands and clamped them tightly around Cameron's neck, choking him. 'You *THINK?!* Don't think!' he bellowed, hurling the Scotsman to the ground in a coughing, spluttering heap. 'Find her!'

# CHAPTER SEVENTEEN

Fatima Ghali – the Turkish girl who had managed all the deliveries from Maria's bakery for the last six years – eyed her newest assistant with envy as she unloaded the two heavy crates from the boat. With her spindly, tattooed arms and slender body, Marta was half Fatima's size and at least twice as fit as her superior, showing no signs of fatigue or discomfort at the backbreaking work. In fact, Marta had been oddly wired all morning, full of nervous energy, while Fatima and their other colleague, Helen, yawned and dozed their way through the uncomfortable, pre-dawn boat ride.

'How much coffee have you had?' Helen had asked her, after they loaded up. 'You do realize it's still only four in the morning.'

'I'm excited to see the island,' Marta replied shyly. She wasn't much of a talker either. 'And the convent. This is all still new to me. We have nothing like this in Patras.'

Helen had scoffed at the idea that anyone could find remote, sleepy Sikinos 'exciting', still less that they might look forward to a backbreaking slog up a cliffside to deliver cakes to a bunch of God-bothering weirdoes in habits and veils. Fatima too found it odd that a city girl like Marta would come all the way to these tiny islands to find work. Although, God knew, times were hard in Greece. Many people traveled many miles these days simply to be able to feed themselves, and city rents were notoriously expensive. At least here on Folegandros one could live on very little.

Now Helen and Fatima carried the heavier crate between the two of them, each resting a corner on one shoulder, while Marta carried the lighter pallet alone as the three women began the long climb from the beach up to the convent walls.

Ella barely felt the weight of the box in her arms as she made her way up the steep steps. All that physical training at Camp Hope had paid off, although in truth at least half of Ella's superhuman strength this morning had to be coming from adrenaline. In an hour, or perhaps only in minutes, she might be coming face to face with Athena Petridis. With the woman who had killed her parents and stolen her childhood. Twenty years of waiting in vain, of not knowing, of feeling different and useless and abandoned and impaired – that might all end today. This morning. The dawn sun rising deep red on the eastern horizon, bleeding its color into the pale blue sky, looked more beautiful to Ella than any she had ever seen. It was rising for her, spurring her on, willing her to succeed, to fulfill her destiny—

'*Ella. Can you hear me?*'

Ella stopped dead. Setting down her box, she put her hands on her temples.

The last time she'd heard Gabriel's voice in her head like this had been on her first 'date' with Makis, the day she'd almost blown her entire cover by blurting out nonsense. Back then she'd been furious that Gabriel was second-guessing her. But today it was a relief to hear his signal, quiet but clear. Just to know he was out there. As long as he didn't start trying to tell her what to do . . .

'Jesus, Marta! Be careful,' Fatima snapped, exhaustion making her sharper than usual as she and Helen almost knocked into her. Ella might be finding the climb easy, but the other girls' labored breathing and flushed faces were a testament to their effort and exertion.

'Sorry,' mumbled Ella, looking around for any signs that Gabriel might be close by. 'You two go ahead of me. I need a minute.'

'Finally, Superwoman needs a break!' Helen panted to Fatima, as the two of them moved slowly up ahead. 'Perhaps we two old tortoises are going to win this race after all.'

'Old tortoises?' Fatima grinned. 'Speak for yourself!'

Ella waited for Gabriel to speak again. As before, she assumed he was using one of the small fishing boats on the horizon as a transmitter. There seemed to be no other signs of life.

'Don't alert the others,' he said, once Helen and Fatima were a good fifty yards ahead. 'But if you're receiving this, raise your hands.'

Ella did as he asked, albeit a little grudgingly. As if she would alert the others!

'Good. I just wanted you to know you're not alone. We have eyes on you right now. But once you're inside the convent walls we'll lose that visual. So please listen carefully now. You already know the parameters of your mission . . .'

*Exactly. So why the mansplaining?* thought Ella, picking up her basket and resuming the climb, her irritation building.

'Try very hard to take a mental snapshot of Sister Elena. You may only have a few seconds but we need a clear picture, transmittable quality.'

*Ten more seconds of this and I'll start tuning him out,* thought Ella, her initial relief at having 'backup' rapidly fading. The fact was, Gabriel couldn't do 'backup'. He had to push his way to the front. Always.

'The most important thing to remember is, whether you positively ID Athena or not, you need to get out of there with the other girls when they leave. No lingering. No heroics. OK?'

Ella kept walking.

'Ella, if you can hear me, raise your hands again.'

She ignored him. A few seconds passed.

'Ella!' His volume crept up as loud as the frequency would allow. 'I know damn well you can hear me. Do you understand the instructions?'

Fatima and Helen were trudging up the final flight of steps, their backs still turned towards Ella. Setting down her crate for a final turn, Ella spun around and extended her middle finger in the general direction of the fishing boat.

'ELLA!' Gabriel roared, so loudly that Ella's brain started to whistle. Counting backwards from ten as Dix had taught her, she successfully turned him down, then off. *I'm getting better at this*, she thought delightedly, following the others up to the heavy iron gate set into almost three-foot-thick stone walls.

'There you are,' panted Fatima. Pausing to catch her breath, she rapped three times on the gate. Moments later, a stooped crone of a nun opened it for them. Without a backward glance, or another thought about Gabriel, Ella slipped inside the fortress and was gone.

'What do you think, Marta?' Fatima asked, noticing Ella's fascinated, roving eyes and feeling more conversational now that she'd finally set down her heavy basket of breads. 'Pretty stunning, isn't it? Is it what you expected?'

'I don't know what I expected,' Ella answered truthfully,

gazing up at the mullioned windows set high in the towering walls of the convent kitchens.

Inside, the Convent of the Sacred Heart felt more like a castle, a fortress of some sort, than a place of worship. The scale of the place was breathtaking, far more so than one might imagine from the outside. Every room, even the kitchens where the girls were now unpacking, seemed to have twenty-foot ceilings, and the long stone corridors that had led them here snaked off into the distance for what felt like miles. Every twenty feet or so, spiral staircases, like something out of a storybook, rose up and up on the right and left into soaring, turreted towers. Presumably there must be some smaller rooms on the upper floors, at the top of these stairs, for the nuns' cells or other private chambers. But the ground floor, with all the communal rooms, was uniformly palatial, and seemed all the bigger thanks to an almost total lack of furniture or adornments of any kind. No rugs were on the floors, and no paintings, not even religious ones, hung on the walls. In the distance, the soft echo of morning matins being sung added to the overall sense of serenity and peace, as did the scent of incense that hung, albeit faintly, in the air of every room they entered. Even the kitchens, although here it mingled with other smells: Freshly picked tomatoes and basil from the gardens; fried onions, perhaps from last night's meal; some sort of smoked fish.

Two nuns in full habit glided silently around the room, fetching plates and cups and tableware, presumably in preparation for the feast day breakfast. They smiled briefly at the three women from the bakery, but otherwise ignored them, going about their business and letting Fatima and her helpers do the same. Ella unpacked her loaves, using any respite to practice taking mental photographs of the two sisters. Dix had made it sound so easy back at Camp

Hope. *'Just use your eyelids as shutters, mentally focus, and blink.'* But in the real world, all sorts of conflicting stimuli ended up blocking or blurring the picture. Besides which, it wasn't that easy to stand stock-still and stare at someone, blinking furiously, without them noticing.

'What's wrong with you?' Fatima whispered in Ella's ear, grabbing a loaf out of her hand and nudging her hard in the ribs. *So much for that shot.* 'Something in your eyes?'

'Just dust I think,' muttered Ella, returning her attention to unpacking and waiting for a suitable moment to slip away and track down Sister Elena. She would head in the direction of the music, which presumably must be coming from the chapel. Fatima, who'd been here many times before, clearly knew her way around the various cupboards and began arranging the madeleines and simple pastries onto long, wooden trays. Helen followed her lead. While both were engrossed, Ella quietly picked up a stack of plates from the cupboard that the two nuns had just opened and followed the sisters out of the room. If anybody challenged her she would say she was helping set up for breakfast and lost her way.

The refectory was down a passageway to the left of the kitchens. Ella remembered passing it on their way, as she'd followed Helen and Fatima. The singing from the chapel came from the opposite direction. Heading right, Ella hurried towards the sound, sticking close to the walls and looking down so as not to attract attention, clinging on to her stack of plates like a shield.

The music grew louder, a hypnotic Gregorian chant comprised of upwards of a hundred female voices. *'Benedictus, Dominus, Deus Israel . . .'* Did one of those angel voices belong to Athena Petridis? To the devil woman whose husband had murdered both of Ella's parents, one of them in front of Athena's eyes? Ella moved towards the sound like a moth to the moon, her heart hammering in her chest.

How would she find Sister Elena, among all the identically robed nuns? And if she did, and Elena *was* Athena, would Ella recognize her? All of the photographs Ella had been shown of Athena Petridis were at least fifteen years old.

Gabriel's words came back to her. '*Whether you positively ID Athena or not . . .*'

'Not' was a possibility, whether Ella liked it or not. She might fail. If she did, all of her training, her time with Makis, her carefully constructed covers as Persephone and now Marta would be for noth—

'No!'

Out of nowhere a man – strikingly tall, dark-skinned, and as out of place in this tranquil, all-female setting as a grizzly bear at a wedding – came staggering out of a side door and crashed straight into Ella. As broad and strong as a boxer, his weight instantly knocked her off her feet. With a gasp of horror, Ella watched in slow motion as the clay plates were knocked out of her hands and fell to the floor, shattering into a thousand pieces, before she too landed on the hard ground. The pain was bearable, she'd just have bruises tomorrow, but the noise was deafening, a cacophony to wake the dead. Within seconds, four or five sisters had come running, all of them looking at the bakery girl with curiosity and confusion as she staggered to her feet.

*So much for keeping to the shadows*, thought Ella miserably. She could hardly have drawn more attention to herself if she'd climbed up onto the altar and started tap-dancing to 'Singin' in the Rain'.

The man who had hit her seemed barely to notice the commotion, however. As he turned briefly to check that

Ella was OK, she noticed that his face was desolate and streaked with tears. He mumbled something that might have been 'sorry', and continued on his way, stumbling towards one of the spiral staircases a few feet down.

'Are you all right?' A gray-haired priest suddenly appeared on the scene. The sisters around Ella immediately stepped back, parting like the Red Sea to make a path for him. 'I'm Father Benjamin.' He had a neatly clipped mustache and a kind face, and looked strangely out of place in his priest's robes, as if he would have been more suited to civilian clothes. 'You look like you twisted your ankle on the way down. May I take a look?'

Ella nodded as he gingerly felt the muscles around her left foot.

'It doesn't look too bad.'

'It's fine. I'm fine, really. I banged my arm a little, that's all.'

An older nun with an air of quiet authority came up and laid a comforting hand on Ella's shoulder. 'It's all right, Father,' she told the priest. 'I'll see to the young lady. You're from Maria's bakery, aren't you?' she asked Ella, as Father Benjamin bowed his head and took his leave.

Ella nodded silently, still in shock, staring after the man who'd knocked her down while the nuns who'd stepped aside for the priest got back to work, calmly cleaning up the mess at Ella's feet.

*There's something familiar about him*, Ella thought. But try as she might, she couldn't seem to retrieve the memory.

'Don't look so worried my dear,' said the older nun. 'It's only a few plates. We have plenty more where those came from. I'm more worried about your bruises. Father Benjamin seemed to think your ankle was all right, but I'd like to see your arm.'

'Honestly, there's no need,' pleaded Ella.

'Marta!' Fatima's voice rang out down the passage. She sounded a lot less sympathetic than the nun. 'What on earth are you *doing* out here?'

'It was just an accident,' the nun began.

'I am *so* sorry, Mother Superior,' Fatima said, glaring at Ella.

'Please, don't apologize,' said the nun, a beatific smile on her strangely bird-like face. 'And you must call me Magdalena. The young lady was only trying to help, setting up our breakfast table. It wasn't her fault the plates fell.'

'Yes, well. Please clean up and then get back to the kitchens, Marta,' Fatima shot Ella a look that clearly indicated she would have liked to say more but was holding back due to present company. 'I know Mother Magdalena appreciates your help, but we're leaving shortly. We still have a full day ahead of us back at the bakery.'

'Yes, Fatima.' Ella nodded dutifully. Once Fatima left, she turned back to the Mother Superior. The two of them were alone in the corridor now, the other nuns having disposed of the broken crockery and then retreated into the shadows as if nothing had ever happened. 'Who was that man?'

'A troubled soul,' Mother Magdalena answered with a sigh. 'Deeply troubled, I'm afraid.'

'What's he doing here?'

'He's come to talk to Sister Elena.'

The name shot through Ella's body like an electrical charge.

'Sister Elena?'

'One of our most blessed, cherished sisters,' Mother Magdalena positively glowed when she spoke of her. 'She has a gift for healing the sick of heart. That poor man lost his family. He's been without hope.' Reaching out, the older woman touched Ella's face compassionately. 'You also look troubled, my dear, if you don't mind my saying so. Perhaps Sister Elena could help you too?'

'Oh . . . I don't know about that,' said Ella, flustered.

She wasn't supposed to confront the target directly. Nikkos had been unusually insistent on that point. But she was supposed to ID her from a safe distance, and take a mental photograph if at all possible. This might be her only chance. Fatima had just said she wanted to leave soon, and Gabriel had made it crystal clear that Ella's future with The Group would be in jeopardy if she wasn't on that boat with the others.

'You know that you and your colleagues are welcome to stay here and pray with us today, or for as long as you'd like,' Mother Magdelena said, sensing the girl's hesitation.

'Thank you,' said Ella. 'But I think the others are eager to get back to the bakery. The feast day's busy for us on Folegandros too.'

'Well,' the Mother Superior smiled. 'Perhaps another time, then. But I know it would be Sister Elena's honor to offer comfort, if she can.'

Nodding farewell to Ella, she wandered away, disappearing somewhere into the recesses of the convent like a ghost. Once again Ella was alone.

Mother Magdalena's words rang in her ears: *'That poor man lost his family.'*

*Just like me*, thought Ella. Was that what had made him seem familiar? Was there some look in his eyes, some unspoken connection that helped loss recognize loss; that made kindred spirits of the suffering?

Hurrying over to the spiral staircase, she began to climb.

Sister Elena's room was at the very top of the tower, set into the eaves of the turret roof. It was circular, and must have been small, although Ella could see almost nothing of the interior through the inch-wide crack in the door. It was only the low, growling sound of the man's voice and his intermittent sobs of anguish that let her know she'd found the right room. Pressing herself back against the stairwell wall, Ella listened.

They were speaking in English, not Greek, and it was a second language for both of them, although Sister Elena's fluency far exceeded the man's. Frustratingly, Ella could only make out every third or fourth word.

'Pain myself . . . lose . . . a child . . .' The woman was saying. 'Unknowable . . . only God . . .'

The man's responses were angry, sometimes incoherent. 'God? NO! . . . kill them . . . my family . . . I can't!'

Ella edged nearer, till she was right outside the door. What about 'a child'? She must hear more.

'Marta! Maaaar-taaaaa!'

*Goddamn it!* Below her, Fatima's raucous, irritated voice drifted up the staircase, ricocheting off the walls, making it even harder to hear. Clearly she and Helen were ready to leave and searching for Marta. *Already?*

'You can,' the woman's voice was saying, clearer now. 'God himself saw his only son die on the cross. I saw my son die. *Only* through suffering can we be redeemed, my son.'

'NO!' The man's voice was rising. 'You don't know—'

'I *do* know. I wear the face of suffering.'

'No, no!' And then, as clear as day, Ella heard a roar of pure rage followed by heavy feet pounding. *He's running at her! He's going to attack her!*

In panic, and not knowing what else to do, she kicked against the door. She'd expected it to be locked but instead it swung fully open, slamming hard against the inside wall. The man who'd run into her earlier turned and stared at her, the carving knife in his right hand still pressed murderously at Elena's throat. Then, without warning, he stepped back and suddenly sank to his knees, sobbing. Turning away from Ella, he gazed bewildered up at the nun, like a pilgrim looking reverently up at a statue, or a savage struck down in awe before an idol. But then Ella looked at the nun's face herself and she realized it wasn't awe on her would-be assassin's face. It was horror.

Like the other nuns at the Sacred Heart, Sister Elena wore a full habit, although hers came with an additional veil, almost like a Muslim hijab, so that only her eyes were visible. In the instant Ella walked in, however, she was pulling off this veil, yanking it upwards over her forehead and hair to reveal a face so grotesquely disfigured, it could hardly be described as human.

'*I wear the face of suffering.*' Ella gasped. Jesus Christ. She obviously meant it literally.

Apparently unperturbed, either by the knife-wielding maniac at her feet or by the bakery girl standing in the doorway, the disfigured sister looked from one to the other before focusing her attention wholly on Ella. Ella stared back, aware of the danger but unable to look away, like a cat mesmerized by the sun.

Was this creature Athena Petridis? This monster? This gargoyle? Surely it couldn't be . . .

Slowly, too slowly, Ella came back to her senses.

*Take a picture. You need to take a mental picture.*

She blinked, again and again, but for some reason the image wouldn't stabilize, wouldn't fix in her brain. *I'm focusing*, Ella thought desperately. *I'm doing what Dix told me. Why isn't this working?*

A crackle in Ella's skull became a voice. Gabriel's voice. In her confusion she must have somehow allowed his signal back in.

'*Ella. Where are you? They're looking for you, they're leaving. You must get out. Get out of there, NOW.*'

'Marta!' Fatima's voice was closer, more insistent, a sound from another world. 'Marta, for God's sake. We have to go!'

Ella blinked again, furiously, her eyes dry and apparently useless, just when she needed them most. Meanwhile, the disfigured nun made no attempt to cover herself and seemed every bit as fascinated by Ella's face as Ella was by hers. Was it Ella's youth and beauty that transfixed her? Or something else? Something more . . . personal?

She was cocking her head to one side, her eyes narrowed, like someone trying to figure out a puzzle. And that was when Ella saw it. *Those eyes!* Cat-like and dancing, the eyes that had hypnotized an entire generation of the world's most powerful men. The eyes Ella had first seen on the plane to Greece, staring out at her from Athena's file. Eyes that no fire could melt, and no surgeon's knife disfigure.

Ella's breath caught in her throat.

*It's her. It's definitely her.*

*It's Athena.*

The moment the thought came to her, she watched, horrified, as the nun's melted face contorted into a smile, at once gloating and repellent.

*She knows. She knows I know.*

Every fiber in Ella's being screamed at her to *do* something. To scream Athena's name out loud. To lunge at her and throttle the life from her evil body with her bare hands. But that smile and the burned skin and the unflinching gaze all combined to paralyze her in some awful way, freezing Ella to the spot in an agony of indecision and immobility.

'MARTA!!'

Fatima's voice broke the spell, but it was too late to act. Instead Ella turned and ran, out of the room, back down the stairs, so quickly she felt dizzy, then back towards the kitchens where Helen emerged and grabbed her, her chubby fingers closing around Ella's skinny arms with surprising firmness.

'Marta! Where the hell have you been?' Picking up an empty crate she shoved it into Ella's hands. 'Didn't you hear Fatima calling? She's been yelling the place down looking for you.'

'Sorry, I . . . I got lost,' stammered Ella.

'Well, lucky I found you because we were about to leave without you. Fatima's probably halfway down to the beach by now. The boat's waiting. Come on.'

In a trance, her mind racing, Ella followed Helen out of the convent, back through the iron gate, past the elderly nun, and down the steep steps they'd ascended less than an hour earlier. Since then the sun had risen fully in the sky and it dazzled now, its light blinding Ella and making her squint like a mole emerging from its burrow.

*I saw her. I saw Athena Petridis. And she saw me!*

She scanned the horizon for the boat she'd seen earlier, that she'd assumed was Gabriel's 'eyes on' her, but it was nowhere to be seen. Ella's heart sank.

*I saw her, but I didn't get the picture.*
*I failed.*

Would Gabriel believe her, without proof? Would any of them?

They had to. Ella must make them. Even without the precious mental picture, she could describe what she'd seen. The charred wreck of a woman. Those eyes. *The way she looked at me!*

She would describe the man too. The giant who'd sounded so threatening, yet whom Ella had found kneeling at the monster's feet, like a supplicant before a saint.

'There you are!' Fatima rolled her eyes at Ella, relieving her of the empty crate and tossing it into the boat before helping her and Helen aboard. 'We were starting to think you'd decided to stay for good. Take Holy Orders and be done with it.'

'Bless me, Sister Marta, for I have sinned!' giggled Helen.

Ella forced herself to laugh, slipping back into her cover character as she'd been trained to.

'I got distracted. Sorry.'

They pushed out to sea, the skipper pulling the cord on the low outboard engine as soon as they were far enough from the beach. Helen and Fatima leaned back against the cushions and closed their eyes, content to rest and let the new sun warm their tired faces. But Ella sat tense and watchful, looking back, her eyes still fixed on Sikinos. They'd barely passed the safety buoys that marked the edge of the bay when she saw it: a town car, dark and sleek and out of place on such a remote island, pulling up outside the convent. A priest stepped out of the driver's door and waved a rushed greeting to the nun on the gate, before a second sister emerged. Ella instantly recognized the second, burka-like veil. *It's her! It's Athena!*

She was carrying a small carry-on suitcase and what looked like a laptop bag. The priest opened the rear door for her and she disappeared into the car. Seconds later they drove away, the road taking them around the headland to the other side of the island.

Ella felt sick. *She's getting away. We're losing her!*

'Wait!' Her loud cry woke the others with a start. 'I forgot something. At the convent. We have to go back!'

'Not a chance,' said Fatima, refusing even to open her eyes.

'Please!' said Ella.

'What did you lose?' asked Helen, who felt sorry for Marta. For such a young girl she seemed awfully tense and stressed out a lot of the time. And she kept clutching her head, like she was in pain, or something was bothering

260

her. It crossed Helen's mind that she'd come to Folegandros to escape from something, or someone. No one was that skittish without a reason.

'My wallet,' said Ella, temporarily lost for inspiration. The town car had disappeared from sight completely now. She wondered how long it would take Sister Elena to board a boat and set sail. Not long, that was for sure.

'Don't worry,' Fatima responded languidly. 'The sisters aren't going to steal your money, Marta. Mother Magdalena will send it back to the bakery if we call and leave a message.'

'But . . .'

'I'll lend you cash if you need any before then,' Helen said kindly. 'But Fatima's right, we can't go back. We're late as it is, and Maria's all on her own back at the shop. Oooo – look at that!'

All three girls looked up. Directly above them, a Bell 525 Relentless, one of the slickest, most expensive private helicopters in the world, swooped gracefully upwards, hovering for a few seconds before taking off toward the mainland with an ear-splitting whirr of its blades.

'Whose do you think it is?' Helen asked breathlessly.

'No one from round here, that's for sure,' observed Fatima. 'Probably some Russian oligarch whose pilot got lost looking for Corfu.'

Ella said nothing. Instead she let her heart sink in silence as the helicopter disappeared from view, swallowed by the limitless blue Greek sky.

'I was right there. Right in front of her!'

Ella's exasperation crackled down the phone line like static.

Gabriel leaned back in his chair in the first-class American Airlines lounge at Charles de Gaulle Airport, listening to

261

Ella's report with increasing alarm. The profound relief he'd felt earlier this morning, when she'd managed to leave Sikinos safely, had swiftly been replaced by a new, graver set of worries.

'It's a pity you never got that picture,' he observed.

'Screw the picture,' snapped Ella, anger hiding her own crushing disappointment. 'It's a pity I didn't kill her. I should have. While I had the chance.'

'What chance?' To Ella's fury, Gabriel sounded mildly amused. 'How were you planning on dispatching her, exactly?'

'*How?* I don't know *how!* What does it matter *how?*' Ella's furious tone strongly suggested that Gabriel might well be her next target.

'You just told me there was a large Arab man in the room with her,' said Gabriel. 'You don't think that between them, they might have overpowered an unarmed, one-hundred-pound woman?'

'Well whose fault is it I was unarmed?' Ella shot back. '"Don't worry, Ella," you said. "We're all cogs in a wheel . . . You just get out of there so the experts can go in and finish the job." Well, guess what? The "experts" are going to be too late, because she's *gone!* And now we have *no idea* where she is.'

Gabriel sighed. It struck him how much easier it was communicating with Ella via brain-transmission, when she couldn't talk back, than it was over the phone. Arguing with the woman was like trying to wrangle live eels in a tub full of olive oil.

'We don't know for sure that she's gone.'

'Are you not listening to me?' Ella ranted. 'I told you, I saw her take off in one of those high-tech, modern choppers, that sure as shit wasn't owned by some priest. They flew right over us!'

'You saw a chopper,' said Gabriel. 'Not who was inside.'

'Now you're just being ridiculous.'

'Am I? You said yourself the "nun" was wearing a burka-like habit.'

'Yeah! Like Sister Elena's!' Ella seethed. 'Why is it so hard for you to admit that you screwed up. It *was* Athena and we lost her. Now I'll have to resurrect Persephone Hamlin and go back to Makis until I can get a new lead.'

Gabriel sat bolt upright as if he'd just been electrocuted.

'You cannot go back to Makis Alexiadis. Not now, not ever. Do you understand?'

'No. I don't,' Ella said bluntly. 'Correct me if I'm wrong, but right now Mak is our only live lead, our only link to Athena. That's what *you* told me, remember? And he trusts me.'

'It's out of the question,' Gabriel said, his fear playing out as arrogance.

'I can handle him,' said Ella.

'It's not feasible. Persephone Hamlin has been retired as a cover persona.'

'So un-retire her,' said Ella.

'No.'

A tense silence descended.

Ella broke it first, and not in the way that Gabriel had expected.

'You know I think I recognized him.'

'Who?' he asked warily.

'The man. The giant. In Sister Elena's cell. I can't place him yet but I just . . . I know I've seen him before somewhere.'

'OK,' said Gabriel, his unease increasing. 'Well if anything comes back to you—'

'It was really strange.' Ella cut him off. 'He was threatening her. He had a knife. I'm sure he'd come to the convent for the same reason I did. He knew who she was. He intended to kill her. But then something happened. Something changed his mind.' She was thinking aloud, talking more to herself than to Gabriel. 'Maybe it was me?' The awful possibility dawned on her. 'Maybe if I hadn't walked in, he'd have finished the job? Maybe I did more than just let her get away. Maybe I *saved* her!'

'Stop,' said Gabriel. 'Those are way too many *maybes*. You don't even know who he was; you can't speculate about his motives.'

'Yes, but—'

'Look, Ella, this was your first mission. It would have been nice to get the picture, but you were under immense pressure. Nonetheless, the intelligence you've provided is valuable and you can rest assured we'll act on it. If you're correct that Elena was Athena, and if you're correct that she escaped—'

'*If?*' Ella spluttered indignantly. 'There is no "if"!'

Looking out of the tiny window in the bedroom of 'Marta's' rented cottage, she watched as a pair of mangy-looking chickens chased each other across a dusty lane, squawking and pecking at one another out of hunger or boredom or both. *I know how they feel*, Ella thought. This island was starting to depress her, but not as much as Gabriel's attitude. This was exactly what she'd feared. That, without the mental picture, the 'proof' that only her special abilities could provide, he wouldn't believe she'd found Athena. It was infuriating, the way he blew hot and cold. One minute he trusted her: '*Only you can do this for us, Ella. You're our secret weapon.*' And the next she was some inexperienced little girl, 'cracking' under pressure. Well she'd had enough of trying to please him, of watching him twist the evidence she presented to get the answers he wanted, even when those answers were just plain wrong.

'I want to talk to Nikkos,' she said curtly. 'He trusts my judgment, even if you don't. He also knows Makis Alexiadis is our only hope of ever finding Athena again.'

Gabriel cleared his throat. 'Ella, I'm sorry to have to tell you this. I meant to say something earlier, but I needed to understand what happened today at the convent and I—'

'Tell me what?' Ella interrupted.

The silence, laden with dread, seemed to go on forever.

Then Gabriel said quietly, 'I'm afraid Nikkos Anastas is dead.'

Ten minutes later, her call with Gabriel over, Ella walked down the creaky cottage stairs and out into the lane. The chickens had gone, and so had their owner, a stooped old farmer ironically named Herakles, who usually pottered around outside her cottage until sunset. All was peace on Folegandros. But, in Ella's heart, war raged.

*Nikkos*. Dear, sweet, incorrigible Nikkos. According to Gabriel he had been tortured before he died, his fat body burned and beaten, the bones of his kind face crushed, his fingers snapped like twigs. Gabriel claimed not to know who was responsible.

'We'll find out, believe me,' he promised Ella. 'But until we do, we must assume it's at least possible that Makis Alexiadis was involved.'

Ella thought about Mak. About his hand, covering hers at dinner. About the hungry hardness of his body, his easy humor, his flirtatious smile. And her own flirtatious smiles back. She'd told herself she was merely playing a role, doing what she'd been trained to do, doing her part to avenge her parents' deaths. But deep down, she knew a part of her had wanted Makis Alexiadis. Liked him, even.

*Mak can't have killed Nikkos. It can't be him. It mustn't be him.*

'Whoever was following "Persephone" was probably doing so at Alexiadis's request. If that person saw you and Nikkos together . . .'

'No. They wouldn't have,' Ella insisted. 'We were careful . . .'

Gabriel could hear the pain in her voice. But she had to face reality.

'You must listen to me, Ella. Nikkos's death means that your identity may well have been compromised. The whole Petridis mission may have to be aborted, or at least put on hold until we know more. But you *cannot* return to Makis. Not now. Not ever.'

Ella was silent.

'You know that the last thing Nikkos would have wanted would be to put *you* in unnecessary danger,' said Gabriel. 'He was very fond of you.'

*And I of him.* Although it struck Ella that the *last* thing Nikkos actually would have wanted was to escape the clutches of the murderous sadists torturing him to death. The thugs who had taken it on themselves to execute an innocent and brave man. To snuff out his big, happy, irrepressible spirit.

Whoever was responsible would rot in hell. Just as soon as Ella Praeger found them and sent them there.

'You must return to Athens tomorrow,' Gabriel informed her. 'A new passport and papers will be waiting for you, along with all your reservations. You're on a flight to JFK first thing Sunday morning. Someone will contact you on Monday in New York about next steps. OK?'

Ella assented to everything. *Yes. Yes. Yes.* It was pointless to argue with Gabriel once he was in order-giving mode, and the news about poor Nikkos had knocked the last vestiges of fight right out of her.

'I'm sorry about Nikkos, Ella. And we will follow up on the intel you provided today. Trust us.'

Walking along the lane, Ella replayed Gabriel's words in her head, trying to make them sound less empty.

'*Sorry.*'

What use was 'sorry' to anyone? Poor Nikkos didn't need The Group's pity. He needed justice. Vengeance. Just like all the other anguished souls whose lives had been ended, or ruined, terrorized by Athena Petridis and her wicked acolytes.

*Like my mother.*

*Like me.*

She had recognized Athena Petridis today. Gazed directly into the eyes of the monster. But that wasn't even the most frightening part.

The most frightening part was the one thing Ella hadn't told Gabriel: The monster had recognized her, too. Or at least something about her. Just as Ella had felt a strange familiarity with the huge man at Athena's feet, so she was sure that the look in Athena's eyes when she studied Ella's face was one of recognition.

*We're connected, Athena and I.*

*There's something between us.*

Until Ella found out what that something was, she knew she could never let go. Not for Gabriel. Not for anyone.

Mark Redmayne was on the NordicTrack in his home gymnasium when Gabriel's text came through.

'E returning to Athens, as requested.'

Turning off the machine, Mark Redmayne wiped the sweat from his brow and hands and tapped out a reply:

'E believes Mission P suspended?'

There was a few seconds pause, then: 'Yes.'

*Good*, thought Mark, hanging up.

Nikkos Anastas's death was unfortunate, as was the snafu with the 'giant' Ella encountered at the convent, and Athena

Petridis slipping through their fingers – for now. But one couldn't control everything. These were irritations, not disasters. And Ella Praeger knew no more now than she had at the start.

He thought briefly about Ella's mother, Rachel. How passionate she'd been, how beautiful, but also how stubborn. Fatally so, as it turned out.

Ella was too valuable an asset for them to lose. On that point, at least, Mark Redmayne and Gabriel agreed.

With the damage contained, he filed it to the back of his mind.

Switching his machine back on, Redmayne started to run.

Makis Alexiadis gazed up at the sunset, bleeding into an azure Italian sky. Lying next to him on the top deck of his yacht, *Argo*, a stunning nineteen-year-old Victoria's Secret model lay sprawled out, topless. Jenna, her name was. Or was it Jenny? Either way, her body was as close to female perfection as one was likely to see on this earth. Yet Makis felt as little desire for her as if she were an overweight, middle-aged housewife from Ohio. Persephone had ruined him, stunted his libido like someone pouring poison into the roots of a once vigorous plant.

The fact that she had run from him was bad enough, after weeks of leading him on and turning him into a horny teenager. But that she had *succeeded* in making her escape, eluding every spy he sent after her? That was the kicker. The bitch might as well have castrated him with her bare hands.

Miriam Dabiri was due to join him tomorrow, once they reached Portofino. If nothing else, Miriam was a more skillful lover than the lingerie model, who seemed to believe that by removing her clothes she'd already amply fulfilled her part of the lovemaking bargain. But even the prospect of Miriam's expert ministrations couldn't completely banish the cloud that hung over Makis. *I must get this woman out of my head.*

A buzzing on his private cell distracted him. It was too bright to see the caller ID on the screen, but on a whim he picked up anyway.

'This is Makis.'

'It's me.'

In two words, Persephone's voice did more to turn him on than Jenna's naked body had been able to in two weeks.

'I'm sorry I've been AWOL. Things have been really stressful with Nick.'

'That's OK,' Mak heard himself saying. 'Where are you?'

'On my way back to Athens. Where are you?'

'Italy. On the yacht.' His voice was so hoarse with desire, it was hard to speak.

There was a pause, and then with a coy hesitance that made his heart do cartwheels, Makis heard her say:

'If it's not too late . . . I'd really like to join you.'

# CHAPTER EIGHTEEN

Vera Pridden, Peter Hambrecht's housekeeper at Windlesham Grange, stripped the bed linen as quickly as she could and put fresh Egyptian cotton sheets on the guest bed. Mr Hambrecht's guest, the poor lady with the burns, would be back from her morning walk shortly, and Mr Hambrecht had given Vera strict instructions to stay out of her way.

'She's a very old friend, and she's come to Windlesham to recuperate after an accident. She needs peace and rest and – above all – privacy. But I know I can trust you with all of that, Mrs Pridden,' Vera's boss had added flatteringly.

'Of course, Mr H.'

Vera Pridden loved working for Mr Hambrecht. She felt important, being the trusted servant of such a great man and important conductor, not to mention the gatekeeper to one of the most beautiful small estates in the Cotswolds. Peter and his guests only used the house at weekends and for occasional summer parties. The rest of the time the idyllic Elizabethan manor house with its wisteria-clad walls, breathtaking gardens and extensive grounds, including thirty acres of ancient woodland and a pretty stream where

270

the burned lady liked to walk, was a private kingdom for Vera and her husband, Albert. Nestled in the dip of a valley, and at the end of a long driveway, completely invisible from the road, the manor house cast a protective shadow over the neighboring gamekeeper's cottage, where the Priddens lived. Windlesham lifted Vera Pridden's heart and spirits every day, rain or shine. She had no doubt it would do the same for Mr H's friend, whoever she was.

Athena waited for the dumpy housekeeper with her tight curls to disappear back into her cottage before emerging from the woodland path and making her way back across the lawn to the house.

She'd always loved early mornings at the convent – the cool air, the smell of warm bread and coffee from the kitchens mingling with incense from the chapel, where Matins marked the start of every new day. But they were just as beautiful here, albeit in a different way. Cooing wood pigeons, mist and wood smoke – those were God's harbingers of dawn in the English countryside.

*God!* Athena laughed at herself. *Would you listen to me?*

Shedding Sister Elena's habit after twelve long years had been no easy feat. Years of dawn wakings had reset her body clock profoundly, and she could no longer sleep past four thirty in the morning, or stay awake later than ten. The God that Athena had stopped believing in the day Apollo died had also managed to worm his insidious way into her thoughts and words and utterances, the natural consequence of long and tedious repetition.

*God be with you.*

*And also with you.*

Wearing civilian clothes again felt simultaneously liberating and strange. Peter had kindly provided a few simple items from Marks & Spencer for her to wear around the estate at Windlesham, including a pair of wellington boots and a hooded parka raincoat, despite it being late August.

'Mrs Pridden can return anything that doesn't fit or that you don't like,' he'd assured her, in a typically thoughtful handwritten note. 'It's not high fashion, I'm afraid, but I guessed you'd prefer comfort, at least while you're here.'

Dear Peter. He hadn't changed. Time might have withered his once smooth, handsome face, but it had had no impact on his kindness, loyalty or discretion. He'd respected Athena's wishes for them not to meet in person, never even asking her where she'd been since the helicopter crash, or why she'd suddenly decided to rise like a Phoenix from the ashes of her assumed death. He knew, instinctively, that she would talk when – if – she was ready. He had even gone so far as to remove all photographs of himself, and her, from the manor – his own home.

'The pictures remind me too much of him,' Athena explained when they spoke on the telephone, her voice as laden with pain as it had been all those years ago. 'Being in England will be hard enough. I hope you understand?'

'Of course,' said Peter. 'Stay as long as you need or want. No one will disturb you there.'

Stepping back into the kitchen, a wonderfully warm, English room with a bright red Aga, flagstone floors, and prints of Irish wolfhounds all over the walls, Athena made herself a mug of coffee, and flipped open her laptop computer. She'd had numerous offers of 'bolt-holes', places she could stay and regroup once she'd decided to leave the convent. Konstantinos Papadakis, an old friend who had been Spyros's best man, had prepared his ultra-private villa in Corsica to be at her disposal. Darling Konsta. She'd seriously considered it, but ultimately she'd decided she needed to be further away from Greece and the forces ranged against her. Besides which, all of Spyros's old friends would be under suspicion, once people realized she was not only alive, but once again at large.

Peter was part of another life. Before Spyros. Before all of the madness. Before Apollo, even – although that Peter and that Athena were long gone now. For better or worse. *No one will look for me here*, Athena thought. More importantly, Peter Hambrecht was one of the very few men on earth that she knew, with certainty, she could trust. Unlike her so-called 'loyal' number two and Spyros's surrogate son, that turncoat snake-in-the-grass Makis.

*He wants me dead*, thought Athena. She'd suspected it before, but events on the morning she fled Sikinos had hardened her suspicion into bitter certainty. There was no way that the surprise visitor had found his way to the convent by accident. Someone from inside the Petridis organization must have leaked her whereabouts, no doubt hoping that the damaged soul would find her and do their dirty work for them. As for the 'village girl' who'd burst in on the two of them, the way she'd looked at 'Sister Elena' – that was more than just shock at her disfigurement. She'd been looking for something, searching Athena's ruined face for clues. The girl's own face had been unusual too, in a different way: searching, intelligent, but also hauntingly familiar. Athena still couldn't place what it was she remembered. But there'd been more to that young lady than met the eye.

Athena could no longer doubt that someone close to her had deliberately betrayed her. With only a handful of people aware of her existence, let alone her identity as Sister Elena, Makis Alexiadis was the obvious culprit.

On her computer, Instagram and Facebook images displayed Mak the businessman, his legitimate alter ego, living the high life on his yacht.

*Fiddling while our business burns*, she thought bitterly.

*Swanning around the Med while everything Spyros built, everything we gave you, crumbles to dust.*

If they didn't act soon, their rivals would establish a stranglehold grip on the Aegean migrant route, and a pipeline worth hundreds of millions of dollars would be lost. She would contact Makis today about this. Let him know, by default, that she'd escaped whatever grisly fate he'd had in store for her at the convent, and begun to reassert her authority.

Her hands twitched with frustration. After so long out of the game, so long in hiding and isolation, she yearned for action. A part of her longed simply to get rid of Makis. She fantasized about a world where he was dead, and she, Athena, could seamlessly take over the reins of the Petridis empire, resuming her role as head of the organization and Spyros's rightful heir. But that was a fantasy. Athena had her loyal supporters, to be sure. But the reality was, after twelve years in day-to-day command, Makis had henchmen of his own. Not everyone would welcome the return of Spyros's wife from the grave.

For the time being, Athena must keep her friends close and her enemies closer. She must approach Makis Alexiadis with both skill and caution, like a male spider perfecting its mating dance, hoping to get close enough to mount the female, but without the risk of being eaten afterwards.

*One step at a time.*

Closing her computer, she took out a pen and paper and began to write.

*She's got a nerve. My God, she's got a bloody nerve.*

Like a petulant child, Mak tore Athena's note into tiny pieces and scattered them over the side of the yacht.

Who the hell did she think she was, chastising him like a schoolboy for 'allowing' the migrant business to slip through his fingers? As if he controlled the tides and storms! As if he weren't already actively sabotaging his rivals' boats, bribing their skippers, and generally doing everything in his power to turn things around.

And meanwhile she, Athena, had inexplicably chosen this crucial moment to upset the apple cart. What did she think she was *doing*, having the Arab children's feet branded like that? Had she hoped that one of them would drown? That by hijacking this very public human tragedy, her coded message would make its way into the media in a suitably macabre fashion, announcing both her glorious return to the Petridis organization, and her willingness to maim and kill to secure her place at the top table?

If so, then her plan had been a resounding success. But at what cost? Thanks to Athena's flare for the dramatic gesture, Makis now had half the world's intelligence agencies sniffing around him, not to mention Interpol, making it exponentially harder to 'lock up' the migrant route, as she claimed to want him to. And she had the nerve to lecture him about neglecting 'our' business?

Mak had never warmed to Athena, even back when Spyros was alive. He was used to the old man patronizing him, and he accepted it, but his much younger wife's disdain was a different matter. Like every other red-blooded male, Mak had wanted Athena back then. He would have walked over hot coals to take her to bed, as he knew many other men did besides her husband. But the bitch had looked through him as if he didn't exist. Athena was only interested in powerful men.

Spyros seemed to tolerate his wife's infidelities with a sort of resigned regret, liberally mingled with adoration. As if Athena were a superior being, a superannuated sexual goddess who could no more be expected to remain faithful to one man than to go without food or water. For such a macho, controlling Greek, it was a strange attitude. But then all men changed the rules for Athena.

*Not any more*, Makis thought, with a warm, cruel glow of satisfaction. He hadn't seen her in person since the accident. Nobody had, except the nuns and priests who – as was proved on Sikinos – had obviously saved and protected her. (The Petridis family had done a lot for the Catholic Church over the years; enough to ensure that they repaid their debts.) But Mak knew that she was hideous now, her once legendary beauty utterly destroyed by the flames that had consumed Spyros, burning him alive. With the resources at her disposal, Athena could easily have undergone reconstructive surgery if she'd chosen to. But instead she had opted to keep her ravaged face, wearing it as a mask, perhaps, something to hide behind? Or as a penance for her many sins?

She wasn't stupid enough to agree to a face-to-face meeting with Makis now, and had deftly avoided all his requests for information on her whereabouts. 'It's safer for us all to keep our distance.' *Safer for you, you mean.* But eventually the time would come. She'd slipped through his fingers at Sikinos, which was irritating, and the person responsible would pay for that. But in the end she would make a misstep. And when she did, Mak would be waiting.

One of the yacht stewards approached him.

'Your drink is waiting for you in the study, sir. Would you prefer me to bring it out to you here?'

'No, John, thank you,' said Mak. 'I'm coming inside.'

Pushing thoughts of Athena out of his mind for now, Mak made his way to his study, a small but perfectly formed wood-paneled room crammed with prints of the great Greek shipping era and models of Aristotle Onassis's most famous yachts. Taking a sip of his perfectly prepared old-fashioned, he turned on his private cell and began skimming through pictures of Persephone Hamlin from earlier in the summer.

Instantly, he felt his mood lifting. What Athena had done to Spyros Petridis, himself a committed playboy when they met, Persephone had done to Makis. They hadn't even slept together yet. Had only once kissed! And yet the feelings he had for her, his need, his longing . . . He hesitated to call it love. But perhaps that was what it was? This strange compulsion to possess. This desperation to be near her.

Tomorrow night she would be here. In his arms. She had returned to him, not because of anything he had done, but of her own free will. Just the thought of it made his heart race and the hairs on his neck and forearms stand on end.

The irony was, she wasn't even classically beautiful. Not in the accepted, marketable way that a girl like Jenna was, or even Miriam or Arabella. Mesmerized by the pictures, he zoomed in on her quirky, off-kilter face with the wide-set eyes and the jutting cheekbones. She was standing on the shore of the tiny island he'd taken her to on their first 'date', when she'd cast her line so elegantly and he'd actually taken up the oars of a boat for her. She'd reminded him of somebody that day, although he never had figured out exactly who it was. *I was too intoxicated*, he reminisced, fondly. *The things that girl does to me. And she doesn't even have to try.*

At lunch, Makis joined the last of his guests for fresh poached lobster and salad. He enjoyed playing host on his beloved *Argo*, and typically had up to ten people staying on board at any one time, partaking of his hospitality, separate from whatever girls he brought on board for his own enjoyment. But with Persephone coming, he wanted rid of them all – the men as well as the women. He wanted to be free to make love to her everywhere – on deck, in the hot tub, the movie theater and in every bed. His guests would all be shuttled by speed-boat tender to Portofino tomorrow morning, and would have to continue their summer adventures from there.

'Great night last night, Mak.' Andrew Simon, a producer from LA and regular summer visitor to Mykonos, raised a glass to his host. 'Could you believe Jorge's girlfriend went home with that guy? The Englishman?'

Mak grinned. That had been a funny moment.

Jorge Colomar, a Spanish billionaire and mutual friend, had joined Mak's group at the restaurant last night, and afterwards at Covo di Nord-Est, where his young Venezuelan date had embarrassingly deserted him for a handsome English polo player half Jorge's age.

'I can believe it,' Andrew's wife, Carmen, piped up. 'The guy was so good looking.'

'Are you saying Jorge isn't?' Mak teased. Everyone knew that in his spare time Jorge Colomar lived under a bridge and ate billy goats.

'What was his name . . . William something,' said Carmen, who was still reminiscing about the polo hunk. 'Was it William Ponsonby?'

'No,' said Andrew. 'You're thinking of Rachel's husband. He's a Ponsonby. This guy was from another one of those old English families. *Coutts!*' It came to him suddenly. 'William Coutts, that was it. Like the bank. Although I doubt he's richer than Jorge.'

Everyone else at the table smiled and nodded their assent, but Mak had fallen deathly silent. All the blood had drained from his face suddenly, and his upper body froze, as though he was in some sort of trance.

Andrew Simon put a hand on his shoulder. 'Makis? Are you OK, man?'

But Mak didn't answer.

*William. Rachel.*

'*You're thinking of Rachel's husband.*'

He stood up abruptly. 'I'm sorry. I have to go.'

Back in the study, it took him thirty minutes to find the images, saved on a backup hard drive from fifteen years ago. But there he was: William Praeger, young and blond and preppily handsome, except for his oddly wide-set eyes. Next to him on one side was his wife, Rachel, a raving beauty with her flowing hair and high, sculpted cheekbones. And on the other side, also looking preposterously young, was that bastard Mark Redmayne.

*The Group.* That's what they used to call themselves. Spyros used to make fun of them in the beginning. No one took them seriously, a ragtag bunch of vigilantes, naïve American rich kids who thought they could succeed where the CIA and MI6 had failed. But Spyros had been wrong.

Staring transfixed at William and Rachel Praeger's faces, Mak realized he'd been wrong too. There could be no mistaking the resemblance.

Cameron McKinley had just finished playing squash when his phone rang.

'Yes?' he panted.

'Praeger. William and Rachel Praeger. I need you to find out everything you can about them.' Mak sounded tense. 'I've just sent you some pictures.'

'OK,' said Cameron. 'Am I looking for anything specific?'

'Yes. I need to know whether they ever had a daughter.'

# CHAPTER NINETEEN

It was already almost dusk when Ella arrived in Portofino. Lights twinkled in the harbor, and the pretty hillside town was bathed in the rich, early evening glow. A warm breeze still lingered in the air, the remnants of the blazing heat of a few hours earlier, and everything smelled of summer: the rich, cloying scent of jasmine mingling with coconut oil and perfume on the women's skin, and the pungent tang of garlic and truffles wafting out from various restaurant kitchens. Underneath it all, the familiar, salt-scent of the sea and the gentle, rhythmic swish of the waves completed the picture of the vacation idyll. This was a place to relax. To exhale. To allow one's senses free rein. To be without constraints.

But not for Ella. Stepping back into the role of Persephone Hamlin so suddenly had been jarring, to say the least. Resurrecting not just Persephone's voice and mannerisms, but her feelings – and in particular her complicated relationship with Mak – was a daunting prospect. And there was no room for error. But it had to be done. *I owe it to Nikkos. And my parents. And myself.* Gabriel had made it clear that the alternative was for Ella to return to the States empty-handed, with nothing concrete to show for any of this but poor Nikkos's death. Ella couldn't allow that.

Still, she wished she could have spent at least one night here in a hotel, going over Persephone's backstory for the hundredth time, easing herself back into the identity before she joined Makis on his yacht. As it was, his eagerness to see her meant he would brook no more delays. 'Call the second you arrive,' he instructed her. 'I'll send someone to come and pick you up in the tender right away.'

'Your check, Ms Hamlin. Can I get you anything else?'

An elderly waiter, with the sort of ancient face that looked as if it had been etched in stone, approached Ella's table. She'd chosen a café near the harbor so that she could tune in easily to transmissions between the various boats while she enjoyed a last meal of *branzino* on the safety of dry land. Once aboard the *Argo*, she would be trapped. Makis's prisoner, albeit a willing one.

'No, thank you. That was delicious.' She reached into her pocketbook for Persephone's credit card, praying suddenly that The Group hadn't already cancelled it. Luckily it seemed to go through the old man's little machine with no problems.

She'd already texted Mak and was expecting one of the *Argo*'s state-of-the-art speedboats to arrive in the harbor for her at any minute. She was to wait for them at jetty five. Pulling her suitcase along behind her, she rattled and rumbled over the creaky wooden boards of the pier, all the while focusing on isolating the *Argo*'s call signal from the rest of the deafening radio chatter in her head.

'*Argonaut II*, are you there yet?' she heard the yacht's skipper signal the tender.

'Almost,' came the reply. 'I think I can see her coming down the jetty.'

*Don't look up*, Ella reminded herself, fighting the urge

to search out the speedboat in the growing darkness. *Remember, Persephone can't hear them.*

Her heart hammered in her chest, powered by a familiar feeling of excitement mingled with fear. Tonight she would be on the yacht with Mak. Though nothing had been spelled out between them, she understood that the time for separate bedrooms had passed. That 'Persephone' was returning to him not as a friend, but as a lover.

Two uniformed men waved as a sleek, sky-blue Wajer 55 tender arrived at jetty 5, with the word *ARGONAUT II* embossed on the side in shiny black lettering.

'Ms Hamlin?' A young, handsome boat-hand climbed up to the jetty, reaching for Ella's bag.

Ella nodded.

'We saw you walking over from the harbor. Perfect timing.' He smiled, helping her down into the boat.

'Thank you for coming to get me,' said Ella.

The second man, who was older and more heavily set, introduced himself with a shake of his hairy, bear-like hand.

'It's our pleasure, ma'am. Mr Alexiadis is looking forward to welcoming you aboard the *Argo*. We're a little further out of the harbor than we'd hoped to be, but we should have you at the yacht in fifteen minutes. In the meantime, please just relax.'

*Relax.*

Sitting back on the rich velvet-cushioned bench, Ella smiled to herself.

The excitement of her new life was becoming addictive. She wondered if she would ever truly relax again.

The little boat took off with alarming speed. Both men remained at the helm while Ella sat at the back, a thick cashmere blanket covering her knees. Turning back, she watched the lights of Portofino harbor recede behind them, like stars in the wake of a warp-speeding *Millennium Falcon*. As they rounded the headland, the last lights to go were those of the sparkling Hotel Splendido Mare. And then there was nothing but open water, the pitch darkness softened only slightly by the light of a pale half-moon.

The roar of the speedboat's engine quickly faded out to become background noise, and the buzzing signals from the harbor traffic also quietened in Ella's brain into more of a low purr, like a contented cat about to fall asleep. In the relative peace, she was able to tune into the *Argo* much more clearly, her mind flipping through the various frequencies like songs on a jukebox, until she stumbled across Makis's own voice – low, gravelly and crystal clear. He was using a satellite phone of some sort, and from Ella's position on the boat the sound quality was perfect. Her stomach gave a little flip when she realized he was talking to Cameron McKinley, the fixer whose goons had followed her, and possibly Nikkos too, in Athens.

Mak's voice came first. '*You are certain?*'

Then Cameron's. '*Yes. The birth was listed in public records. There's been no attempt to conceal it as far as I can see. Praeger, Ella Jane. Born 28 May 1994, to Rachel, née Franklin, and William.*'

At the sound of her own name, Ella felt her stomach liquefy with fear.

There was a pause on the line, then Mak spoke again. '*The same age as Persephone . . .*' He sounded thoughtful. '*Any pictures?*'

'*Two. One from Paradise Valley High School Yearbook. Another from Berkeley. It appears Ms Praeger attended in 2012 as a computer science major.*'

This was bad. Very bad.

'*And?*' said Mak.

Ella couldn't breathe as she waited for Cameron's answer.

'*It's her. There's no question. It's the same girl.*'

A deafening silence followed. In the distance, Ella could make out the lights of the yacht where Makis was waiting for her. Where she would be trapped, helpless, with no hope of escape.

'*What would you like me to do?*' Cameron asked.

This time's Mak's answer was instant. His voice was resolute and his tone harder than Ella had ever heard it, every shred of his legendary warmth gone, squeezed out like pips from a crushed lemon.

'*Nothing. I'll take care of it.*'

'*Be careful, Makis. It would be safer – cleaner – if you kept some distance. Let my people handle this. It's what we do.*'

'*I said I'll take care of it!*' Makis snapped. '*We'll talk again in the morning. When it's done.*'

The line went dead.

For a moment, Ella froze, paralyzed with panic.

'*I'll take care of it.*'

'*When it's done.*'

*He's talking about me. About killing me. He wants to do it himself.*

She thought back to all the horror stories she'd read about Spyros Petridis and the ways in which he disposed of his enemies. Torture. Strangulation. Burying alive. Drowning.

*Like my mother.*

Mak had been Spyros's enforcer back then, the servant, learning his tradecraft at his master's feet. Now, he had enforcers of his own to do his dirty work, men like Cameron McKinley and his 'people'. They'd almost certainly killed Nikkos. '*It's what we do.*' But this was different. This was personal. 'Persephone' had betrayed Makis Alexiadis, made a fool of him. He must mete out her punishment himself, look her in the eyes as he hurt her, terrorized her, extinguished her life with his own bare hands . . .

Ella sat bolt upright, shaken suddenly from her trance. If she wanted to live she must act, and act now. But what could she do? No one knew where she was. She was unarmed, alone, and with no hope of rescue. The *Argo* was clearly visible up ahead of them, vast and impressive, looming like a great white death star from which there could be no escape. In less than two minutes they would reach it.

*I'm as good as dead.*

The boss was shouting. Screaming, in fact.

Gabriel held the phone away from his ears. He'd landed back in the States yesterday, exhausted and emotionally drained by the grim circumstances of Nikkos Anastas's murder and having to break the news to Ella. Everything in Greece was unraveling faster than ball of yarn tossed from a clifftop, and Gabriel couldn't shake the sinking feeling that worse was yet to come.

Checking into a cheap hotel near JFK, he'd taken a pill and slept solidly for fourteen hours. When he woke, it was to Mark Redmayne's borderline hysteria.

'She's gone!' he bellowed, as if shattering Gabriel's eardrums was going to solve the problem. 'Ella's gone. She gave the new handler the slip in Athens and she never showed up for her flight.'

'Shit,' muttered Gabriel.

'You lost her!' Redmayne roared. 'How the hell could you have lost her?'

'Sir?'

'You told me you'd convinced her the mission was aborted!' Redmayne boomed. 'That she was coming back here. You said it was sorted.'

'I thought it was.' Gabriel rubbed his eyes blearily. If Ella hadn't caught her flight to New York, there was only one place she was headed.

Redmayne was still incandescent, expletives firing off his tongue like bullets from a machine-gun, as if indiscriminate anger was going to help the situation. Not for the first time, Gabriel wondered how this man had ever risen to become head of The Group.

'Be quiet,' he said eventually and with characteristic bluntness, his need to think overriding everything else. 'We need to find her and get her out of there.'

'*Do you think I don't know that?*' Redmayne's decibel levels were reaching dangerous proportions. 'The question is, where the hell is she?'

'She's with Makis Alexiadis,' Gabriel answered instantly. 'We need to track down his yacht.'

Mak watched from the upper deck as the tender approached. He first made it out from almost a mile away, a mere speck of light flying over the tops of the waves like a skimming pebble. Inside him, he felt the monster start to grow.

It was a feeling he used to know well, but one that he rarely experienced nowadays. The excitement, quasi-sexual, of exerting the ultimate dominance over another human being. Since rising to such dizzy heights of power, the physical rush of killing was something he largely delegated to others. He hadn't missed it. In fact, it had been a relief to take a step back, to be able to conduct the operations of the Petridis empire as if it were any other business. These days, in middle age, Mak had the luxury of indulging in reflection, and introspection. If he'd never met Spyros, if his life had taken a different, more prosaic turn, might he never have killed at all? He did not, after all, consider himself innately violent, or criminal, or cruel. It was more that, like

286

a kitten watching its mother hunt mice, he had *learned* those skills – learned to trap, to terrorize, to kill, to devour – and he had also learned to develop the emotions that went with them. He wasn't a monster. But he did have a monster inside him. Over the years, his evil, abhorrent feelings had become entwined with all his other regulated emotions, so that he could no longer fully separate the normal from the abnormal, the acceptable from the psychotic.

Waiting for Persephone to arrive – he would always think of her as Persephone, right to the end – he felt both sickened and aroused. Angry and excited. Longing, yet full of a hatred so poisonous it threatened to burn through his skin like lava spewing through the cracked earth.

He let his mind roam ahead, picturing himself greeting her, touching her, seducing her and then, once he'd taken everything he wanted, everything she owed him, killing her, as slowly and painfully as he could. *Lying bitch.*

The *Argonaut II* was drawing nearer now. Mak could clearly see Ioannis and Evangelos, his crew members, at the helm. All he could make out of Persephone was a slumped figure at the back of the boat, wrapped in blankets against the cold. Soon she would be warm and naked in his bed. For the first and last time.

After what felt like an age they pulled up alongside the yacht.

'Finally,' Makis beamed, walking down the steps to the deck to greet them.

Ioannis tethered the tender while Evangelos walked to the stern to help Ms Hamlin up. When he turned around, he looked like a ghost, his face drained of color.

'What is it? What's the matter?' Makis demanded. Every sinew in his body had tightened like an overstrung violin. Jumping down into the boat himself, he pushed past both men.

287

Persephone's suitcase was propped against the bench. Next to it, a pile of cushions lay covered with Makis's monogrammed blankets.

'Where is she?' Mak growled menacingly.

'She . . . We picked her up at the harbor . . .' Evangelos stammered. 'She was sitting right there.'

'So?' Mak bellowed, the unsated monster roaring out in fury from within. 'WHERE . . . IS . . . SHE?'

At first the water felt like her enemy.

Slipping silently off the back of the boat into its dark embrace, the paralyzing cold knocked the breath from Ella's body. Her clothes coiled themselves around her like deadly snakes, encasing her, gluing her limbs to her sides, dragging her down. Waves that had seemed so shallow, so gentle from the safety of the boat, now loomed like monsters over her, crashing painfully over her head and robbing her of what little sense of orientation remained. She no longer knew up from down, still less which direction led back to shore and which to open water. While her heart raced in panic, the rest of her body and mind slowed, first to a crawl, and then to a total stop.

The speedboat had gone. Ella was alone in the world. Everything was darkness and cold.

And then, just as suddenly as it began, the panic left her. The painful aching of her frozen limbs switched off like a light – *gone*. Her body was numb, her mind and spirit calm, and her heart barely beating, its rhythm slowed to a barely discernible *boom, boom, boom*, as much of an echo or a memory as an actual sound.

*I'm drowning*, thought Ella. *And it's OK. It's peaceful. All I have to do is let go.*

Images stole into her brain, freeze-frames from a slow-playing home movie.

*Her mother, holding her, gazing into her eyes.* Ella was a baby, an infant. She felt safe and cocooned in her sea-swaddled limbs. The water and darkness surrounding her became a womb, and the soft *swoosh* of the tide her mother's heartbeat. For a moment, it was lovely. All Ella had to do was let go and she could live in that state forever. Returned to her mother. To Rachel. The idea was intoxicating. Wonderful.

Ella's lungs emptied. She began to sink, deeper and deeper into nothing, the beckoning abyss.

But then, unbidden, new images came.

Her mother again, but this time fighting for breath, for her life, struggling vainly against the strong, male arms that held her down.

Athena Petridis, standing on the shore, watching.

Gabriel, standing in her apartment in San Francisco, his handsome features turned witheringly towards Ella as he mocked her attempts to resist joining The Group. She could hear his voice now: *'That's not what I would call a life. But perhaps we have different standards?'*

After that, other voices and faces forced their way into her consciousness.

Nikkos, screaming as the hot metal burned into his flesh, pleading for his life.

The little boy washed up on the shore, sightless eyes staring upwards at the blue sky, pleading for justice. For vengeance.

*They all want vengeance. And I'm their weapon. I'm their avenging angel. If not me, then who?*

Ella's eyes snapped open.

*I can't let go. Not yet!*

She began to move, to kick. First her feet, then her lower legs, then her whole body, arms, neck, head, straining upwards. It was too dark to see the surface, to know how far it was, or whether she would make it or not. All she could do was try, to reach up blindly, clawing her way back to life and breath and all the pain that went with it . . .

'*Ahh!*' Her upper body shot out of the water like a breaching whale, or a submarine-launched missile. Gulping down air, her lungs filled painfully. It felt as if her chest might explode. She could picture her ribcage shattering, the bones flying left and right. All at once the cold was back, and the fear. A desperate alertness took over.

*Think, Ella. Don't panic. Think.*

She was a decent swimmer, but her chances of making it back to the shore from this distance and in these temperatures were nil. She needed rescuing.

Makis might already have boats out looking for her. She must avoid those at all costs. Better to drown than fall into his sadistic, murderous hands. Closing her eyes, she let herself float still for a moment as the waves calmed. Remembering the techniques Dix had taught her back at Camp Hope, she let her conscious mind switch off while she tuned herself into any surrounding signals.

At first all was quiet. But within a few minutes she was picking up shipping signals, both radio calls between different fishing boats and the coastguard or harbormaster, and the more sophisticated satellite communications from larger vessels. There was one, very faint signal from a lifeboat crew, doing their routine nightly check of waters where foolhardy teenagers sometimes attempted to paddleboard at night. But they were more than halfway back to Portofino, an impossible swim.

Then it came to her. Something else Dix had told her, back at Camp Hope, the day they first met. He'd been riffing about her visual capabilities and how far they might take her, beyond what even her parents had envisaged. Something to do with satellite technology . . .

*You could use satellite coordinates to navigate, for instance. To visualize vast areas of land or sea, or even space.*

Satellite coordinates. That was it! Like a GPS. If she could receive the boats' satellite signals, she could accurately work out which one was closest – theoretically at least. Where she was. Where they were. All she had to do was keep calm. Clear her mind. Let the data flow into her, like the lapping waves. Let the map appear, like a vision of stars in the night sky. She could save herself. But she had to believe it. Believe in her powers. Believe in her gifts. Believe she would survive.

*Do you, Ella?* A voice from inside her seemed to be asking, as the cold salt water splashed her face. *Do you believe?*

She closed her eyes and let the magic begin. It wasn't one sense but all five, mingled inexplicably into an explosion of stimuli, a beautiful web of data, its myriad threads all pulling Ella towards hope, towards rescue. Lights at first, pinpricks in the darkness. Then numbers. Coordinates. Patterns, flying at her like shooting stars. Sounds too: the rhythmic *whoosh* of the waves melded with Ella's heartbeat, and her breath, and the numbing cold that froze her limbs, yet somehow liberated a deeper energy within her, a deeper determination to live. To conquer. To win.

One light, red, brighter than the others, called her on.

*A boat. The closest boat. A chance.*

Turning towards it like a moth to the moon, commanding her paralyzed body back to life, Ella began to swim.

# CHAPTER TWENTY

Mark Redmayne turned the incline on his NordicTrack to the maximum fifteen and increased his pace. Hill running had become his therapy, and he found himself turning to his treadmill more and more, the burning of lactic acid in his thighs and the painful constriction in his lungs providing a welcome distraction from his growing anxiety. Things in Europe were spinning out of his control at an alarming rate, and for once Mark Redmayne was unsure what to do about it.

Nikkos Anastas's death had been unfortunate. Losing Ella Praeger was potentially catastrophic, although he still hoped to rectify that situation sooner rather than later. And today he found himself dealing with the fallout following Noriko Adachi's unfortunate death in London, at the hands of one of Athena Petridis's thugs.

Katherine MacAvoy, who usually wouldn't say boo to Redmayne's goose, had suddenly decided to take umbrage at the boss's tactics regarding the illustrious Japanese professor.

'You sent that poor woman to London as a lure,' MacAvoy had accused him on this morning's conference call, a call that had been joined by a large number of The Group's senior leadership. 'You threw her to the wolves!'

'Not at all,' Redmayne had replied coolly, keeping his head. 'Noriko was following up on a lead.'

'What lead?' demanded MacAvoy.

'A lead regarding Athena's potential operations in the UK and northern Europe,' Redmayne answered vaguely. 'And, as tragic as it was, Professor Adachi's death and the letter branding on her body have provided us with the clearest evidence yet that Athena has indeed taken back personal control of her criminal network from Big Mak, *and* that she's keeping tabs on everyone she considers a threat to her power. Including us.'

'And an innocent woman's life was worth that, was it?' Katherine MacAvoy's emotions were getting the better of her, unusually for the Camp Hope chief. 'Did she know she was being sent in as bait? As a canary into Athena Petridis's mine, which we all know is a black hole from which hardly anyone emerges alive?'

'As I said Katherine, Noriko was following up a lead.' A steely edge had crept into Redmayne's voice that was not lost on any of the call's participants. 'She volunteered to join us because she wanted to do something concrete to avenge her son's death. The woman was being eaten alive by grief when I met her. Trust me on that.'

*Grief which you exploited*, thought Katherine MacAvoy, but she said nothing further. She already knew she'd gone too far.

'I think Katherine's right to raise concerns though, sir.' Anthony Lyon, The Group's London chief of staff, piped up, his cut-glass British accent further fraying Redmayne's nerves. 'Professor Adachi's murder was particularly gruesome. We must do all we can to reduce this sort of collateral damage. Apart from the moral considerations, we now have the Metropolitan Police sniffing around our operations in London, which we could do without.'

*Moral considerations*, Redmayne thought bitterly, increasing his speed yet again. *Pompous prick*. At the end of the day, he and he alone led The Group, and he expected loyalty from his senior lieutenants. Even so, he recognized that Noriko Adachi's death was bad news, on a number of levels.

Athena Petridis must be stopped. That much was clearer than ever. But the currents swirling around her were as strong and as dangerous as ever, For all Mark Redmayne knew, Ella Praeger, The Group's most precious weapon, was out there being sucked down into the maelstrom right now, this very instant.

It didn't bear thinking about.

The first thing Ella saw was light. Not blinding, or constant, but low, flickering, a sort of warm glow that faded in and out, on and off, like the dying embers of a fire.

For a moment she wondered whether this was heaven. But then she heard his voice and realized categorically that it wasn't. If there was such a thing as an afterlife for the virtuous, there was no way on earth that *he* would be in it.

'Ella? Can you hear me? Ella!'

The touch of his hand made her start. So the voice wasn't in her head this time. He was actually here. With an effort she opened her eyes.

'*You.*'

'No need to sound so pleased to see me.'

Gabriel's face looked darker than she remembered it, more tanned, as if he'd just returned from a vacation. When he smiled, as he did now, he was still provokingly handsome. Christine Marshall's 'Ryan Gosling' comment floated back into Ella's mind.

*Camp Hope.*
*Christine.*
*Lunch with Gabriel at that adobe farmhouse down the coast.*

How long ago all that felt now.

'I'm not pleased to see you,' Ella said sullenly, turning her face away. She wasn't sure why she was angry with him. Some lingering distrust, perhaps, but mingled with other, deeper, more troublesome feelings that she didn't want to think about.

Looking around her she took in her surroundings. The bare white walls and clinical smell suggested she was in a hospital, although her wooden bed with its expensive linens said otherwise, as did the stunning vase of peonies propped on the small rococo table beside her bed. A single window set high in the wall was the source of the golden light, but provided no clues as to her whereabouts. From Ella's prone position all she could see was an evening sky, and even that was half hidden through slatted blinds.

'Where are we?'

'At a private clinic in Genoa,' Gabriel replied. He was still smiling, apparently unoffended by Ella's standoffishness. 'You realize you're lucky to be alive? The lifeboatmen who pulled you out of the water took almost a full minute to get you breathing again.'

'And you?' Ella looked up at him, realizing belatedly that his hand was still over hers. 'How did you find me? Did you bring me here? I don't remember anything.'

'That's not important,' he replied, with typical arrogance. 'I *told* you not to go back to Makis. I *told* you you would be in danger. What were you thinking?'

'I was thinking that without Mak we had no leads to Athena. None!' Ella shot back angrily. 'I was thinking that Persephone might give me a way back in.'

'So what happened?' Gabriel asked.

Ella blushed and looked away. 'I overheard him on the phone to Cameron McKinley. He knows who I am. Who my parents were.'

Gabriel withdrew his hand. Clutching his head he let out a long, low groan.

'I know,' Ella said meekly. 'It's bad.'

'You actually heard him use the word Praeger?' Gabriel asked, still too depressed to look up.

'Yes,' said Ella. 'On the speedboat on my way out to the *Argo*. He knows I'm William and Rachel's daughter. I don't think he knows anything about . . . you know . . . my gifts. But he knows I'm connected with The Group. If I'd boarded that yacht, he would have killed me.'

'No question,' said Gabriel.

'So I jumped. I didn't know what else to do.'

Gabriel stood up and started pacing. Ella assumed he was working on a plan, what to do next. But when he turned back to face her, he surprised her.

'Did you sleep with Makis Alexiadis?' he asked Ella bluntly.

'No! Never.'

'Were you planning to? When you joined him on the yacht?'

Ella hesitated for a second before answering. 'Yes.'

Gabriel took an audible breath, as if he'd just been punched in the stomach.

'He would have expected that from Persephone. Demanded it, I think,' said Ella. 'I had to get close to him, to regain his trust. I'm not saying I *wanted* to sleep with him.'

'But did you?' Gabriel's eyes bored into hers. 'Want to?'

Ella thought guiltily about all the times she'd fantasized about making love to Makis. About the electric jolt of longing she felt whenever his hand touched hers, despite knowing he was a murderer. The only other man she'd ever felt that much attraction for was the one grilling her right now. But she wasn't about to give him the satisfaction of getting her to admit it.

'No,' she lied. 'Of course not.'

'Good.'

It was the closest he'd ever come to acknowledging his desire for her. But the moment this intimate exchange was over, it was straight back to business.

'Mak knows who you are. Obviously that means you're in danger,' he began.

'From Mak, yes,' agreed Ella. 'But not necessarily from Athena.'

Gabriel shook his head. 'It's over, Ella. The boss wants you back in the States, as soon as you're well enough to travel. I'm to deliver you there personally this time.'

'And what if I won't go?' asked Ella indignantly.

'You will go.'

'Says who? I'm a free agent, you know. I'm not a piece of freight that you guys get to ship around at will.'

'Don't yell at me. I'm just the messenger. Redmayne won't let you compromise the safety of The Group, and that's that. He has countless operatives to think of, not just you.'

'Redmayne can go to hell!'

Gabriel sighed. 'Do you *ever* simply do what you're told?'

'No. Do you?'

He grinned. 'Not very often.'

With an effort, Ella sat upright, hauling herself back against the stacked goose-down pillows. 'I know you don't like Redmayne.'

'How could you possibly know that?'

She tapped the side of her head. 'I know a lot of things about you.'

His eyes narrowed playfully. 'Oh yeah? Like what.'

'I know Gabriel's not your real name.'

He looked at her, trying to fathom whether this was intuition speaking or whether, somehow, she'd actually found out information about his past. The latter possibility was deeply troubling.

'Lots of people change their names when they get older,' he said, trying to sound casual about it.

'Only if they have something to hide,' said Ella. 'Or run away from.'

'Bullshit,' he countered. 'What if they were christened Humperdinck? Or . . . Derek?'

His ploy worked. Ella laughed loudly.

'Is that your real name? Derek?'

He rolled his eyes. 'Sure, Ella. If you want it to be. I'm Derek Humperdinck, if that makes you happy. But weren't we talking about Mark Redmayne?'

The laughter died.

'I don't trust him,' said Ella.

'OK.'

'And I know you don't either.'

'Doesn't matter,' said Gabriel, not denying it. 'He's our boss.'

'You trust me, though?' asked Ella.

'I worry about you,' Gabriel answered truthfully, after a pause.

Ella was touched. Apart from her grandmother Mimi, and Bob back in her old life in San Francisco, no one had ever worried about her.

'Tell me what you know about Athena.'

'Ella . . .'

'Tell me everything. Including the things Redmayne told you not to.'

He hesitated, but she could see his resolve was weakening.

'Trust *me*. Not him. Trust me, so I can trust you. And then – maybe – I'll do what you tell me.'

'I'll believe that when I see it,' he grinned. 'But OK. This is what we know today: Athena's no longer in Greece. She left the country the day after you saw her on Sikinos—'

'So it *was* her on Sikinos! You admit it!' Ella jumped in.

'Of course,' said Gabriel. 'Please stop interrupting.'

'Sorry.'

'We don't know where she is. The couple of leads we had on possible safehouses all came to nothing. But we're confident she'll resurface soon.'

'Why? It took her twelve years last time.'

'That was different. For whatever reason, back then she didn't want control of her husband's empire. Now, she does. What we're witnessing now is the beginning of a civil war between Athena and Makis. It's being fought through proxy armies – her people versus his people – and it's going to get bloody.

'Nikkos was an early casualty. It looks as if Athena's – not Makis's – loyalists were behind his death.'

'Which means . . .'

'That she probably also knows who you are. Or at least suspects it. The only plausible motive for Nikkos's murder lies in his connection to you.'

*So it's my fault either way*, thought Ella. *And my job to avenge his death.*

'Did she get a good look at you that day at the convent?'

Ella's mind flew back to 'Sister Elena's' room. Her grotesque, melted face. Her eyes, neither angry nor frightened, but calm, curious, searching, looking over Ella with a sort of fascinated surprise as Ella stood, frozen, a deer in the headlights.

She nodded. 'Unfortunately, yes.'

'And what about the man? The one who knocked you over and attacked Sister Elena with a knife.'

'What about him?'

'Can you describe him? You said he was tall.'

'Not just tall. He was enormous. Broad shouldered. He looked like a giant.'

'Age?'

Ella shrugged. 'Early thirties? I'm not sure. He was dark skinned. I'm guessing Arabic. He had dark hair but I didn't get a good look at his face. I was too focused on her.'

'That's OK,' said Gabriel, lapsing into a thoughtful silence.

It sounded like him. Like the man Redmayne had warned Gabriel about, and had already, privately, asked him to track down urgently. But he mustn't jump to conclusions. Nor could he allow himself to sidetrack Ella.

'I can't go back to New York.' Ella's voice broke his reverie quietly but with intent. It wasn't just that she couldn't let Athena go, although that was certainly a part of it. She couldn't go back to the person she had been before. To the frightened misfit with a head full of jumbled noise. The lonely observer who saw the world only in black in white. Now, for the first time, Ella's world was in glorious color, and she was *in* it, a part of it, doing something meaningful, not standing on the sidelines. Maybe one day she could go back, but not yet. Not until her transformation was complete.

'I hope you understand. And I'm sorry if it gets you in trouble. But I can't go back until Athena is dead. For my mother. For Nikkos. For myself. I have to see this through.'

To Ella's surprise, Gabriel made no protest. 'OK. You can stay. I'll handle Redmayne.'

'Really?'

'Really,' he said gruffly. If he was going to track down

Redmayne's target, he would need Ella to keep the hunt for Athena alive while he was gone. 'But from now on, the two of us work as a team. No going rogue. No disappearing into the night on your own, unarmed, to have sex with psychopaths.'

'OK. But that has to work both ways,' Ella countered. 'No more half-truths and withholding information. No more, "You'll be told when the time is right".'

Gabriel nodded grudgingly. Then, opening up a large file of pictures on his iPhone, he handed it over to Ella.

'These are all known and active members of the Petridis organization. Most work for Makis, but one or two go way back and are fanatical Athena loyalists. Do you recognize anyone?'

Ella began scrolling through the images. There were a lot of them, over a hundred faces. None leaped out at her.

'Right now, officially at least, they're still all one big happy family,' said Gabriel. 'Big Mak is "delighted" about Athena's return to the fray, and excited about the two of them wreaking havoc together. But behind the scenes it's daggers drawn, and these guys are starting to choose sides. Once they—'

'Him!'

Excited, Ella passed the phone back to Gabriel.

'This guy?' He zoomed in on the face of a bland, nondescript-looking gray-haired man in his mid-fifties, with a neatly clipped mustache.

'He was at the convent.'

'*This* guy?' Gabriel asked. 'You're sure?'

Ella's expression darkened. 'Again with the sure? Yes, I am sure. That's the priest. Father Benjamin. He felt my ankle, when I was hurt.'

Leaning down, Gabriel took Ella's face in both his hands and kissed her on the top of the head, unable to conceal his delight.

'Well *Father Benjamin* also goes by the name of Antonio Lovato. Believe it or not, he used to be Athena's personal trainer back in the day. Rumor had it their training sessions got to be *mighty* personal, but Spyros turned a blind eye. Athena set him up in business, bought him a chain of gyms all across Italy that Spyros used to launder money through. Lovato made out like a bandit.'

'I remember thinking he didn't look especially holy,' Ella mused. 'His robes didn't seem to suit him.'

Gabriel smiled wryly. 'I guess you could say that about a lot of priests these days.'

'So he's a lead, then?' asked Ella.

'Oh he's a lead, all right,' said Gabriel. 'Even better, he's a lead that Mak knows nothing about. And it just so happens . . .' he made a few more taps on his phone, his long fingers rapid-firing like pistons, 'that I also have . . .' *tap, tap, tap*. He handed the phone back to Ella with a look of triumph. 'An address. How would you feel about a trip to London?'

# CHAPTER TWENTY-ONE

Dimitri Mantzaris held the note up to the light with shaking hands. At eighty years old, the former premier's eyesight wasn't what it used to be. But it was good enough to read the four lines in front of him, lines that filled him with a mixture of anticipation and dread.

Written in a code Dimitri hadn't encountered for many, many years, the note said simply: *I am coming.*

*Soon.*

*Need your help.*

*Contact to follow.*

It wasn't signed. It didn't need to be.

The enormous breakfast the old man had just eaten – six *bougatsa*, traditional Greek breakfast pastries, filled with custard and rolled in powdered sugar – churned in his distended stomach now like sour milk, all the pleasure they had brought him gone. Not even the soothing sound of the waves crashing on his beloved Vouliagmeni beach could calm his jangled nerves.

Athena's last 'message' had been indirect, a sign sent to the world. But now she was reaching out to him directly, enticing yet deadly, like a black widow spider, eager to mate.

Unlike the male spider, however, Dimitri Mantzaris did not have the option of refusing her.

It was too late to run, and he was too old to hide.

Athena was calling in a debt, and Dimitri must prepare to honor it.

On the northern bank of the Thames, not far from Vauxhall Bridge, Dolphin Square in Pimlico was one of London's iconic addresses, considered a landmark example of 1930s architecture. Once the height of modernity with its red-brick façade, grand art-deco arches and, to modern eyes, tiny windows, the flats had become synonymous over the year with political intrigue. Occupied by the Free French in the 1940s and a temporary home for General de Gaulle, and later by Mandy Rice-Davies and Christine Keeler, the girls at the center of the Profumo scandal, according to Ella's *Hidden London* guidebook, Dolphin Square was also the London address of Maxwell Knight, the inspiration for 'M' in Ian Fleming's James Bond books.

A jaded lothario and former personal trainer like Antonio Lovato might not merit a mention as one of the famous flats' 'celebrity' residents. But one could argue he had earned his place as part of Dolphin Square's long tradition of secrecy, espionage and dirty politics. Like just about everyone who had once been part of Athena Petridis's inner circle, a strong whiff of corruption surrounded him and his growing empire of gyms and 'wellness centers'.

Ella landed at Heathrow on a Monday afternoon, and spent the night at one of the countless Pimlico bed and breakfasts surrounding Victoria Station. Her room was dingy and depressing and smelled of wet towels, and the breakfast was quite the most revolting mess Ella had ever seen on a plate, consisting of congealed animal fat, deep-fried stale bread and something that might or might not have been an egg. But the Excelsior Guesthouse did at least provide a quiet space where she could practice tuning in and out of different frequencies amid the deafening clamor of London's unrelenting data traffic. Dix's techniques had worked faultlessly in the relative peace of Camp Hope and the remoter Greek islands. But Ella had yet to put them to the test in a major metropolis, and she had to admit that a growing part of her was excited by the prospect. So far Athens had been the only urban center she'd spent time in whilst in the field, her first taste of city life since San Francisco, back when the signals she received had been a frightening, debilitating jumble of white noise. But comparing Athens to London was like comparing the 'Moonlight Sonata' to hardcore thrash metal, cranked up to full volume. This was going to be a challenge.

If she were going to be able to isolate any of Antonio Lovato's emails, texts or phone communications, she would need to get physically closer to him. Tailing him in the street or on public transport would have been the simplest way to achieve this, but by Wednesday he hadn't left his flat once, other than for two short excursions along the river to walk his Pekinese, Mitzi.

'He's a recluse,' Ella complained to Gabriel, after a second fruitless day of observations from a café across the road. She was itching to make a move, to feel the adrenaline rush she'd started to learn to love, just as her parents had. 'Not one trip to his new London gym. No coffees with a friend, no shopping, no nothing. What the hell is he *doing* in there all day?'

'I don't know,' said Gabriel. 'But he may be contacting Athena. Can you really not pick up *anything* from his devices?'

'I'm trying!' Ella said defensively. 'It's not like tuning in a radio, you know. It's like trying to isolate one instrument in a concert hall the size of two baseball fields, where ten symphony orchestras are playing different pieces, all at once. I need to get inside the building.'

'So?' Gabriel hit the ball back to her. 'What's your plan?'

Antonio Lovato pouted at his reflection in the mirror as the doorbell rang. He resented being disturbed, almost as much as he resented the deep grooves on his forehead that would insist on returning each time his Botox wore off, or the fact that, no matter how many crunches he did, his 'six-pack' was now forever destined to be marred by his sagging, aging, paper-dry skin. Age was a ruthless enemy, and one against which his vanity had no adequate defense.

'Yes?' Opening the door of flat 49B, he barked at the intruder.

'Sorry to trouble you, sir. But I'm afraid we've 'ad a complaint.' Alfred, the fat building supervisor, hovered obsequiously on the doorstep. 'Mrs Burton from the flat below.'

'Well, what about her?' snapped Antonio.

'Well, sir, it seems she's been 'aving problems with 'er dining-room ceiling, sir. Damp patches and that. Looks like it might be a problem with the pipes under your floorboards. We've called in a plumber to 'ave a look. If it's convenient . . .' he added, wilting under Antonio Lovato's disdainful glare.

Antonio opened his mouth to explain forcefully that it wasn't convenient, nor would it ever be convenient; that there was quite plainly nothing at all wrong with his pipes and that Mrs Burton was an appalling, desiccated old hag with nothing better to do than invent problems and bother her neighbors in a pathetic and disruptive attempt to draw attention to herself; when fat Alfred stepped aside and the 'plumber' stepped forward. Hovering shyly on Antonio's doorstep was a quite breathtaking girl in her twenties, blonde and elfin, wearing a charming pair of tomboyish overalls that Antonio felt an instant and overwhelming urge to remove, and carrying a toolbox (which, if this were the opening scene in the porn movie already playing in Antonio's mind, ought surely to contain a variety of dildos and sundry other sexually explicit gadgets).

For half of a moment, he felt as if he'd seen her before. But his had been a life so full of young, attractive women, whom in his youth he'd consumed as greedily and prolific-ally as a whale gulping down plankton, she was as impossible to place as a single star in the sky. The important point was that this was not what plumbers looked like in Italy. Or anywhere else, in Antonio's experience. His aging reflection forgotten, he felt suddenly cheered. What a marvelous city London could be!

'I see,' he demurred. 'Well, it's not terribly convenient. But as you've already called this young lady out, I suppose she may as well take a look. Follow me.'

With an openly lecherous smile at Ella, he shut the door firmly in fat Albert's face.

Gabriel sat glumly at a table in the back of Mehmet's Café in the upmarket Istanbul suburb of Ortaköy. Usually he'd be happy to be in Turkey, a country he'd always loved for its warmth, both literal and metaphorical, its rich, melting pot of a culture, its gorgeous, curvaceous, sensual women and perhaps, above all, its coffee, so strong and sweet you wanted to drink it with a spoon. But today, he had multiple reasons to be depressed.

Number one, according to the balances on his phone's internet-banking app, his funds were severely depleted. This was mostly down to poor investments, stock-buying deci-sions that he hadn't had time to check properly since being on back-to-back missions over the summer. But it didn't help that Mark Redmayne, in an epic fit of pique, had made good on his threat to stop Gabriel's regular monthly payments from The Group.

'You're paid to work for us, on specific assigned missions. Not for yourself,' Redmayne had reminded him caustically during their last telephone conversation, the day Ella left the Genoa hospital and, as far as Redmayne was concerned, disappeared.

'I'm hardly working for myself, sir,' Gabriel countered. 'I've been tracking Mood Salim, like you asked me to.'

'Well, now I'm asking you to stop.'

At first, Gabriel had resented being asked to pause the hunt for Athena in order to track down Salim, a Libyan migrant whom The Group had tried to recruit months ago, after his family drowned on one of the Petridis organization's migrant boats. By all accounts the man was a walking mountain of rage, hell-bent on avenging his wife and daughters. And yet, after some initial, tepid interest in joining The Group, Salim had vanished, with various reports suggesting that he was responsible for a string of subsequent murders connected to Athena's network.

'If he's acting alone, that's one thing,' Redmayne told Gabriel. 'But he seems to have access to some very sophisticated intelligence that suggests otherwise. He's a loose cannon and I want him watched.'

Whatever annoyance Gabriel had felt at the boss's paranoia evaporated once he heard Ella's description of the 'giant' at Sikinos. It had to be Salim – there weren't that many six-foot-seven Arabs out there hell-bent on murdering Athena Petridis. But Redmayne was right: there was no way an uneducated Libyan migrant would have found 'Sister Elena' on his own. Which meant there was more to Salim's story than met the eye. So when Gabriel obtained some good intel of his own last week, placing Mood Salim in

Istanbul, he had jumped on the first flight. Only, infuriatingly, to find himself being slapped down by none other than Mark Redmayne.

'You know how crucial it is to act quickly on leads like this, sir,' he pleaded. 'I missed him in Italy, and in France, and in Germany. He's been all over the map since Sikinos. He's definitely working for someone, although whether that's—'

'You're not listening to me Gabriel,' Redmayne interrupted. 'You have been *recalled*. Forget Salim, forget Athena. I expect you back in the States within forty-eight hours. You *and* Ella Praeger, I know damn well you know where she is.'

'I'm sorry. We can't come home, sir. Not yet,' Gabriel replied, triggering an explosion from the boss the likes of which even he had never heard before. Apparently it was his use of the word 'we' that rankled most. Ella was The Group's single most valuable asset, not part of some sort of rogue duo with *him*. Gabriel had 'zero authority' to engage her on missions without The Group's consent – which meant Redmayne's consent.

'We'll find her and bring her back by force if we have to,' Redmayne threatened, adding ominously. 'And we'll cut you off. You're expendable, Gabriel. She's not.'

Evidently stage one of 'Operation Cut-Off' was to be Gabriel's money. No one joined the Group to get rich, but at the same time it rankled to be spending grueling days risking one's life to rid the world of evil, and then told to pay for your own Turkish coffee.

Gabriel's second reason to be depressed was the fact that, having risked so much to follow him to Istanbul, Mood Salim's trail had suddenly gone ice cold. All the leads that had seemed so promising last week, the whispered sightings and overheard conversations that had seen Gabriel flit from

Genoa to Paris to Munich and finally here, to a former ISIS sleeper cell of disaffected young Muslim youth on the outskirts of the city, had petered out like a dried-up river, leading him nowhere. If nothing came up in the next twenty-four hours, he would fly to London and rejoin Ella, who'd already begun her surveillance of Athena's former flame, the dreadful Mr Lovato.

If Antonio Lovato was involved enough to have posed as a priest, of all things, to help spirit Athena out of Sikinos, it stood to reason that he knew where she was now. But so far, Ella had been frustratingly unable to gather any new intelligence. And with Redmayne no doubt scouring the globe for her as Gabriel sat here, sipping his coffee, and quite possibly planning some rendition-style kidnap to smuggle Ella back to New York and 'safety', their time might well be running out.

Just as he was mulling over this dispiriting thought, his new burner phone rang. Ella was the only person who had the number.

'Any news?'

'Yes! Finally.' The excitement in her voice was palpable, and contagious. 'I got into the flat while he was there and was able to blink-scan some documents.'

'While he was *there*? You mean he saw you?'

Ella sighed. It really was uncanny the way that Gabriel never failed to pick up on the one thing she was hoping he might miss. The man was like a heat-seeking missile of disapproval.

'Don't worry, he didn't suspect anything.'

'But Ella, he saw you before! At the convent.'

'Trust me, he barely glanced at me,' Ella lied. 'In any case, the point is he's been corresponding with a private surgery facility on Wimpole Street on behalf of a Mrs Hambrecht.'

Gabriel felt the hairs on the back of his neck stand on end. Athena had been 'Mrs Hambrecht' once, before she met Spyros, before the whole nightmare began.

'Lovato's been negotiating the price on a whole bunch of procedures,' said Ella. 'I think it must be for Athena.'

'I agree.' Tossing down a few coins on the table, Gabriel stood up and walked outside. He couldn't imagine either of the wizened old Kurdish men playing chess in the corner were tuning into his conversation, but you could never be too careful. 'Do you have the name of the clinic?'

'Yes. And the surgeon,' Ella said triumphantly. 'I'll pay him a visit tomorrow. See what I can find out.'

'Be careful,' Gabriel said. 'Doctors aren't usually in the habit of letting slip information about their patients. And if anyone suspects you, you could be in danger.'

Ella's gifts were incredible and her instincts often good. But when her blood was up, she had scant concern for her personal safety. Worse, Gabriel was starting to pick up on a certain thrill-seeking streak in Ella that seemed to have grown exponentially since she left Mykonos. The fact that it mirrored his own didn't make it any less worrisome. Ella was her mother's daughter in more ways than one, and it wasn't just Mark Redmayne who had trouble getting through to her. Treating these missions like a role-playing adventure game was not a helpful trait when you had Makis Alexiadis's trained killers out hunting for you, not to mention Redmayne determined to implement a 'rescue' at any cost.

'I'll be fine,' said Ella, with worrying nonchalance. 'I'll let you know what I find out.'

Before Gabriel could say another word, she'd hung up.

Dr Mungo Hansen-Gerard gazed admiringly at the young woman sitting opposite him. She was American, rich (at least if the diamonds sparkling on her fingers and ears were anything to go by) and far too beautiful to be in need of his services. With her pretty, elfin features and slim athletic body, her skin still bearing the smooth tautness of youth, she was an 'after' picture, not a 'before'. But Dr Mungo Hansen-Gerard hadn't got to where he was today by looking gift horses in the mouth, however attractive or delusional they may be.

'What is it I can help you with, Miss Yorke?' He leaned forward, flashing his most avuncular smile.

'Oh, I don't know. A few things, I guess,' Ella sighed. 'This.' She tapped the bridge of her nose. 'And these.' She ran a long finger down from the side of her nose to the outer edges of her lips, feigning displeasure with the faint line that ran between the two. 'And, you know. My breasts could be bigger.'

Looking round the room, she scanned everything she could visually, while simultaneously trying to tune in to the phone and email data whirling around her, both from Dr Hansen-Gerard's personal devices, and from his PA's workstation on the other side of the door. Holding a conversation with the surgeon at the same time wasn't easy, but Samantha Yorke was the ditzy, easily distracted type. Ella imagined Dr Hansen-Gerard must be used to those.

'Well, breast size is of course a very personal matter,' he was saying suavely, while Ella mentally searched for his schedule for the next two weeks online. Helpfully, his efficient PA sent him nightly reminders of the following day's work, but so far the magical word *Hambrecht* had not come up. 'If you do opt for an augmentation, there are a number of factors to consider. Did you know if you wanted a silicone or a saline implant, for example? And had you thought about shape? Round or teardrop? Textured or smooth? Nowadays a number of my patients opt for what we call "gummy bear" augmentations . . .'

*Hambrecht! Mrs A.* There it was! She was scheduled for preliminary blood work next Monday and surgery the following Tuesday, the eighteenth. Dr Mungo Hansen-Gerard had the entire day's surgery reserved for her that day – nine hours in theater.

'I guess I maybe haven't done enough research,' Ella said, getting up and reaching for her purse, eager to go now she had the information she needed. 'I'm wasting your time, doctor.'

'Not at all, Miss Yorke, not at all! And please, call me Mungo.' Sensing he was in danger of losing her, he was at his most ingratiating. 'Most of my patients are uncertain on their first visit. Part of my job is to guide you through the various options. I've done the research so you don't have to.' He gestured for Ella to sit. 'You mentioned you were also considering rhinoplasty?'

'Mmm hmm,' said Ella, sitting back down reluctantly. At this point, it didn't make sense to draw attention to herself by bolting out of there, much as she wanted to race into the street and call Gabriel. She'd come here as a prospective patient, and she must behave like one. Besides which, it wouldn't hurt to see more of the facility, become familiar with Athena's likely movements on the day. 'If I went ahead with that, would the actual surgery be done here? And could you do it on the same day?'

'Yes. And yes, it could, although I probably wouldn't advise that,' Dr Hansen-Gerard replied, delighted to have brought his prospective patient back into the fold. 'I advise most patients to wait at least a week between procedures.'

*Not Athena Petridis, though*, thought Ella. *She's in a rush for a whole new look.*

After fifteen more minutes talking about the various noses, lips and injectable fillers available to today's affluent, insecure narcissist, 'Mungo' offered Ella a brief tour of the clinic. Set behind a classical Georgian façade on Wimpole Street, just a stone's throw from the more famous Harley Street, the London Aesthetic Clinic was in fact three former townhouses knocked together and extended backwards into what had once been gardens and then a mews to create two separate surgical suites, a recovery and a preoperative room, six private patient bedrooms, a nurses' station, and a large 'consultation wing', consisting of Mungo's private office and those of his junior partner, a front office for the PAs and a light and airy waiting room, hidden from the prying eyes of the street by antique Belgian lace curtains.

Mungo talked 'Samantha' through the protocols for each operation and explained exactly what happened to each patient from their arrival for a procedure until their ultimate discharge. By the time they were done, Ella had a clear idea of exactly where Athena ought to be and when on the eighteenth. Armed with this information, she hoped that she and Gabriel together would be able to come up with a detailed plan.

'It's been a pleasure to meet you, Miss Yorke.' The surgeon shook his prospective patient's hand at the door to his consulting room, ushering her back towards the front office. 'Make a follow-up appointment with the girls and in the meantime I'll send you links to some of the options we discussed.'

Itching to escape, Ella nonetheless did as she was asked and headed to the office. While she was standing at the desk, filling out the PA's follow-up form, she saw a man in dark green overalls tinkering with what looked like a fuse box at the back of the room. She couldn't put her finger on it exactly, but something about him seemed familiar. He had his back to her, so that 'something' must have been connected to his movements, his body language . . . Ella couldn't place it, yet she felt herself shudder as if a spider had just scuttled up her arm.

'Are you all right, Miss Yorke?' the receptionist asked. She must have sensed something too.

'Fine,' said Ella, signing her name quickly at the bottom of the paper and, in the same instant, instinctively pulling up the silk Hermès scarf she wore around her neck, covering the entire lower part of her face.

When she spoke, the overalled man spun around, as suddenly as a snake pouncing on its prey.

*He couldn't see my face*, Ella reassured herself as she bolted out of the building and straight into one of a string of black cabs streaming down Wimpole Street. *He didn't know it was me.*

Even so, she heard herself telling the driver to drop her at Oxford Circus, which was nowhere near her guesthouse, because she suddenly felt the need to lose herself in a crowd.

She could only pray that the overalled electrician hadn't recognized her. But Ella had certainly recognized him, with his pale, see-through skin, like a maggot's, his wispy red hair, and his ice-blue, watery, emotionless eyes.

She waited until she was deep in a throng of noisily giggling Japanese tourists before she dared to pull out her phone.

This time, when Gabriel heard Ella's voice, he knew that the undertone wasn't excitement.

It was fear.

'She's going in on the eighteenth,' she panted. 'Mrs Hambrecht. I got a tour . . . I think I know where we can . . . how we can . . .'

'Ella.' His voice was low and calm, like a father's hand on a hysterical daughter's shoulder. 'What's the matter? What happened in there?'

Reaching out, Ella steadied herself against a wooden bench. She felt dizzy all of a sudden.

'I saw . . .' She inhaled deeply, almost gasping for breath. 'I saw . . .'

People around her began to give her funny looks.

*Am I having a panic attack?* Ella wondered. She'd never had one before, but there was a first time for everything.

'What did you see?' Gabriel asked patiently.

'Not what,' she wheezed. 'Who. Cameron McKinley. He was right there, at the clinic! Not six feet in front of me.'

Then she said something Gabriel had never heard her say before.

'I'm scared.'

His own heart raced. *You should be.*

'Don't be.'

'What if Mak knows I'm here? What if Cameron followed me to London? To the clinic? Mak wants me dead.'

'More likely he followed Athena,' Gabriel said, projecting a confidence he didn't feel. 'But we need to take extra precautions, either way. I'll be in London by tomorrow morning. But for now, don't go back to Pimlico. Check into another hotel, somewhere small and nondescript. And wait for me to call.'

For once, Ella was compliant, agreeing to follow his instructions without a word of protest.

*She really is scared*, Gabriel thought.

In that moment, so was he.

# CHAPTER TWENTY-TWO

'Good morning. Checking in?'

The receptionist smiled brightly at the male nurse and his charge, a slight woman in a wheelchair with a heavily bandaged face.

'Yes.' The nurse, a stocky Filipino man in his late twenties, was wearing green scrubs and a gold necklace with the word 'Jesus' spelled out in elaborate cursive script. 'This is Mrs Hambrecht. She's scheduled for a procedure with Dr Hansen-Gerard at nine.'

'Lovely,' said the receptionist. 'One of our admissions team will show you both up to your room shortly. If you'd like to take a seat.'

Makis Alexiadis paced anxiously in his bedroom at Villa Mirage, his cell phone in his hand. Since returning from his yacht, Makis been sleeping poorly, wracked by dreams about 'Persephone' and Athena Petridis, the two women that some vengeful God had seen fit to send up from Hades to torment him. In some of the dreams, the two of them had teamed up, laughing at him together as he tried in vain to pursue them. Usually in these 'chase' dreams, Makis

317

found his legs became mired in treacle so he would run and run and get nowhere, driven on by rage and frustration. He would wake from these nightmares dripping in sweat, and with his heart pounding impotently to a wild beat that made further sleep impossible.

It was still only seven in the morning, but he'd already been awake for hours, waiting restlessly for Cameron's call. When at last it came, he was so amped up he was practically vibrating.

'Is your man in there yet?' he demanded.

'He is.' The fixer's voice was as relaxed and even as ever, his soft, Scots brogue in sharp contrast to Makis's agitated Greek growl. 'He had no problems as the substitute agency nurse. He's been in the building since the shift started at five a.m.'

'And you're in contact?'

'Yes. His earpiece is working beautifully. Mrs H has checked in and is on her way up to her room. Once the operation's over, he'll wheel her out of the recovery room while she's still sedated, and take the service elevator down to the goods entrance. I'll be waiting there with the van. Try to relax, Mak. There's nothing to worry about.'

*Nothing to worry about!* If he weren't as tense as a taut rubber band, Makis might have laughed. With Athena Petridis there was always something to worry about. Always.

Would he finally be rid of her today? He hardly dared believe it.

He *mustn't* believe it. Not until it was done.

The receptionist stole a glance at Samantha Yorke, who was flipping nervously through an old copy of *Vogue* magazine.

*Poor thing.* It was obvious Samantha didn't really want to be here. Apprehension was written all over her beautiful

318

face. Patients like Samantha made the receptionist feel guilty that she worked here. That she was part of an industry where rich successful male surgeons who should know better, like Dr H-G, preyed on the insecurities of beautiful young women who no more needed surgery than they needed to fly to the moon.

*Get out of here!* she longed to tell Samantha. *Run, while you still can.*

She wasn't here for a procedure today, only for a longer consultation with another of the clinic's surgeons, the nose job specialist Dr Henry Butler. But she still had that look about her, as if she were about to face the firing squad. *Why on earth couldn't these women trust their own instincts?*

Samantha approached the desk. For one, hopeful moment the receptionist thought she was going to cancel and leave. But instead she asked where the ladies' room was.

The receptionist pointed to a door across the hall. 'But I believe somebody's in there at the moment.'

'Is there another one? I'm sorry but I . . . I need to go urgently. I think I might be sick.'

'Here.' Reaching into a drawer, the receptionist handed over a key. 'Patients aren't really supposed to use it, but if it's an emergency.'

'Thank you,' Samantha grabbed the key gratefully.

'It's on the first floor, next to the pre-op suite,' the receptionist told her. 'Turn right at the top of the stairs.'

Halfway up the stairs, Ella leaned back against the wall and took a moment to compose herself. So far, everything had gone remarkably smoothly. She'd had a Plan B in place, in case the receptionist had refused to direct her upstairs. Together with Gabriel, she'd identified three different windows of opportunity for encountering Athena when she would be both alone and incapacitated. But her nerves were already starting to get the better of her, and she was relieved to be able to act now.

In her right hand, she clutched the bathroom key. In her left, thrust deep into her jacket pocket, she felt the contours of the syringe.

'It's incredibly simple,' Gabriel had assured her over dinner last night at Hakkasan in Mayfair. Relieved to have abandoned his wild-goose chase in Istanbul, at least for the moment, he was sipping warm sake as if the next day's assassination attempt was just a regular day at the office. 'You use it like an epi pen. Stab her anywhere at all on her body. Through clothes is fine. You just stab, push and go.'

Ella climbed the stairs and turned right. The ladies' room was in front of her to the left. Pre-op was straight ahead. If the schedule was going according to plan, Athena should be in there right now, heavily sedated, and alone.

*You just stab, push and go.*

*Kill and go, you mean*, thought Ella, moving towards the door. Gabriel had probably done this sort of thing scores of times. But for Ella it was all new, and a step she couldn't take back. Once she had 'stabbed' and 'pushed', Athena Petridis would be dead and she, Ella Praeger, would be a killer. A murderer. Yes, she was avenging her parents' deaths, and ridding the world of an evil, dangerous woman. It wasn't that she was having second thoughts about the morality of what she was about to do. It was more that she knew that from this moment on, her life would forever be divided into 'before' and 'after'.

The hallway was deserted. A whiteboard on the wall outside the room had the word 'Hambrecht' scrawled on it in marker pen.

*This is it*, thought Ella. *Stab, push and go. Stab, push and go.*

Try as she might, she couldn't seem to stop her hands from shaking.

Parked outside the back entrance to the clinic in a nondescript white Ford transit van, Cameron McKinley felt his mouth go dry and his heart begin to beat uncomfortably fast.

'Are you certain?'

'Yes, sir. Quite certain. It's her. What should I do?'

*Shit*, thought Cameron. *Shit, shit, shit.*

Ella Praeger was there. In the clinic. Right now. How was that possible?

It had been a long time since Cameron had stooped to become personally involved in hit jobs for Makis Alexiadis, or any of his clients for that matter. But after the debacle with the Praeger girl in Italy, when those cretins managed to 'lose' her from a moving speedboat, he couldn't afford another screw-up. One more mistake would cost him not just this most lucrative and loyal client but, in all likelihood, his life. He had to get this right.

Last week he'd gone into Wimpole Street himself, posing as an electrician, to get the lie of the land and to make sure everything went smoothly on the day of the kidnap. Once Athena Petridis was safely unconscious and in the back of his van, he would drive her out to a secluded, private woodland in Essex, shoot her himself, and bury her with his own two hands. Only then would he feel confident that Makis could truly forgive him. Only then would he be safe.

'Sir?' Roger Carlton, Cameron's partner for today's job, was one of his most senior and trusted operatives. 'Sorry, but I have to go back inside soon or I'll be missed. I need an answer.'

'OK,' said Cameron, beads of sweat forming on his brow. 'Hold on. I'll get back to you.'

If Ella Praeger was here, it must be for the same reason they were: to kill Athena. Cameron McKinley could not let that happen.

Stomach churning, he called Mak.

'Kill her. Do it! Kill them both.'

The excitement in Alexiadis's voice was terrifying. He sounded manic. Deranged.

'Mak, we can't kill her. We're not equipped. Roger isn't even armed.'

'He can strangle her,' said Mak, so matter-of-factly that it made even Cameron's blood run cold.

'No. He needs to focus on Athena,' Cameron pushed back. 'She's our target. Once I've got her in the vehicle, I can have Roger follow Ella—'

'NO!' Mak shrieked, like a maddened chimpanzee. 'Don't follow her. Kill her. I want her dead. Today. We'll never have a better opportunity.'

'But, Mak—'

'Tell your man I'll pay him a million-dollar bonus, cash, when he sends me a picture of Ella Praeger's corpse.'

Cameron hung up. It was like trying to reason with a rabid dog.

There was nothing for it. Between them, he and Roger would have to try and kill Ella and Athena. His cunning mind raced. Within thirty seconds, he called Roger back.

'OK,' he said with a calm he didn't feel. 'Change of plan.'

With one last glance behind her at the empty corridor, Ella opened the door to the pre-op suite.

Inside, all was quiet. Athena lay on her side, apparently sleeping with her back to Ella. Her facial bandages had been removed and her hair covered with a surgical mesh cap. A machine attached to her finger measured her blood pressure and

322

heart rate, and the only movement was the soft, slow rise and fall of her chest as she breathed, obviously heavily sedated.

*Stab, push and go.*

One of the medical staff might come back in at any moment. It was now or never. Pulling the syringe out of her pocket, Ella walked towards the sleeping form. She would do it in the back or shoulder, through her surgical gown, just like Gabriel had shown her. Easy. Instant. Painless. *'It's better than Athena deserves, Ella. Remember that.'*

Ella lifted the syringe.

As she did so, Athena stirred, turning over suddenly as if aware of her presence. When her eyes blinked open, it was like the wakening of the dead. 'Nurse?' she queried groggily, eyeing the fatal syringe.

Ella found herself looking at her victim, face to face.

She was young, dark haired and rather plain looking.

And she was not Athena Petridis.

Outside in the corridor, Ella slumped against the wall, her legs like Jell-O.

*I could have killed her! I was this close. I could have murdered an innocent woman.*

Bile rose up in her throat. With shaking hands, she texted Gabriel.

'It's not her. We've been set up. Lovato duped us.'

The reply was instant. 'OK. Abort. Get out of there.'

*With pleasure*, thought Ella. *Just as soon as I can stand.*

'Miss Yorke? Samantha?'

A tall, effete blond man with a cut-glass accent emerged from a door down the hall. Ella stared at him as if he'd just landed from Mars. 'Yes?'

'I'm Dr Butler. No need to look so terrified, my dear. Come on in.'

*

Roger Carlton waited for Henry Butler's door to open before hitting the call button for the elevator. Number 77 Wimpole Street had one of those beautiful 1930s London lifts with metal concertina gates at each floor that had to be opened and closed fully before the elevator itself would move.

Roger's palms were sweating as he gripped the laundry cart in front of him. He was nervous. It was more than five years since he'd killed with his bare hands. The technique for breaking a woman's neck was simple, but he was out of practice and would have very little time. Less than forty seconds to kill her, deposit her body in the hamper and cover it with loose sheets, before he opened the grille on the ground floor and wheeled her out to Cameron's van.

Nothing could go wrong. She mustn't struggle. She mustn't scream. No one else must enter the elevator. He mustn't botch the move. This was a one-shot thing.

'*A million dollars cash, Rog. He's good for it, believe me.*'

Dr Butler's Eton-educated drawl reverberated down the corridor behind him.

'Lovely to meet you, Miss Yorke. I'll be in touch.'

Ella waited for the elevator in a trance. She remembered nothing of her twenty-minute interview with Dr Henry Butler. He, no doubt, had talked about rhinoplasty. She had sat and stared and nodded and tried to swallow the fact that she had come within seconds, *seconds*, of ending another human being's life. *By mistake.*

Was this really what her 'gifts' were for? For killing? For vengeance?

Had her parents truly wanted that for her? And even if they had, did that really matter? This was her life after all, her choices. If 'Mrs Hambrecht' – whoever she really was

– had wound up dead today, then she, Ella, would be responsible. Not Rachel or William Praeger.

*Me.*

Were these awful choices what her grandmother Mimi had been trying to save her from for all those long, lonely years? Had Mimi tried to protect her, in her own way, by isolating her from the world up at Paradise Ranch? Perhaps Mimi had been the only one who truly loved her, after all.

*Today was a wake-up call*, Ella decided, letting the laundry man into the elevator before turning around to pull the metal gates closed. *I'll tell Gabriel I've changed my mind. I'm out. It's not my 'destiny' to kill anyone. I'll go back to San Francisco and my old life. To Bob and Joanie and . . .*

It happened so suddenly she had no time to react. Strong, male hands grabbing her from behind, one across her chest pinning both her arms to her sides, the other clamped hard over her nose and mouth. The doors were closed and the elevator was moving, grindingly slowly. The man with the laundry hamper had her completely incapacitated. Ella felt his knee dig into the small of her back and his left arm, the one forming a straitjacket across her torso, begin to move upwards, towards her neck. She knew then that he was going to try to kill her. She'd done it herself, to injured livestock on the farm. She'd used her knee as a brace, gripped the head and pulled sharply around and up, snapping the neck.

*Not me. Not today.*

Unable to breathe, she thrust her jaw forward and bit hard on the fingers covering her mouth. Blood spurted everywhere and her assailant let out a muted scream of agony.

'Bitch!' he muttered under his breath, using his other arm to take a firmer grim on Ella's entire skull. Ella's heart pounded. One well-timed twist and she'd be dead. She had to break free from that grip right now.

With a strength and agility she didn't know she had, she drew one leg up behind her in a painful reverse twist and shot her foot as fast as she could, jack-rabbit style, into what she hoped were his genitals. A second scream, louder this time, signaled she'd found her target. His arm involuntarily loosened just a fraction, but it was enough for Ella to drop down to her knees, slipping her head free from his grip. Reaching down, maddened with pain, he changed tactics and wrapped both, bear-like hands around her neck, squeezing her windpipe until Ella could feel her eyeballs bulge and the blood throb in her temples. She flailed her arms and legs as the elevator cranked slowly down, down, but it was no use. She'd be unconscious, if not dead, by the time they reached the ground.

Looking up into his eyes, she could see her attacker's anger turn to satisfaction and finally to a sort of sadistic triumph. *He's enjoying it. He's enjoying killing me.*

Without making any conscious movement, her jerking arms found their way to her pocket. She felt the syringe against her fingers, just as everything around her was starting to turn black. Flailing out wildly, she plunged it into his forearm and pushed.

Outside on Wimpole Street, Ella calmly crossed the road at the zebra crossing and walked round the corner onto Mansfield Street, where she took the first in a long line of waiting black cabs.

'Hampstead Heath, please,' she told the driver, simply because it was the first destination to pop into her head. Only once they'd passed the Langham Hotel did she allow herself to exhale, reaching up and touching the ring of livid bruises around her neck from where the man's fingers had tried to choke her.

They would have found his body by now, slumped behind the laundry cart.

So Ella had killed today after all.

Later, up on the heath, she would text Gabriel. For now she was content to lean back in the cab and enjoy the luxury of her own breath coming in and out, in and out.

*I'm alive. I survived.*

Perhaps this stuff really was her destiny . . .

# CHAPTER TWENTY-THREE

Mahmood Salim jumped off the side of the fishing sloop into warm, waist-deep water and waded slowly towards the shore, his backpack slung over his broad shoulders.

It felt strange being back in the Greek islands. Strange and unnerving, as if some dark force, some unnamed fates kept demanding his return, pulling him in like a magnet to the place where his darling girls had left this earth. Of course, this was Mykonos, not Lesbos. And this time Salim was not a helpless North African migrant, but a legitimate French citizen enjoying his vacation, complete with all the requisite forged paperwork and fifteen thousand euros in cash and traveler's checks, should he need them.

Another man – a man who still had something to lose – would doubtless have been frightened at the task that lay ahead. But Mood Salim was past fear, just as he was past pain, or joy or despair. All emotions were dead in him, as dead as his beloved Hoda and their children. What was left was his giant's body, battle-scarred but mighty. And that body was a machine, programmed for one thing and one thing only: revenge.

His work had begun as soon as he'd broken out of the

detention center, a surprisingly simple matter of physically incapacitating two semi-drunk night watchmen and convincing a naïve American charity worker to give him a ride to the mainland.

Killing the Kouvlaki brothers had been surprisingly easy. Perhaps too easy. Armed with Andreas's memory stick and his frozen index finger in a zip-lock baggie, Mahmoud had arrived in Athens soon afterwards, ready to dispose of Makis Alexiadis at his townhouse and finish the job.

But it was in Athens that it all went wrong. Overconfident after his successes with Perry and Andreas, Mood had been too trusting in the latter's information and had seriously underestimated both the scale and the sophistication of Makis Alexiadis's security arrangements. He barely made it into the grounds with Andreas's code before he was Tasered to the ground, disarmed, bound, beaten, and finally dragged like a sack of rocks before Big Mak himself. He never even got a chance to use the stupid finger.

Prepared for death and not remotely afraid, Mood's defiant attitude and physical courage made an instant impression on Makis. Rather than shooting him at once, Makis began to question him, curious about this fearless, angry giant of a man and what drove him.

'You came here to kill me?'

'Yes.'

'Because?'

'Because you killed my family.'

Salim's eyes bored into his with laser-like hatred.

'You're mistaken,' said Makis. 'I don't even know your family.'

'That doesn't matter. You're responsible for their deaths. For so many deaths.'

The whole story came out then. Makis listened, fascinated. Not only to the horrors of the overcrowded migrant boats – this man's wife and children had been among the lost cargo on one of their Aegean shipments – but how it was *he* who had tracked down Perry and Andreas Kouvlaki, murdering both and then branding them with letters 'in memory' of the drowned Libyan boy. This lunatic had been using Athena's calling card *without even knowing it!* Tit-for-tat brandings! The whole thing was so ironic, you couldn't make it up. 'A' had been for Ava, and 'P' for Parzheen, his drowned daughters. Makis, presumably, was to have been marked with an 'H' – for Hoda, the man's dead wife.

It was amusing to think that all this time Mak had been second-guessing Athena, trying to piece together a code that was indeed about loss and rage – just not hers!

But Makis didn't laugh. Instead he listened intently to Salim's story. And then he told Mood a story of his own. It was a story that changed everything. A story that reframed what had happened to Hoda and Parzheen and Ava that terrible night, and that provided Mood with a new focus, a new enemy: Athena Petridis.

It was Athena, Mak explained, who had masterminded the people-smuggling operation. Athena who was obsessed with gaining overall control of the Aegean route. Athena who had branded children like animals, like cargo, to stake her claim over their lives, and deaths, and whose calling card Mood had unwittingly hijacked.

Makis Alexiadis had not sought to exonerate himself. That part was crucial for Mood. Unlike the Kouvlaki brothers, he hadn't needed to. He wasn't begging for his life. On the contrary, it was Mood whose life was in *his* hands. Makis could have shot Mood in the head then and there if he'd chosen to. But he didn't.

Instead, he made him a deal.

Makis would spare Mood's life, *and* direct him to the

real mastermind behind his family's deaths. In return, Mood would make no further attempt to kill him. Makis explained to Mood that if he, Mak, were to die, then Athena would assume total control of the Petridis empire and the drownings would only multiply.

The new plan was for Mood to go to the convent at Sikinos, with Makis's help, find and kill Athena – aka, 'Sister Elena' – and bring irrefutable evidence of her demise back to Makis. In return for this task of Hercules, Makis would pull the Petridis organization out of the migrant business altogether and revert to his core areas of expertise – fraud, extortion and drugs. He would also donate $2 million to 'Open Arms', the charity that rescued Mood, pulling him from the water on the night of the drownings. 'Because even if we withdraw from the business, others won't,' Makis reminded him. 'And you can't kill them all, my friend.'

Makis Alexiadis would never be Mood Salim's 'friend'. But the deal he offered was a good one. Mood believed him about Athena, for the simple reason that, as far as Mood could tell, he had no reason to lie.

The world Mahmoud Salim had come to know was full of evil, full of enemies. Makis was one of them. But he was also right: Mood couldn't kill them all. He had to pick and choose. And if he could kill Athena – the worst of them all, the queen bee of the whole revolting, murderous hive – then surely he would die knowing he had avenged his girls?

That would be enough.

It would have to be.


That meeting had been two months ago. But again, Mood had been overconfident, and much had changed since then.

Athena Petridis was still alive.

Mood had failed in his mission to Sikinos.

331

According to their 'deal', this meant that, officially at least, Makis owed him nothing. And that he, Mood, owed Makis nothing, other than not to try to kill him again. They had shaken hands on that agreement, and Mood Salim's word was his bond.

Any other man would have left Greece, left Europe, run as fast and as far as he could from the murderous crime boss who had miraculously spared his life once, but would not do so again. But Mood Salim was not any other man. He needed to see Makis. His work wasn't done. He needed another chance. To put things right. And so he stepped ashore on Mykonos, preparing to walk once more into the lion's den.

The doctor looked at the reading on his blood-pressure monitor and frowned.

'Are you taking your simvastatin?'

Makis Alexiadis gave a grunt that might have been 'yes'. Or 'no'.

'What about your diet?'

They were in the study at Villa Mirage, with the vast modern picture windows tinted dark for privacy, and a stunning bespoke concrete and linen couch serving as the patient's examination table. In the past, Makis had agreed to come into the surgery for his regular check-ups, drawn at least in part by the lure of Dr Farouk's extremely attractive but depressingly attached receptionist, Mariette. But ever since the dismal failure of Cameron McKinley's London operation, Makis had been too depressed to get out of bed most days, let alone leave the villa.

How could it be? How was it *possible* that not only Athena, but Ella Praeger too, had slipped through his fingers? Again! He hated himself for caring more about Ella's escape than he did about Athena's. The slippery little witch was proving as cunning as her mother had been before her. Not only had she got away, but she'd managed to kill Roger Carlton, a seasoned operative and reliable assassin with more than two decades' worth of experience. As for Athena, once again Makis now had zero idea where she was, or whether or not she even knew that an attempt had been made to kill her. Thanks to Cameron's incompetence, he'd been left naked. Exposed. Vulnerable.

Was it any wonder his blood pressure was through the roof?

'My diet's fine,' he growled at Dr Farouk, a slight, immaculately dressed Egyptian who always smelled of a distinctive mixture of expensive cologne and camphor. 'Same chef. No changes. I've been a little stressed.'

'More than a little,' Dr Farouk said, removing an old-fashioned thermometer from his battered leather doctor's bag and inserting it under Makis's tongue. When it came to medical care, Makis preferred tradition. 'I don't suppose you'd consider taking a vacation?'

'This is a vacation,' Mak mumbled around the thermometer.

'I'm serious, Makis,' frowned the doctor. 'These numbers aren't good. I know you keep fit, but you're not a young man any more.'

A knock on the door interrupted this dispiriting conversation.

An ashen-looking lackey stuck his head into the room. 'Sorry to disturb you, sir. But a man's been detained at the gatehouse.'

'And?' Makis snapped, as Dr Farouk removed the glass vial from between his lips. 'Can't security deal with it?'

'Well, yes, sir. But they thought . . . I thought . . . you would want to know. It's the man. From Athens.'

'What "man from Athens"? What the hell are you talking about? There are three million men in Athens, you cretin!'

Dr Farouk watched with alarm as his patient's face began to turn a violent puce. It wasn't healthy how quickly Makis Alexiadis could go from calm to apoplectic in a matter of seconds. He didn't think he'd ever known a man with less emotional regulation. For all the outward trappings of success and good health, the man's inner life was clearly a wild and uncontrollable storm.

The poor lackey swallowed nervously. 'The man . . . the very tall Arabic man. He was stopped in the grounds of the mansion?'

Makis's eyes widened. 'You can't mean Salim?'

*He's here?*

'Yes, sir. And he's asking to see you. He says it's urgent.'

Makis frowned, then laughed. Did the idiot have a death wish? Not many men would be brave – or foolish – enough to dare come crawling back to Makis Alexiadis having failed at a job as important as the one Mood Salim had been given.

He turned to Dr Farouk. 'We'll have to finish this later.'

For a moment, the elegant little medic considered protesting. But only for a moment. There was a steel in Mak's eyes that spelled danger.

'Show Salim in,' he barked at the lackey. 'Then leave us.'

Mood gazed around him at the opulence of the villa as he followed Makis's manservant down a long, light-filled hallway. This wasn't opulence in the Libyan style. There was no gold, no rich rugs or priceless antique furniture or chandeliers. This was starker, sleeker, altogether more modern. And yet the endless expanses of marble and glass, and the two vast, abstract stone sculptures at either end of the corridor spoke just as eloquently of wealth, status and power. Perhaps more so. After all, who needed art when one had the limitless blue Aegean sparkling on the other side of windows so enormous and brilliantly clean they were practically invisible? Everything about Villa Mirage was impressive in a clean, controlled way.

'In there,' the manservant nodded towards a set of walnut double doors.

Steeling himself for the encounter ahead, Mood pushed them open effortlessly with his weightlifter's arms and closed them behind him.

Makis, business casual in his shirtsleeves and suit trousers, had his back to him and did not turn around when Mood entered, continuing to stare out of the window.

'You came back.'

'Yes.'

'You failed. You let Athena get away. But you still came back.'

Mood was silent. As this wasn't a question, it didn't seem to require an answer.

'You know I could kill you?'

'You could try,' said Mood.

This seemed to amuse Makis. He spun around, smiling broadly. 'You don't think I could succeed? I have ten, armed, former Mossad agents on this property, ready to put a bullet in your brain at a snap of my fingers!'

The big man shrugged. His indifference to his own life and safety was impressive, and obviously utterly genuine. 'I need to know where she is,' he explained matter-of-factly. 'I need to try again.'

'Yes, well. Thanks to your failure at the convent, I don't know where she is,' said Makis, a sharper edge creeping into his tone. He wasn't about to tell Salim the truth, or share any more intelligence with him about Athena's whereabouts after the last debacle. 'And even if I did, what makes you think I'd trust you to kill her? You had your chance, Salim. I have other men, better-trained men—'

'No.' Mood's voice was firm rather than angry, but it boomed around the room, ricocheting like a bullet off the wood-paneled walls. 'I will do it. I will kill her. My girls cannot rest in peace until I do.'

Makis slammed his fist down on the desk so hard he could have cracked it. 'What the hell happened at the convent?' he demanded. 'What went wrong?'

For the first time, a pained look came over the giant Arab's impassive face, a flash of the anguish that drove him. He seemed to want to explain, but was struggling to find the words.

'Let's walk and talk,' said Makis. 'We'll go to my private beach.'

Opening his desk drawer, he pulled out a gun and a silencer, tucking both into the waistband of his pants with no more ceremony than if he were grabbing a packet of tissues or a box of breath mints. Once again, though, if Mood was intimidated he didn't show it, nodding silently as he walked ahead of Mak out of the door.

The two men proceeded in silence through the villa's gardens and down the winding, private steps to the sand. Mood couldn't see the security detail watching them, guns poised, but he knew they were there. He also knew that once they rounded the headland to the next cove, if Mak took him that far, that they would be out of sight and out of range. He wondered how many souls, men and women, Makis Alexiadis had killed on this beach, dispatching them to their maker with no more qualms of conscience than if he were shooting a duck or a deer? If what Mood had heard was true, this windswept strip of white sand was where he came to be alone and to indulge his pleasures. To walk. To think. To make love. To kill.

But none of that mattered.

Only Athena Petridis mattered.

As they walked, Makis asked again what had happened at the convent. And this time Mood answered, explaining calmly how there had been a diversion: a girl. And afterwards how a priest had come in and spirited 'Sister Elena' away before he'd had time to act decisively; how he'd lost her in the endless maze of ancient passages that led from the nuns' cells down to the beach.

'I wanted to hear her admit what she'd done,' he told Makis, his voice trembling. 'I needed to hear her say it. But she wouldn't.'

'You wasted time,' Makis responded angrily as they rounded the headland. 'I told you to do it the second you were alone with her.'

'I know.' Mood hung his head. 'It was a mistake.' Looking up he added, 'I won't make it twice.'

'No,' agreed Makis. 'You won't.'

In one swift, seamless moment, he pulled the gun from his waistband, spun around and pointed the barrel right between Mood's eyes. He waited for the big man to flinch or cringe or close his eyes. To exhibit any natural instinct in the face of imminent death. But instead Mahmoud just stood there, unblinking, unruffled. His breath didn't even quicken.

*Perfect.* This was the kind of man who could finish Athena Petridis.

He lowered the gun. Smiling, he handed it to Mood. Then, reaching down again, he passed him the silencer. 'Do you know how to use one of these?'

Mood shook his head. 'A silencer, yes. But not this model.'

Taking back the Ruger, Makis attached the shining silver cylinder to the barrel with expert fingers, then removed it again before handing both pieces back to Mood. 'Now you try.'

Mood followed Alexiadis's lead, screwing on the silencer with no difficulty.

337

'Good.' Makis nodded approvingly. 'Athena made contact with me this morning. Unfortunately, she survived a second assassination attempt in London and has since gone to ground. However, the good news is she has no evidence to link either operation with me – London or Sikinos – so we're still in contact over business matters, albeit sporadically.'

'Where is she now?' asked Mood, fingering the gun lovingly.

'I'm not certain yet. But I hope to have a confirmed location soon, some time in the coming days. In the meantime you need to eat, sleep and train. Hard. You can do all of that here.'

'Thank you,' Mood murmured, still mesmerized by the gun in his hands.

'For what?'

'For giving me another chance.'

Extending his arm, Makis patted him on the shoulder in an almost avuncular manner, all trace of his earlier anger gone. What a bizarre man he was!

'The only thanks I want is success,' he told Mood. 'Do not fail again, Salim.'

Now it was Mood's turn to smile.

'I won't.'

Pressing the gun against Makis Alexiadis's temple, he pulled the trigger.

The shot was silent. Even the explosion of Makis's skull as blood and brain tissue splattered out over the white sand was no louder than a dropped watermelon splitting open on the ground. The soft lapping of the waves and the cawing of the gulls overhead easily drowned out the sound.

Laying the gun on the sand, Mood stripped off, waded into the surf and washed the blood from his hands, face and torso as best he could. Then he returned, pulled the clean clothes from his backpack and put them on, laying his blood-stained shirt and shorts over what was left of Makis's head. Retrieving the gun and his packet of forged papers and money, he walked calmly to the far end of the cove.

The speedboat was exactly where Athena had said it would be, tethered beneath the roots of a cypress tree at the edge of the shore. Athena was his commander now. His mistress. His purpose. With his family gone, he'd had no reason to live – until Athena saved him. Her voice, her words . . . it was impossible to explain. But there had been magic in them, some healing power that had stopped him from hurting her back at the convent. That had transfigured him. He couldn't define it, or rationalize it, but nor could he deny its truth. He could hear her voice now in his head like an angel's, guiding him:

'*I lost a child too. My only son. I died that day. But I was reborn. God brought you to me, Mahmoud. He brought you to me for a reason. We are bound together in loss. We are one. Our pain is our power.*'

He had listened, entranced, while Athena told him the truth about Makis Alexiadis. How it was he, and not she, who had profited from the evil migrant trade; he whose greed and avarice and ruthlessness had led directly to Hoda and the girls' deaths.

'He had my husband killed too,' Athena told Mood. 'And did *this* to my face.' Lifting her veil, she had shown Mood her appalling scars, the melted ruin of her once beautiful face. 'I was a sinner back then myself. But I've repented. I've changed. And so can you, Mahmoud. But first you must avenge the ones you lost. Just as I am.'

Climbing inside the boat, Mood started the outboard motor.

*I've done what you asked, my Athena. I've done God's will. The beast is dead.*

With a feeling of deep peace, he sped off into the limitless blue.

# CHAPTER TWENTY-FOUR

Athena sat up in her four-poster bed, leaning back against two cloud-soft goose-down pillows, and turned up the volume on her TV remote. The converted water mill Peter had rented for her recuperation in rural Burgundy was about as remote as one could get in France, but he'd made sure Athena had access to the British news as well as CNN.

'And here we have the first glimpse of the suspect as he attends the initial hearing, in a case that has once again reopened the bitter debate about asylum seekers all across Europe,' the BBC reporter was saying in his clipped, public school accent.

Athena watched as Mahmoud Salim, looking enormous and dark and menacing, if a little confused, emerged from a German police van in handcuffs. She'd allowed two days, enough time for Salim to reach Berlin, before alerting the German authorities to his true identity, as well as to his involvement in the brutal slaying of 'respected businessman' Makis Alexiadis on Mykonos, a murder still dominating the Greek news more than a week later.

Part of her felt sorry for Salim. His grief had blinded him and made him pathetically trusting. Even now, according to Dierk Kimmel, the German lawyer Athena had hired to 'defend' him, Mood still believed that she was on his side. That together they'd been part of an underground resistance determined to destroy Makis Alexiadis and put an end to the evil trade in migrants for ever.

'He keeps asking when you're coming to see him,' said Dierk. 'I'm not sure he's entirely mentally well.'

*Are any of us? w*ondered Athena. Her qualms over having exploited the grief-addled Salim were tempered by the fact that she knew Mood would be perfectly indifferent to spending the remaining years of his life in a German jail, or a Greek one for that matter, if the new president's extradition request were honored. Salim might be confused, but he wasn't suffering. He was beyond suffering. *Like me.* And he had certainly done the world, as well as Athena, a service, by murdering that treacherous snake Makis Alexiadis. *May he rot in hell.*

'Now, what's all this?'

Mary, the fearsomely efficient English nurse that Peter Hambrecht had hired to tend to Athena while she recovered from her extensive facial surgeries, bustled into the room and looked disapprovingly at the television.

'I'll take that, if you don't mind, madam.' She held out her chubby hand for the remote, which Athena meekly handed over. 'You still have thirty more minutes of rest time before your stretches. Rest means rest.'

'I know. I'm sorry. I needed a distraction.'

'Tsk,' said Mary dismissively. 'Stuff and nonsense. Everything will be fine, you'll see.'

Athena liked Mary with her starched uniforms and her pocket watch and the military precision with which she performed all her duties. Every morning, at seven o'clock sharp, the curtains were drawn back and Athena was helped to wash and perform her limited toilette before breakfast in bed at 7.30. 'None of this French nonsense. Bacon, eggs and fried bread. You need to build up your strength.' There were scheduled times for rest, for movement, for pain medication, for everything. Athena found the routine comforting, a reminder of life in the convent. At times she still missed the rhythmic peace of the Sacred Heart. But at other times she felt the thrill of being out, of being free and back in the driver's seat of Spyros's empire. *My empire now.*

She'd outsmarted Makis, just as she'd outsmarted so many enemies before him. But with her would-be rival gone, it was more important than ever for her to take back the reins of the business herself. There was so much to do.

'I suppose you won't get back to sleep now,' Mary grumbled, helping Athena to sit up while she re-plumped her pillows. 'Shall we take a look at how things are healing, then?'

Athena nodded, a sick feeling of apprehension mingled with excitement churning in the pit of her stomach. This morning, for the first time since leaving the Paris clinic, Mary would remove her bandages completely. Athena would be able to see her 'new' face, the image that would represent her new identity, for the rest of her life. She'd re-invented herself before, of course. Risen like a phoenix from the ashes of her childhood, her son's death, the helicopter crash that had so nearly killed her . . . But not like this. Today she would be reborn an entirely different person, utterly unrecognizable as the Athena of old. Today, Athena Petridis would truly and finally die, and a new woman, a stronger, wiser, invincible woman, would emerge to take her place. If all went well . . .

Propping a mirror at the foot of the bed, the nurse began to unwind the dressings encircling Athena's forehead, nose, mouth and chin. She worked slowly and methodically, her

343

fingers deft and light, like an archaeologist unwrapping a fragile Egyptian mummy. As she got close to the skin she slowed even further, watching her patient's reactions carefully for signs of pain or discomfort.

'If anything pulls or stings, tell me at once,' she instructed a mute Athena.

Nothing did. Instead, Athena stared in wonder as, little by little, a woman's face appeared in reflection. First came the smooth, wide forehead. Then the long, slender nose – so different to how it was before! The skin on this new woman's cheeks was taut and had a slightly waxen look, but that too was unrecognizable from the burned, melted ruin that had gone before; nothing short of a miracle. Finally, the lower face emerged, still bruised and with markedly fuller lips and a more pronounced chin, possibly the result of some sort of implant to replace lost tissue. Taken together, despite the residual swelling and some small scars along the hairline and under the jaw, it was the face of a moderately attractive, middle-aged woman.

Athena's eyes welled up with tears.

It was the most beautiful thing she'd ever seen. And she had Peter to thank for it. *Darling Peter*. He was the only really true friend Athena had ever had in this world. Spyros had loved her, in his own way, and he had saved her when she needed saving, after Apollo died. But like all the other, lesser men in Athena's life – Dimitri Mantzaris, Larry Gaster, Antonio Lovato, Spyros had wanted something in return for his love. To possess her. To own her. To suck her dry from the inside out until there was nothing left. No heart, no soul, no identity of her own.

Peter had never wanted her like that. Only Peter had ever loved her unconditionally. Although, of course, there was so much Peter didn't know, so much he would never understand about her life since she left him, no matter how

Athena tried to explain it. Peter Hambrecht didn't know her dark side.

Spyros knew it. He knew it and understood it and nurtured it, like a precious plant, a rare flower. But Spyros was gone now. She was on her own.

'Hmmm. Yes. That all looks good to me,' Mary clucked approvingly as her fingers moved from scar to scar, her critical eye assessing the degree of healing. 'How do you feel?'

'Incredible,' the woman in the mirror answered, her voice choked with emotion. 'Like I could take over the world.'

Mary laughed. This friend of Mr Hambrecht's was a funny one. All meek and mild one minute, and then coming out with things like that the next. *Take over the world, indeed.*

'Let's see if you can manage a proper shower first,' said the nurse, carrying away the used bandages and scrubbing her hands with carbolic soap up to the elbows in the bath-room sink. 'And then I'll bring you a nice cup of tea.'

Later, her face freshly dressed with smaller bandages and her newly washed hair combed up into a tidy bun, Athena won Mary's permission to get dressed and take a 'gentle' stroll in the grounds. 'Nothing strenuous – I mean it. Don't make me ring Mr Hambrecht and tell him you're refusing to rest, because if I do he'll have both our guts for garters. Back in bed by six sharp.'

Athena promised solemnly. She would miss Mary, and this place, and of course Peter. He hadn't wanted to deceive Antonio and set up the whole London clinic arrangement as a decoy, while secretly making alternate arrangements with a top plastic surgeon in Paris. 'Is all this subterfuge really necessary?' he'd asked Athena in one of their last phone calls, while at the same time booking the Mill House and dutifully arranging a small private plane to fly her into Le

Touquet. 'I know you're lying low from the police, but must you really double-cross your friends as well?'

'Until I'm safe, yes,' Athena told him.

'And when will that be?'

'Soon,' she promised him.

'And when you're "safe", I can see you? Face to face?'

She hesitated.

'You promised, Athena,' he reminded her. 'That was your part of the deal. I miss him too, you know,' he added, in the face of her silence. 'But do you think our son would have wanted his death to keep us apart for ever? I don't want to lose you again. I can't . . .'

'You won't,' said Athena. Then, not wanting her last words to him to be a lie, she added. 'I love you, Peter.'

Strolling down past the old mill wheel, still and silent now, to the shallow, rushing brook that snaked along the floor of the valley, Athena drank in the joy of the moment. The warm sun on her back, the heady scent of earth and grass and new life rising up from the ground, the softly lowing calves on the hillside, calling to their mothers. This place was beautiful. Life was beautiful. Her face was beautiful.

But there was much to be done. First, she must leave here and return to where she could reestablish her old networks. After that, she would secure her hold on the coveted migrant routes by doing what Makis had been too short-sighted to do: by running their people-smuggling like any other Petridis business. That meant focusing on quality, from top to bottom. Better boats, better conditions, a safer passage for more 'high-end' stock. No more half-starved children being shipped to pimps in Eastern Europe. That was simply bad business. They needed fewer, more discerning clients, willing to pay a premium for high-quality, reliable shipments of healthy adult workers. Forget the sex trade. The big profits were in illegal slave labor, and the biggest and best buyers in that market were independent farmers and factory owners, struggling to compete with their larger, multinational rivals.

*That's who we should be targeting. It's so obvious!*

Adrenaline coursed through her body as she visualized the challenges to come. Rebuilding Spyros's empire. Creating something meaningful, something lasting of her own. Her life had already been an incredible journey, a story no one could have scripted or even imagined. But she wasn't done yet.

She was alive and free, and Makis Alexiadis was dead.

It was time for the final chapters to begin.

# CHAPTER TWENTY-FIVE

Three men and one woman sat in an uneasy circle in the grand living room of Nathan Maslow's Nantucket beach house. Number 2 Lincoln Circle was a sprawling, gray-shingled estate with a long shell drive, stately grounds and picture-perfect views across the Nantucket Sound. It was a fittingly impressive vacation home for billionaire investor Maslow and his wife, Jane, and the living room was the perfect space for parties with its floor-to-ceiling windows, spacious high ceilings and endlessly comfortable couches.

Today's gathering, however, was not a social event. It was an urgently convened business meeting, and the mood was grim.

'Twenty-six years of work, Mark. Twenty-six years of waiting, of biding our time. And it was all for nothing.'

Nathan Maslow glowered at Mark Redmayne accusingly. As The Group's single largest financial donor, Nathan felt entitled to an explanation as to how, exactly, Ella Praeger had been allowed to simply 'disappear'.

'It's not for nothing,' Redmayne countered, his jaw rigid with tension. He resented Nathan Maslow's assumption of superiority, especially coming from a man who dressed like a buffoon in 'Nantucket red' shorts, docksiders, and a polo shirt covered in lobster motifs. 'I'm as frustrated as you are, Nathan, but we'll find her.'

'Will we? I don't see how, when she can tune in to every communication we make, every attempt to track her down.'

'That's not strictly true . . .' Redmayne ventured, but Nathan wasn't done yet.

'The fact is she should never have been on active operations in the first place!' he snapped. 'Her entire value is as a reconnaissance tool. To gather intelligence.'

'With respect,' Professor Dixon interjected from his seat by the door, 'the way Ella's abilities function mean that she *has* to be in relatively close proximity to any target signal in order to intercept it. We were working on increasing her range, but unfortunately we ran out of time. She was always going to have to accompany an agent on ops.'

'Not this agent,' Nathan growled, simmering with bottled anger like an over-boiled kettle. 'Everybody knows Gabriel's the biggest womanizer in your entire organization. Right, Katherine?'

Katherine MacAvoy blushed vermilion. How on earth had Nathan Maslow got wind of her affair with Gabriel? It was almost a decade ago and almost nobody knew. She glanced suspiciously at Mark Redmayne. The bastard must have let something slip on the golf course! 'That's certainly his reputation,' she answered cautiously.

'That's what's happened here, isn't it?' said Nathan. 'She's fallen for him and now he's calling the shots. They're together somewhere, and they're going to try to go after Athena Petridis with no backup, and Ella's going to get herself killed!'

Mark Redmayne stood up and walked over to the window, his hand thrust deep in the pockets. He longed to be able to turn around and deliver a stinging comeback, to put Nathan Maslow in his place. But the fact was, his biggest donor had just neatly articulated his own fears in a nutshell.

'Look,' he said brusquely. 'I won't sugar-coat it. Ella's disappearance is a blow.'

'You think so?' Maslow sneered.

'And yes, she could be at risk,' Mark went on, ignoring him. 'But I am confident that the situation is salvageable. We will find her, and Gabriel. In the meantime, let's try to focus on the positives. Makis Alexiadis is dead, which is good in itself, and even better in that it means Athena is going to have to start making moves, reaching out to allies and so forth. She can no longer stay invisible, not completely.'

'Hmmm,' Maslow grunted. 'We'll see.'

'When we find and kill Athena, Ella will have no reason to stay on in Europe.'

'Sure she will,' said Nathan. 'She'll have lover-boy.'

'No,' Mark Redmayne contradicted him bluntly. 'She's there to avenge her mother's death. That's her primary motivation. Whatever she feels for Gabriel will evaporate once Athena's been liquidated and the adrenaline rush of the mission is gone. Ella will return to the States. Then we can work on undoing whatever damage Gabriel may have done.'

'I agree,' Professor Dix said quietly. 'The file we gave her on Rachel Praeger's murder was compelling. Ella's doing this for her mother's sake – not for ours, or Gabriel's, or anyone else's.'

'I agree too,' said Katherine. 'And, even if we're wrong, he will tire of her once Athena's dead,' she added, knowingly. 'His big sexual motivator is danger, the thrill of the chase. After that's gone, so is he.'

Nathan Maslow withdrew into angry silence. Mark

Redmayne continued to stare out to sea, his gaze fixed on a lone sailboat, barely visible on the shimmering horizon.

He hadn't said anything to Nathan Maslow, or the others, as he didn't want to raise anyone's expectations. But just a few hours ago he'd gotten word of a possible new location for Athena. Admittedly the address he'd been given seemed wildly improbable. Not even Athena Petridis would be *that* bold, not when she knew The Group would be looking for her.

On the other hand, it was good intelligence from a trusted source. And it was Athena who'd brazenly sent the message alerting the world to her return, with the brand on the little boy's foot. *She wanted us to know she was alive. That we failed twelve years ago. She wanted us to hunt her.* Like Gabriel, it seemed, on some level Athena Petridis must get off on the thrill of the chase.

Well, now the chase was on.

All Mark Redmayne had to do was find her before Ella did.

Ella called Gabriel from her London hotel room.

'Why are you calling me?' His voice sounded more amused than annoyed. 'I thought we agreed no voice calls unless it's an emergency.'

'I forgot. What are you doing on Saturday night?'

'No fixed plans,' Gabriel drawled. 'Are you asking me on a date?'

'Peter Hambrecht's conducting in Oxford. An intimate chamber-music concert at Magdalen College,' said Ella, ignoring the innuendo. 'I'm going to see what I can pick up.'

Gabriel sighed. 'He's no longer in contact with her, Ella. You know that. You've been tuning into his devices for weeks.'

'I think Oxford will be different.'

'It won't.'

'Well, I'm going.'

'You're wasting your time. We should go back to other known contacts. A Japanese professor, Noriko Adachi, was found dead in London. She lost her son to the Petridis's drug empire years ago and had been in England asking questions about Athena before she went . . . Ella? Are you there?'

A single, long beep answered the question.

Peter Hambrecht gave a few light twitches of his baton as he guided the musicians effortlessly through the last bars of Handel's *Messiah*. It was glorious to be back in Oxford, and specifically in Magdalen chapel, a baroque masterpiece that was surely the most fitting setting possible for one of Peter's very favorite pieces of music. The ancient stone walls, the faint, lingering smell of incense and candle wax, mingled with women's perfume, and the joy of doing the one thing he knew he could do perfectly and effortlessly – conducting an orchestra – all helped ease the pain. The terrible pain of Athena.

'You bring it on yourself you know, my love,' Paolo, Peter's bookseller boyfriend of almost a year, told him reprovingly last night, right before Peter took his chauffeured car to Oxford. 'I don't know this woman at all, but I do know you can't save her.'

'How can you possibly know that?' Peter challenged.

'Because no one can ever save another person from themselves,' Paolo said simply. 'Besides, from everything you've told me, salvation isn't what this lady wants.'

He was right. Absolutely right. The other things Paolo had said had been right too. About Athena being toxic to Peter's happiness, about her dragging him back to the past, about his need to focus on his present life, his glittering career, their relationship.

But Athena's latest betrayal still hurt.

She'd gone. Disappeared like a thief in the night from the house in Burgundy, just as Peter had helped her to disappear from Antonio's flat, and just as Athena had promised, *sworn*, that she wouldn't do to him.

Poor Mary was convinced that she was to blame. 'I don't know what happened, Mr H. Truly I don't. It was a day like any other. She seemed well. Calm. When I found her gone at six the next morning, I assumed she'd gone for an early morning walk in the grounds, but there was no trace of her.'

'It's quite all right, Mary,' Peter had reassured her. 'I'm afraid Athena is a master at this. Her life has always been rather . . . complicated. She'll show up eventually.'

'Yes, sir, I daresay, but she still needs medical attention, that's the thing! She thinks she's well but she isn't. Her operation scars aren't healed yet. Without proper nursing they could easily get infected. And she's supposed to have physio for her walking as well, that limp she has on the left side? We'd only just started the exercises. But she's so stubborn.'

'That she is,' Peter had agreed with a light laugh. But inside, his own feeling of dread was building, and it only grew greater as the days passed. Slowly it dawned on him that Athena had never had any intention of recuperating in private. The new identity he'd helped her to forge – the new face, new name, new papers he'd spent so much money and effort procuring for her – had never been so that she could live out the remainder of her days in peace and safety, as Peter had hoped.

*The surgery wasn't her ticket out of her old life of crime with Spyros. It was her ticket back into it.*

*She used me.*

Spyros Petridis might be dead and gone, but the changes he'd wrought in Athena's psyche were not so easily reversed. The Athena Peter had grown up with in Organi was still there, deep inside. But she'd long since been subsumed by this other Athena, this dangerous, vengeful, duplicitous Athena, who had learned to love power for its own sake and to wield it without mercy or compassion.

Lowering his baton as the dying notes of the Handel subsided into a breathless silence, Peter closed his eyes and waited for the inevitable eruption of the audience.

'Bravo, maestro!' They yelled and whistled from the pews. 'Encore!'

Tears coursed down Peter Hambrecht's cheeks. Only one member of the audience surmised that they weren't brought on by the sublime music.

Ella waited outside the vestry that served as the conductor's dressing room, poised to intercept any signals from Peter Hambrecht's phone. She didn't have to wait long.

'Mary?'

'I'm sorry to ring you again, Mr H.' The nurse's voice rang out as clearly in Ella's head as if she were standing in the same, cold stone cloister. 'But something came back to me. I don't know if it's relevant.'

'What is it?' asked Peter, unable to keep the hope out of his voice entirely.

'I overheard her talking on the phone. Not the day before she left but earlier in the week. I don't know what she said, I'm afraid. I only remembered it at all because she was speaking Greek. But she was talking to someone called "Jimmy". I wondered if that might mean anything to you?'

'Thank you,' said Peter, his heart sinking. He had no idea who 'Jimmy' might be, and with no further clues he had no way of finding out. 'I appreciate the call. I'll give it some thought.'

There were no other calls. Ella waited till Peter Hambrecht left the college and followed him back to the Randolph, but after a single lonely brandy at the bar, he turned his phone off and turned in for the night.

Depressed, Ella pulled on her jacket and summer scarf and headed back towards her own room, a tiny Airbnb above a bookshop on the other side of Christchurch Meadows. Gabriel was right. It had been a wild-goose chase coming to Oxford, a foolish exercise of hope over experience. Clearly Athena had used her ex-husband and moved on, just as she'd done with all her other old lovers. Trust and loyalty were either qualities she didn't understand, or luxuries she couldn't afford. With Makis Alexiadis dead, there was nothing to stop her coming back to reclaim her rightful place as mistress of her late husband's empire. Nothing except the terrible facial burns that would make her instantly recognizable to her many enemies lurking in the shadows.

Peter Hambrecht had helped his former wife and child-hood playmate overcome that problem. Having set up an effective decoy in London, he had spirited her away for reconstructive surgery somewhere else. Unfortunately for Peter, now that she had a new face and name, Athena didn't need him any more. Evidently she'd moved on to 'Jimmy' as her confidant of choice, the next pawn in her endless game of chess, staying one step ahead of her pursuers. No doubt he was another former lover . . .

Walking past the Radcliffe Camera, its domed roof dream-like in the misty moonlight, it came to Ella suddenly, staring her in the face like the answer to a crossword clue, insultingly obvious now that she'd seen it.

*Another former lover. And what had Mary said? 'I only remembered because they were speaking Greek'?*

There weren't any Greeks named Jimmy. *Dimi*, on the other hand, short for Dimitri, had to be one of the most common Greek names of all. No doubt in her sexual heyday, Athena Petridis had bedded more than one Dimitri. But if Ella remembered correctly from Athena's file, there was one in particular who would have both the financial means and the contacts to be able to help her, even now. One who'd been deeply enough embroiled in the Petridises' criminal dealings to be afraid of Athena's Lazarus-like resurrection, and what it might mean for his own reputation and legacy.

Quickening her pace, she ran up the High Street to Carfax, turning left past Tom Tower and left again along Christchurch Meadows until she reached the tiny cobbled lane where she was staying. Once safely in her room above the bookshop, she locked the door, drew the curtains, and flipped open her laptop, messaging Gabriel on their private, encrypted service. She could see at once that he was already online. Gabriel was always online. *Like a low-tech version of me.*

'Is Dimitri Mantzaris still alive?' Ella typed.

The reply came back within seconds. A thumb's-up sign. Then, 'He's eighty.'

'Where does he live?' Ella followed up.

A few more seconds. 'Vouliagmeni. Near Athens. Why?'

*Would Athena return to Athens?* She might. It was the sort of move she was ballsy enough to pull off, although Ella still felt it was more likely she would pick somewhere quieter and more remote, especially if she were going to base herself in Greece. She also couldn't imagine her living as the houseguest of a figure as famous as Dimitri Mantzaris, the former prime minister.

'Any other property?' she asked Gabriel.

This time a full three minutes went by before he answered.

'No. Goodnight.'

Ella shut down the computer, irritated. Her elation of earlier had evaporated now, her balloon pricked by both Gabriel's monosyllabic lack of enthusiasm and by the difficulties involved in following up Dimitri Mantzaris as a lead. For one thing she would have to tread carefully if she returned to Athens or anywhere in Greece, knowing that Redmayne had agents from The Group swarming like maddened ants, hunting for her and Gabriel. For another, as a former premier, Mantzaris was bound to have extensive security, making it harder to get close enough to him to pick up any communications he might be having with Athena. All this assuming, of course, that Mantzaris *was* 'Jimmy'. She'd felt so certain about it all on her way home from the Randolph. But now, just like Peter Hambrecht, she could sense her hopes fading.

*I'll sleep on it*, she thought, undressing and dropping her clothes mindlessly in a heap on the floor, before removing her make-up, cleaning her teeth and climbing into the creaky single bed. Turning her phone to silent, she plugged it in to charge in the alcove next to her pillow when it suddenly buzzed in her hand.

'Why are you calling me?' She mimicked Gabriel's tone from their last call. 'I thought we agreed the phone was only for emergencies.'

'You turned off your computer,' he answered matter-of-factly. 'And you didn't answer my question. Why are you interested in Mantzaris? Is she in contact with him?'

'Maybe,' said Ella, too tired to explain everything tonight. 'I'll message you in the morning.'

'Don't message,' said Gabriel. 'Come back to London. I did some more digging just now. Turns out he does own other real estate, through an offshore trust in Cayman. He's actually a remarkably active investor for an eighty-year-old.

357

And you'll never guess which property he picked up in private sale just this week, for twice its listed value?'

'Which?' asked Ella grumpily. She'd never enjoyed guessing games.

'Number 24 Liasti Beach Road.'

Ella's heart leaped into her mouth.

'Otherwise known as Villa Mirage. Now who do we know who'd pay twice what it's worth to get hold of Makis Alexiadis's former center of operations and take it over, lock stock and barrel?' Gabriel chuckled. 'Nice work, Miss Praeger. It looks like we've come full circle. And now you and I have some travel plans to arrange.'

# CHAPTER TWENTY-SIX

Athena Petridis tightened her silk kimono robe around her slender waist and opened the sliding glass doors to the deck, taking her coffee with her. It was her favorite time of day: early morning, an hour or two after sunrise, when the warm promise of the day to come hung soft and sweet in the air, but the ocean breeze made the heat comfortable rather than cloying. And this morning was even lovelier than usual, with one of those spectacular, pina-colada skies that only the Greek islands could produce, an almost tacky riot of azure blue and soft pink and burnt-sienna orange bleeding out from a lazily rising sun.

All the tourists and villa owners were still in their beds, sleeping off the excesses of the prior night's drinking and dancing and general indulgence. But the army of workers on whose backs the island was run – the garbage collectors and delivery men and fishermen and boutique owners – they were all awake and buzzing around in the streets below Villa Mirage, their mingled shouts and idling engines and clattering crates of produce providing a background soundtrack of life and vibrancy to the otherwise tranquil scene.

*It's good to be alive*, Athena thought. *And even better to be waking up here, in the house that Makis Alexiadis built.* She felt like a conquering empress, or a goddess atop Mount Olympus. Powerful. Protected. Reborn.

Leaning back on one of Makis's ultra-modern sun loungers (some of the furniture would have to go; she would speak to Dimitri Mantzaris later, have one of her people send through a list of changes), Athena gazed down at the glorious manicured gardens that spilled in terraces down the cliffside until they seemed to merge with the tranquil blue of the sea. There was no doubt about it, this was an incredible house, and a fitting center of operations for the rebirth of an empire.

It pleased her that Dimitri had bought it for her. That, despite her new face, new life and new identity – Athena Solakis, as she would henceforth be known – she would still maintain some links with the past. Her affair with Dimitri felt so preposterously long ago now. And of course, it was. Dimi had been president then, a powerful, virile man in his mid-fifties. Now he was old and fat and walked with a cane, crippled by an arthritic knee, sustained only by memories of past glories.

*His race is run. But mine isn't. The fates have not yet finished paying for what they did, for taking Apollo from me.*

The ancient Egyptians believed that 'true' death came only after your name was forgotten, no longer written or spoken out loud. By branding the letters of her son's name onto the bodies of her victims (P on the Japanese woman who'd followed her to London, L on the migrant child, As and Os on countless others'), Athena had made sure Apollo lived on. She had vented her anger, hit back at the fates, and created a memorial to her darling baby, engraved not in stone but in the flesh of her enemies. Spyros's old calling card had inspired her, helping to obfuscate the true meaning of Athena's coded message. But the longer it took the world to figure it out, the longer Apollo's soul would live on. Athena would keep writing his name until she, too, had left this world. Until her son's spirit and her own were finally reunited, never again to be torn apart.

Sipping her coffee, the strong, black Turkish blend that Spyros had got her hooked on twenty years ago, Athena contemplated the day ahead. This morning she must talk to all her South American suppliers about the unconscionable hikes in cocaine prices, and pay bonuses to two of her top enforcers in the Czech Republic for securing a valuable piece of commercial real estate from a 'reluctant' seller. After that she had two hours of physiotherapy with the local girl she'd hired to take over where the indomitable Nurse Mary had left off in Burgundy. *Sweet Mary.* Athena had far preferred Peter's English nurse to Helen, the sullen, shaven-headed Mykonos girl that her private doctor, Farouk, had recommended to help her combat the limp in her left leg, a hangover from the helicopter crash that remained the last, telltale giveaway to Athena's old identity. To Athena's eyes, Helen seemed deeply distasteful, all puppy fat and attitude. But apparently she had a stellar reputation as a physio, renowned for fast and lasting results. And now, at the moment of her rebirth, that was all that mattered.

Draining the last of her coffee, Athena turned to go back inside. Catching sight of her reflection in Makis's gleaming glass doors, she stopped and did a double take. This last week at Villa Mirage had helped not just to heal her bruises but to tan her face a light nut-brown. Her newly dyed dark hair, cut in a feathered bob, framed her face beautifully, and though she would never again boast the radiance of youth, her green eyes shone with hope and the promise of great things to come. Her figure, of course, had always been excellent, slim and toned and with none of the middle-aged spread that other women her age succumbed to so meekly, relinquishing their last vestiges of attraction or claims to male sexual interest without so much as a fight.

Not Athena. *You're beautiful again*, she told her reflection. Her legendary allure, in hibernation for twelve long years, was coming back to life like a delicate snowdrop tentatively unfurling its petals in the first thaw of spring after a long, hard winter. Perhaps, once the hard work of regaining her iron grip on Spyros's empire was complete, she would consider finding a lover? Someone younger, perhaps, but not so young that they couldn't challenge her. A world of possibilities awaited.

The physiotherapist walked into the kitchen, her sneakers squeaking and squelching in an irritating rhythm with each step.

They were only halfway through the physio session, but already Athena felt drained, not so much by the monotony of the repeated exercises and stretches, but by the young therapist's almost comical lack of personality. Helen wasn't rude, or at least not to a point where one could reasonably object to her manner. When Athena asked her a question, she answered politely. And if Athena exhibited any pain or exhaustion with a certain exercise, the physio instinctively paused, waiting uncomplainingly for her patient to regain strength. Yet despite this, almost everything about Helen irked Athena, from her butch hairstyle and gait, to her ugly, shapeless clothes – loose green scrubs hid what Athena could only assume were fat legs, if the blubber rolls around the girl's belly were anything to go by. Her face might have been pretty, even though most of the time it was half hidden beneath a mannish baseball cap. The only really striking feature was her oddly wide-set eyes – familiar eyes, Athena thought, on the rare occasions they made direct contact with her own. But Helen was nothing if not professional, and made a point of focusing most of her attention on the motion of Athena's left knee and ankle, rather than on her newly beautiful features.

Perhaps that was what irked Athena the most: the fact that this uniquely un-compelling young woman should find *her*, the legendary Athena, uncompelling too. No more noteworthy or interesting than any of her other charges.

'What are you doing in there?' Athena demanded now. Perched on the edge of one of Makis's ornate, silk-covered footstools, she gingerly stretched her aching leg out in front of her.

'I'm getting you something for the pain,' replied Helen, in her grating island accent.

'Don't bother. I don't do painkillers,' Athena called out bluntly from the other room. 'I need a short break, that's all.'

'No need to worry,' said Helen. As if she, this young nobody, possessed the ability to worry Athena Solakis. 'This isn't an opiate or anything addictive. It's a homeopathic powder I use with all my clients. I mix it with fish oils for overall joint health and a custom blend of multivitamins for energy. It works.'

Athena grunted gracelessly, still unsure why she felt so annoyed. This was the most she'd heard Helen speak during their time together, and if her magic powder really did work, it might escalate her recovery. The pain in Athena's leg was mild but it was persistent, no doubt a contributor to her present bad mood.

'All right, but hurry up,' she commanded. 'I have a busy schedule this afternoon and we need to get these stretches finished.'

'Of course, Ms Solakis,' the girl said obediently. 'I won't be long.'

A few moments later, she emerged, waddling in with a glass of unappetizing-looking sludge-brown liquid fizzing in her hand.

Frowning, Athena reached for it.

'What? What's the matter?' she snapped. As her long, bony fingers wrapped themselves around the glass, the girl's pudgier ones refused to let go. Almost as if she didn't want Athena to drink it. Their eyes locked, and for a moment Athena could have sworn she saw something searching in Helen's gaze. An unspoken question. A hesitation, but with a hint of something deeper. Fear? Pleading?

'Nothing,' said the girl. But she was still holding on to the glass. 'Nothing's the matter.'

'In that case . . . may I?' Athena looked slowly from the girl to the glass and back again. Those wide eyes were beginning to haunt her.

Finally, as if released from a trance, the physio released her grip. 'Of course. It doesn't taste very nice I'm afraid.'

Raising the noxious-looking liquid impatiently to her lips, Athena downed it in two swift gulps, grimacing as the last bitter drops descended into her stomach.

'Revolting,' she muttered. 'But I think I'm OK to resume now. Shall we go back out to the terrace?'

Helen had turned away. When she spoke her voice sounded different. Less grating, somehow.

'I'd give it a minute or two if I were you,' she said softly.

'I don't *want* to give it a—' Athena began, but her words were cut short by a strange, cramping sensation in her stomach. It was swiftly followed by a tingling in the tips of her fingers and toes that was hard to describe but was distinctly unpleasant, like a sort of burning numbness.

She groaned, clasping her hands to her belly.

Helen turned around slowly. She made no reaction to her patient's obvious distress. Instead, removing her baseball cap, she placed it deliberately on the table beside her, and ran a hand over the fuzz covering her shaven skull.

Athena grimaced. 'Call Georgiou,' she hissed, through clenched teeth. 'Tell him . . . Dr Farouk . . .' She was fighting for breath now, gasping like a stranded fish. The numb heat in her fingers and toes was spreading along her arms and legs, making it difficult to move, and her lungs and chest felt painfully constricted.

*What's happening?* She fought back a surge of panic. *Am I having a heart attack? Or a stroke? Am I going to die?*

Wide-eyed and frightened, she stared helplessly at Helen. Why was the stupid girl just standing there doing nothing? Surely she could see something was very wrong? Why hadn't she gone to fetch Georgiou, the butler, as Athena had requested? Opening her mouth to protest, Athena found her jaw was suddenly clamped shut. A rigor-like tension was setting in to her neck and facial muscles in some awful, painful paralysis. Flailing her arms, she clutched wildly at a side table, missed and landed with a thud on the carpeted floor.

Immobile, eyes glazed, she watched as dumpy Helen stepped over her, with no more ceremony than if she were a sack of rubbish or a rolled-up rug. Walking slowly over to the door, Helen locked it with an audible *click*. Then she flipped a switch to darken the windows to blackout and turned on the overhead lights.

*She knows her way around the house*, thought Athena, clocking the girl's sure, confident movements as she glided around the room, straightening a tablecloth here or a framed photograph there, taking her time.

Finally satisfied, Helen sat down and gazed impassively at Athena, lying motionless on the floor. Athena's sense of foreboding grew. Something clearly wasn't right. *Why won't the fat slug help me?* A dribble of saliva escaped Athena's lips as she struggled again to speak. And then, suddenly, through the fog of terror and confusion, it dawned on her.

The powder. *'I use it with all my clients.'*

*She's poisoned me. The bitch has poisoned me!*

Even in the throes of panic, Athena's sharp mind raced. Who was this girl? 'Helen' knew where all the switches and systems were inside the villa. She'd clearly been here before. Had she worked for Makis? Was she loyal to him, perhaps, or to someone else within his faction? Dr Farouk had recommended her. Had *he* been on Makis's payroll too? Perhaps they were both part of a rebel clique within the organization still plotting to overthrow her, a hardcore Mykonos inner circle? Dimitri had warned her about coming here to Makis's own lair so soon after her rival's demise. If only she'd listened!

Removing her cap, Ella leaned back and shifted forwards in her chair, trying to find a less uncomfortable position. The prosthetic fat rolls she wore under her scrubs chafed everywhere and made every small movement more difficult. But as she'd learned at Camp Hope, changing one's body language and walk could be two of the most important elements in a successful disguise. Being heavy and ungainly had helped her *feel* like Helen, and that alone had been enough to pull the wool over Athena's self-centered, narcissistic eyes.

She'd imagined this moment countless times: revealing herself to Athena as she lay dying, so that the monster's final thought on earth would be that Rachel Praeger's daughter had outsmarted and destroyed her. That she, Ella Praeger, had fulfilled her life's destiny and avenged her mother's murder at last. But now that it was actually happening, the closure she'd dreamed of eluded her. She felt no pity for Athena. She deserved none. But although it pained her to admit it, Ella found herself disappointed, even regretful, that their cat-and-mouse game should be coming to an end. For better or worse, there had been a connection between the two of them. Ella had felt it back at the convent, and she was sure Athena felt it too: a toxic yet magnetic pull towards each other. An intertwining of their lives and fates and purposes, so that only one of them could ultimately survive. Athena's death would mean that Ella had won. But it would also mean the game was over. It shocked Ella to realize just how desolate that made her feel.

'You!' Athena gasped, the effort of forming and expelling the word almost more than she could bear. Soon, she knew, speech would be impossible. She must try now.

'You recognize me, then?' the girl asked, but in English this time, the flawless English of a native-born American. Her eyes bored defiantly into Athena's own. How could she not have seen it before? The high cheekbones, those wide-set cartoon eyes . . .

*'You're the girl from the convent,'* she tried to say. *'The bakery girl!'* But what actually came out was a slurred mass of words, barely comprehensible.

With an effort, Ella caught the word 'bakery'.

'That's right. Very good. I was the girl from the bakery on Folegandros. You saw me at the convent that day.' Heaving herself out of the chair, Ella kneeled down so that her face was only inches from Athena's. 'I ought to have killed you then but I was too inexperienced. I wasn't prepared, and I was following orders. Not any more, though. I play by my own rules now.'

She smiled, reflecting for a moment that it was actually she and Gabriel who had set the agenda for today's strike. The reality was it was *their* rules now, not just hers. Almost without her noticing, their relationship had shifted from 'mentor and recruit', to allies, to true partners. Even so, killing Athena Petridis was personal to Ella Praeger in a way that it could never be for Gabriel, no matter how much he hated her.

Reaching down, she slipped her hands under Athena's armpits and dragged her across the room, before pulling her up into a sitting position and propping her back against the base of an armchair. Her paralysis was almost complete now, so it was like moving a dead weight.

*This woman murdered your mother*, she reminded herself, determined not to allow any glimmer of compassion to creep in and derail her. *Rachel had begged for her life. She had pleaded with Athena – as a woman, as a mother – to spare her. But Athena had just watched while Spyros held her head under the water. While he drowned her like an unwanted cat in a bag.*

Strengthened, Ella began the monologue she'd been rehearsing in her head for days.

'You have between five and fifteen minutes left, in case you were wondering,' she told Athena. 'Nobody's coming. These are your last moments on earth. I'd like you to think about that.'

The slumped figure made a low, groaning noise, mostly through her nose, but that was all.

'The liquid you just drank contained a nerve agent. It's similar to Novichok, which I know you're familiar with,' Ella went on. 'It's fatal, irreversible, and reasonably painful. Although not as painful as you deserve. The cramps are from your stomach starting to hemorrhage, although your lungs or heart are likely to give way before that kills you.'

Another groan and the rolling of the eyes triggered a seizure-like spasm, stiff and uncontrolled. Foam had begun to appear at the corners of Athena's newly perfected lips, a sign that things were progressing more swiftly than Ella had intended. There wasn't much time.

'My real name is Ella. Ella Praeger,' she said quickly, scanning Athena's expression for a reaction. But all she could make out was the generalized fear and dilated pupils of a person anticipating imminent death. Had she left it too late?

But no. Athena ought to be lucid, right to the end. The poison Ella had administered had no effect on the cognitive function of the brain. Victims were supposed to be able to hear, see and understand perfectly, despite the pain.

'My mother was Rachel Praeger,' Ella pushed on, tears streaming down her cheeks. 'You stood by and watched while your husband drowned her on a private beach near Athens. Do you remember?'

Athena let out a dreadful, guttural sound that might have been a death rattle. Mucus streamed from her nose, but her eyes remained fixed on Ella's. She couldn't seem to respond, but she was listening.

'Rachel worked for The Group, back in the 1990s, and her dream was for me to work for them too. So now I do. We're the ones who brought down your helicopter by the way, in case you never figured it out. We destroyed your evil husband and now I'm here to finish the job. You are about to die, Athena.' Ella's voice broke with emotion. 'Is there anything you want to say to me?'

Athena's eyes glistened with tears. Her lips were moving, faintly and apparently silently. Ella brought her ear as close as she could, straining to hear. And at last she did, a single, breathy word.

'*Apollo.*'

Rage flowed into Ella's body like lava. *No. No, no, no!* The monster's last word could not be about her dead son.

About *her* loss. She didn't deserve that! It was Ella's loss that mattered now. Ella's pain. Ella's vengeance.

Clamping Athena's face between her hands, she forced her to look at her.

'Do. You. Remember. My. Mother?' she demanded, stabbing out each word like a switchblade.

Athena's lips parted. For the last time, the two women looked at one another, face to face. Then, with a final effort of will, defeating the demands of her collapsing body, Athena's bony fingers grasped Ella's collar and she whispered back a single, Greek word. A word that meant that she, Athena Petridis, would not let her killer win. That the last laugh, even in death, would be hers.

'Όχι.' She breathed defiantly at Ella.

*No.*

# PART THREE

# CHAPTER TWENTY-SEVEN

**Six weeks later . . .**

Ella sat in the back of the UberX, her face pressed to the window as the rain streamed down. Outside, the streets and beaches of East Hampton were deserted, the wet October weather leaving an eerie, glistening sheen on the grand, weather-boarded homes with their drenched gardens, ghostly visions of green and white beneath a brooding, gray sky.

Once again Ella reflected on the unlikely series of events that had brought her here. How utterly crazy everything had been since Mykonos, and the fateful day of Athena's death. *Not death*, she reminded herself, her gaze fixed on a single raindrop snaking its way down the car window. *Murder.*

*I murdered Athena Petridis.*

One day, Ella imagined, those shocking words would have the effect they were supposed to. They would elicit some profound feeling in her. Not guilt, perhaps, because there was no question that Athena deserved to die. But awe would surely be appropriate? Awe for the magnitude and finality of what she had done, of ending another human life. It worried her that right now she felt nothing at all beyond a nagging discomfort that Athena's last word on earth – 'no' – had been a denial of the admission Ella had so desperately craved.

No, she didn't remember Ella's mother.

No, Rachel Praeger's drowning had not been a significant event in her life. Losing Apollo, her own son, *that* was what she remembered, *that* was what she cared about. Not Ella's mother, or any of her myriad other victims.

'Forget her,' Gabriel had told Ella robustly as they boarded the seaplane back to the mainland, just hours after the murder. Ella had been voicing her disappointment, although she'd wisely omitted the part about already missing the thrill of the chase. 'She's dead, and nothing she said or did matters any more,' said Gabriel. 'Besides, who knows what she really meant by that one word? People aren't rational in the moment of death. Or when they're in pain. Athena was experiencing both.'

Ella nodded mutely. He was right. It just didn't make her feel any better. It occurred to her that she might be in shock. Her teeth were chattering, and the heavy wool blanket Gabriel had wrapped around her shoulders was doing nothing to alleviate the chills. Sipping hot, sweet tea from the flask he'd given her, she looked down at the procession of police cars and ambulances making their belated way up the cliff towards Villa Mirage, trying desperately to shake off the feeling of misery that engulfed her.

*What's done is done and can never be undone.*

Where had she learned that? At school?

And just like that, flashes of another life began to come back to her: Mimi, the ranch, high school. How different she'd been. How 'other'. How unexplainable, even to herself. She remembered her desperation to get away, to leave Paradise Valley and her lonely existence there. The thrill of college at Berkeley, swiftly followed by the misery of her debilitating headaches, the shame and isolation of hearing 'voices' in her head and worrying about her mental health.

Then she thought about her life in San Francisco. Gary Larson, her awful, lecherous boss at Biogen; Bob and his wife Joanie, her first true friends. And Mimi's death. The funeral, the day that changed everything. The first time she'd laid eyes on Gabriel . . .

She turned and looked at him, sitting beside her in the cramped seaplane, her thoughts bringing her full circle. Even in Athena's dying moments, the most significant event in her life to date, Gabriel had been on Ella's mind. Almost as if he were a part of her, as if his irritating, transmitted 'voice' had become internalized, a permanent fixture of Ella's inner life. They'd grown closer in the last two months, since breaking away from The Group, that was for sure. They'd both learned to communicate better, their common goal of finding and killing Athena and keeping one step ahead of Redmayne ultimately overcoming their former rivalry and distrust. And yet, despite this closeness, this fragile brotherhood, it struck Ella that she still knew almost nothing about this man who had changed her life so profoundly. This infuriating, yet addictive person who had led her here, introduced her to The Group and encouraged her to use her abilities, her extraordinary gifts, to serve a higher purpose. This man – who had told her the truth about her parents and convinced her it was moral to kill another human being if it were done in the name of justice – remained an enigma.

Thanks to Gabriel, Ella Praeger had been born again, for better or worse. She had risen like a phoenix from the ashes of her old life. And yet in so many ways, all the important ways, he was a stranger.

'*Who are you?*' Ella had wanted to ask him. But she knew that, if she did, she would probably get only half an answer. She consoled herself that maybe that was all he had to give. After all, *she* barely knew who *she* was any more: a grieving daughter?

A cold-blooded killer? A genetically modified freak? Perhaps, imperfect as it was, the bond she and Gabriel had formed would have to be enough.

When they landed at the same private airstrip in Northern Greece that they'd flown out of together just weeks before, Gabriel handed Ella a fresh weekend bag full of new clothes, papers and cash. Then he helped her into the back seat of the jeep that would take her to Athens's international airport, and her flight to Stockholm, where they'd agreed Ella would lie low until the mysterious death of 'Athena Solakis', Dimitri Mantzaris's reclusive tenant, died down. Once the news cycle moved on, Ella would be free to return home to San Francisco, if that's what she wanted. At some point she would have to decide what she intended to do with the rest of her life. Whether she would return to The Group, rebuilding bridges after her flagrant rule-breaking with Gabriel, and allow her 'gifts' to be used on other, future missions. Or whether avenging her mother's murder already marked a fitting end to the bizarre chapter in her life that had begun with Mimi's death and ended with that of Athena Petridis.

Climbing wearily into the car, she turned to Gabriel and asked the unspoken question hovering in the air between them.

'Will I see you again?'

Reaching into the back seat, he touched her cheek lightly

with the back of his hand. It was an unusually intimate gesture for him – loving, even. To Ella's embarrassment she felt tears welling up in her eyes and a lump forming in the back of her throat.

'I'm sure you will,' he said gruffly.

'When?'

'I don't know.' He forced a smile. 'That might depend on our friend Mr Redmayne. But soon I hope. Once it's safe. Take care of yourself, Ella.'

Now, reminiscing in the back of a different car, and safely on US soil once again, the finality of Gabriel's parting words hit Ella forcefully. In his own repressed, stiff-upper-lip way, he'd been saying goodbye.

Ella hadn't seen him since that day, and she had no idea where he was.

From the moment she'd landed in Stockholm, none of Gabriel's cell phones or email addresses worked. He had simply disappeared, like a ghosting lover, melting out of Ella's life as swiftly and completely as he had first materialized in it. Walking alone through the cobbled streets of Stockholm's romantic old town, Gamla Stan to the locals, muffled up against the autumn chill, Ella could almost believe that the entire last six months of her life had never happened. That it had all been a crazy, elaborate dream. Without Gabriel, none of it seemed real.

Only her ability to isolate and interpret the signals in her head, now almost second nature, reminded her tangibly that what had happened was no fantasy. Camp Hope and Professor Dixon were as real as she was. Thanks to them, Ella no longer suffered from headaches, or nausea or panic attacks. Now she could tune in or out of private electronic conversations at will, be it eavesdropping a lovers' texted tiff at a café, or checking the speed of the electronic transfers being sent from her bank. From time to time, as her

Swedish improved, she amused herself by tuning in to the police radio and following the dramas of drug busts or immigration raids as they unfolded in real time. Anything to distract her from her conflicted feelings about Athena, or from the total radio silence from Gabriel.

It was about two weeks after she arrived in Stockholm that Bob turned up. Ella found her old friend from San Francisco sitting waiting in the lobby of her hotel, as if it were the most normal thing in the world for him to be there, a smiling, khaki-clad ghost from Christmas past, looking like every American tourist with his fanny pack and camera and his San Francisco Giants baseball cap, worn at a jaunty angle.

'Hello, stranger.' He smiled at Ella. 'I've come to take you home.'

According to Bob he'd been contacted out of the blue by 'a weirdo', who from his description could only have been Gabriel, and who informed him where Ella was and that she was waiting for a signal that it was safe to return to the States.

'He never explained why it *wouldn't* be safe,' said Bob, over an enormous plate of meatballs at the Julius' Café. 'He never really explained anything, in fact. He just wired me a boat-load of money, like, a *lot*, and an air ticket, and gave me the address of your hotel. So here I am.'

'Joanie didn't mind, you just taking off for Europe to find me?' Ella asked, trying to picture the conversation between husband and wife. 'And what about your shifts at the café?'

'I was owed time off,' Bob shrugged. 'And yeah, Joanie thought it was weird. I mean, it *is* weird. But for the kind of money this nut-job was offering us, what were we gonna do, say "no"? Besides,' he grinned, depositing the last of the delicious meatballs into his mouth and swallowing greedily before he went on. 'Joanie's missed you. We both have. I'm happy to be the guy who busts you out of Jonestown, or whatever kind of a mess it is you've been sucked into over here. I don't suppose you want to tell me what the hell's been happening since May? Or what this "danger" is that you were in?'

Ella shook her head. 'I can't.'

'Or you'd have to kill me, right?' said Bob, cheerfully accepting that the conversation was now closed and showing zero inclination to press her. 'But you're cool to fly back with me?'

'Yes,' said Ella, partly because she was so very happy to see him, and partly because at that moment, she couldn't think of a reason not to go.

The flight back was long and uneventful. Gabriel had sprung for first-class seats and, to her own surprise, while Bob watched back-to-back movies, Ella fell asleep almost immediately after takeoff and didn't wake until the cabin lights came back on for the coffee service pre-landing.

Settling back into her apartment and daily life in San Francisco was harder. She didn't need to find work right away. Helen Martindale, her realtor, had found a temporary renter for Paradise Ranch, which meant Ella had a modest but steady stream of money coming in.

'I don't know where you've been all this time,' Helen complained, when Ella finally returned her calls 'but I've had to turn down two huge offers from developers over the summer, wanting to build homes up there. If I'd been able to reach you—'

'It wouldn't have made any difference,' said Ella. 'I've changed my mind. I'm not selling, at least not yet. And certainly not to a developer.'

Some decisions, like that one, felt good. Easy. Black and white. Others – like what to do about The Group, and how

379

to spend the rest of her life – were harder. Grayer. Part of her hoped that the decision would be taken out of her hands. That someone from The Group would contact her, either to congratulate her on completing the Petridis mission solo and try to coax her back into the fold, or to berate her for going rogue with Gabriel and banish her from their service for ever. But as the days and weeks passed and nobody called or showed up on her doorstep, it dawned on her that, as far as The Group was concerned, the ball was in Ella's court.

When the invitation finally arrived in the mail – a stiff, formal card in a crisp white envelope, old fashioned and elegant, like something out of *The Great Gatsby* – Ella was astonished to receive it. It was from Mark Redmayne himself, inviting her to a 'private lunch' at his Hamptons estate, Oakacres, as if there had never been any problem between the two of them. Folded inside the printed card was a handwritten note, in beautiful cursive script.

*Dearest Ella*, it read. *While your attendance is purely voluntary, I do hope you will come. I believe we would both benefit from discussing certain recent events in person. With warm regards, and in gratitude for your service, Redmayne.*

There really wasn't much to think about. Mark Redmayne was the one person who should be able to tell her where Gabriel was, or at the very least to reassure her that he was safe. That alone would make it worth the trip. But beyond that, after all this time, Ella was wildly curious to meet the elusive Mr Redmayne in person, this shadowy figure who seemed to be disliked by so many of his operatives, and yet whose authority almost everyone unquestioningly accepted.

'Nearly there.' The driver spoke over his shoulder to Ella,

whose drumming fingers and bitten lower lip suggested growing impatience with the journey. 'You know what Long Islanders are like in the rain. Everybody slows down to a walk.'

At last they turned off in front of a pair of tall, wrought-iron gates, which swung open to allow the car inside. A long, sweeping driveway led up a gentle slope to a classically designed, white clapboard house, vast and sprawling and with spectacular sea views.

'Welcome to Oakacres.' A uniformed manservant opened the door and took Ella's coat, before leading her through a grand, marble-floored reception room to an elegant conservatory at the back of the house. Part sitting room and part dining area, the furniture was an eclectic mix of antiques and more modern beach pieces. There was a voluminous white sofa, covered in pretty silk cushions, an eighteenth-century card table set up for a game of bridge, and a charming round oak table laid with big bowls of salad and various platters of meat, cheese and poached lobster, already expertly cracked. Scattered around the room were a selection of 'trophy' pictures of Mark Redmayne and his attractive, expensive-looking wife, Veronica. In one they were shaking hands with the president in the Oval Office. In another they were laughing with Prince Charles at a polo match. A third showed Veronica by Angelina Jolie's side at a UN conference. There were no children, Ella noticed, nor even any natural, happy, family shots. She found herself wondering whether Mr and Mrs Redmayne's marriage was more of a business arrangement than a love match.

'Ah, Miss Praeger.' Mark Redmayne walked in, all smiles, and extended a manicured hand in Ella's direction. 'We meet at last. Welcome and thank you for coming.'

Ella shook his hand, her eyes scanning his features for

anything that might fill in the blanks around his shadowy identity. He was attractive for an older man, handsome despite the lines etched at his eyes and across his brow, with a strong jaw and the straight white teeth and trim figure that spoke both of wealth and of discipline. *He takes care of himself. Or perhaps his wife takes care of him.* Ella had heard that Redmayne could be both charming and ruthless. Gabriel, in particular, had stressed the latter, but only the former was on display today as he fixed Ella a drink and pulled out a comfortable chair for her, before sitting down himself.

'So. I suppose I should start by saying congratulations,' he said, raising his glass to hers once they were both seated. A silent stream of serving staff seemed to have materialized suddenly, filling Ella's plate while the two of them toasted. 'To your successful mission, even if the methods were a little unorthodox. Thanks to you, the world is finally rid of Athena Petridis. You've done a great service to mankind, Ella.'

Ella glanced uneasily at the servants.

'It's all right,' Redmayne assured her. 'You can speak freely here. Everyone on the property belongs to The Group.'

That struck Ella as a distinctly odd turn of phrase. *Belongs.* As if they were slaves, or property themselves.

'Remember, I didn't defeat Athena alone,' Ella told him, running a hand through her still-short hair, grown out now to a rather fetching pixie cut. 'Gabriel and I worked as a team.'

'Yes,' muttered Redmayne, his expression visibly darkening at the mention of Gabriel's name.

'I couldn't have done it without him. Where is he, by the way?' Ella asked bluntly. 'I haven't been able to reach him since I left Greece. Is he back in the States too?'

Mark Redmayne grimaced, stabbing a chunk of lobster

meat with a tiny silver fork. Evidently things were already veering off-script. 'No.'

Ella waited for Redmayne to elaborate, baiting him with silence.

'He's in London. On assignment,' he said brusquely.

'You don't like him, do you?' Ella heard herself asking.

Redmayne sounded shocked. 'Is that what he told you?' When Ella didn't answer, he went on. 'Whether I like him or not isn't relevant,' he said pointedly – and not denying it.

'It's relevant to me,' said Ella, deciding at last to throw caution to the wind. 'I mean, it's all very well you congratulating me on the mission now, inviting me out here to your beautiful home. But when Gabriel and I were out there, risking our lives, you did everything you could to thwart us. You were furious. You threatened us. You had us followed. If you'd had your way, Athena would have escaped. Again. And then where would we be?'

Mark Redmayne shook his head. He looked more wounded than angry. 'That's not true, Ella. May I call you Ella?'

'Of course,' said Ella, frowning. She mustn't allow herself to be charmed.

'I was furious with Gabriel. That much is true. I still am, as a matter of fact. But not with you. Your job was to gather data using your remarkable abilities, something you achieved to great effect. *His* job was to protect you. And he didn't.'

'I'm here, aren't I?' said Ella.

'You are,' agreed Redmayne. 'But no thanks to him. Believe me when I say I'm as delighted as anybody that Athena has been liquidated, and that you've returned home safely. But it could very easily have gone differently. I had sound reasons for wanting to abort your mission. As an experienced agent, Gabriel knew that.'

'What reasons?' demanded Ella. But Redmayne was on a roll, venting his anger at Gabriel, his fists clenched with tangible rage.

'His insubordination, his *arrogance* . . . He took risks with your life that were not his to take, and that's unacceptable in an organization like ours. Secrecy. Trust. These things are crucial to our work. *You* are crucial to our work, Ella.'

A suited man came in and discreetly tapped Redmayne on the shoulder, whispering something in his ear. He was rewarded with a look of intense irritation.

With great effort, Redmayne calmed himself before turning to Ella, a model of composure once again. 'Will you excuse me?' he asked smoothly. 'I won't be more than a few minutes.' And he swiftly disappeared.

Ella glanced around the room. Waiting staff were still flitting in and out, which meant she couldn't snoop around as much as she wanted to. But she did see that Redmayne had left his tablet lying on the desk near the window. Picking up a copy of *Town and Country* magazine, Ella pretended to read it while mentally scanning all the boss's emails from today and yesterday, sent and received. There were a vast number, most of them business related. At first nothing leaped out at her. But after about a minute, she picked up an exchange between Redmayne and a km@hope.org from late last night. *KM*. Ella wracked her brains and focused on the known identities within The Group . . . Katherine MacAvoy? The thread was entitled 'EP meeting'. It was short but anything but sweet.

Mark Redmayne had opened the exchange. *EP expected here tomorrow as you know. Any final briefing for me? M.*

Camp Hope's head took a full hour to send her first response. *No further information, or contact with EP from our side. Surveillance reports as before.*

*Surveillance reports?* Ella bristled. *So they've been watching me.* The fact of it didn't bother her so much as the realization that she'd had zero idea she was being tailed. She hadn't even thought to check, in fact. It was embarrassing, after everything she'd learned in the field, that she'd allowed herself to switch off like that. To go back to the naïve young woman she had been before Gabriel, before The Group, before any of it.

But Redmayne's next message quickly jolted her out of her self-reflection.

*In your view, then, the deception has been successful?*

And MacAvoy's reply. *Yes, sir. EP unaware, you are good to go tomorrow. Good luck.*

Ella's stomach lurched and a shudder of nausea ran through her. For a moment she feared she might vomit, but thankfully the physical sensations passed. Mentally, however, she was still in shock. She re-scanned the messages twice, to be sure she hadn't missed anything. But no, the words were there in black in white.

*Deception.*

*EP unaware.*

What 'deception' was she 'unaware of'? What the hell was going on?

'So sorry about that.' Mark Redmayne glided back in before Ella had a moment to process what she'd read any further. 'An urgent business matter, I'm afraid. Now, where were we?' He frowned, belatedly noticing how pale Ella had gone. 'Are you all right? You look as if you've seen a ghost.'

'I'm fine,' said Ella, deliberately reverting to the exact tone and manner she'd been using before Redmayne left the room. 'I felt a little nauseous earlier but it passed.' Clearly she'd made a huge mistake over these last weeks, letting her guard down and forgetting her training. She wouldn't let it happen again. *You're angry and concerned about Gabriel*, she reminded herself.

'We were talking about Gabriel.' She leaned forward in a mildly confrontational manner.

Redmayne stiffened. 'Were we? I thought we'd moved on.'

'You may have,' said Ella, forcing what she'd just read out of her mind for the moment. 'I'd like to know when I'm going to be able to see him. We developed a way of working that—'

'You will not be working with Gabriel again,' Mark Redmayne cut her off, bluntly asserting his authority. 'Ever. You are simply too important an asset. I can't allow those sorts of risks to be repeated. I'm sorry.'

*Like hell you are*, thought Ella. But something about his tone gave Ella the sense that she must tread very carefully from here on in.

'Is he really in London?' she asked, her eyes narrowing.

'Of course he is. I already told you.' Redmayne played the ball back with a straight bat.

'You haven't hurt him, have you?'

'*Hurt* him?' Redmayne did his best to sound appalled. 'Don't be so ridiculous. Good God. Why would you ask that? What on earth has he been telling you?'

*Unfortunately, nothing*, thought Ella. *Nothing concrete anyway.* If only Gabriel had shared more with her about his life and background, she might have been able to find him herself. And help him if he needed it, which she increasingly suspected he did. Instead, she was being forced to rely on the word of a man whom she now knew for a fact had deceived her; and who was still deceiving her, with The Group's active help, although about what and to what end, Ella wasn't yet sure. In the past she'd questioned Gabriel's portrayal of Mark Redmayne as some sort of duplicitous, power-hungry, stop-at-nothing fanatic. She'd assumed he was exaggerating. But now, her antennae were well and truly up.

'Gabriel is in London, Ella, I can promise you that,' said Redmayne, adopting a more conciliatory tone in the face of Ella's sullen silence. 'And, as far as I know, he's safe and well, although his current mission *is* a challenging one, something he knew before accepting it. But I didn't ask you here solely to talk about Gabriel.'

'I understand that,' said Ella, deciding it would be a smart move to back off a little herself. At this point she wanted to keep Redmayne talking. Perhaps he would unwittingly give away the nature of The Group's 'deception'? This secret that he and Katherine MacAvoy and God-knew-who-else were keeping from her.

'Before we start thinking about your next mission for The Group, I was hoping you could debrief me in person about exactly what happened on Mykonos,' said Redmayne. 'A minute-by-minute walk-through, if you like, from your arrival on the island, through to Athena's termination and finally your escape.'

'But surely Gabriel walked you through all this already?' Ella asked.

'He did,' acknowledged Redmayne. 'In fact he turned in a very thorough written report, I'll give him that. But Gabriel wasn't in the room when Athena died. Things can get missed. I'd like to hear your first-hand account, Ella, if you don't mind.'

Ella didn't mind. She didn't trust Mark Redmayne as far as she could spit, but it was still a release finally to go through everything hour by hour, moment by moment, laying it all out for another human being without emotion or self-judgment or omission, but as a story, a chronological sequence of factual events. Redmayne listened, calmly but with visible intensity. Occasionally he made notes in a small, Moleskine notepad that he brought out from a dresser drawer, but most of the time he simply sat still while Ella spoke.

Only when she reached the very end of the story – relaying Athena's final, gasped but emphatic 'no' – όχι – did the dynamic between them change.

'I have been wondering about that,' Ella mused. 'Why do you think she said "no" when I asked if she remembered Rachel Praeger?'

'Who knows?' Redmayne gave a nonchalant shrug. But Ella had picked up on the stiffening in his neck and jaw. He was unnerved by the question. 'Perhaps she was confused by the poison. She was dying, after all.'

Ella shook her head. 'Perhaps. But I don't think so. I think she meant it.'

'Well, that's also possible.' Mark Redmayne leaned back in his chair and readjusted his cufflinks – nervously, Ella thought. 'But just because Athena Petridis meant something doesn't mean it was true. Don't forget, this woman was a pathological, lifelong liar.'

'Yes, but why lie about that?' Ella pressed.

'Why not?' Turning around, Mark gestured to one of the waiting staff to bring a second round of coffees. 'If I may say so, Ella – and don't take this personally – you're still new to this game, but you're making the classic mistake of looking for rational reasons behind the words and actions of a psychopath. *You* know that Athena Petridis knew your mother.'

'More than knew her,' Ella corrected him hotly. 'Athena was there in *my mother's* dying moments. She stood by and did nothing while her husband drowned my mother like an animal.'

'Quite.' Mark Redmayne flexed his knuckles with an

audible crack. 'So what does it matter if Athena said otherwise? She wanted to deny you the satisfaction of an admission. Big deal. You killed her, Ella. You won. Ah. Coffee. Excellent. Will you have another cup?'

Ella watched as Redmayne shooed away the waiter, picking up the silver coffee pot himself and pouring them both a fresh cup. Not a drop was spilled as the stream of hot, black liquid splashed down into the white porcelain, swirling in an elegant, circular motion to exactly three quarters of the way up the cup. He added the cream and sugar with the same care, the same controlled, elegant motions, performing the simplest of tasks as if it were a ballet.

*He's too slick. Too perfect*, thought Ella. *He's putting on a show. And I'm the intended audience.*

For the first time, she began to have an inkling that this 'deception', whatever it was, concerned both her mother and Athena. She decided to push things a little further.

'Mr Redmayne.' She leaned forward.

'Mark,' he corrected her.

'Mark,' Ella smiled sweetly. 'Before I commit to returning to The Group permanently, I wonder, is there anything else you can tell me – anything at all – about my parents?'

The nerve on Redmayne's jaw was twitching rapidly now. *I'm getting closer*, thought Ella.

'I'd like to know more about their lives in The Group. Other missions they were involved in. Their friends and colleagues. Right now I feel like I know more about their deaths than I do about their lives. I understand that the three of you were close once.'

Redmayne took a long, slow sip of his coffee.

*Playing for time.*

'Who told you we were close?' His voice was languid, studiedly casual.

'A few people,' Ella said vaguely.

'Gabriel?'

'Oh no.' Ella shook her head convincingly. 'Other people. At Camp Hope. Gabriel's not what you would call a big talker.'

She smiled conspiratorially and Redmayne returned the gesture. He was giving nothing away, but Ella was sure he was rattled.

'So *were* you? Close to them?' She pressed him.

'Not really,' said Redmayne after a pause. He appeared to be choosing his words carefully. 'That's the problem with rumors, you see, Ella. Things get exaggerated. I knew them, of course. And we did work together, your mother and I. But I wouldn't call us close.'

'No?' Ella waited for him to elaborate.

Redmayne cleared his throat and carried on.

'There weren't many married couples in The Group back in those days. Or today, for that matter. Your parents were one of the few, and they were certainly the most well known.'

'Because of their intellect?' asked Ella.

'Yes. And because of you. Their grand experiment. *The wonder child.*' Redmayne gave Ella a wry smile. 'What I'm trying to say is, William and Rachel were close to each other. They were a team. Tightknit. Inseparable, some might say. There wasn't really space for anyone else.'

'Inseparable, eh?' Ella cocked her head to one side. 'Well that's nice.'

*Liar!* She remembered vividly Gabriel telling her the opposite. That her mother became senior to her father within The Group, and that they were regularly sent on separate missions as a result. And that it had driven a wedge between them.

Leaning towards her, Redmayne bestowed his warmest,

most charismatic smile upon Ella. 'I lost my own parents young, you know,' he told her.

'Really?' said Ella, wondering whether this too was a lie. Oddly, she thought not.

'Yeah.' He nodded somberly. 'So trust me, I know what it's like to lie awake at night, wondering. Poring over every detail. But the truth is, Ella, The Group has already shared all the information about your parents with you. William and Rachel were brilliant. They were devoted to The Group and our work. To justice. Ultimately, tragically, they died for the cause. But their loss wasn't in vain. Because now we have you.'

Standing up, he opened his arms wide and pulled Ella suddenly and unexpectedly into a hug. Ella allowed herself to be held. Closing her eyes she decided he smelled of expensive aftershave . . . and bullshit.

'If I could tell you more, I would,' he assured her, his breath warm against her ear. 'But there's nothing more to tell. You know what I know, Ella. Believe me.'

*'Believe me.'*

All the way to the airport for her flight back to San Francisco, Redmayne's parting words rang in Ella's ears. While she was waiting at the gate, and walking on to the passenger ramp, and taking her seat. And still now, as she sat with her face pressed to the plastic window, staring down at a blanket of cloud so thick it looked solid, like a celestial snowdrift, she heard them:

*'Believe me.'*

*'Believe me.'*

*'Believe me.'*

Then she thought about his emails with Katherine MacAvoy.

*In your view, then, the deception has been successful?*

391

*Yes, sir. EP unaware, you are good to go tomorrow. Good luck.*

The bastard was going to need more than luck when she found out whatever it was he'd been hiding. Something about Athena. Or Ella's mother. Or both.

She would rejoin The Group. But from now on, until she learned the truth, Ella would consider herself a double agent. Her new 'mission' was to get to the bottom of Redmayne's deception. And to find Gabriel.

*Gabriel.*

She missed him.

Running a hand through her newly regrown hair, Ella felt immensely tired suddenly. Tired and sad and lonely. She tried to picture Gabriel in London – was he really there? In his hotel room or out pounding the streets? But his image eluded her. As if, even in her imagination, she was losing him.

*What if I never see him again?*

Closing her eyes, she pushed the thought away.

# CHAPTER TWENTY-EIGHT

'It's good to see ya again, kiddo.'

Jim Newsome warmed his hands around the steaming mug of coffee that the waitress had just poured him, still cold from the chill morning air outside, and beamed at Ella.

'It's good to see you too, Mr Newsome.'

Last week had seen the first full frost in Paradise Valley, the landscape turned as stiff as the old rancher's knee joints. Benny's Diner, the only option for a hot breakfast on Prospect Road, was doing a roaring trade. Every booth was filled when Jim walked in, but a group of young ranch hands gladly gave up their seats for Mimi Praeger's old neighbor. Everybody in the valley liked and respected Jim Newsome, even the ones who had fallen foul of his wife's sharp tongue. When Ella walked in a few minutes later, greeting the rancher like an old friend, all eyes turned to look at the pretty, elfin young woman in black corduroy pants and a bottle green turtleneck.

Ella sat down and a second cup of coffee magically appeared, so thick and strong you could have eaten it with a spoon.

'I was surprised to get your call,' she told Jim.

'Yes, well . . .' Newsome muttered something incomprehensible and looked down awkwardly at his napkin. 'Maybe I should-a called you sooner. I wasn't sure what to do for the best, you see.'

Ella reassured him that she understood his predicament perfectly. It turned out Mimi had written him a letter, which he received from her attorney about a month after her funeral, entrusting some 'personal items' to his care for safekeeping. '*They were my son's things, mostly,*' she wrote, '*and though I wouldn't want them destroyed, I also don't want Ella to be upset by them. Perhaps, in the future, if Ella marries, they could go to her children? But I trust you to handle that, Jim. Just keep them safe and dry and use your best judgment. With all good wishes, Mimi Praeger.*'

He'd been specifically asked, from beyond the grave, *not* to show the things Mimi had entrusted to him to Ella. And though she hadn't said it in so many words, he'd read it as implying that *he* wasn't to open the boxes or look at the contents either, or at least not yet, but rather to squirrel them away until some unspecified time in the future.

The problem was, how was he supposed to use his 'best judgment' when he had no idea what it was he was judging?

Needless to say his wife, Mary, felt it was an open-and-shut case. 'You have to honor Mimi's requests, Jim. It's not complicated. This was her property, after all. She trusted you to do what she asked.'

'Yes, but what *did* she ask, exactly?' Jim challenged Mary.

'For you to put the boxes away and forget about them.'

For a few months, Jim Newsome had managed the first part, putting the crates, unopened, into the rafters in one of his dry barns, far away on the part of his property where nobody ever went. But 'forgetting about them' was never an option. On the one hand, he naturally wanted to do right by his friend. But on the other, these things had in fact belonged to Ella's parents. Wouldn't they have wanted their only child to have them? Allowing her to make up her own mind about whatever it was that had been hidden inside? Jim Newsome felt guilty that he, a virtual stranger, should be in possession of things that, by all natural laws, ought to have been Ella's. Mimi Praeger wasn't infallible, after all. What if her desire to protect her granddaughter was unfounded in this case? What if the contents of the boxes provided a link to Ella's parents, to her past, that would prove vital to her future happiness?

What if . . .?

There were too many 'what ifs' for Jim Newsome's liking. So early last Sunday morning, he'd walked up to the barn, opened just one of the four boxes, and come to a decision. The next day he'd telephoned Ella and arranged today's meeting.

'I apologize for meeting you here and not at home,' he said quietly, his thin lips barely opening wide enough to let the words out. 'But I daren't tell Mary I contacted you. She means well, but she doesn't see this the way I do. I wouldn't want to upset her none.'

'Of course not,' said Ella. She didn't want to upset Mary Newsome either, or risk having the meddlesome, disapproving old biddy looking over her shoulder when she read . . . whatever it was she was going to read. *God, she was excited!*

It had been torture since she'd met with Mark Redmayne in the Hamptons a few weeks ago, exchanging polite encrypted messages about possible future missions and 'next steps' for her training with The Group, while being unable to discover anything further about the 'secret' being kept from her. (Or about Gabriel's whereabouts, for that matter.) Ella had gone over every possible scenario in her mind that might conceivably have involved both Athena Petridis and her mother – anything that Mark Redmayne would *want* to conceal from her. But nothing seemed to stick. Besides, until she was summoned back to active duty with The Group, until she was in a position to intercept more data traffic on the matter, it was all conjecture anyway. Blind guesswork. Ella had been climbing the walls with frustration when she got Jim Newsome's call. But how wonderfully ironic it would be if she learned the truth about her parents, not from the duplicitous Redmayne or his acolytes at Camp Hope, but from her parents themselves? What if Jim's boxes, his precious papers, held the answers she was looking for? What if they'd been there all along?

'I'll drive out to the barn the back way like you suggested and park where I can't be seen from the road,' she reassured Jim. 'I'll spend a few hours going through what's there, and take anything really important with me when I'm done. I'd appreciate it if you wouldn't mind holding on to the rest for now, just until I move into a bigger place with more storage.'

Jim Newsome nodded. 'Surely. Mind you, I don't know myself what's in all of 'em. Felt it wasn't my place to pry more than I needed. So I'm not sure exactly what you're gonna find.'

'I appreciate that,' said Ella.

'If you'd like me to keep you company, I'd be happy to.'

'Thank you.' She squeezed his hand, genuinely grateful. 'That's really kind. But I'll be OK. This is something I need to do on my own.'

Ella Praeger had changed since Jim Newsome last saw her, back at Mimi's funeral. Physically: her hair was shorter and dyed a dark brown that suited her, and she looked fit and lean, like an athlete. But it was the personality changes that struck Jim the most. Almost all the rough edges were gone, all the weird, uninhibited behavior. Sitting opposite him now was a mature, rational, poised young woman. Confident and calm, the kind of person who could handle a lot more than her grandmother might have imagined. Jim wanted to tell Ella all this, but the words stubbornly refused to arrange themselves into the compliment he intended. Settling instead for an awkward hug, he handed her a hand-drawn map to the hay barn and a set of keys to the locks on all four boxes.

'You know where I am if you need me,' he told her. 'Good luck.'

Jim's map was excellent and, despite the winding, single-track roads, Ella found the hay barn relatively easily. She vaguely remembered seeing it during her childhood on one of her long, aimless rambles around the valley, but she'd never been inside the traditional red-timber structure with its pitched roof and wide-plank doors. Other than the addition of electricity – no heat, but three bare light bulbs operated from a single switch located by the door – it had been virtually unaltered since it was built in the late 1800s, although, like everything else on the Newsome ranch, it was in excellent repair; as 'safe and dry' a storage solution as Mimi could have wished for.

It was cold though, bitterly cold, and Ella was glad of her fingerless gloves and her expensive goose-down puffa jacket as she climbed the wooden ladder into the loft where Mimi's boxes were lined up like soldiers against the back wall of the barn.

Fumbling for the keys with half-numb fingers, she crouched down and unlocked all four in turn before lifting the lid of the first box, slowly and with infinite care. The boxes themselves were identical, antique, mahogany by the looks of them, and with a simple but pretty gilt inlay forming a border around the lids. Each one was about two feet wide and perhaps ten inches tall, so clearly there were no large objects inside. Some books maybe, or jewelry, or a few small items of clothing folded up. Hopefully some photographs. Unearthing Redmayne's secret was important, of course. But there was more to Ella's excitement than the chance to outsmart The Group and play them at their own game. That was only one piece of her life. The thing she longed for above all else were more images of her parents: fresh pictures with new and different expressions, to breathe new life into her stale fantasies. Letters would be wonderful too, or keepsakes, trinkets; anything truly personal that could form a bridge between the dead and the living, spin a gossamer spider's web to connect the present with the past, what was still here with what was forever gone, never to return.

The first box, the one Jim had opened, was a surprise and a delight. There were no dark secrets here. Instead it contained what must have been Rachel's wedding veil, simple netting trimmed with antique lace, as well as an order of service from the church, some dry pressed flowers, presumably from the bouquet, and an entire small album of photographs from Ella's parents' wedding.

Ella's stomach lurched with emotion, as if someone had thrown a medicine ball at her stomach. There was her mother, laughing, her long, wild blonde tresses tumbling over her face and shoulders beneath the veil as she leaned in towards Ella's father, towards William, her naughty, intimate expression completely belying the demure look of her floor-length gown. Where was that dress now? Ella wondered.

Her father's face was equally mesmerizing, lit up with love and adoration. How young and happy and *certain* they both looked. Equally interesting was Mimi, in the front pew of a church Ella didn't recognize. She looked small and out of place in her staid cotton dress with the high collar, and later at the reception with a glass of champagne in her hands that almost looked as if it might have been Photoshopped on. She had a sour look on her face, likely brought on, Ella mused, by her having to mingle with the sort of people she would usually have avoided like the plague. Bohemians. Fashionable types with flowing robe-like dresses and tattoos, many of them smoking what looked suspiciously like joints. *My parents' friends*, thought Ella. Scientists and doctors, presumably, letting their hair down at a party. But it was crystal clear from the pictures that Mimi didn't approve.

Had her parents already joined The Group by then, or did that come later, after their marriage? Ella scanned the faces of the guests for anyone else she recognized but there was no one she knew. Putting the album carefully down to one side, so she would remember to take it back with her to the city tonight, she gingerly closed the lid of the first box and opened the second, then the third, alternately amused, touched and entranced by what was inside. So much so, she almost forgot about Mark Redmayne and his 'deception'. A lot of what was in the boxes was junk – old books and clothes and tax returns, carefully filed for a future that never came. But here and there were nuggets of pure gold; priceless treasures from a childhood lost. There was the hospital bracelet Ella had been given at her birth, and a tiny heart-shaped box containing what must have been one of her baby teeth. An engraved watch, its strap broken, that had been given to her father as a college graduation present. A notebook of her mother's with some doodles in it and what read like snatches of song lyrics.

Lovely things. Personal things.

Ella frowned.

*Why on earth would Mimi have wanted Jim to keep all this from me?*

*What could possibly upset me here?*

As she opened the last box, Ella's heart beat a little faster. Right at the top, tied neatly with a ribbon above some ancient teddy bears and baby blankets, was a bundle of letters. Ella recognized William's handwriting immediately, with its distinctive looped Gs and Fs and the left slant that made it look as if all his words were hurtling too fast onto the paper and trying desperately to apply invisible brakes. Untying the bundle carefully, running her fingers over the envelopes with reverence, Ella suddenly stopped and did a double take.

The postmark.

*No. That must be a mistake.*

She checked the second letter, then the third and fourth. All the envelopes were dated within three months of each other, in the spring of 2003.

Ella closed her eyes and tried to steady her breathing.

That wasn't possible. It couldn't be. Her father was shot and her mother was drowned by Spyros and Athena Petridis in Greece in 2001.

Ella tried to think rationally. Had someone found and posted these letters after their deaths? With trembling hands, she pulled out the folded notes one by one. But no. The dates at the top of the letters bore out the ones on the envelopes: 2003. Most had been written by her father to her mother, but two – short, loving missives in a rounder, neater hand – were clearly signed 'Rachel xox.'

Ella's parents had both been alive in 2003. Two years *after* she'd been told the Petridises had murdered them.

So *that* was the lie! The 'deception' that Mark Redmayne and Katherine MacAvoy had been emailing about.

*Athena Petridis didn't stand by and watch my mother*

400

*drown. Because my mother didn't drown. It never happened!*

Bile rose up in Ella's throat and she sank to her knees. Her mind raced, terrible images and possibilities swimming before her eyes. Athena, dying and desperate, her eyes pleading for help. Poisoned for a crime she never committed. Poisoned by *me*.

The Group had turned Ella into a murderer, and they had done it based on a lie. A terrible lie, a lie that exploited Ella's greatest weakness – her love and longing for her lost family – and that had utterly betrayed her trust.

Shaking, Ella tried to trace the deception back to the beginning. Where had she first heard the story of the drowning?

*On the plane to Greece. The briefing files.*

And who had given her those?

Not Redmayne.

Not MacAvoy.

She let out a cry that was part anguish, part raw fury as the awful truth hit home.

It was Gabriel.

*Her* Gabriel

Gabriel had personally handed her those files. He had planted the lie! The fact that it was probably at Redmayne's bidding did nothing to lessen the betrayal. He'd doubled down on it, too, the bastard. How many times had he referenced Ella's mother's drowning during their work together? Three? Four? More?

The pain was unbearable. The one person in The Group that Ella had come to trust implicitly. The one person she had really believed was on her side. Who she'd come to care about. Even to love. How ironic that she could admit it to herself now, thought Ella. Now that it was too late. Now that Gabriel had proved himself a liar and a manipulator and a . . .

She clenched her fists so tightly they ached. This wasn't over. Gabriel would pay for what he'd done. They all would. But right now she needed to calm down. Keep her head.

With considerable effort, she picked up the letters again and began reading each of them, slowly, from beginning to end. Any one of them might contain a clue as to what had *really* happened to her parents. Or reveal what connection, if any, they had had with Athena Petridis.

Most of the notes were short, exchanges of news and love between the couple during times apart, presumably on separate missions for The Group. But two, the bottom two of the pile, dating to the fall of 2003, were from William to his mother Mimi. The gist of both of these was Ella's father defending his marriage. Specifically, defending his wife to his mother, who had obviously expressed her disapproval of Rachel in previous notes.

From what Ella could make out, the letters were written after her mother had mysteriously gone missing. William was clearly concerned for her welfare and convinced of an innocent explanation. But Mimi seemed equally convinced that her daughter-in-law, far from being at risk, had simply abandoned her family.

*I know she's been troubled,* William wrote. *And it's true things have been strained between us. But Rachel would never desert Ella, Mother. I know she wouldn't. Something's happened to her, and I can't rest until I find out what it is.*

In the last letter, he alluded to depression and even possible suicide, railing against what he saw as Mimi's lack of compassion.

*Until you've felt that darkness, Mother, how can you know? How can any of us know? I won't let you be around our child if you continue to say these things. Please stop.*

It was dark by the time Ella stopped reading. Dark and

so cold that her fingertips and toes were completely numb. Like a tennis ball, or a bullet ricocheting off the walls, her mind flitted back and forth, trying and failing to process all that she'd learned in the last few hours:

Both her parents were still alive in the spring of 2003.

By the fall of that year, her mother had gone missing.

Gabriel had lied to her.

Athena Petridis had not killed her mother.

She, Ella, had been tricked into murder.

Retying the letters with the ribbon, she slipped them into her bag along with the wedding photographs and baby bracelet and tooth box that had seemed so meaningful and important a few hours ago, but now felt like trivial post-scripts to a nightmare that was only just beginning to unfold. Carefully replacing the lid on the fourth box, she noticed what felt like a tiny indentation beneath her fingertips. Pressing down, she was astonished to feel a sliding sensation. A hidden panel, no more than two inches long, moved to one side like the lid of an old-fashioned wooden pencil case. In the cavity beneath was yet another letter – this one without an envelope or dates and torn at the edges. It was also signed by Ella's father, but unlike the others it had been typed.

*Take care of Ella*, it read. *I've found Rachel. She's in North Africa, and she's with M. I know how you feel about her, Mother. But she isn't well. She's besotted with M, but she has no conception of how dangerous he is. I have to get her away from him and out of this group we're involved with. I have to get us both out, for good. And I will, I promise. As soon as it's safe and I have Rachel, we'll come back for E.*

*Wish me luck, Mother. I love you. Will.*

Ella held her breath. Tears welled up in her eyes.

So her parents *had* intended to come back for her! They

403

had. But something – or someone – had stopped them. William's letter clearly implied that that 'something' was The Group. And was that 'someone' the mysterious 'M', who had brainwashed and spirited away Ella's mother?

*My father wasn't loyal to The Group*, Ella realized. *He was trying to escape them!*

She thought back to the footage she'd watched, on the USB stick that Gabriel had given her after they'd first met, with William waxing lyrical about The Group and how it was Ella's 'destiny' to join them. Had that been made before he lost his faith? Or had he been pressured into saying it?

What if the video wasn't real at all, but had been doctored, digitally altered in some way, as a sick piece of propaganda, designed to draw her in? If it was, it had worked.

But now Ella's eyes had been opened. Her father had wanted to escape The Group. Which meant that the very last thing he would have wanted was for The Group to get their talons into her as well.

Could it really be true that these people who had transformed Ella's life – who had turned her into a vigilante, a killer, a human weapon – were not the good guys at all, but were in fact responsible for destroying Ella's family?

*Who was 'M'?* Ella mused. *And why was he so dangerous?*

She had to find out what had happened to her parents after her father wrote that letter. Because William and Rachel never did come back for her. And they would have done if they could, Ella felt sure of it.

Driving back to the city, with the bag of letters and trinkets on the passenger seat beside her, Ella felt oddly alert, despite her physical exhaustion and the lack of food in her stomach. She knew more now than she had ever known in her life about the family she had lost. And yet, in a way, she also knew less. About her parents. About The Group. About herself. About Gabriel. And about Athena Petridis, and what the whole past year of her life had *really* been about.

The dreadful, inescapable fact was that Ella had become a killer. An assassin. She hadn't avenged her mother's death at all. Instead she had murdered the 'wrong' person, based on a lie. And yet there *had* been a connection between her and Athena. Some sort of recognition, some link with her parents and her past that Ella had felt so strongly, she couldn't relinquish it now, even in the face of all today's evidence.

Waves of fatigue washed over Ella. But she knew how much work she still had to do. And *that* was what was keeping her going, giving her this strange sense of energy that prevented her from falling asleep at the wheel.

She had come so far.

But her journey wasn't over, nor her mission even close to complete.

Father Michael Murphy blinked blearily at the young woman standing in the parsonage doorway. It was the middle of the night – two in the morning, to be precise – and her ashen face looked as eerily white as the moon.

'Can I help you?'

'I need to confess.'

'OK.' Father Michael pulled the belt on his dressing gown tighter against the cold and ran a hand through what was left of his hair, trying to shake off the sleep that still clung to him. 'And it can't wait till morning?'

The woman shook her head.

'I see.' Father Michael put a hand on the woman's shoulder. 'Well, no sin is beyond God's forgiveness.'

'Even murder?'

Wide awake now, Father Michael looked at her more intently.

'Even murder.' He chose his words carefully. 'You are

welcome to come in, and I will gladly hear your confession, whatever it is. However, you should know that if a priest suspects a serious crime has been or may be committed, we're required by law to report it.'

She processed this. 'I see.'

A pause.

'So you're not like lawyers?'

Father Michael smiled. 'No. We're not like lawyers. On all sorts of levels.'

'I see,' she said again. She turned to go, looking back across the street towards her parked car, her troubled expression still clearly visible beneath the porch lights.

'God's forgiveness is boundless,' Father Michael called after her. 'All He wants is contrition. For you to be truly sorry for what you've done. To try to make amends. And not to do it again.'

*It's the last part that's the problem*, Ella thought, as she drove away. Because right now the only way she could think to 'make amends' for killing Athena Petridis was to kill the man who'd tricked her into doing it in the first place.

The man who'd lied to her about her parents' murders, about The Group, about Athena, about everything.

The man she'd almost believed might be her future.

Confession would have to wait until after she was done sinning.

First, Ella had to find Gabriel.

# CHAPTER TWENTY-NINE

Christine Marshall pulled her skintight Hello Kitty T-shirt in the vague direction of her midriff and straightened her pleated miniskirt nonchalantly as she swung her hips back and forth, happily aware of the men from the building site ogling her as she passed. She was all for #Metoo and women's empowerment, but Christine's own particular 'power' had always come from the effect she had on red-blooded males. By using that power in the service of The Group – using it to do good and to make a difference – she'd succeeded in building a life for herself that was full of meaning, full of purpose, even if it had involved other sacrifices. *And* she'd done it all in kitten heels and exquisite underwear, which in Christine's world had to count for something.

Of course, she wasn't a heavyweight like Ella Praeger. Although Christine and Ella had only been roommates in Camp Hope for a few short weeks, a time during which Ella's abrupt manner and simmering anger had frequently frightened Christine, she nevertheless believed the two of them had forged a significant connection. She was honored when Katherine MacAvoy, the Camp Hope supervisor, had summoned her personally to her office and told her that Ella, probably The Group's single most important asset *of all time*, felt the same way about her.

'We all noticed how well the two of you got along during Ella's training,' Katherine told Christine, flicking a stray piece of lint from her disappointingly frumpy knee-length skirt. 'Now that Ella's indicated a willingness to recommit to The Group, we thought it would be a nice touch to have *you* make the first, personal contact. Welcome her back to the family, as it were. You'll go to San Francisco, take her out for a meal and then hand over the detailed brief for her next assignment.'

Christine could scarcely credit that she, of all people, would have been selected for such a prestigious assignment. 'Are you sure it shouldn't be someone more senior who goes, ma'am?' she asked meekly.

'Quite sure,' Katherine MacAvoy assured her. 'Ella asked specifically after you and Jackson when she was debriefed by Mr Redmayne a couple of weeks ago.'

Christine flushed from ear to ear with pure pleasure. *Mr Redmayne? The big boss knows my name?*

This just got better and better.

But today was the best of all. A cloudless, blue-skied, crisp fall morning in San Francisco had provided the perfect backdrop for what Christine hoped would be her and Ella's joyous reunion. Christine wouldn't be so inappropriate as to ask Ella about her most recent, fabled mission in Europe, or to quiz her on her rumored extrasensory 'superpowers', and how she'd used them to outwit the evil Athena Petridis. But she would demand an update on Ella's love life; whether the mysterious 'Gabriel' had ever made a move. Or maybe some British lord or French count had swept her off her feet while she was over there, Meghan Markle style? Christine did hope so. Ella had a lovely side to her, but

Christine couldn't help feeling that the love of a good man might help to knock off some of those rough edges. Very rough, if memory served.

Christine looked up at the smart, red-brick apartment building to her right. According to her phone, she had arrived at her destination. Ella's new digs were in an expensive neighborhood on a clean, tree-lined street, with doormen outside the front doors and new model Teslas in all of the on-street parking bays. So Ella was rich as well as beautiful, thought Christine, but without envy. Envying Ella would be like envying a bird its flight, or a fish its gills. One couldn't compare oneself to a creature so utterly different, and special and superior in every way. Her excitement building, she practically skipped into the lobby.

'I'm here to see Ms Praeger,' she told the elderly man on the front desk. 'Apartment 12B.'

'Okey dokey.'

Christine signed in in an old-fashioned visitors' book, and was directed towards a bank of elevators. *Not exactly state-of-the-art security*, she thought. Someone needed to talk to Ella about that.

Up on the third floor, she rang the buzzer of Ella's apartment, waiting outside nervously, like a first date. After what felt like an age, it opened.

'May I help you?'

The woman in front of Christine was around Ella's age, with shoulder-length chestnut hair and an attractive, intelligent face. She wore an expensive cream shift dress and suede pumps and she radiated elegance, wealth and class. Christine had never seen her before in her life.

'I don't know. I'm . . . looking for Ella,' she said, peering over the woman's shoulder into the recesses of the apartment. 'Is she home? I'm an old friend.'

The woman frowned, confused. 'Ella?' Then it dawned on her. 'Oh! You must mean the owner. Ms Praeger?'

'Yes, that's right. Ella Praeger.'

'She doesn't live here, dear.'

Christine blinked stupidly for a moment. 'Ella doesn't live here?'

'No. She's the landlady. She lets the place out,' the woman explained kindly. She sensed that the pretty girl on her doorstep might possibly be a few sandwiches short of a picnic. 'This is my apartment now. I signed a year's lease last month.'

Christine looked pained. 'I see. Well, do you have an address for her? For Ella?'

The woman shook her head. 'Sorry. Everything's done through the accountants. You could try them, I suppose. But I believe Ms Praeger's out of the country at the moment. Europe, I think.'

'All right Christine. Well, thank you for trying. I'll take it from here.'

Katherine MacAvoy hung up the phone, a feeling of apprehension rising in her stomach, like foul water in a flooded drain.

Mark Redmayne had told her to act quickly. To get Ella safely distracted with another assignment before any more questions about Athena or her mother occurred to her. Or worse, before she figured out a way to make contact with Gabriel. They both agreed that that man had become a dangerously loose cannon. His feelings for Ella, and hers for him, now posed the biggest threat to The Group's ability to hold on to Ella as their 'secret weapon'.

The plan had been to distract Ella by pairing her with another suave, attractive agent who could seduce her, getting Gabriel out of her head. Katherine had found the perfect

410

candidate. But it had taken her a couple of weeks to convince him, bring him back from Tokyo, and brief him fully on Ella Praeger's history and special 'gifts'.

A couple of weeks too long, it now turned out.

*Oh God.* Katherine MacAvoy put her head in her hands. Ella Praeger had slipped through their fingers. Again.

How the hell was she going to explain this to the boss?

# CHAPTER THIRTY

Gabriel stood beneath a lamppost, waving as the black cab pulled away.

He felt good.

Content. Satisfied. At peace.

There was something almost postcard romantic about the scene. The moonlit Mayfair street, on the corner of a cobbled mews. Gabriel's Savile Row suit. Even the light drizzle helped with the general atmosphere of a classic London romance. And then of course there was the poignant look of farewell on Daisy's pretty, wholesome, girl-next-door features as she looked through the rear window of the taxi, waving goodbye.

*Ah, Daisy.* Twenty-eight, an officer's daughter with a degree from the Courtauld and a job at Christie's, she was the sort of girl featured on the engagement pages of *Tatler* magazine. The sort of girl that an upper-class English boy should bring home to mother, marry at an ancient village church in Hampshire, and go on to produce a large family of children with names like Torquil and Hermione.

If Gabriel, in the guise of 'Jeff Mason', an American businessman, had been a blip in Daisy's perfect English dating CV, then she had been a refreshing interlude in his jaded, world-weary womanizing. They'd met at Annabel's one Saturday night, and enjoyed a passionate two-week fling that both of them knew couldn't last. Tomorrow 'Jeff' left London for the States. But their brief affair had been enough to give Daisy a taste of an exotic 'other' world she would never again experience. And for Gabriel, it had achieved the minor miracle of banishing thoughts of Ella Praeger from his head, at least temporarily, and putting a dent in an obsession that was bordering on seriously problematic.

The taxi turned out of sight. Time for bed. It was only a few blocks to Gabriel's hotel and the rain was light, so he decided to walk. He did, in fact, have a flight back to the States tomorrow, his first trip home in almost four months. It was hard to believe he'd already completed two missions since Mykonos – since Ella. At first he'd resisted Redmayne's decision to get him 'out of sight, out of mind'. He'd refused to accept that his closeness to Ella had somehow endangered her safety, or her efficacy as an agent.

'You could easily have let something slip, going rogue the way you did,' the boss yelled at him.

'Yes, but I didn't,' Gabriel yelled back. 'We got Athena, for God's sake. Isn't that what you wanted?'

'It was the first thing I wanted,' Redmayne growled. 'But not the only thing. It wasn't worth the *risk* you took, Gabriel.'

'So much for gratitude,' Gabriel seethed.

'What did you expect? A medal?'

'Maybe,' Gabriel shot back. 'Why not? It wasn't easy, you know.'

'Well you've earned a medal for bull-headed arrogance, I'll give you that,' Redmayne snapped.

'I'm going to Stockholm to get her,' said Gabriel.

'No you are *not*,' Redmayne insisted.

At the time, Gabriel was furious about his new

413

deployments, but now he admitted grudgingly that, on this occasion, the boss may have been right. He'd needed to break ties with Ella, more than he'd realized. His current London trip was a detour, tying up a few loose ends on his way back from a dangerous assignment in Moscow. That had gone well. Along with a small team, Gabriel had successfully 'neutralized' a group of assassins targeting Western journalists and filmmakers who had dared to criticize the Kremlin regime. It was dirty work. But the mission had gone as smoothly as could be hoped, and it reminded him that the life he had chosen – working for The Group, taking on forces of evil that even security services were afraid to target – was valuable and important. Yes, sometimes the 'means' sucked. Sometimes, oftentimes, you had to be shitty and duplicitous and immoral and violent to people who might not deserve it. But we lived in a shitty, duplicitous, immoral and violent world. The bottom line was that the 'ends' of The Group's missions were always justified.

Well. Almost always. And that was good enough for Gabriel.

He still hated Mark Redmayne on a personal level. And every time he thought about Ella, and his role in dragging her into all this, he felt a knife twist in his heart. But with each passing day it hurt less, as his old, self-sufficient persona regained strength. The work had helped. Time had helped. Daisy had helped. Tonight, for the first time in a long time, Gabriel felt light. Free. He would return to the States renewed, refreshed, and ready to be of service.

'Evening, Mr Mason.'

The receptionist at the Dorchester greeted him coyly, making no effort to hide her blatant sexual interest.

'Hello, Anna.'

'Are you turning in for the night? Can I . . . get you anything?'

Gabriel thought about it. She was a seriously beautiful girl. And he missed Daisy terribly already.

'Not tonight, thank you,' he said regretfully. 'I've a horribly early start in the morning.'

Anna sighed. 'Sweet dreams, then.'

She would miss Jeff Mason.

Upstairs in his suite, Gabriel poured himself a whisky from the minibar, drank it, stripped and showered. Powerful jets of hot water pummeled his aching shoulders, expelling the last traces of tension from his body. Stepping out, he reached for the oversized Egyptian cotton towel hanging on the rail when a movement in the mirror caught his eye.

'Don't move.'

He'd already spun around but it was too late. The Glock, complete with silencer, glinted menacingly about six feet from his face, pointed right between his eyes.

'One more step and I'll kill you.'

His eyes met those of his attacker, flashing a mixture of surprise and amusement as his fear dissipated.

'Oh, I doubt you'll do that, Ella.'

'Try me.'

In skintight dark blue jeans and a white tank top streaked with red and gold, with her short hair slicked back and her shooting arm fully extended, she looked stunning – lithe and tiny and exotic and deadly, a jungle mamba ready to strike. In other circumstances he would have been overjoyed to see her. But the loaded gun, snarling voice and eyes ablaze with hate put a bit of a dampener on the joyous reunion.

'You're angry.' He raised his hands, and stepped back, like a footballer admitting a foul. The step was a mistake. Without hesitation Ella fired, a barely audible shot that missed his foot by millimeters.

'Jesus!'

'I SAID DON'T MOVE!'

Gabriel's amusement turned back to genuine fear. She wasn't kidding around.

'Ella—' he began, but she cut him off.

'You lied to me! About my parents. And Athena. You *lied*.'

He returned her stony stare but didn't deny it.

'Athena Petridis never drowned my mother. My mother was still alive, two years after that summer. That whole story, the file you showed me, the pictures, the "evidence". It was all faked. Wasn't it? WASN'T IT?'

'Yes.' There was no point denying it. She clearly already knew the truth. And it was freeing in a way to be able to admit it, even if he was about to have his head blown off for it.

'And you knew from the beginning?'

He *could* deny that part, or at least try to. But that might anger her even further. He decided he might as well risk the truth.

'I did. Yes.' He looked down, conscious suddenly of his nakedness. 'May I get a towel?'

'NO!' The shout vibrated with rage. 'Don't move. I mean it.'

'Well would you throw one to me, then?'

Ella hesitated for a second. Then, grabbing a hand towel from the basin behind her, tossed it towards him.

He caught it one-handed. 'It's not very big.'

Ella looked directly at his penis. 'Yes, I've certainly seen bigger.'

Despite himself, he grinned, tying the tiny towel around himself as best he could.

'Come on, Ella. Put the gun down. You don't really want to kill me.'

'Don't I?' Anger burned in her eyes. 'You deceived me,

in the worst way imaginable. I killed a woman because of you. You made me a killer.'

'Athena was a monster,' Gabriel shot back. 'She deserved to die.'

'That's not the point!'

'It is the point. Do you regret it?'

Ella stared at him in astonishment. 'Of course I regret it! Do you think I enjoy murder?'

'Well, you certainly enjoyed the thrill of the chase.'

Ella blushed scarlet, hating the fact that this was true.

'That's not fair and you know it! I thought I was avenging my—'

He hit her before she knew what happened, flying across the bathroom, the full force of his still-warm body slamming into Ella's, pinning her back against the tiled wall. She felt a sharp pain in her back and head, heard the gun clatter to the floor. He kicked it away, securing her arms behind her back and manhandling her effortlessly into the bedroom.

'Stop fighting me,' he commanded. 'Stop it or your arm will break.'

He forced her onto the bed, his face inches above hers.

'Listen to me, Ella.'

'No!' She shook her head furiously, closing her eyes like a petulant child, refusing to look at its parent. 'I won't listen to you, ever again. Why should I? You're a liar.'

Gabriel let out a groan of exasperation. 'You're right. I am a liar. I lied to you, to get you to join The Group, to get you to help us. I had to.'

'You didn't "have to". You had a choice and you made the wrong one.'

'No, Ella.' His voice softened. 'That's not how it works. If the boss gives an order, you follow it. The Group votes for the leader, but day to day we're not a democracy. We're an army. It's the only way we can operate and stay safe.'

'Bullshit.' Ella shot back. 'You break plenty of rules. We broke them together.'

'That's true,' he admitted. 'But that was different.'

'How?'

He closed his eyes and shook his head. It was hard having a rational conversation with someone whilst trying to restrain them from clawing out your eyeballs.

'Because *you're* different, Ella. Your gifts, what you bring to The Group, to our work. Your potential. That's more important than anything else. I *did* feel bad, colluding in the lie about Athena killing your parents. And I did argue with Redmayne about it. So did Nikkos, and other people who knew. But you know what? We were wrong. We were wrong and the boss was right. Your anger for what you lost and your need for vengeance – those were your drivers, your most powerful emotions at the time of your recruitment. The Group has always worked by identifying people's drivers and harnessing them.'

'Manipulating them, you mean,' hissed Ella. 'You manipulated me, sucked me in, just like you did to my mother and father.'

'We used your rage and anger and pain to perform a great good,' Gabriel countered.

'I didn't perform a great good' Ella sobbed. 'I murdered somebody.'

'Technically, perhaps. But killing Athena Petridis was justified, Ella. It was a collective goal for The Group. It was right. All the more so because it enabled your initiation. You're one of us now.'

'No.' She shook her head again. 'I'm not. I'm not one of you.'

'Oh yes you are.' His face moved closer. 'You destroyed your enemy, you defeated evil, and it felt good. Admit it. You can blame me if you want to, Ella. Or Redmayne, or anybody else you want to. But the truth is, *you* felt that rush of power and *you* loved it, the same way we all love it. The Group is your calling. It's your destiny, what you were born to do. And your powers are greater than any of ours. Your powers could change the world, Ella.'

When his lips first touched hers, Ella flinched. She didn't want to change the world. She didn't want to be part of a group that had trapped and terrorized her parents, lied to her, and – for all she knew – was still lying, however much 'good' they did in the world. But she did want him. She wished she didn't, but there could be no denying it now. She wanted Gabriel. His mouth, his body, his scent. She wanted to know him. The real him, not just the avatar he became on missions.

'Close your eyes,' he whispered gruffly, sensing the change in her emotions, her body.

This time, Ella did as he asked, losing herself in the physical, the intoxicating feeling of his hands on her body, shedding her clothes like a snake slipping off its skin. There had been so much held back between them, so many lies, even in their closest moments. But *this*: his body around her, inside her, her hands in his hair pulling him closer, deeper. *This* was truth. *This* was reality. The past – her parents, Athena and the enormity of what she'd done – all fell away, overwhelmed by a present so blissful and powerful that there was no room for anything else. No doubts. No regrets. Even the white noise in her head, the signals that ran through her brain constantly like the background hum of a generator, had been pushed aside. All that was left was sweat and heat and pleasure, two animals pulled together by a life force stronger than either of them.

'Ella!'

Her name rang out like an echo in the darkness, but she pushed that out too, putting a hand to his lips.

*No words. Words aren't the truth.*

They made love for hours, more times than Ella could count. Afterwards, words began to come back to her. Questions, half formed through exhaustion, but urgent again, demanding to be heard like impatient children.

Did he know what had *really* happened to her parents? Or who the 'M' might have been that her father referred to in his letters, as her mother's 'dangerous' lover? She couldn't yet allow herself to hope that maybe, just maybe, her mother and father were still alive, still out there somewhere. But the possibility hovered in her subconscious like a shimmering cloud, its silver glow refusing to fade completely, despite the odds.

Gabriel stroked her hair, pulling her damp, spent body closer against his own.

'I don't know, Ella. All of that was long before my time.'

'Is that the truth?' she mumbled, sleep already overtaking her. 'Or another lie?'

'It's the truth. I swear to you. No more lies.'

'Promise?'

'Promise.'

Closing his eyes, he inhaled the scent of her, hoping with all his heart that it was a promise he might be able to keep.

It was gray when Ella opened her eyes. Heavy, laden rainclouds hung over the London skyline and a film of drizzle coated the windows. Gabriel was already up and dressed, standing next to the opened curtains in chinos and an open-necked shirt, sipping a cup of coffee and staring at Ella lovingly. A wave of desire tore through her.

'Sorry to wake you.'

She sat up, rubbing her eyes blearily. 'What time is it?'

'Early.' Pouring a second cup of coffee for her, he brought it over to the bed. Sitting beside her he smelled of lemon verbena shower gel and toothpaste. *Delicious.* 'I have to go,' he whispered, setting the mug down on the bedside table. 'My flight's in an hour.'

Ella felt as if she'd been punched. 'Flight? What flight? To where?'

'Washington.' He took her hand and squeezed it.

Ella squeezed back miserably. She could already feel him slipping through her fingers. 'Can I meet you there?'

'There won't be time. I'll only be there a day or two."

A day or two. That was good. That was OK.

"After that they're sending me on a new assignment.'

Ella's face fell. 'A new . . . where?' She hated how desperate she sounded, but it was too soon for this. Too soon for him to go. To leave her again.

He looked pained. 'I can't tell you that.'

'Well how long will you be gone?'

'I don't know. But when I'm back, I'll come and find you. OK?'

'No!' Ella snatched away her hand and sat up, pulling the sheet around her to cover her nakedness, which was ridiculous after last night, but she was angry. 'It's not OK. None of this is OK. I can't live like this.'

He looked at her bemused. 'Of course you can. This *is* how we live, Ella. It's what we do. You'll be on a new assignment yourself soon.'

She shook her head. 'Oh no I won't. My only 'assignment' is to find out what happened to my father and mother after Rachel went to Africa with "M". For all I know, The Group could be behind their disappearance.'

Gabriel rolled his eyes. 'Come on.'

'"Come on" what?' said Ella. 'They could be. So until I know exactly what happened, I'm not going anywhere.' She pouted petulantly. 'And neither you nor Redmayne can make me.'

To her annoyance, Gabriel erupted into loud and very genuine laughter.

'I don't see what's so funny.'

'I know you don't.' He kissed the top of her head affectionately. 'It's one of the many things I love about you.'

Reluctantly, he got to his feet. 'I have to go.'

'Fine,' Ella said grumpily from the bed, still refusing to look at him. Did he really think he'd placated her with last night's promises? That she would forgive and forget Redmayne's deception, and meekly return to The Group, ready to do their bidding? If he did, then he didn't know her half as well as he thought he did. Whoever "M" turned out to be, he had better be looking over his shoulder. Because Ella Praeger wouldn't rest until she found him. She might love Gabriel, but from now on she trusted nobody but herself.

'I could have killed you last night, you know,' she reminded him.

Gabriel grinned. 'You very nearly did.'

Ella tried hard to stop it but it was no good. The smile crept over her face anyway.

He opened the door, wheeling his suitcase behind him.

'I just realized," Ella called after him, an urgent thought suddenly occurring to her. 'I still don't know your real name.'

'Ah.' He bit his lip awkwardly. 'That.'

Ella sat up in bed. 'Yes. That. So, what is it? What's your name?'

'My name?' He looked at her adoringly. God he wished he didn't have to catch that plane. 'The thing is, my darling, that's kind of a long story.'

# ACKNOWLEDGEMENTS

With sincere thanks to Alexandra, Mary and the whole Sheldon family for their continued support, encouragement and trust in me. Also to everybody at HarperCollins for their hard work and dedication, especially my editors Charlotte Brabbin and Kimberley Young. And to my fantastic agents, Hellie Ogden in London and Luke Janklow in New York. Finally, as always, I would like to thank my family, especially my husband Robin and our children, Sefi, Zac, Theo and Summer. I love and adore you.

This novel is dedicated to my son, Zac, who often gives me ideas for stories and who lights up my life in every way. So much love to you Zac, and I hope you enjoy the book.

# Discover more suspenseful thrillers from the master storyteller

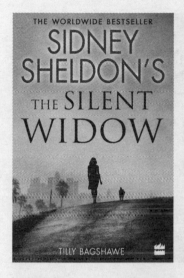

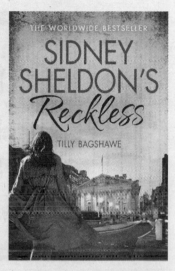

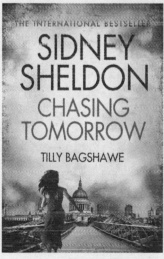

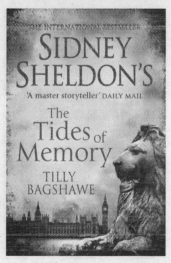

# All available to buy now

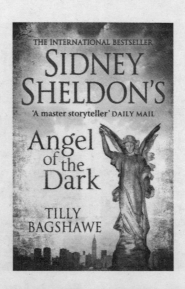

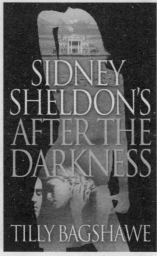

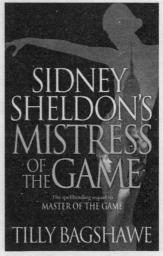